I0726416

PRINT EDITION

Ghosts & Exiles © 2018 by Mirror World Publishing and Sandra Unerman

Edited by: Robert Dowsett
Cover Design by: Justine Dowsett

Published by Mirror World Publishing in April 2018

Mirror World Publishing
Windsor, Ontario, Canada
www.mirrorworldpublishing.com
info@mirrorworldpublishing.com

ISBN: 978-1-987976-40-3

Ghosts & Exiles

by

Sandra Unerman

M|W mirror world publishing

One

Stephen Cole would never have asked for help on his own account, not from strangers and especially not from a woman and a couple of young boys. Since his slow recovery from his experiences in the trenches during the First World War, he had devoted himself to his work at the Bar and had spent little time in the company of women or children. But the help was for his nephew, Hugo, and by the time Stephen arrived at the Grays' house in Highgate one Sunday morning in November 1933, he did not know where else to turn.

When he was shown into the drawing room, Stephen looked round to try and gain an impression of the family. He decided that the room had been decorated about ten years ago and hardly changed since then. The yellow and grey curtains had lost their bloom and the wooden feet on the armchairs were scuffed, but the parquet floor round the carpet was thoroughly polished, as were the tiles inset into the fireplace. Mrs. Gray must have had skilled and hardworking servants, not as easy to find as they would once have been. Botanical illustrations hung on the panelled walls. Stephen had no time to notice more before Mrs. Gray entered the room.

Her appearance took Stephen aback. When he had been told she was a widow, somehow he had pictured a middle-aged woman, dumpy and depressed. Maybe he had been thinking of Queen Victoria, even though he had seen enough war widows in the early days of his practice to know they came in all shapes and styles. Matilda Gray was tall for a woman, with light eyes and a pointed chin. Her pale brown hair was bobbed and smooth. She wore a fawn twin-set and a brown skirt, not new or fashionable but shapely and trim.

'Thank you for seeing me on a Sunday, Mrs. Gray,' Stephen said. 'It's your son, Nicholas, I'd really like to talk to. He is home for the weekend, isn't he?'

Hugo lived at school all term, and often in the holidays as well, but Stephen had been told that the Grays were weekly boarders.

'The boys are at breakfast, Mr. Cole.' Mrs. Gray looked as wary of him as he was of her.

'I hope your maid gave you my apologies for disturbing you.'

'It doesn't matter, but you will have to explain what this is about before I decide whether Nicholas should be involved.'

'Very well, although he is already involved in a way.'

She frowned and raised her chin at that but she said, 'Please sit down.'

Stephen folded himself into the nearest chair as his hostess settled down opposite.

'I'm here on behalf of my nephew, Hugo. He's at school with Nicholas and he's in trouble. The school is threatening to send him down.'

'And you believe that Nicholas has something to do with this?'

The words were chipped out of ice. Stephen took a breath and sat back. 'I'm not suggesting your boy is to blame, Mrs. Gray. I'm just trying to understand what happened.'

'Did the school send you here?' She sounded politely incredulous and he did not blame her.

'I asked if I could speak to some of Hugo's friends and the school refused. But they did say he only appeared to have one friend and that was Gray Major. They wouldn't give me the address but Hugo did. It was about the one thing he was willing to tell me. He hardly knows me so I'm not surprised he doesn't trust me.'

'I take it his parents are away?'

'In China. They haven't been home for six or seven years, since they brought Hugo over to start him at school. I haven't been in touch. I was – preoccupied after the war and I've never had much to do with children. My mother used to deal with Hugo, but she is not at all well now, so there's nobody else.'

'That is difficult for you but I still don't understand how we can help you.'

'I'm hoping Hugo might have confided in your son. But even if he doesn't know what happened last week, if he can just talk to me about Hugo and what might have got him into this state, I'd be grateful.'

Mrs. Gray looked down at her hands for a long moment. Then she nodded. 'Please wait here for a moment.'

When Mrs. Gray came back into the room, two boys followed her. They were about the same height, one dark-haired and solid, the other brown-haired and bony. Both were neatly dressed in flannel shorts, shirts and ties, outfits hardly to be distinguished from their school uniform, except that their jerseys were navy instead of grey. Stephen could not tell which was which until the brown-haired boy said, 'I'm James, Mr. Cole. I'm in the form below the others but I expect you'll need me as well as Nick, to explain things.'

Stephen glanced at Mrs. Gray, whose smile was brief.

'Let's see how we get on,' she said and sat down.

The boys ranged themselves one on either side of the fireplace and gazed at Stephen. He would have liked to stand up and roam about but he could not make himself so much at home. He concentrated on the dark-haired boy.

'The school sent for me last week, Nicholas, because I'm Hugo's uncle. I'd like to hear his explanation for what happened but he won't talk to me. Do you know what he did?'

Nicholas thought this over. James said, 'He set fire to a heap of books in the school library.'

'So they told me. But why? What drove him to do it? Was it a dare or a quarrel with other boys?'

They looked at him steadily and said nothing.

'I'm not trying to put the blame on anyone else, but Hugo does not strike me as a mischievous boy or a malicious one,' Stephen said.

Nicholas looked at his brother, who said, 'Everyone calls him Howler, not Hugo. That's what he's used to.'

'Howler? Why?'

'He goes into rages. Sometimes he can keep the lid on but others he works himself into a fit and howls until they cart him off to the sanatorium.'

'I didn't know.' The school had said the boy was subject to nervous attacks but this was worse than Stephen had realised. 'But the fire?'

Nicholas spoke for the first time. 'He was angry about the ghost stories.'

'What do you mean?'

'He didn't want to listen when Mr. Fletcher read ghost stories to us after prep, but he wasn't allowed to leave the room all week. He couldn't bear any more so he tried to burn all the books with ghosts in them.'

'It wouldn't have worked,' James said, 'but being haunted makes it hard to think logically, I expect.'

Mrs. Gray's body tightened but her voice was neutral. 'What does that mean?'

James looked surprised. 'It was only a little fire, Mother. But anyway, the books could have been replaced. Old boys are always giving books to the library.'

'Not that, James.' Stephen leaned forward. 'Are you saying Hugo is haunted?'

'He doesn't like talking about it.' James grimaced. 'That's why he keeps getting into trouble.'

Stephen looked across to Mrs. Gray, whose face was stiff, and then at Nicholas, who might have been listening to his brother conjugate Latin verbs. 'Is this a joke, boys? Because I really am worried about Hugo.'

They both shook their heads. Stephen tried to think back to his own schooldays and decided that, if they had been teasing, they would have protested noisily. 'All right, then. What makes you think he is haunted?'

James looked at Nicholas, who shrugged and said, 'I can tell.'

'But how?' Stephen tried not to shout. 'They say he talks to you. Is that what he told you?'

'He didn't need to,' Nicholas said.

'It's the other way round,' James said. 'Howler talks to Nick because he already knows about the ghosts.'

The room felt cold suddenly, bleak as the bare trees out in the garden. Stephen wished himself back in Chambers, insulated by the shelves of Law Reports in their leather bindings. 'And where do you come in?' he asked James.

'I'm interested in Howler as a scientific study. He's in the wrong form, of course, but one doesn't let that interfere with anything important.'

Nicholas had resumed his silence. Stephen could not read the look on Mrs. Gray's face but he hurried to speak before she could. 'Then please will you explain. Has Hugo seen a ghost at the school?'

'Wherever he goes, not just at school. They won't leave him alone but nobody else can see them or hear them. They curse at him and make fun of him: that's what he can't stand.'

'Enough!' Mrs. Gray's voice was not loud but sharp. 'James, if you are making up this nonsense, I'm ashamed of you.'

James looked wounded. 'That's what people say to Howler whenever he tries to explain.'

'Some people don't believe in ghosts,' Stephen said, 'especially if they can't see anything themselves.'

James stared at him. 'Do you believe in them, sir?'

Stephen did not know how to answer. For years, the War had brought him nightmares which seemed as real and as painful as the encounters with ghosts some of his old comrades described, but he did not want to talk about that now. 'Isn't it what Hugo believes that matters?'

'He's not making it up,' James said, 'Nick can tell.'

The others turned to look at Nicholas, who shrugged. 'I can sense the ghosts.'

'Sense them how?' Stephen asked. 'What exactly have you seen? Or heard?'

Nicholas shrugged again.

'I will not have this,' Mrs. Gray said. She looked at her hands gripped in her lap and spoke more to herself than anyone else. 'I thought better of the school than to let the boys fall into this kind of hysteria.'

'Forgive me for asking but does your faith prohibit a belief in ghosts, Mrs. Gray?' Stephen asked.

'I lost my faith some years ago, if I ever had any,' she answered and he was shocked that she should speak so openly in front of the boys, 'but I know what troubles people inflict on themselves if they let imagination run riot.'

She stood up and Stephen rose with her as she said, 'I'm sorry, Mr. Cole. Whatever is wrong with your nephew, he is plainly doing Nicholas no good. I think they should be kept apart from one another.'

Nicholas did not speak but the force of his frown pushed the air back, as though a thundercloud had gathered in the room.

James did not frown but he bounced up and down and went red in the face. 'That's not fair, Mother. None of this is Howler's fault.'

Mrs. Gray drew a harsh breath and then paused. 'Maybe not,' she said. 'Maybe he needs help, but not from Nicholas. Or you.'

'The boy's in a wretched state. I'm afraid of what it will do to him if I forbid him to speak to your sons,' Stephen said.

'You've never met him, Mother,' James said. 'You shouldn't punish someone you don't even know.'

'I don't mean to punish him. I simply think a separation is necessary, in Nick's interests and very likely in his as well.'

'There's nothing wrong with Nick.' James glared at his brother, maybe willing him to speak. Nicholas's frown filled his whole body but he said nothing. James carried on, 'Anyhow, it will be a punishment to Howler. Shouldn't he be allowed to put his case before sentence is passed?'

'Don't argue with me, James!' The shadows on Mrs. Gray's face deepened and her eyes glittered. James opened his mouth, looked at her, and shut it again.

Stephen felt he ought to leave but he was desperate. 'I don't suppose – I realise it's too much to ask, Mrs. Gray, but it would be such a help…'

'I beg your pardon?'

'If you could spare the time to meet Hugo, I would be most grateful.'

James bounced up and down again but had the wit to keep quiet. Mrs. Gray settled into stillness, her eyes on Stephen's. When she spoke, her voice was cool. 'Whatever he tells me about ghosts, I won't believe.'

'But you are used to dealing with boys, and not mixed up in what happened last week, like the masters at school. Just your opinion would be a great help to me in deciding what to do next.'

She hesitated. She did not care about any of that, Stephen thought, but she did care about her sons' opinions of her. While he waited for her answer, Nicholas spoke.

'Please see him, Mother. You might like him.'

From the jerk of her head, Mrs. Gray was as startled as Stephen felt. She turned to Nicholas and said, 'Liking won't help matters.'

He did not answer. Mrs. Gray sighed and nodded at Stephen. 'Very well. I'll see him if you wish, but I make no promises after that.'

Two

After she had taken the boys back to school that evening, Tilda Gray went upstairs to talk to her sister-in-law, Rowan. She found her busy in her painting studio, a north facing room, which had once been the spare bedroom.

When she opened the door, Tilda, who was not a smoker, recoiled from the fug of tobacco mixed with paint and turps. Rowan looked round. 'Good lord, I didn't notice how sordid it is in here. I'll open a window.'

'I'll do it.' Tilda let in the cold night air. She leaned against the windowsill and watched Rowan for a while, a wiry, dark-haired figure, who looked younger than her twenty six years. Rowan was dressed in her usual painting clothes: boy's trousers and an open-necked shirt. She must have been working furiously this evening, to judge from the lipstick stained cigarette stubs in her glass and onyx ashtray. When she was dawdling, Rowan put her cigarettes into a holder.

'We had a visit from a stranger this morning,' Tilda said.

'When? Why didn't you wake me?'

'He was much too early for you, and I doubt he'd have welcomed an audience.'

Rowan had come to share the house three years ago, after her brother Alick, Tilda's husband, had been killed in a motoring accident. The arrangement suited both women but they lived separate lives. Now that the boys needed her less, Tilda kept busy with a mixture of good causes, from support for the League of Nations to the relief of poverty in the East End. Rowan, by contrast, was determined to build a career as a professional artist, though so far she had experimented with one style after another without settling on any. She spent most of her evenings with a crowd of students and struggling artists, so she preferred to sleep late in the mornings, but she took a kindly interest in Tilda's more sedate life. Now she put down her brush and came to perch on the end of the couch facing Tilda.

'Which one of your committees was he from?'

'None. He was a complete stranger.'

'Go on.'

'His nephew is in the same form as Nicholas at school.'

'His nephew?' Rowan raised an eyebrow. 'Is he married? How old is he?'

'My dear Rowan, how could I tell?'

'What did he look like?'

'Worried,' Tilda answered and smiled at Rowan's grimace. 'A big man, with a creased face. Well turned out, but a bit old fashioned. Dark hair.'

'Going grey?'

'Not quite yet.'

'Hmm?' Rowan reached for a sketch pad and pencil. 'Don't move for a minute. I like the wavy reflections in the glass. 'What did he want?'

When she heard the story, Rowan said, 'I wonder what the Exiles' Club would make of this Howler. Maybe I should take him there one Saturday.'

'I don't think so.'

Rowan kept her eyes on her sketch. 'They'd like to hear about him.'

Tilda's neck was cold. Shreds of mist were coming in and thickening the air instead of clearing it. She pulled the window shut and said, 'They wouldn't do him any good.'

'They understand about hauntings,' Rowan said, 'and the younger ones can be good with children.'

'I didn't know you ever went there.' Tilda kept her voice neutral. She had been grateful that Rowan never spoke about Spellhaven, the strange island from which the Gray family had fled many years ago. When she had come to London, Rowan had cut her hair, changed her name from the sentimental Rowena to the enigmatic Rowan and thrown herself into the life of a modern art student. Family history or history of any other kind never seemed to interest her.

Now she said, 'Their painting techniques are hopelessly old-fashioned, but I drop in to the Club now and then to catch up with the gossip. Although not so much lately, because the talk is gloomier every time I go. The place is full of people who have given up life in Germany or Italy and are afraid of what could happen here.'

'They're lucky to have somewhere to go.'

'They know that, in a way, but coming back here makes them think of Spellhaven more than ever, even the ones who scarcely remember the city.'

'London is full of people trying to help friends on the Continent who can't get away, or working to prevent the whole of civilization collapsing in another war. Wouldn't the Exiles be less miserable if they joined in with something real?'

'Spellhaven is real to them, more real than anything else.' Rowan put down her sketchpad and looked Tilda in the face. 'I see Alick's friends at the Club sometimes. They would like to get to know his sons.'

Tilda turned towards the window, though she could see nothing but reflections of the lamps in the room.

'Did your mother tell you what happened after Alick died?'

'When you stayed with my parents in the country? I remember feeling a brute because I bolted back to town after a few days. I couldn't bear to stay any longer.'

'I didn't know what to say to your parents or how to comfort them. So when your mother asked me to visit the Exiles' Club with her, I agreed. We came up to spend the day there. Only I couldn't endure it. I ran away.'

'Hadn't you been there before?'

'Alick took me once or twice when we first married. I never liked it much and he was happier going on his own. I didn't mind. He needed to talk sometimes about the place where he grew up. But I never understood – I never realised what went on there until I met those men who said they were his friends.'

Rowan pushed her hair up into spikes with her pencil. 'They haven't told me much. They think I'm still a child.'

Alick had been ten years older than his sister. When Tilda had first met him, after the war, he had seemed full of enthusiasm and humour, better company than any of the other young men of her generation, who were only slowly leaving the War behind them. The complications of Alick's past had only become visible after they were married and Tilda had done her best to accept them, but the more he told her about his former home, the more she had disliked the place.

'They wanted to work witchcraft,' Tilda said.

Rowan frowned. 'Magic, not witchcraft,' she said. 'Nobody from Spellhaven believes in witches.'

'They told me Alick had discovered some method for going back into the past, to bring Spellhaven back to life. They implored me to help reconstruct what he'd done.'

'That's the dream,' Rowan said. 'Everyone who goes to the Club has that in mind, though some are more preoccupied than others.'

'But it's impossible.' Tilda took a deep breath. 'Alick used to have nightmares about the earthquake and the waves that drowned the city.'

'So did I.' Rowan had been nine years old when the city was destroyed. She began to work on her sketch again. 'In the early years. Hardly ever now, thank goodness.'

'Then you must know it's impossible.'

Rowan did not look up. 'Didn't Alick talk to you about the Lords Magician?'

'I couldn't make any sense out of that.' Alick had worn out Tilda's patience on the matter. Even now, three years after his death, she had not much to offer Rowan. 'Whatever happened on the island, there is no magic here, in twentieth century London.'

'There was for a while,' Rowan said and Tilda's heart sank. 'When the Exiles first washed up here, a few found ways to call on the help of Unseen spirits before their powers faded. Only for a little while and for little things, but that's what's so tantalising, do you see?'

'Not really.'

'My parents gave up going to the Club and moved out of town, because they did not want to wear their hearts away in longing. I suppose my mother must have changed her mind, when she lost Alick as well.'

There had been other brothers and sisters who had not survived the destruction of Spellhaven. Tilda had avoided talking to her parents-in-law about them or about the city as much as she decently could.

'Your mother stood beside me while those men talked about a ritual to summon Alick back from the dead. They wanted to take me to his grave and teach me to dance and sing at him. I stopped them before they could explain the details and they argued with me, so I ran away. I apologised to your mother later and she only said she had not intended to upset me.'

'They would never have made that work.' Rowan sounded surprised. 'They must have really thought Alick was onto something.'

'I don't want anything to do with those people, Rowan, and I won't let Nicholas or James go near them.'

Rowan shrugged. 'That's for you to decide, of course. But won't unhealthy curiosity be more likely to germinate if they are told nothing?'

'They see your parents regularly. Your father can tell them whatever he likes.' Tilda owed a great deal to her father-in-law. His allowance made it possible for her to carry on living in London and he paid for the boys to stay at the school Alick had chosen. His only stipulation had been that Rowan should give up her room in a women's hostel to keep Tilda company, a plan Tilda had welcomed. He was not an easy man to talk to, all the same. Tilda would not have dreamt of trying to stop him telling his grandsons whatever he thought fit about the past, but she hoped he would not want them to waste their lives hankering after superstitions. Alick's mother was a sad, quiet woman, even more withdrawn since Alick's death. She was kind to the boys but unlikely to spend much time with them.

'Righto.' Rowan stood up and stretched. 'I'm all for thinking about the future and not the past. And the boy Howler?'

'I've agreed to see him tomorrow.' Tilda walked to the door. 'I don't know how I can help but I'll have to do the best I can.'

Three

In the Monday morning chill of her drawing room, Tilda considered Howler and wished her sons had never met him. His uncle had left him here and was to call back later. Tilda had decided to see the boy alone, so that she could attempt to make sense of his story without heroic interventions by James or outbreaks of anxiety from Mr. Cole. Rowan was out at a class this morning, but now that the boy was here, Tilda hardly knew what to do with him. He was small and thin, with grey-brown hair and a scrap of a face. He stood with his head up and his hands clasped behind his back but he quivered, his mouth pinching at every breath.

He would never talk while they stared at one another. Tilda had no wool for winding and if she took out her mending, the boy would have nothing to do. Then she thought of something else.

'I intend to clean the silver this morning. Will you help me?'

He looked surprised but he nodded.

In the dining room, Tilda set out the silver, mostly jugs and pots she and Alick had been given as wedding presents. Helping the servants clean the silver had been a treat to her as a small child, growing up in the country. From the beginning of their marriage, she and Alick had never had what the previous generation would have regarded as a satisfactory complement of servants and Tilda had reduced her household still further after Alick's death. She had decided then that cleaning the silver would be a task she could take on herself, though she did not do it often enough.

She showed the boy what to do and then gave him the teapot to work on while she tackled the coffee jug. Once they were both warmed up, she spoke without looking at him. 'Did your uncle explain why I wanted to see you?'

The boy's voice was high but steady. 'Gray Minor told you about last week.'

'And that worried me. Will you please tell me as best you can what has happened to you?'

The boy rubbed away fiercely for a while. Then he said, 'I don't want to see any more doctors.'

Tilda glanced at him. 'Why should you?'

More rubbing before he said, 'Old Digger said you don't believe in ghosts but you're more sensible than most grown-ups. But every time I've tried to explain to anyone, they take me to another doctor. I've had my ears and eyes tested, and my nerves, and answered silly questions about my dreams. I hate doctors.'

'Old Digger?' Tilda asked.

'Gray Major.' His voice eased a little. 'Because he's so deep, you know.'

'I know.' The boy sounded perfectly rational, even mature for his age. On the other hand, that was not how he had behaved. 'You might have burned down the school.'

'The fire was in the grate.' He stopped work to glare at her. 'It was a stupid thing to do but it wasn't dangerous.'

Tilda rubbed at smears of polish in the fluting at the base of the coffee pot. 'You must have been very unhappy to do such a stupid thing.'

'I'm used to being unhappy,' the boy said. 'I was angry.' He turned back to the silver. 'Those books made people believe ghosts can be funny or exciting, but Mr Fletcher thought I was cheeking him when I said he was leading our minds astray.'

'Why did you care so much?'

Hugo shook his head. He bent forward over the polishing but Tilda could see his mouth working. She waited, her own hands still, until at last he whispered, 'I never meant to summon a ghost. I made a mistake'

'What kind of mistake?'

'I tried to make white magic.'

'Not you as well,' Tilda said and the boy looked at her in puzzlement. She heard the fury in her voice and sat back. 'Who has been talking to you about magic?'

'It was in a book. A grown-up book about primitive tribes. I didn't think it would work nowadays, though.'

So the Exiles had nothing to do with this. In any case, as James had guessed, drat him, she could not be angry with this child. Tilda picked up her polishing cloth and spoke as neutrally as she could. 'Then what made you try it?'

'I suppose I was even more fed up than usual. I'd had to stay on at school by myself over the summer holidays, not this year but the one before, because Granny was ill. I did a lot of reading, which was all right, but I started counting the days before the other boys got back. Then I remembered how none of them would be pleased to see me.'

He sounded embarrassed, as though his loneliness was his own fault. Tilda thought back to the times in her childhood when she had belonged to no one. 'What did you do?'

'I made a kind of game from what I'd been reading. I went out onto the Heath to do an invocation for someone to come and keep me company, to be with me for always. I didn't expect it to work.'

He was trembling now and sweating, his voice indignant. Tilda pretended not to notice. 'Then what happened?'

'The ghosts came and snarled at me. Ghosts of people who have died on the Heath, murdering gangs who quarrelled and stabbed one another, and robbers who were hanged on gibbets at the top of the hill. At first, I could hardly understand what they said, they speak so rough, but I could tell they were angry. I ran away but they came after me. They never leave me, though it's worse at night.'

'Why are they angry?'

'They don't want to be companions to a boy, a namby pamby weakling. They say they were better off wandering lonely on the Heath. Once I got used to the way they talk, I begged them to tell me how to release them, but they only laughed.

'"You've made your bed," they said and "Try if that little penknife can reach your heart. Then you'll be one of us and never whimper in fright again."

'I tried another invocation like the first one. And I've tried other things, from different books. Nothing works. Even Digger doesn't know how to banish my ghosts.'

Tilda pushed back her chair and stood up. She put a hand on the boy's shoulder to keep him where he was and then paced round the table. She had to clench her teeth to swallow her disgust but she could not tell where to begin unravelling the boy's tale. Was he suffering from delusions or merely an overactive imagination working on unhappiness? Maybe a responsible woman would insist that he saw an alienist, but it sounded as though whatever had been done in that direction had only made matters worse. As for Nicholas, he had never mentioned ghosts before and she did not want him tormented for the sake of a few words. Besides, she could hardly call in a doctor without explaining the costs to her father-in-law. If that led to more talk about Spellhaven and the Exiles, it was bound to do more harm than good. To gain time for thought, she asked, 'Do they hurt you, these ghosts?'

'They don't touch me,' the boy said. 'They jeer and make fun of me, mostly, or tell me stuff I don't want to know about other people.'

'Was it their idea to set the books on fire?'

'No. They liked the stories.'

Tilda returned to her chair and looked at him carefully. He was holding himself together, though he seemed frailer than when he had arrived, as though a breeze might blow him apart. Maybe it would be better to let the boys find their own way to tell the difference between make believe and reality. On the other hand, this one needed practical help of some kind.

'You can't banish the ghosts. What else have you tried?'

'Nothing!' he looked startled. 'I can't fight them or scare them.'

Tilda picked up the coffee pot and frowned at the blotchy surface. 'This looks worse than when we started. I wonder, would it help if you had a dog?'

The teapot was in a better condition but the boy went back to rubbing it.

'I don't think so.' He almost managed to match Tilda's tone. 'Dogs on the Heath avoid me now. I think the ghosts frighten them.'

'What about a bargain? Is there anything you could do for the ghosts to persuade them to bother you less, even if you can't get rid of them entirely?'

'I don't know.' He stared at her. 'I never thought.'

'Could you ask them?'

'Maybe.' He looked alarmed and then determined. He reached out for the coffee pot. 'Let me finish that for you, Mrs Gray.'

At this time of year, the school grounds were in full darkness by half past four in the afternoon. James Gray was supposed to be at music practice but he had arranged for a couple of his friends to make enough noise for three. With any luck, nobody would go to check up on them. He scrambled through the secret hole in the hedge and ran up the road onto the Heath. He was the first to arrive at the rendezvous by the dead oak, which he did not mind, but he had not put on his coat and the night was cold. He jigged up and down, his hands tucked into his armpits, while he tipped his head back to gaze at the stars. His form had been given a lecture about astronomy, illustrated with charts, but he could not fit the patterns he half-remembered into anything he could see.

'Don't fall over.' Nick arrived silently, as usual.

'Which one's the North Star?' James asked and his brother shrugged, visible as a solid bulk with a pale face. James gave up on astronomy for the moment. 'Are you sure he's coming? What did the note say?'

'He's on his way. He wants our help.'

'Will he be able to get away from the uncle, though? The uncle looks haunted himself, according to my observations. He hunches his shoulders and sort of broods inside whenever he mentions Howler. Maybe he killed people in the War and they won't leave him alone. Maybe that could be why none of his family ever come to see Howler, because they are all haunted. Do you think Mother's afraid our Pater might come back as a ghost? Motor crash accidents–'

'Shut up, James.' Nick spoke decisively, but without heat, and James closed his mouth. In the private challenge he set himself every week, he scored a point when one of the other boys told him to be quiet, in whatever words, and five points if it was a schoolmaster. An instruction from Nick counted for ten points. On the other hand, Nick was capable of cutting James for a whole weekend if pushed too far, even though he needed him here tonight. James jigged up and down and flapped his arms in silence, until he heard the pelting of footsteps up the hill.

Howler speeded up as he drew near and had to brake hard. 'I wasn't sure you'd come.'

'Ease up.' Nick took one of Howler's hands and James took the other. They joined in a circle and began to tread round clockwise. After a moment, Howler's breathing steadied and the bitter cold loosened its grip on James, although they were not moving fast. He could see more clearly now, as if their circle were a pool of starlight. This was why he was here, James knew. A circle of two did not work, Nick had told him, and after dark the ghosts were stronger. Howler could not think out here, without some protection.

'What happened?' Nick asked.

'It's all gone wrong. I don't know what to do.'

'Didn't Mother see you?'

Howler's white face jerked up and down. 'You were right about her, but I've made things worse again.'

The subject was exhibiting his usual tendency to panic, James noted, writing up his observations in his head. Then, since Nick was silent, also as usual, James said, 'Just tell us what happened.'

'Your mother said I should make a bargain with the ghosts, if I couldn't fight them. Find out what they want and make them promise to go away in exchange. So I asked them.' Howler's voice wobbled. 'Their wishes are disgusting. They want me to knife Mr. Fletcher or put rat poison in the juniors' milk and steal their clothes. They think I could sell the clothes for a fortune and ride in a gold coach. And they jeer worse than ever when I refuse.'

They trod round in their circle until James began to feel dizzy and said, 'If they won't go away, what would they take to be quiet? What can you do that cheers them up?'

'I don't want to do anything for them.' Howler broke the circle and stood with his head in his hands, rocking to and fro. James had scarcely time to steady himself before Nick pinched his arm and set them moving again.

'If you want to make a serious bargain,' Nick said, 'you have to pay a price. Ask them again.'

'I don't know if I can bear it.'

'I'll help you,' Nick said.

'And me,' James said.

'No.' This time it was Nick who pulled them to a halt. 'You should get back to school before they miss you.'

'That's not fair,' James said, but he could feel the dark and the cold ready to swallow him up, and his protest was not as iron-clad as he would have liked.

'You won't be able to see anything,' Hugo said.

Nick added, 'If you go now, I'll tell you the whole thing at the weekend. Go on.'

It still wasn't fair but the more he argued, the more annoying it would be to lose. James snorted and set off without another word.

Hugo Cole listened to the footsteps running down the hill. Now that the circle was broken, the ghosts pressed round him. During the day, the apparitions were faint, almost cloudlike, though their voices were sharp and persistent. But at night, they shone in their own light, their faces blue and bloated or eaten away to show their skulls, their bodies twisted under layers of filthy rags. Hugo kept his glance on the ground, so that he did not have to look at their eyes.

'Can you see them?' he whispered.

'Just about.' Digger Gray's voice was thoughtful. 'What happens when you're asleep, Howler? They can't see into your dreams, can they?'

Hugo shrank from the thought. The ghosts said nothing but he felt their scorn slacken for the first time since he had summoned them.

'There are pills that can send you to sleep, you know, or you could drink brandy. You'd only really need to wake up to eat, and you could sleep the rest of the time until they get bored and leave you alone.'

He would never be allowed to live like that but Hugo kept his mind away from that knowledge. He tried to copy Digger's practical tone and said, 'Sleeping all day might be a bit boring but it would be better than what I put up with now.'

The ghosts could not touch him. He knew that because they had tried before to punch and kick him in vain. But as they squeezed inwards, shoving each other towards him, he felt the bruises in his mind. He forced himself to stay upright, his hands clenched at his sides.

'They'll be sorry, I suppose,' Digger said. 'While you are awake, they must see and hear a lot more of the world than they did out on the Heath.'

The voices were harsh, as two or three spoke at once and interrupted one another. By now, Hugo was used to picking out the sense of what they said.

'A cold world, a ruined world. Why should we care about that?'

'If you don't care, why don't you leave me alone?' Hugo asked and they laughed.

'You summoned us. You wanted us for your companions.'

'I made a mistake!' Hugo shouted and the laughter grew.

'What do they care about, I wonder?' Digger asked.

The voices muttered. From a tangle of words and snarls, Hugo made out, 'Our stories. You never listen when we tell you our stories.'

'I can't,' Hugo said. 'They are all hateful. I don't want to hear them.'

'Is that what they want?' Digger asked. 'Could you promise to listen to them before breakfast in the mornings if they keep quiet for the rest of the day?'

Hugo tried to think. 'I don't know.'

'Not long enough,' the voices muttered.

'Maybe you'd rather sleep,' Digger said.

'We'll find a way into your dreams,' the voices snarled.

Hugo could not endure much longer. 'You haven't so far,' he said. 'If I promise to wake up an hour earlier every morning and listen to whatever you say, however horrible, until I go to breakfast, will you keep silent for the rest of my time awake?'

He looked up then but the ghosts were too close and he had to shut his eyes.

'Make them say the words,' Digger said.

And after more grumbling and snarling, they did.

'The chrysanthemums are magnificent, Mr. Cole.' Rowan smiled at him and he looked pleased. Tilda could not tell what they made of each other. The flowers had arrived two days ago and Rowan had persuaded Tilda to invite the man to tea. 'I wanted to dismantle the arrangement as soon as they arrived but Tilda wouldn't let me.'

He seemed no more than politely puzzled. 'Don't you like the foliage, Miss Gray?'

'Do call me Rowan, everyone does. They're too difficult to paint meaningfully in a vase. I want two or three against black velvet, I think, with a box of matches and a cigarette lighter.'

'You're thinking of fireworks,' Tilda said. 'Have some more tea, Mr. Cole.'

He was thinner than he ought to be for his height and broad shoulders, but less of the weight of the world was pressing down on him today than when they had first met. Rowan looked at him keenly, though he must be considerably older than her usual escorts. Maybe she wanted to paint him.

'How is your nephew?' Tilda asked. 'Your note said he was better?'

'Much better. I can't tell you how grateful I am, Mrs. Gray. He is more anxious and quiet than other boys, but he doesn't panic or throw fits. I can't make out what went wrong, even now, but it seems best to let him forget about the past.'

'I'm glad.'

'The school have agreed to take him back.'

'Is that a good idea?' Rowan asked and scowled when they both turned to look at her. 'They haven't done him much good up 'till now, from what I've heard of the story. Not that it's my affair, of course, but somebody needs to ask the question.'

Stephen Cole did not look surprised. 'I doubt I have the authority to move him until I write to my brother. Besides, I have a busy practice at the Bar. What could I do with a twelve-year-old boy except put him in another school, where he'd be a complete stranger?'

'Could you find time to visit him?' Tilda asked. 'He is lonely in the holidays.'

'I must,' Cole said. He frowned and Tilda smoothed out her face, ready for an unwelcome request. 'But the boy is good friends with both your sons. Would it be asking too much for you to have him here now and then?'

'I'll do what I can,' Tilda said.

When he had gone, Rowan said, 'I thought you liked the boy.'

Tilda turned to look out of the window. 'He's over-imaginative and unhappy. I'm not sure that's the company we need in this house.'

'James will cheer him up,' Rowan said. 'What did you think of the uncle? Why has he never married?'

Four

Tilda found it hard to sleep through the night, especially since her husband's death. Sometimes when she woke she would sit up and read in bed, but that was liable to result in a headache next morning. So often, when she could lie still no longer, she would sit on the window seat in her bedroom to watch away the rest of the night.

In mid-March she felt the chill in the air as soon as she pushed back the blankets, but she had equipment ready for that: two pairs of socks, a sweater over her pyjamas, and a quilted dressing gown, along with a shawl and woolly mittens. Once she was wrapped up, she settled in her usual place, her feet on one side of the window and her back propped against the other. The garden was a mass of shadows when she looked out and pale clouds swept across a deep blue sky. The moon must have been shining somewhere out of sight. She could make out the geometry of the houses at the back of hers; long rectangles, irregular chimneys and uneven roofs. But no windows were lit tonight, so maybe nobody else was awake. The leafless trees away on the Heath creaked and rattled in the wind.

She must have fallen into a doze, until the call of a blackbird roused her. The sky seemed no brighter now but she could distinguish the shapes in the garden more clearly. Stiff and cold, she decided to go back to bed but a movement caught her eye, as a figure separated itself from the darkness of the house and moved into the middle of the lawn.

She could not see who stood there. The bulk was too small for Rowan or Cook and James would never keep so still. Nicholas, then, who was another light sleeper and who did not mind the cold. As she watched, he stretched his arms wide and a bird flew down to perch on his wrist; a robin, she thought. Then another bird came, and another, and another, until they sat in rows along his arms and on his shoulders; blackbirds, thrushes, and others she could not recognise. They roused into full song, so that the dawn chorus from all over the Heath seemed to be gathered here in one garden. Minute by minute, Tilda could make out more details as the night faded into a pale morning. Nicholas stood motionless, his feet bare, his head tipped back, while the birds jostled round him. They pushed one another off their perch, flew away and came back again, or swooped under and over his arms in widening and then narrowing circles. Then the bigger birds joined in, pigeons, crows, and magpies. Tilda saw a woodpecker land on Nick's chest to drum on his ribs and she grew uneasy, but he seemed untroubled. He made no attempt to push the birds away, even when the wings flicked close to his eyes.

A pair of gulls landed on his head. Nick folded at the knees and sank back onto the grass, his arms still outstretched. Tilda could not see his face and she could hold back her alarm no longer. She pushed her window open and shouted out, 'Leave him alone.'

She ran downstairs and out through the side door, which Nick must have left unlocked. By the time she reached him, he was alone and up on his feet. She gripped his shoulders and held him away to look at him.

'Are you all right?'

He was breathing hard but seemed quite steady. 'I didn't know I could do that,' he said.

His pyjamas were stained with birds' mess and so was his bristling hair but Tilda could see no scratches.

'I thought they would hurt you.'

He shook his head. 'They were only playing. I'm sorry if I frightened you.'

Tilda let go and smiled at him. 'You weren't to know I was watching. How did you draw down all those birds?'

He shrugged. 'They just came.'

She found she did not want to ask any more. 'You'll get chilblains,' she said. 'Let's go and warm up.'

Once or twice a week, when they both happened to be home, Tilda and Rowan would lunch together, as they did a few days after Tilda had seen Nicholas in the garden. She seldom had much appetite lately, so she cut her omelette into small pieces and ate slowly. Rowan, as usual, had had no breakfast and ate with relish, but after a few mouthfuls, she paused to say, 'Stephen Cole telephoned. He wants to know if you and the boys will go out with him on Saturday afternoon. He's taking Howler to a Trade Fair at the Agricultural Hall in Islington.'

'A Trade Fair?'

'For Games and Toys. Did you know April is the month when manufacturers take orders for the Christmas after next? Stephen has a friend who has invented a new Board Game.'

'James would like that, but Peter and Agnes are in town this weekend. I promised to have tea with them on Saturday.'

'Couldn't you put them off?'

Peter was one of the cousins Tilda had grown up with in Gloucestershire after her parents had separated. Tilda and her sons visited her uncle's farm every summer and Tilda remained grateful for the kindness they had shown during her childhood. They all came up to town as seldom as they could, so she did not see them often.

'They're only here for a few days. But I suppose they might not mind if they don't see the boys this time.'

'Can Stephen master the three of them on his own?'

'Would you like to go with them? You might find some new subjects for painting.'

'Stephen invited you, not me.'

'I'm sure he'll be glad to have your company.'

'Poor old Stephen. I'll go, if you ask him to supper afterwards.'

Tobacco smoke hung in a cloud under the chandeliers and the hall was noisy with voices shouting, boxes banging, and the clatter of footsteps on the wooden floor. Stephen Cole wished himself away as soon as he saw the rows of stalls with the crowds milling round them. As he hesitated, Rowan took his arm.

'Do we have to look at everything before they let us out?' she asked.

'With a prize for who goes the fastest.' James sounded enthusiastic. 'They should have thought of that.'

Stephen felt better. Rowan was not as reassuring a presence as Tilda, partly because he felt old and staid beside her. Her hair was too short under a lopsided hat and her jacket was made of some sort of art silk in blotchy blues. She wore a necklace of wooden beads, which hung nearly to her knees and clanked as she moved, but she was easy to talk to and competent with the boys.

'I have to find old Jenkins in aisle seven. The rest of you can pick what you want to see as we go along.'

'Must we stay together?' James asked. 'We're bound to choose different things.'

'I'd rather have you in sight,' Stephen answered. 'We needn't hurry.'

But down in the crowd, the heat brought out smells from sweat, perfume, leather, and wool, and made Stephen, at least, reluctant to linger. His companions browsed at different paces. Nicholas found a demonstration of wood carving and seemed unwilling to move on, however much the others fidgeted. With Hugo at his side, James darted from one stall to another to examine both the wares and the visitors. Rowan was horrified by the faces of the dolls on display, which she said were a betrayal of artistic principles as well as feminism; she wanted to survey all the doll makers, to see if she could find any better ones.

They bumped their way unevenly down one aisle and then discovered that Nick had gone back to watch the wood carving for the third time.

'Maybe we could split up and arrange to meet in an hour under that Clock,' Rowan said.

'Or in the Tea Room up on the Balcony,' Stephen said. There were other schoolboys about and not all were obviously attached to an adult. All the same, he was doubtful as he looked at his nephew. 'Hugo?'

At once James said, 'He can stick with me. That'll be all right, won't it, Howler?'

Hugo nodded.

'Will you give us your word not to leave the Hall?' Rowan asked. 'And not to touch anything without permission.'

James huffed. 'We're not babies, Aunt Rowan.'

But they promised and so did Nick, when they told him, though he did not turn his head to look at them.

Rowan stayed with Stephen to be introduced to his friend. When they tracked him down, Jenkins was in the middle of an earnest discussion with a pair of Americans who admired the ocean painted on his board but had trouble understanding the rules of his treasure hunting game. Rowan and Stephen tried to help by playing a round under Jenkins's instructions, but the pirate ships and the Spanish galleons were easily confused and so were the seven different types of coins. The Americans started making suggestions for improvement which Jenkins contested. Stephen decided it would be tactful to wish the man luck and move on. When they were safely away, he slowed down and was relieved to see Rowan's smile.

'How I longed to explain that sort of game goes much better when everyone's drunk, but I was afraid your friend would be upset,' she said.

'The Americans wouldn't have liked it,' Stephen agreed. 'What now? Would you like to look for more dolls?'

She shook her head. 'It's not worth making a fuss.'

'Then shall we go upstairs and have some tea? We can order more when the boys arrive.'

They found a corner where they could look out over the exhibition hall. The crowd was less oppressive up here and the air was cooler. They sat in silence until their tea arrived and they had each drunk the first cup. Rowan poured out more and said, 'Tell me about life at the Bar. Do you have lots of exciting cases?'

'Not if I can help it. Excitement is not what I'm aiming at.'

'But how do you avoid it if you have to act for crooks and murderers?'

'I specialise in property law. Much more interesting, as it happens, and more profitable.'

'More interesting?'

'Disentangling the complications of statute and common law, and trying to make sense out of clients who don't know what they want or how to achieve it.'

'But not matters of life and death?' Rowan put a slice of a cake on her plate and poured more tea. 'James is hoping for tales of blood and thunder, when he gets to know you better.'

'James did not have to live through the War, and I hope his generation will never have to know its like. The less they hear about killing, the better.'

Rowan's frown was impatient. 'Surely men will never let themselves be led to the slaughter so easily again.'

'It does no good to talk about it.'

Stephen looked at his watch and leaned over the railing. The boys should have been on their way up but he could not see them.

'They'll likely set off from wherever they've got to when the time is up, not before,' Rowan said.

Stephen nodded but he did not sit back. They watched the crowd until Nicholas appeared, climbing towards them. They waved to catch his attention and Stephen rose to greet him. 'There you are. Have you seen the others?'

Nick shook his head.

'They can't be long now,' Rowan said. 'Come and have some tea.'

Stephen beckoned to a waitress but remained on his feet. 'Perhaps I should go and look for them?'

'Not yet,' Rowan said. 'Let's not treat them as infants.'

An hour later, Stephen returned to the balcony from an anxious prowl up and down the aisles. Nick and Rowan sat in a glum silence, both craning forward to gaze between the railings.

'Nobody seems to have noticed them,' Stephen said. 'The woodcarvers remember you, Nick, but that's no help.'

'They promised not to leave the Hall. James wouldn't break his word,' Rowan said.

'Is there a basement?' Nick asked.

They looked at him.

'I suppose they might think the promise covered the whole building,' Rowan said. 'Could James have decided to investigate the plumbing or something of that sort?'

Nick shrugged and Stephen said, 'I'll go and make inquiries. Will you stay here, just in case?'

Five

'There aren't many scientific games.' James stood on tiptoe to read the list of exhibitors pinned to the notice board facing the aisles.

'There's clockwork sets,' Howler suggested.

'They're never usually strong enough to run a proper mechanism, but we can go and look if you like.'

Howler shrugged, so James went on studying the list.

'I can't tell what half of these are about.' He turned round and surveyed the Hall. He wanted a plan, because if they only had an hour they might not have time to see everything, especially with the crowd to slow them down. 'They ought to clump things together, according to subject. Then people wouldn't waste time wandering past teddy bears when they want train sets.'

'I can see model aeroplanes. Big ones,' Howler said.

James looked at him. Howler was a lot better than he used to be. Liable to shy now and then without warning, but his interest in the planes seemed uncomplicated.

'Let's go that way then.'

They did not hurry but pottered past a stall of playing cards decorated with caricatures of famous sportsmen, a racing game with miniature horses on wooden rods, and displays of skittles and bagatelle sets. Then they came to a stall which puzzled them. Face down on a drab cloth lay a single mirror, the spoon-shaped kind. It looked to be made of silver and its back was decorated with a maze of wiggling lines, from which claws, fins, and snake tails reached out at irregular intervals. The sign above said Lyulf Lyulf, Purveyor of the Unexpected, but the stall holder was nowhere in sight.

They stared.

'It can't be real silver,' Howler said.

'There's nobody here to ask for permission,' James said, as much to himself as Howler He let his fingers rest on the handle. 'It feels slippy, like ice.' He turned the mirror over, his other hand ready to catch in case he lost his grip. Then he lifted it up, forgetting his caution. 'I can't see anything!'

'Does it need cleaning?'

James tipped the thing towards Howler. The mazy frame ran for a couple of inches round a circle of glass which shone dark and clear. Their faces were not reflected in it, nor was the bustle in the Hall behind them.

'Get away from it!' Howler said.

James tipped the mirror back and bent his head over it. 'But I don't understand. Why doesn't it reflect?'

'Put that down,' a new voice spoke. The curtain across the stall was pulled back and a face peered at them. 'I don't want any more boys.'

James lowered the mirror onto the cloth but did not let go. 'Are you Mr. Lyulf? How does it work?'

'Curiosity is not good for little boys. Go away.'

James straightened up, prepared to argue. Lyulf Lyulf looked younger than he sounded, not tall, with a head that seemed too large for his body. He had a square black beard, though his hair was reddish, and he wore a brown smock. He might have been one of Rowan's arty friends, except that they were usually thinking about something else when they looked at James. The glint in this man's eyes was searching and uncomfortable. All the same, James said, 'Our schoolmasters approve of curiosity, sir. One needs to acquire the habit when one is young. Where would the human race be, if

Newton hadn't been curious about the apple? Or if the Wright Brothers had never-'

'Let go of the mirror,' Lyulf said and James released his hold.

Howler tugged at his arm.'Come away.'

Lyulf leaned forward. 'I didn't see there were two of you.' He reached forward and pinned down James's hand. 'Come and join your friend.'

Howler stepped closer to James, who said, 'He didn't touch anything, and I haven't done any harm.'

'You talk too much. I want your friend to speak.'

'Please, we didn't know the mirror wasn't meant for us,' Howler said.

'Maybe I was wrong about that,' Lyulf said. His voice was growly but he spoke like a gentleman. 'Come closer.'

James tried to push Howler behind him. 'Who is it meant for?'

'I wanted girls today. I have secrets and delights not meant for common boys, but your friend is a different matter. Let him pick up the mirror.'

'Leave him alone.' James squirmed without shifting the man's grip.

'If I do, please will you let James go?' Howler asked.

'He's not hurting me,' James said.

'But you were the one who wanted to know how the toy works. Let your friend look and I'll show you both something worth seeing.'

'It's not a toy,' Howler said and the stallholder nodded.

'Not only a toy, clever boy.'

That made the thing all the more intriguing. Nick would have known what to do but James meant to show that he could manage without Nick. He nodded to Howler, who picked up the mirror and held it so that they could both see.

The surface wrinkled and broke into jagged lines, long and dark, and then the glass cleared. James saw Howler's face briefly, before a multitude of other heads pushed in front of it, grinning skulls with worms wriggling in the eye sockets, blue and swollen faces clotted with earth, and battered hats tilted over bony jaws. James's own face was nowhere in sight.

Howler cried out and dropped the mirror, which would have fallen if James had not caught it. The metal was burning cold now but he managed to steer it onto the cloth. He turned to follow

Howler and run away but Lyulf had come outside his stall and gripped Howler by the shoulder.

'Easy now,' the man said. 'Don't you care for the looks of your pals?'

James was about to drag Howler away but he stopped and said, 'Could you see them too?'

'They're not my pals,' Howler said. 'I never wanted them.'

'So much the better,' Lyulf said. 'Would you like to be separated from them?'

Howler stared at him with his mouth open.

'Do you know how to banish them?' James asked. 'Nobody else does.'

'That would be more than I should care to undertake.' Lyulf let go of Howler and folded his arms. 'I spoke of separation.'

'What's the difference?' James asked.

'I could not send those spirits anywhere they did not wish to go, but I can make sure your friend is not troubled by them.'

'But how? If they are determined to stay with him-'

'Do you mean it?' Howler interrupted. 'Could you stop me from seeing and hearing them? I can't pay you anything.'

'You needn't worry about that. You will be contributing to my work – my scientific experiments, shall we say?'

'What would I have to do?'

'Come with me and I'll show you.'

'We can't leave the hall,' James said.

Howler looked at him. 'Could you explain to my uncle?'

'I'm coming with you.'

'If you must,' Lyulf said. 'Into the back, here.'

At the back of the stall was a sort of cupboard without a ceiling, scarcely wide enough for the three of them to stand together between the stacks of boxes on the floor. One lay open and James bent down to examine the contents; glass balls like giant marbles. Lyulf tapped him on the shoulder.

'You'd better go first. Take this and follow where it leads.'

He handed James the end of a rope, frayed and chewed-looking. James was disgusted.

'Is this a game?'

'Explanations later. Do as you're told.'

The deep voice pushed him onward. James looked back at Howler, who said, 'I'll be all right.'

The rope led James through a narrow slit into a dim passage. Nobody was about. He hurried on, winding up the rope as he went. He came to a succession of doors, each slightly ajar to let the rope through, each opening into a space narrower and darker than the one before. The rope zigzagged round corners, so that he soon lost any sense of direction. He must still be in the Hall, he thought, because the stale air smelled of disinfectant and the floor was smooth underfoot, but he could not imagine the purpose of such a complication of spaces. Even the corridors at school that connected different buildings were not so confusing. He slowed down and realised he could hear nothing but his own uneven breathing. He was not sure when he had been cut off from the hum of the Exhibition but no noise reached into this darkness, not even the clank of pipes or the rattle of traffic from the street.

He doubted he would know how to retrace his steps from here. If he saw a window or a door aside from the rope trail he could try it, but by now he was feeling his way forward, hardly able to see anything. Then he noticed a gleam in the distance, a watery light which spread towards him along the rope. His pace quickened. He passed through more doors and now they seemed to increase in size and weight, so that he had to use both hands to open them wide, and the handles were above his head. He was impatient to reach the light, which grew stronger as he went along, though it fluttered in a way that he could not identify. It was not red enough for firelight, too pale and unsteady for gas or electricity.

He was going too fast to stop himself when the floor tilted suddenly downwards. He slid forward and stumbled, landing on his back. When he climbed to his feet, light was all round him but he could not see out. He was in a circular dip, with glass walls curved round him and above his head. The glass was smooth but cloudy, marbled with lavender and grey.

The rope had vanished and so had the passage inwards. James tried to scramble up the sides of the glass and fell back. He banged on the floor and shouted for help. The reverberations hurt his ears but he kept going until he felt pressure from the other side of the glass. Beyond the marbling, he saw wobbling flesh and a squashed mouth. Lyulf Lyulf's voice reached through the glass with the same echo as his own. 'Shout louder.'

James stopped shouting and banging. Instead, he whispered, 'Let me out.'

'Not after all the trouble you've caused. I didn't want you in the first place but I'll make the best I can of you now.'

'Let me out! What have you done to Howler?'

'He's a coward, your friend. His little collection of haunts would never have reached him inside my glass bubble but he lost his nerve.'

'You tricked us. What have you done to him?'

'You can forget about him. Or curse him for deserting you, if you like. The livelier you are, the better the price you'll fetch. You can practice while you wait.'

The pressure shifted and the face was gone. James fought himself to a standstill and tried to think. If Lyulf wanted him to make a noise, the chance that he could summon help must be small, unless the man was bluffing. He wondered how much air he had inside the bubble and how long he could shout without losing his voice. He had the wristwatch he had been given for his last birthday and it seemed to be working. He resolved to shout and stamp for five minutes in every half hour and rest in between. He felt cold now and stupid. He sat down and curled himself up while he swallowed his tears.

Six

'I'm sorry, Mrs. Gray, Mr. Cole. I don't think there is any more we can do tonight.' The Fair Manager looked at Stephen, not Tilda. Stephen found it hard to look at her himself, at her clenched face and white knuckles. Instead, he looked round the deserted stalls of the Exhibition Hall and then at the uneasy faces of the men who had just finished searching the building.

The police constable called in to help took this as his cue to speak. 'Ten to one your lads are on their way home by now by themselves, sir, madam.'

'They promised not to leave the building,' Stephen tried to keep the anger at the repetition out of his voice, 'and nobody saw them go.'

Tilda had been summoned by telephone and had sent Rowan home with Nicholas, though both had wanted to stay. Since then, she had settled into a stillness so deep she scarcely seemed able to use her voice.

The Fair Manager mopped his face. 'Nobody we have spoken to so far,' he said. 'The stallholders will be here in the morning to pack up. We can ask more questions then.'

'I want to look for myself,' Tilda said.

They all twitched, as though she had bitten them.

'Look where, ma'am?' the constable asked.

'Anywhere in the building where they might have got stuck. Any holes or machinery they might have fallen into.'

The caretaker, already indignant, snarled at this. 'They had no business playing around in here.'

'I had no business letting them, but that doesn't help us now,' Stephen said.

'We don't know what they did,' Tilda said. 'I want to look.'

The manager said, 'One more walk through, then, but after that, we must lock up for the night.'

They found nothing. In the taxi on the way back to Highgate, Stephen could not bear the silence beside him. 'It wasn't Rowan's fault. I should have known better.'

'We haven't found out what happened yet,' Tilda said.

'Whatever happened, I'm sorry you must go through this.'

'I could say as much to you.'

'It's not the same.' She knew the differences as well as he did but he wanted to keep talking. 'I'd hardly seen Hugo until last winter. I quarrelled with my family during the War and I'd scarcely been in touch since then until my mother became ill.'

'That's a long time for a family quarrel.'

'I couldn't forget the way they treated my fiancée while I was in the trenches.'

'I didn't know you were married.'

'They drove her away and she went off and married another man.' He had not thought about Helen for a long time. Now his grievance seemed immature and he could not think why Tilda should be burdened with it.

'My husband was at the Front.'

'Rowan told me. Not my Regiment.'

'Rowan disapproves of War.'

'And you?' Stephen asked.

Tilda turned her head towards him, though he could not make out her expression in the dimness.

'How old was your fiancée when she promised to marry you?'

'I was just turned nineteen. I think she was a year younger.'

'I was twenty one when I married Alick. We should have waited.' Her voice was bleak but rational. Before Stephen could decide how to respond, the taxi pulled up at her house. He arranged to call for her in the morning and set off on the long walk home to his flat.

The stall between the jigsaw puzzles and the religious tracts display was blank, an empty grey shelf.

'What was meant to be here?' Tilda asked.

The assistant manager consulted his list. 'Mr Lyulf, Purveyor of the Unexpected. He was here: I've marked him off.'

They had already spoken to the jigsaw man, who had noticed nothing useful at his own stall. Now he leaned over. 'That chap's already gone. He left early.'

'This morning?' Tilda had been told that all the stallholders would be asked to wait.

The jigsaw man shook his head. 'Yesterday, before closing time. He just packed up and went.'

'Was anybody with him?'

He shook his head. 'I'm sorry, missus. He loaded a stack of boxes onto a trolley and struggled off with it. I thought to myself he could do with a lad to help him but I never saw sign of one.'

'But why did he leave so early? Surely that's unusual?'

'I never worked out what he was doing here in the first place. Wouldn't talk about what he was selling or even pass the time of day. Maybe he decided the whole thing was a mistake and cut his losses.'

'He should have reported in to the office,' the manager said, 'but that's of no interest to you, ma'am.'

'I wonder,' Tilda said. 'What was on his stall?'

'A few bits of glass and a mirror, as far as I could see,' the jigsaw man answered. 'Nothing to make a proper display.'

That didn't sound helpful but it was the only anomaly Tilda had encountered so far this morning.

'Can we look inside the stall?'

The narrow cubicle was empty. Tilda was about to turn away when Nicholas, at her side, said, 'They were in here.'

She frowned at him. 'How do you know?'

'From the smell.'

Tilda sniffed but could only smell cloth and common sweat. Nick's nose might be sharper but she had never heard of a boy who could act like a bloodhound. She did not think he would lie but he might delude himself in his desire to help. Even so, she was willing to investigate this stallholder a little further.

'Did the man spend time anywhere else in the building?' she asked.

'He had a crate to unpack in the storerooms, like everyone else,' the manager said, 'but we've already looked there.'

'May we look again?'

The storeroom was full of men in a bustle but the corner allocated to Lyulf Lyulf was vacant. Tilda had left Nicholas upstairs in the main hall, at the manager's insistence – no boys allowed in the back - so she was on her own, as she stood and gazed round. She hardly knew what she hoped to find. Anything unusual would be worth questioning but she did not know what that would be in a place like this.

A heap of curtains lay against the wall, a few feet from the space Lyulf had occupied. Dusty and crumpled, they might have been left there months ago. Tilda walked over for a closer look only because she was not yet ready to move on. Then she saw the cloth twitch.

'Please be careful, ma'am.' The assistant manager spoke from behind her. 'We do our best to keep out the mice but it's not easy.'

Mice would not have pulled back when Tilda tugged at the cloth. She pulled harder and uncovered Hugo Cole, pressed into the angle between the wall and the floor, his head turned away from her.

She cried out and crouched down beside him. 'Here you are! Where's James?'

He did not answer, except by squirming away into a gap that wasn't there. Tilda steadied her voice. 'Are you all right, Hugo? What happened?'

He began to weep, without turning round. Tilda stood up and looked at the astonished manager.

'He must have had a shock,' she said. 'Will you please fetch his uncle?'

When he was calmer, Hugo said, 'James is in Lyulf Lyulf's trap. He tricked us both but I was frightened when James disappeared. I ran away and now I don't know where they are.'

The rest of the story made no sense but Tilda had not the patience to disentangle it. She obtained Lyulf's address from the Fair's Secretary and set off to visit him, while Stephen and Rowan stayed behind with Hugo.

Seven

Tilda took Nicholas on the journey to visit Lyulf Lyulf chiefly because she could not bring herself to let him out of her sight for long. But as the taxi took them into a dingy street in Hoxton, crowded with families out for a Sunday walk, she grew doubtful of the wisdom of her decision.

The address she had been given belonged to a shop, its front made of old fashioned bottle glass, covered with a wire mesh encrusted with grime. Tilda was afraid it would be closed but she knocked and was surprised at the prompt response.

Inside the light was dim. Tilda stood with Nicholas at her side and tried to look round.

'Are those sparklers real?' The man who had let her in came close to squint at the rings on her fingers, the only jewellery she wore. Nick pushed in front of her and she put her hand on his shoulder.

'Mr Lyulf?' she asked.

'If you have a few more like that, you might have the means to be a customer of mine. Otherwise you're wasting my time.'

The man was bigger than she had expected from the jigsaw man's description but the beard was right and the smock.

'I'm afraid I'm not a customer but I hope you won't be a waste of my time, Mr Lyulf,' she said. 'Were you at the Games Fair yesterday?'

'Maybe.'

He backed away and sat down. Tilda could see now that the room contained no shop counter but a large round table, with three heavy chairs placed round it. The walls were hung with leather curtains, stamped with a maze design, which also covered the table top. No goods for sale were visible.

'I believe you saw a pair of boys in school uniform,' Tilda said.

'I didn't go to the Fair for boys.'

Tilda advanced to the table and grasped the back of a chair. She had no desire to sit down in this place but she wanted to show that she would not be dislodged easily.

'One of them has come back to us.'

'Told you a story, has he, madam? Is it the kind you can believe?'

His speech was educated, Tilda thought, and his appalling manners were deliberate. She glanced at Nicholas, who had gone into one of his stony trances, his eyes heavy, his body unmoving.

'What should I believe, Mr Lyulf?'

'That depends. Are you sure you're not willing to be a customer of mine?'

'Are you offering to sell me news of my son?'

Lyulf's eyes narrowed. 'How much would you be willing to pay?'

'Nothing. Not unless I had proof that it was true.'

'And if we can get over that difficulty?'

Tilda pulled out the chair and sat down. 'You'd have to explain why I should not simply call the police and let them question you.'

'You'd never find anything out if you did that.' Lyulf grinned and ran his fingers along the lines on the table top. 'I mostly prefer to deal with the Connoisseurs. They are so appreciative, but I could make an exception for the right price.'

Without leaving his seat, he reached behind the leather hanging at his back and brought out a glass ball, which he handed to Tilda. 'Look there.'

The thing was about the size of a man's fist; a cloudy glass bubble, with movement inside it. Tilda had seen snow globes but not ones that moved if you did not shake them. She lifted the ball up to look more closely and found herself staring at a cat's face, its mouth wide open in a scream. Its claws scrabbled at the inside of the glass and its tail thrashed back and forth. She put the ball down in a hurry.

'What has that to do with my son?'

'Pick it up again and hold it to your ear.'

Now she heard a cat wailing and snarling.

'Suppose I can show you your son, cosy in his own little bubble, how much would that be worth?'

Tilda felt sick. 'How is it done? Is it a film?'

'Think of it that way if you like.'

'Then I don't believe you. You had no camera or filming equipment at the Fair.'

'Give me your rings,' Lyulf said, 'and I'll show you what you want to see.'

He had supplied the Fair with the right address, so he could not be worried about being tracked down here. Maybe, in fact, there were no connoisseurs and the whole business was in tricking people, but Tilda still did not have enough information to let the police find James quickly. Her fingers were thinner than they used to be. The rings slipped off easily: the sapphire engagement ring, the amethyst she had inherited from her grandmother, and the gold band of her wedding ring. She put them on the table but kept her thumb on them.

Lyulf fetched a box from behind the curtain and took another glass ball from inside it. He handed it across to Tilda but did not let go. She looked down and then up at Lyulf's face.

'Nicholas,' she said, 'go and fetch a policeman.'

Nick did not move. Lyulf sat back in his chair.

'Don't be absurd. If you bring the police here, you'll leave with nothing.'

'James must be somewhere in this place. How did you get him here? What have you done to him?'

'He's in the glass. I told you that already.'

He was not joking, Tilda realised, in which case he must be mad, but if she and Nicholas left now, she was afraid that Lyulf would clear out before she could come back with reinforcements.

'If you want to be paid, you must tell me how to get him out of the glass.'

Lyulf shook his head. 'The maze leads one way only. Think how much better off you'll be. You'll always know where he is from now on. You can look at him or listen whenever you wish and put the box away when you don't.'

Tilda swallowed a heave of revulsion and said, 'There must be some way of reaching him. Please.'

'The balls can't be broken.' Lyulf said. 'Look.'

He picked the thing up and dropped it on the table. Before he could reach it, Nicholas lunged forward and seized it. Tilda sprang to her feet.

'And what can you do with that?' Lyulf asked.

Nick said nothing. He held the ball between his hands and stared at it. Tilda was afraid that Lyulf would attack him but she forgot her fear as Nick's fingers sank into the glass as though into sand. Then he twisted his hands and the glass exploded. Something fell out, impossibly large. Lyulf lifted up a chair to swing at Nick but Tilda punched him in the stomach and he struck at her instead.

'Here,' Nick called and she turned to see him drag James to the door. Tilda snatched up the only weapon she could see, the leather box on the table, and flung it at Lyulf, before she ran out behind the others.

'I've run out of questions.' Tilda looked at the three boys, who sat in an uncomfortable row in her drawing room late that Sunday afternoon. Even cleaned up and fed, none of them seemed happy. They were due back at school in an hour and had spent the afternoon with an irritable policeman, sent round after Tilda had telephoned the Fair organisers. Since the policeman had departed, Tilda and Stephen Cole had been trying to make sense of the boys' story. Rowan watched in silence, after she had been politely discouraged from asking questions about magic.

'We wouldn't lie to you, Mother,' James said.

'Then you must have been hypnotised. Or drugged. Can't you remember anything that would explain what that man did?'

'He trapped me in a glass bubble. You saw me fall when Nick broke the glass.'

'You saw the cat,' Nick said. 'I wanted to free the cat as well but there wasn't time.'

'That simply isn't possible,' Tilda said.

'We need more information,' Stephen Cole said. 'Maybe the police will be able to tell us more soon.'

But for the loss of her rings, Tilda guessed the police would have preferred to forget the whole episode. As it was, she hoped they would raid Lyulf's shop, though she could not imagine what they would find there.

'But what about the cat? How can we rescue the cat?' James asked.

Hugo had spent most of the afternoon staring at his feet. Now, without looking up, he whispered,

'He had more glass bubbles. I should have taken one to show you.'

The adults glanced at one another.

'It doesn't matter, Hugo,' Tilda said.

He shook his head. 'And I should have come straight to find you. Or Digger. If I hadn't been in such a funk, James would not have been trapped for so long.'

'I was all right,' James said. 'Scientists have to be prepared to experiment on themselves, so it was good experience.'

'You'll do better another time,' Stephen Cole said. 'Don't brood over it now.'

'We should all stop brooding,' Rowan stood up. 'Shall we raid the kitchen for cocoa before you get ready for school?'

Eight

Hugo sat on a bundle of sacking opposite the easel in Rowan's studio. Dust sheets were draped over the furniture behind him. His mouth twitched and his eyelids flickered now and then, but he did not fidget.

Rowan nibbled the end of her brush as she studied him. James was at choir practice this Saturday afternoon and Nicholas out for a walk with his mother, while Stephen Cole was busy in chambers. So Rowan had asked Hugo to sit for her, partly to leave Nicholas and Tilda free for a long tramp by themselves, but mainly because she saw his potential for the picture she had in her mind. He was a co-operative model and had not objected when she asked him to replace his school tie and blazer with a ragged, brown jersey several sizes too large. Carefully arranged, it hid his shorts and the shining knobs of his knees. Even so, the picture was not turning out as she had expected.

On the canvas, thunder clouds, broken masonry, and dead weeds were shaped by broad strokes of paint. In the middle, a small boy sat and stared at the viewer. Rowan wanted a figure there to give focus and perspective to the ruins, not to take attention away from them, but somehow the tilted head and bleak face compelled the eye so that it was hard to notice all the rest. Or maybe it only seemed that way because she had been working on the figure so intently.

A thump sounded at the door and Rowan went to let in James, who carried a tray of lemonade. Over her shoulder, she said, 'Jolly well done, Hugo. You can stretch now.'

'Tea is in half an hour,' James said, 'but Mother thought you'd be thirsty.'

He was in his school uniform but was too well-mannered to comment on Hugo's garb. Rowan poured glasses of Cook's cloudy, homemade drink and the boys thanked her.

'May we see the picture please, Aunt Rowan?' James asked.

'Mmm?' Rowan frowned and then nodded. 'Let's see what you make of it.'

She turned the easel round and waited. After a long pause, James said, 'He looks like that at school sometimes.'

'But school's not a ruin,' Hugo said quickly. 'I'm not frightened at school now, not so much any more, I mean.'

Rowan abandoned the problem of the picture for the moment and considered the two boys. In the six weeks since their adventure at the Games Fair, they had recovered their confidence and their ease with one another, even if James continued to worry about the cat. What Nicholas thought about it all, nobody could tell, as usual. When the three were together, Nicholas was the ringleader, but it might be easier to tackle the others without him.

'I want to talk to you two,' Rowan said.

They were on the alert straight away. Rowan put the lemonade tray on the floor and sat down on the couch, so that she did not loom over them.

'I've been trying to get a handle on that man, Lyulf Lyulf. I've had no luck at all.'

The Exiles' Club had proved a disappointment. All his life, her brother had maintained that if ever you wanted to find out anything, somebody at the Club would be able to help, especially over anything odd or strange. Rowan had respected Tilda's wish not to involve the boys but she had made some inquiries about Lyulf Lyulf, which had been met with blank denials.

'We saw his name painted up,' James said, 'and it was on the manager's list as well. Mother told me.'

'Which makes his disappearance a little sinister, don't you think? And that reinforces your version of the story.'

The boys looked at one another.

'We didn't think of that,' Hugo said.

James shook his head. 'It all depends on one's definition of the impossible, whatever Sherlock Holmes said. If one adopts the wrong definition, one eliminates the wrong things.'

'So we need more clues,' Rowan said. 'If we could find the man, we could gather more evidence.'

James frowned. 'What kind of clues?'

Rowan settled back in her seat and spoke gently. 'I wondered about your ghosts, Hugo. Didn't they see Lyulf, if they are with you all the time?'

Hugo stared at her and his lemonade glass trembled in his hands. James bumped the rim of his glass against his mouth and said nothing.

Rowan went on, 'Couldn't the ghosts find him? Or tell us how to find him?'

'No.' Hugo's voice creaked and he started again. 'I mean I won't ask them, Miss Gray. I won't ever ask them for anything.'

'I should like you to tell me why not,' Rowan said.

'I mustn't give in to them. Not ever,' Hugo said.

Rowan looked at James, who said doubtfully, 'But you made a bargain with them, didn't you?'

'Once, so that I don't go mad. Asking for anything else would be different.'

'I suppose if they had dropped any hints, you would have told us,' James said. 'Aren't they interested in Lyulf Lyulf?'

Hugo shook his head. He looked shrunken, Rowan saw, and he could not hold his glass steady. She jumped up and took it from him.

'Never mind,' she said. 'Thank you for sitting for me, Hugo.'

When the boys had gone, Rowan turned back to her canvas and frowned at it. Eventually she found a stick of charcoal and began to sketch over the surface of the paint. She drew large cloudy faces round the central figure, some grinning, some with mouths open in a scream. Their bodies floated in the air. At first she worked tentatively and then with grim enthusiasm.

The exhibition was a shared one between five artists, of whom Rowan was one. From the outside, the small gallery looked much like the run-down shops in the rest of the street. Indoors, new owners had done their best to make it inviting within their limited means. They and their friends had experimented by painting the walls and floors themselves with white paint. It had been a surprisingly messy job, and even now you could see streaks and knobbly patches if you looked hard enough, but the exhibits covered the worst bits and the money saved on decorators had been spent on ceiling lights, triple circles of frosted glass.

The Private View was crowded. Tilda wore her new hat, a present from Rowan, an amber wedge carefully tilted over one ear. Her coat and skirt were three years old but of excellent cut and the honey colour flattered her skin. Her gloves were also new, so that altogether she felt she could live up to the occasion. Rowan's friends had their own style, of course, flamboyant and bohemian. That might be cheaper to maintain, but Tilda suspected she would make herself ridiculous if she tried it. She usually enjoyed meeting the crowd, however, and today she was cheered by the way they made her welcome. She saw Rowan from across the room and threaded a way towards her. Perhaps to claim her place among the exhibitors, Rowan had chosen to wear a fancy version of her painting clothes; steel blue trousers which fell in wide folds and a matching waistcoat, scavenged from a theatrical costumier. Her hat was a white saucer, like a lopsided halo. The look suited her skinny frame and Tilda smiled to see her listen intently to three people at once. Then Tilda noticed the picture behind Rowan.

'Remarkable, isn't it?' said a voice she did not know.

'The most interesting thing she's done. A real breakthrough,' said another.

'You're here, Tilda. Thank you for coming.'

Rowan was at her side but Tilda did not turn to her.

'You never showed me this.'

'I only just finished it in time to hand it in.' Rowan's voice was light and a little flurried. 'The Unconscious is a tricky subject. I wasn't sure how well it would turn out.'

'The Unconscious?' Tilda repeated.

'Have you read Freud, Mrs. Gray?' someone in the crowd asked. 'There's a lot more going on inside us than we have an idea of.'

Tilda's teeth locked together so that she could not speak. She shook her head and turned to walk out of the Gallery.

By midnight, Tilda's drawing room was cold, even at the end of June. Tilda had kept herself busy since her return home but the committee correspondence from families seeking to emigrate from Germany only increased the darkness of her mood. Now her head ached and she sat with only one lamp alight, rubbing her fingers to warm them.

She heard the front door open and a brief exchange of voices as Rowan dismissed her escort. She did not call out but Rowan must have seen the light and came in, brisk and bright-eyed.

'Are you all right? I'm sorry I couldn't get away sooner.'

'That picture, Rowan. What have you done?'

Rowan unpinned the saucer hat and rubbed up her hair. 'Painted a work of the imagination. A brilliant one. Everyone is thrilled by it.'

'Why didn't you warn me?'

'Warn you about what? Nobody would have dreamt there was anything to get upset about until you walked out like that.'

'What did they say?'

'It doesn't matter. I told them you'd been feeling poorly.'

'It would have been worse if I'd stayed. Did you show the picture to Hugo? Or his uncle?'

'Not since I painted in the ghosts.' Rowan crouched down by Tilda's chair. 'Nobody will know about Hugo. I haven't painted a portrait. The boy could be any child with a nightmare.'

'It's Hugo's face. And the look in his eyes.'

'That's what you see. Nobody else will think along those lines.'

'Except the boys. And Stephen Cole. And how many of your crowd know families with boys at the school?'

'They'll have to understand about art.' Rowan stood up and wandered round the room, picking things up and putting them down again. 'I painted the ghosts I imagined, not Hugo's.'

When Rowan made her feel ancient, Tilda was usually inclined to suppose that she herself had grown stuffy and old fashioned. Not this time.

'I wish you had not done it.'

'I won't withdraw the picture.' Rowan turned round with a scowl.

'I daresay that would only make matters worse.' Tilda could imagine the fuss. She leaned her head back and shut her eyes. 'You had better warn Mr. Cole. He may not want Hugo to go to the exhibition.'

Nine

Stephen Cole visited the exhibition on Thursday afternoon, as he made his way back from a court hearing out of town. He arrived in a teatime lull. The art crowd tended to come later in the day and friends or family up from the country in the mornings. The near empty rooms made Stephen feel even more out of place than he had feared in his pinstriped trousers and black jacket, like an elephant in an aviary. This kind of show was outside his experience and he did not want to attract further attention by heading straight for one picture. In fact, his solemn scrutiny of everything on the walls was more puzzling to the Gallery's assistants and the few other visitors. They were used to people who were interested only in the work of their friends. The occasional critic might pace round slowly, if he wished to display his diligence, but Stephen did not look like a critic and he took no notes. So they watched him and leaned towards one another to mutter, until the hairs prickled under his hat.

He forgot the watchers when he came to the picture labelled Eyes in the Shadows. He understood at once what the trouble was. On the telephone, Rowan had been abrupt and cryptic. 'Tilda thinks you ought to see the picture before the boys do.' He had arranged to collect the three boys from school on Saturday, take them out for lunch with Mrs. Gray, and then bring them here. He had not supposed the boys would care much about the paintings except for a mild curiosity about Hugo's appearance. After the phone call, he had nearly decided not to bother with the preview. He did not think anyone would mind if Hugo had been painted with three noses or turned into a violin, but something in Rowan's voice, as well his respect for Tilda Gray's judgement, had made him rearrange his conference in Chambers this afternoon so that he could call in here. Now he saw that Saturday's expedition would have to be cancelled.

For over twelve years, Stephen had thought about nothing but his career. Legal problems, chambers politics, and the petty tyrannies of judges had thickened into a bulwark against his memories of the War and of the person he had once hoped to become. When he answered the summons from Hugo's school, he had had no intention of letting the boy interfere with his life, but turning his back on Hugo would have reminded him too much of the men he had failed to save from death or madness in the trenches. At the beginning, he had told himself his intervention was temporary, a stopgap until his brother made better arrangements. More recently, he had given up hope of explaining what needed to be done in letters to China. But he had been unexpectedly glad to see Hugo calm down, and he had enjoyed his encounters with all the Grays. Now he wished he could retreat into isolation, maybe in a six month hearing in the Court of Appeal, but he was too cowardly to invent one.

'Are you a friend of Rowan Gray?' The speaker was a round woman, her arms loaded with bangles. 'She'll be here soon.'

Stephen had no desire to encounter Rowan. He could not believe she had painted this picture to torment Hugo or display his troubles to the world, but how had she not realised what would happen?

'I'm afraid I can't wait,' he said and turned away. Then he thought of something. 'May I ask, do you know if this painting is for sale?'

'Eyes in the Shadows?' The woman looked flustered. 'Not at present, I'm afraid. At least, I'm not in a position to say that it is.'

'What do you mean?'

'It was for sale.' She twisted her bangles around. 'Eyes had a lot of attention and we were sure it would make a sale. Then yesterday

Miss Gray said she had decided to make it unavailable. So difficult and disappointing. We're hoping she'll think better of it. So if you are interested, Mr.?'

Stephen gave his name and said, 'Yes, if she decides to sell, please let me know.'

Saturday was the last day of the exhibition. By the evening, the gallery was more crowded than ever and several paintings had actually been sold. The gallery owners did not expect to make a profit but they were confident now that the show would enhance their reputations. Not many of their undertakings did this well. They brought out bottles of wine and trays of cheese. Both were cheap and sour but Rowan had not eaten for hours and her mood had darkened steadily throughout the day. She was determined not to sulk because Stephen Cole had cancelled today's visit with the boys. Her parents had come up to town yesterday and Rowan had known from their greetings that Tilda had not complained to them. Even so, they had seemed troubled when they looked at Eyes.

'Have you shown this to the Exiles' Club?' they asked and when Rowan shook her head, her father said, 'Maybe better not. You don't want to stir up memories after all this time.'

'It's a work of the imagination,' Rowan had said. 'Nothing to do with the Exiles.'

Her parents had not argued, which meant that they did not believe her. Rowan had taken refuge in the company of her friends but for once she could not share their humour. The more they speculated about the psychological impulses behind Eyes or offered suggestions for the next painting, the more irritable she felt. She drank a couple of glasses of the rough red wine before she lost count and swallowed handfuls of cheese cubes. Then she began to feel sick.

'Miss Gray?' The speaker was a sturdy man with a mismatched beard. His smock might have belonged to an acolyte of Eric Gill but not the brilliantine on his hair or the shine on his shoes. Something about him stirred in Rowan's memory but she could not think what.

'How much do you want for that picture?'

'I'm afraid Eyes in the Shadows is not for sale.' Rowan was tired of being polite on this subject. She put down her glass and prepared to walk away. Then she decided it would be safer to lean back against the wall.

'You can't drive the price up that way to me. I'm Lyulf Lyulf, Miss Gray. I'm sure you've heard of me.'

Rowan was furious with herself for feeling unwell at such a moment.

'Don't go away,' she said and reached out a hand to the nearest sensible person, Daphne, the Gallery owner's wife. 'Help me, please.'

At least she made it to the lavatory before she vomited. Afterwards her throat hurt and her head ached, but she could think again. She sat in a side office with a cup of the bitter mud Daphne called coffee and looked at Lyulf. They were alone. Rowan did not blame Daphne for wanting Eyes to be sold so that the Gallery could take its commission, but even so she was prepared to be ruthless about interruptions.

'Ready now, Miss Gray?' Lyulf did not sound sympathetic.

'The police are searching for you,' Rowan said.

'Not with much persistence, I assure you. They are too busy to waste time on a matter they could never bring to court.'

Stephen Cole had said much the same but Rowan was not prepared to acknowledge the force of the argument yet.

'In that case, why did you empty out your shop in such a panic?'

'Why should I tell you my business? I'm here to buy your picture. Nothing else, Miss Gray.'

Tilda had said the man was a bully. Rowan drew herself upright in her chair, despite her headache.

'The picture's not for sale.'

'The Exiles' Club won't want it, you know. They'll have no idea what to do with it.'

How did he know about the Club? Rowan guessed that he was in his thirties, if not older, so he might have come from Spellhaven himself and somehow contrived to keep a portion of the island's magic alive. She had never heard of such a thing but it would explain what had happened to James. But in that case, why was nobody in the Club willing to talk about him?

'What would you do with it?

'None of your business. You should be glad I'm willing to pay for it. Your family owe me recompense for wrecking my shop and breaking my glass bubbles.'

'Don't be absurd.' Rowan took a sip of the bitter coffee. It didn't improve the headache but the action helped contain her anger. 'You caught my nephew in a trap. You deserve punishment for that, even if the police won't act.'

'Your nephew, is he? What about the others?'

She had not meant to give away any information, although once he had her name, he could have probably found out about the rest of the family in any case. Meanwhile, she had learnt nothing about him at all. In her vexation, she did not answer him.

'They are both trouble, those two,' he said after a moment. 'You'll have to let me at them sooner or later if you want to live in peace, you and the faded Snow Queen.'

'You stole her rings,' Rowan remembered. 'The police will understand that, at least.'

'How did the dark boy break my spells? If you knew, any of you, you would have taken him to the Club to be fussed over. And if you don't know, what are you going to do next time he goes mad?'

Nicholas never went mad, however inexplicably he behaved, but the rest of the world might not find that easy to believe. Rowan closed her eyes and asked, 'What did you do with the cat?'

'What cat?' for the first time, Lyulf sounded taken aback.

Rowan looked at him. 'You had a cat in one of your glass bubbles, Mr. Lyulf. Is it still alive?'

He snorted. 'Cats fled from Spellhaven before the people could get away. You're not too young to remember that.'

Rowan remembered the night of the drowning as seldom as possible, and she had heard more than one story about the fate of Spellhaven's cats.

'That hardly entitles you to imprison a cat today. Where is it now?'

'I'll give you the cat for the picture.'

James would like that but Rowan would not trust Lyulf with the picture on any terms. 'No,' she said.

'Then let me talk to the dark boy. Bring him to meet me and I'll show you the cat.'

Rowan's headache had changed from a dull throb to a stabbing pain behind her left eye. She wanted to get something out of this encounter before she gave up. 'What do you want with him?'

'To fathom his powers. He needs training.'

'And you expect us to trust you?'

'Who else is there?' Lyulf leaned forward and thrust his beard at Rowan. 'Meet me somewhere you feel safe. A Lyons' Corner House, if you like. What harm can I do there?'

Ten

'But I've never followed anyone in my life, old girl. I don't know how to set about it.'

'What do we do if he spots us lurking about?'

Rowan looked from one of her aides to the other. Vernon Swift and Henry Bailes were among the least disreputable looking of her friends, even if their jackets were on the baggy side and their ties were loud. Also, they were known to play cricket occasionally and were out and about during the day, when other artists were asleep. She had expected the opportunity for a small adventure to appeal to them. Indeed, they had been eager to offer their support, until she explained what she wanted.

'Lurking should not be necessary,' Rowan said. 'Just stroll about idly, until I send the man away. Then follow him as far as you can.'

They looked at one another.

'Why don't we stick with you?' Vernon asked. 'Maybe we can persuade the blighter to cough up his ill-gotten gains.'

'No.' Rowan had not told them everything about Lyulf Lyulf. She had said only that she suspected him of a connection with the theft of some jewellery and she wanted to find out where he lived. 'We have to do this my way. If you don't want to help, I'll ask Pongo and Tim.'

They argued some more but Rowan did not listen.

The meeting place was in front of the Albert Memorial. Rowan disliked the thought of sitting down again with Lyulf, even over a cup of tea. Here in the Park, she and Nicholas could move away the moment they felt threatened, or summon help from passersby. Vernon and Henry had promised to stay well back but their presence was an additional safeguard.

The afternoon was warm but overcast. As Rowan expected, the area was busy. Nannies did not encourage their charges to play round the Memorial but they went by on their way to Peter Pan. So did students, couples out for an airing, and visitors seeing the sights, the men hot and sticky in their town clothes while the women wore summer cottons, which looked limp and grubby under the dull sky.

James's choir was performing at the Albert Hall this afternoon and Tilda was watching. In principle, Nicholas would have been content to go too but he wilted every time he had to spend hours in a crowd. Rowan had offered to bring him to meet the others at the end of the concert. She had not told Tilda about the rendezvous with Lyulf. She had waited until they were on the bus from Highgate to ask Nicholas if he was willing to face up to Lyulf.

Nicholas had frowned. 'Aunt Rowan, I won't tell him about Howler.'

'You don't have to say anything to him, if you don't want to. I'd like to find out what he wants with you, that's all.'

This proposition sounded less convincing to Rowan today than in her fevered state at the gallery two weeks ago, but she had explained the scheme for following Lyulf when he left and Nicholas nodded at that.

They arrived early at the Memorial but Lyulf was waiting for them nevertheless. He stood under the soot caked frieze, squat and unmoving, in a smock of mustard yellow and brown trousers. He might have been an allegorical figure from one of the gaudier corners of the monument, cleaned up and come to life. His arms were folded and he did not so much as nod his head to acknowledge their arrival, but his eyes glittered as he said, 'Come closer, boy. I want to look at you.'

Rowan put her hand on Nicholas's shoulder.

'Good afternoon, Mr Lyulf. I believe you can see well enough already. Do you have something to show us?'

Lyulf did not turn his glance towards Rowan. 'You look no more than commonplace now,' he said. 'Show me your hands.'

Nicholas clasped them behind his back. 'Did you bring the cat?' His voice sounded high and thin after Lyulf's deep growl.

Lyulf grunted. He brought out a glass ball from a trouser pocket and held it out to Nicholas, but Rowan stepped forward.

'Looking is all I promised,' Lyulf said, 'so you'll have to come close if you want to see.'

They bent their heads over the thing together. Rowan kept her hand on Nicholas's elbow, ready to push him aside if Lyulf grabbed at him. Inside the glass, a cat's mouth gaped at them and a tail thrashed. They had no time to see more before Lyulf pulled his hand away, but Rowan was jolted by a sudden glimpse of what James must have felt, trapped and off balance. She had not been properly frightened of Lyulf until now.

Lyulf put the ball away and took out something else.

'What's that?' Rowan stepped back and Nicholas moved with her.

'Watch.' Lyulf held a twist of grey wool, which he hooked onto the fingers of both hands and then twisted, loop over loop. Rowan had played cat's cradle years ago. This was not quite the same but she could not pinpoint the differences.

'See now, my hands are occupied, so I can't touch you,' Lyulf said. 'Talk to me, boy.'

'What are you making?'

'Don't they teach manners at your school? Don't you call a man sir, when your aunt brings you to apologise to him?'

'That's not why we have come,' Rowan said.

'What are you making, sir?' Nicholas asked.

Lyulf's thick fingers went to and fro. The grey thread seemed darker and stronger as it grew into a complicated web between his hands. 'Unguided magic is dangerous. You'll hurt yourself before you're much older.'

'I don't know anything about magic.' Nicholas sounded surprised.

Lyulf stared at Nicholas, his head thrust forward though his fingers continued to work. 'Who taught you how to break my traps?'

Nicholas shrugged. 'Nobody.'

'Seven years ago I learned how to make them and paid a price for it. Men with hammers and explosives, chemists, and old fools who were once Lords Magician have tried to break them and failed. How did you do it?'

'If I knew, I wouldn't tell you.'

'You're a child of the Exiles. Don't pretend to be an ignoramus as well as a fool.'

'That's all in the past. Mother says it is best forgotten.'

'When a boy grows up, he stops listening to his mother. Who else do you listen to?'

Nicholas shook his head. Rowan would have liked to see his face but she could not lift her gaze from the cobweb between Lyulf's fingers. She thought she should take Nicholas away but her body felt too heavy for her legs to carry. She smelled rotting seaweed, so strongly that she choked and jerked forwards. Nicholas grasped her elbow, just as Lyulf held out his hands to them both.

'Take a loop,' he said, in a new gentle voice. Rowan reached out instinctively in response but Nicholas pushed her sideways.

'No!' he said.

'Then I'll drag you,' Lyulf said.

The cobweb stretched out into a net, which he threw over Nicholas's head. Lyulf pulled at the net but Nicholas did not budge. Rowan grasped Lyulf's arm but he shook her off and she fell.

'Help!' she shouted.

There was a moment when nobody moved. Passersby looked but did not act. Lyulf's wrists bulged and sweat trickled down his forehead as he tugged at the net. Nicholas breathed as slowly as if he were asleep.

'Coming.' Henry and Vernon rushed round from the other side of the Monument and various strangers joined them. Lyulf grunted, snatched back his net, and tried to move away, but now Nicholas reached out to hold onto him and did not let go, even when Lyulf punched him. Henry and Vernon joined in, only to fall back from a whirl of blows.

Lyulf was a strong man, not tall but broad shouldered and fit. He ought to have been able to shake Nicholas off quickly but he could not. Rowan scrambled to her feet as both Lyulf and Nicholas sank into the stones under their feet. They went slowly but every jerk or twist from Lyulf took them further down, until they were embedded up to their ankles. Everyone else backed away, staring in alarm and bewilderment.

Rowan reached out, trembling, and patted Nicholas's shoulder. 'Nick,' she said. 'Stop, please. Can you stop?'

She was not sure whether he heard her. Lyulf was the one who discontinued the struggle.

'Fool boy! Let me go.'

Nicholas's face was glassy. Blue veins showed under his skin and his eyes were nearly shut. He did not answer.

Lyulf glared at Rowan. 'Make him let me go.'

'Keep still,' Rowan said. She steadied her breathing, continued to pat Nicholas and studied the ground. The sinking had come to a halt, she decided, but she had no idea how to reverse it. The two bodies looked like double stems which had grown up through holes in the paving. The stones were cracked and tilted round their legs, as though they had enlarged the holes as they grew. She knelt down and tried to push the cracks further apart but the stones were too heavy.

'Does that hurt, Nick?' she asked but received no response. Then a policeman pushed his way through the growing ring of spectators.

'What's going on here?'

Rowan stepped in front of Nicholas, suddenly conscious that she had torn her stockings when she fell and knocked her hat awry. Henry and Vernon came heroically to stand either side of her and Henry said, 'It's all right, officer. At least, it's going to be. We'll sort things out, if you'll give us a few minutes. Won't we, old girl?'

He was babbling but Rowan appreciated the gesture. Before she could decide what to say, Lyulf spoke. 'He's misleading you, officer. You should take this boy into custody for wanton destruction and malice.'

'Liar!' Rowan said. 'This man attacked us. He's a thief and a brute.'

She turned round to glare at Lyulf and saw that his net had disappeared. His hands were empty.

The policeman walked round to her side for a clear view of Lyulf and Nicholas.

'Hello!' he said. 'Who did that? Who's been damaging the Park grounds?'

'The boy.' Lyulf's voice was savage.

Rowan backed up to put her arm round Nicholas's shoulders. 'How could he? Where's his hammer?'

Nicholas's head was bent and he looked as if he had gone into hibernation.

'I'll have to report this to the Park Rangers,' the policeman said. 'Come along out of there and follow me.'

'We're stuck here, you oaf,' Lyulf said. 'Dig us out if you can.'

'Now then, sir.' The policeman's tone was a rebuke.

'All the same, I think they really are stuck, officer,' Vernon said.

He crouched down and tried to shift the stones round Nicholas's ankles without success. The crowd of bystanders had swollen in the last few minutes. Now someone called out, 'It must be a trick.'

'A publicity stunt.' That was someone else. 'What's the show, kids?'

The crowd laughed and the policeman looked round at them.

'Move along now, please. No loitering here, move along.'

Henry went to the Albert Hall instead of Rowan, to fetch Tilda. Before she came, two Park keepers arrived to investigate and the crowd dispersed, although little knots of people gathered at a distance and stayed a while, before becoming disheartened by the lack of action. Lyulf demanded that the keepers fetch picks and spades to lever out the stones, but they wanted to find out first how the stones had been broken. They asked questions and treated Lyulf's answers with growing incredulity. Rowan decided to say as little as possible and was soon too worried about Nicholas to pay attention to anything else. He was upright, so she thought he must be conscious, but he did not move or speak. His skin was cold, though the afternoon had become oppressively muggy. Rowan took off her linen jacket to put over him and Vernon added his blazer, which was a little more substantial, but Nicholas's deep chill did not change.

Tilda hurried into the Park, glad that she had chosen to wear walking shoes today and not anything smart enough to slow her down. She had not understood Henry's story but had decided to come and see for herself without wasting time. As soon as she had arranged for James to go home with a friend, she dashed across the road.

She saw Lyulf first and then Rowan's unhappy face. Then she saw Nicholas's head, atop a bundle of clothes. He stood solid and steady in the earth, while Lyulf twisted and flailed about. Tilda took a deep breath and walked forward to hug her son.

'Nicky, dear Nicky.' She pushed away the extra coats and folded her arms as close round him as she could. 'Everything's all right. You're going to be all right.'

She felt him turn his head up, so she eased away slightly to look at his face.

'Are you tired, Nick? Or hungry? Would you like to go home?'

He frowned. 'Thirsty,' he said.

Rowan burst into tears and other voices babbled but Tilda took no notice. 'Can you move the stones, Nick? Do you want people to dig round you?'

'Stones?' His voice was slow and dark. Then he said, 'Stones, stones, stones,' in a chant which quickened and grew brighter. He switched into Latin 'Saxa terraque,' he chanted, over and over.

Tilda felt his body shift against hers as he rose upwards and the stones crunched out of the way. He stepped free of the ground and at the same moment, Lyulf lurched forward. Before anyone was ready for him, he ran off, out of their reach across the Park. A couple of the men turned to chase him but gave up after a few steps.

Nicholas stopped chanting. Everyone stared at the ground, where the stones lay broken. The gaps in which Nicholas and Lyulf had been trapped were no longer to be seen.

'What kind of trick is this?' one of the Park Keepers asked.

'Excuse me, gentlemen,' Tilda said. 'I must take my son home.'

Eleven

Tilda leaned back against the door inside the studio and looked at the smoke from the cigarette between Rowan's fingers. For a moment, she wondered whether tobacco would make her feel better, but she had no cigarettes of her own and she was in no mood to ask for one of Rowan's.

'Are they all right?' Rowan looked up from her sketch pad. She had changed into her painting clothes and sat cross-legged on the couch, surrounded by crumpled sheets of paper.

'Both in bed,' Tilda said. Nicholas had been too exhausted to talk when they arrived home. James was in a sulk at being left out of the afternoon's excitement but he should have been tired enough from his singing to go to sleep. 'Have you got rid of those absurd young men?'

'They've gone. They were only trying to help.'

They had helped. Tilda could not remember which was which but one had brought her home with her sons in his car. The other had stayed in the Park to help Rowan deal with officialdom and then come back with her, but then they had lingered around, anxious to talk.

'The one in the car asked me if I had put a chemical on the soles of Nicholas's shoes,' Tilda said.

Rowan frowned at the open page of her sketch pad, which was covered with cross-hatching, shapeless and heavy. She tore the page out and crumpled it.

'They must have thought I planned an ambush with you and I had not told them.'

'Whereas…' Tilda could not keep her voice steady.

'I never meant to put Nick in danger.'

'Didn't you? What did you intend?'

Rowan drew rapid swirls and loops with a thick pencil and then scribbled over them. She did not look up.

'To find out more about Lyulf Lyulf. Maybe even track him to his lair. That's why I dragged the chaps along.'

'They are old enough to look after themselves. Nicholas is not.'

'Lyulf could not hurt Nick. You saw how he ran away as soon as he could.'

'I wasn't watching,' Tilda said. 'I was busy with Nicholas.'

The scribbles grew darker and heavier.

'Nick frightened himself. I didn't know he could do anything like that.'

'Then how could you know he would be safe?' Tilda wanted to sit down but not close to Rowan. She went over to perch on the windowsill. 'And how could you use my son for bait without asking my permission, without even warning me?'

'You wouldn't have listened.'

'I beg your pardon?'

'You wouldn't have let me tell you.' Rowan stubbed out her cigarette and swivelled round to face Tilda. 'You didn't believe James was trapped by magic. You will not talk about the Exiles' Club or about Spellhaven. If I had tried to explain, you would have said it was all nonsense and stopped Nick from coming with me. Then we would never have found out anything.'

'So you went behind my back, just as Alick did.'

'I didn't mean it like that.'

Tilda shut her eyes. 'I never forgave Alick. I never had the chance.'

'Tilda, old dear!' Rowan's arms came round Tilda in a hug. 'I'm sorry, I'm sorry. Don't let me upset you like this.'

Tilda had not realised she was cold but Rowan's warmth was an unexpected comfort.

'I must have been wrong about the magic. Wrong about Spellhaven. But it's worse if it's real. What he did was worse.'

'Come and sit down.' Rowan pulled Tilda over to sit on the couch and wrapped a shawl over her shoulders. 'Shall I fetch you a whisky? Or some cocoa?'

Tilda shook her head. The drinks were downstairs and she did not want to be left alone just now, ridiculous as that was. Rowan must have guessed, because she did not press her offer but sat down on the floor close by.

'I didn't know about Alick,' Rowan said. 'Did you two have a fight about Spellhaven?'

'About the boys.' Tilda's voice was thick and she swallowed hard. 'That evening, the night he died, I waited for him to come home so that I could quarrel with him. A Tuesday it was, and I had been waiting since Sunday morning, because of something James told me.'

'And Alick was away?' Rowan did not look round but her shoulder touched Tilda's knee.

'He had been down in the country for the weekend, showing off a new motor to some clients.' Alick worked as a salesman for his father's company, which had a reputation for making fast, well-designed motor cars. 'He enjoyed those trips and I did not want to go with him. I was happier at home with the boys.'

'What did James tell you?'

'He was eight years old and small for his age, which he hated. I said, "You'll soon grow," and he said, "When I'm nine. Then Father will let me help with his grand design, like Nick."

'I didn't know what he was talking about and I couldn't make much sense of his explanation, except that when Alick took the boys out, he sometimes left James alone with one of the engineers, while he and Nicholas went off together. I asked Nick, who said that what they did was a secret. Alick had made him promise not to tell anyone about it, not even me.

'So the boys went back to school and I waited for Alick. I was furious with him for leaving James behind and for putting the burden on Nicholas of keeping a secret, whatever it was. When I tackled Alick that evening, I made him furious with me: for questioning him, not trusting him, jumping to unwarranted conclusions.'

'I never saw him angry, that I can remember,' Rowan said.

'He was at his ease with you,' Tilda said. 'He was comfortable with me most of the time but he hated arguing.'

'He didn't have to take me seriously,' Rowan said. 'I was so much younger. I remember him sullen and miserable when we first came to London, but not angry.'

'I should not be talking to you about him like this.'

'Because he was my brother? Queen Victoria's dead.' Rowan sat up and twisted round to look Tilda in the eye. 'And I turn feelings into art. Whatever you want to say about Alick, I'm tough enough to hear.'

'What good would it do?' Tilda tried to think through the painful muddle of her feelings. 'I've never told anyone about that night.'

'Then you have bottled it up for far too long,' Rowan said briskly. 'Besides, I think it might be important. I don't know anyone at the Exiles' Club who could do what Nick did today.'

Sooner or later, they would have to face up to that. If Rowan had not taken Nicholas to meet Lyulf, something else would have happened to bring out the strangeness in him.

'Alick didn't tell me much,' Tilda said. 'He thought he had found a way to bring supernatural creatures under his control, just as the magician lords did in Spellhaven, but he needed Nick's help. He was teaching him, he said, and maybe James could join in later, but they couldn't have James interrupting them meanwhile. The experiments were too difficult and sensitive.'

'What experiments?'

'I never asked.' Tilda shut her eyes. 'I thought he was deluding himself. I told him occultism was poisonous rubbish. And I said my sons should not grow up unable to distinguish between truth and unhappy dreams, like his inadequate friends at the Club.'

'Ouch!' Rowan said.

'Alick said they were his sons too and he would make sure they learned about their inheritance in spite of me. I reminded him how little attention he paid, how often he promised to be at home with them and then let them down.'

'You were always so loving together,' Rowan said. Tilda looked up and saw that she was more puzzled than disapproving.

'We were too young. I thought Alick was wonderful when I married him, and he never stopped paying me compliments or courting me when he was at home, but he would not listen to me. I told myself I was lucky to have such a fond husband, but that night I was in despair.'

'What happened?'

'Not much more. We said the same things over and over again, until Alick decided to go out for a drive. To cool down, he said.' Tilda's throat dried and she whispered, 'He liked driving around at night. I thought he would be back in the morning, the same as ever.'

Instead he had run into a collision at a crossroads and died at the scene.

'You couldn't have known,' Rowan said.

Tilda was not prepared to talk about her misery as she had waited for him or her guilt and anger, as she realised their argument would never be resolved.

'I didn't believe in him,' she said. 'I was sure he was wrong about Spellhaven and about the magic. I've fought to keep the boys away from all that. Now what am I to do?'

'Lyulf will be keener than ever to lay a trap for Nicholas now,' Rowan said. 'You were right. I should not have interfered.'

'You didn't start this.'

'Nick will need help. Has he ever told you any more about Alick's experiments?'

'I never asked,' Tilda said. 'I wanted him to forget about it all.'

'Then maybe we can ask him tomorrow.'

James woke up, sure that someone had just blown in his ear. That should have meant he was at school, with some ass playing games after lights out, but when he opened his eyes, nobody was near him. His pillow smelled of lavender, not the carbolic they used in the school laundry. Moonlight came in through a slit in the curtains, so that he could see the jumble of stones on his bedside table at home and the wobbly model crane propped against the wall. The only other person in the room was Nick, who lay in his own bed and rolled from side to side, groaning.

James sat up and looked across. Nick's face turned in and out of the shadows, his eyes tight shut and his teeth bared. He held his arms up and jerked them to and fro, while his fingers clutched at nothing. He had thrown off his covering and his legs thrashed up and down. In the ordinary way, James knew better than to disturb his brother but this was not right.

'Nick! Hey Nick, wake up!'

The thrashing speeded up. James scrambled out of bed and went across. He called again with no result, so after some dithering he made a grab for Nick's feet. He caught hold of a big toe and pulled.

With a great start, Nick sat upright. He seized James's arm and shook him.

'Stop that, you fool.' James tried to twist out of the way. 'It's only me.'

Nick opened his eyes. He stared at James and relaxed his grip.

'James? Get out of the way!'

'When you have woken up.' James stood still. 'Are you all right?'

'I don't know.' Nick let go and looked round the room. 'I was in a fight.'

'You were having a nightmare.' James dropped his voice, in the hope that the grownups had not been roused up yet. 'Nobody else is here.'

Nick rubbed his hands over his face. 'I never have nightmares.'

'Where's the fight, then?' Nick did not answer, so James asked, 'Where did you think it was?'

Nick shrugged.

'Who were you fighting? Did you have a sword? The way your arms moved was more like wrestling. Or ju-jitsu, maybe.'

'I don't know ju-jitsu.'

'You might believe you did, in a dream. What did you see?'

Nick sat back against the wall. 'It's all gone now.'

James retreated to his own side of the room. 'Was it to do with the Park? Did you dream about Mr Lyulf?'

Nick shook his head.

'What happened in the Park? Did you hit Lyulf this afternoon?'

'I don't want to talk about this afternoon.'

'That's not fair! You know all about what he did to me.'

Nick said nothing. James thumped down onto his bed.

'How can anybody investigate anything without adequate information? I was the one caught in that man's trap. I ought to be the person to make a proper scientific investigation of his tricks.'

'He doesn't do tricks.' Nick stood up and went over to the wardrobe. 'I forgot. I've got something for you.' He found his trousers and felt in the pockets. 'Here.'

He held out a glass ball. James carried it over to the window and they both looked at it in the moonlight.

'How did you get this?'

'Snatched it before he ran away.'

James was too fascinated to ask for a fuller explanation. Inside the glass, a cat's mouth pressed towards them, stretched in a scream wider than its head. Its claws flashed in and out, useless against the glass.

'Shall I let it out?' Nick asked.

'Can you?'

'Maybe. I was too tired earlier.'

He took the ball between his hands and frowned at it. For a moment, nothing happened. James could hear his own breathing, fast and shallow, so he slowed down, to match his brother's deep, steady breaths.

Nick's fingers sank into the glass. A twist and a crack and the glass splintered. The cat dropped to the floor. Now they could hear its screams, sharp and furious.

'It's hurt,' James said and tried to pick it up. The glass splinters turned to grit in his hands. Claws dug deep into his arm and he yelped. The cat made a leap at the moonlight between the curtains but it failed to reach the open window and bounced back onto Nicholas. It swiped its claws across his knees and then twisted about to cut at James, just as his hands closed in on its body. The cat's screams turned to a high, continuous wailing.

'Not us,' James said as he crouched down. 'We won't do you any harm.'

The cat ricocheted round the room.

'Leave it alone,' Nick said.

'But it's injured.' They could see bald patches on its tail and one ear was torn. 'It needs cleaning up.'

They heard the creak of the door too late.

'Don't come in,' they both called out, but the door opened and the cat shot out onto the landing.

'What was that?' Their mother stumbled back and then entered the room. 'What's all the noise?' She switched on the light. 'You're bleeding, both of you!'

'We must catch the cat.' James went past her and ran down the stairs. Crashes and thuds directed him, but at this time of year doors and windows were left open to air the house. The cat slipped into the dining room and found a way up to cling under an open casement. James arrived to see it pour through the gap and drop down into the garden.

James' scratches were worse than Nick's. When they were both bandaged, Tilda allowed them to go out and search for the cat, but it was hopeless. The darkness was lifting by then but they could not see under bushes or among the flowerbeds. The screaming had stopped but they could hear scurrying and bird alarms, which might have been stirred up by the cat, or might not.

'Can we put out some milk?' Nick asked.

'That seems reasonable,' Tilda said, 'but you are not to sit and watch for the creature. Back to bed for you both. I want you clear-headed for a talk in the morning.'

'You held Lyulf's wrists. Do you remember that?' Rowan asked.

Nicholas looked at Tilda. 'He took your rings, Mother. I wanted to stop him getting away.'

Tilda did not care about the rings but she could not easily explain that. The drawing room was warm, even so soon after breakfast, and everyone was slippery with sweat. Tilda decided not to interrupt and Rowan said, 'Then you both sank down into the earth. How did that happen?'

Nicholas did not answer. He looked lumpish and heavy-eyed this morning. He stood in front of the fireplace, his head bent and his shoulders hunched, as though ready to fold himself up and disappear into the chimney. James stood beside him, jigging from foot to foot and often glancing over to the windows.

'It seemed as though your chant pulled you up, as far as I could tell,' Tilda said. 'Did you learn that from your father?'

'No.'

'Then how did you know what to do?'

'I didn't.' Nicholas thought this over and added, 'It felt right.'

Tilda could not see that this conversation was leading anywhere. Maybe she should have taken Nicholas for a walk and not pinned him down here, but she had wanted to clear matters up quickly so that the boys could return to normal for the rest of the day. Besides, Rowan and James had to be included somehow.

'Nicholas, we are worried about what that man may try next. Isn't there anything you can tell us about what you did to him?'

Nicholas shook his head.

Rowan leaned forward. 'I'm sorry I took you to him, Nick, but he was interested in you already. He asked me questions about you. Now he's bound to be even more eager to lay traps for you and we don't know how to stop him.'

'I'll be all right.'

'If we could find the cat,' James said, 'we might discover some of Lyulf's secrets.'

Tilda gritted her teeth. She did not blame the boys for setting the cat loose but she did not want to worry about it now. There had been no sightings this morning, though James had been out before breakfast to call and to examine the garden for traces of the beast.

'It's only a cat,' Nicholas said.

'But it was in that man's trap for weeks or longer.'

'True enough, James,' Rowan said, 'but you couldn't tell us anything useful about him when you escaped.'

'In any case, we can't find the cat,' Tilda said, 'or communicate with it if we do.'

'Unless Nick can?' James asked.

'Nicholas is not a conjuror,' Tilda snapped and the boys stared at her, wide-eyed.

'That's not what people are going to think he is,' Rowan said, 'but they will be interested. There's bound to be talk, even if I put the dampeners on Henry and Vernon.'

Tilda appreciated her tact. She did not want to talk to the boys about the Exiles' Club just yet. 'Term ends next week. Rowan, would your parents care for a visit, this early in the holidays?'

'From the boys?'

'And from me. Isn't your father the best person to advise Nicholas now?'

'I'm not sure,' Rowan said. 'He hasn't had anything to do with such matters for a long time, but he can tell you about the family and the powers we used to have. Maybe that will help.'

Twelve

Elephant Cottage was bigger than Tilda's house in Highgate, a red brick building on the edge of a Hertfordshire village. Ivar and Beatrice Gray had moved there soon after Alick's marriage. Tilda and the boys visited regularly, though they seldom stayed for more than a few days. This time, they went down by train and were met at the local station by one of the Gray cars, which took them up the hill. The hedges were thick with dust and the car went faster round the narrow bends than Tilda liked. The boys sat beside the chauffeur, where they could study his actions and watch the instrument panel. They were silent, as they had been all morning, but the drive was a short one and the air fresh and cool when they disembarked.

Mrs. Gray was in the front garden to greet them.

'We're delighted to see you, my dears. Ivar is at the works but he has promised to come home early for tea.'

She bent down for a brief embrace with each grandson and then straightened to shake hands with Tilda, who was the taller by a head. Tilda took off her glove and Mrs. Gray's eyes widened.

'Your rings?'

'I should have written to you about that,' Tilda said. 'May I tell the story later on, when your husband is here?'

'You're wearing no rings at all. You haven't come to say you are going to marry again?'

'Nothing like that.' The thought had never occurred to Tilda. She reached forward to clasp Mrs. Gray's hands. 'I didn't mean to frighten you.'

'Of course not.' Mrs Gray's smile did not quite restore her to cheerfulness. 'Come inside and wash off the journey.'

After tea, they gathered in the back garden, in the shade of an elm tree. Ivar and Beatrice sat side by side on the bench built round the trunk, while Tilda faced them on a wicker chair and the boys sat on rugs beside her. The tree filled Tilda's vision and the sky behind it, wider and clearer than in London. The breeze was slight but enough to set the elm leaves ashiver. The call of the wood pigeons and the buzz of insects should have provided refreshment from the heat and noise of London, but Tilda had never found Alick's parents easy to talk to and now she could hardly see their faces in the shade.

They listened as she described James's disappearance and her visit to Lyulf's shop. James was enough in awe of his grandparents not to interrupt. When Tilda told how Nicholas had broken the glass ball and let James out, Ivar Gray sat forward.

'That is not possible. Such things can never happen here.'

Tilda would have expected disbelief from anyone else but not the Grays.

'I thought the same at the time. Let me tell you the rest.'

When she came to what she had seen in the Park, Mr. Gray broke in, 'Rowena knows better than this. Where is she?'

'She offered to come but I wanted to talk to you by ourselves first,' Tilda said. 'I saw Nicholas and the man Lyulf sunk in the ground. I'm sure of that. And I saw them rise up when Nicholas chanted.'

'You must have been tricked somehow.' Mr. Gray sounded angry as well as disbelieving, and he reminded Tilda suddenly of her husband. She had not noticed much of a resemblance while Alick was alive but now she could see him in his father's long limbs and square shoulders. Ivar Gray was in his sixties but fit and quick-moving. He sat back now and Tilda sensed that he would rather have been pacing up and down, as Alick would have done.

'You boys,' he said. 'What kind of game were you playing?'

'We were not playing, Grandfather.' James was almost too indignant to be polite. 'We despise practical jokers, and we wouldn't have known how to do any of that.'

'Nicholas, what did you do?'

'I don't know,' Nicholas said. Mr. Gray glared at him and he added, 'James is right. We weren't playing.'

'Then you must all have been hypnotised.'

Tilda enjoyed walking into the wind, but this was like a gust coming sideways to knock her over. She had fought so long against Alick's belief in magic, until she had been convinced by what she had seen with her own eyes. Either she and her sons, and Rowan too, were seriously unwell or the magic was real. She realised the rest of the world might not understand but she had thought Alick's parents would be eager to accept her belief.

'Alick told me magic worked in the city you came from,' she said.

'Indeed it did.' Mr. Gray sagged back against the tree trunk and his voice darkened. 'Spellhaven was founded in magic and destroyed by magic. That's why I'm sure this tale of yours cannot be true.'

James bounced where he sat. Tilda frowned at him and he kept quiet, though his chin quivered with fury. Nicholas had shut himself down, his head bent, his shoulders slumped.

'I don't understand,' Tilda said.

Mr. Gray drew in a deep breath and glanced at his wife, who had scarcely moved as she listened to Tilda. Now she winced and looked away, out over the garden. She did not speak.

'What do you know about our city?' Mr. Gray asked. 'What have you told the boys?'

'Alick told them he was born in a tower on a marvellous island ruled by magicians, and he made a bedtime story out of the way you all escaped when the city was drowned.'

'Not all of us.' He glanced at his wife again. 'Alick's brothers and his older sister, Stilicho, Kendric, and Ismene were killed that day, and more of the Graysteel Clan besides. And Beatrice's family.'

'I'm sorry,' Tilda said. 'The boys were so young, Alick could not tell them too much. And since he died, I have not talked to them about his background.'

Mr. Gray grunted. 'In Spellhaven, the Unseen inhabitants, the Spirits great and small, were bound to the protection of the island and to the service of the Lords Magician. With their aid, I could work marvels beyond your imagining, although I was never among the greatest of the Magicians. Spirits away from the city were never so bound, but when we travelled they would converse with us and help us for the sake of their cousins on the island.'

His voice was deliberate and his face stern. He might have been a doctor reporting on the onset of a dangerous illness. 'When the binding spells were broken, the Spirits were angry at their long captivity. Fire erupted from under the earth and monstrous waves crashed down until the city was broken apart. Many people drowned but others escaped.' He paused. 'Is that what your father told you?'

Nicholas nodded.

'I tried to find Spellhaven on a map of the British Isles,' James said. 'It's not there. Father said it was peripatetic.'

'That was part of the magic,' Mr. Gray answered. 'A magician could find his way home by travelling any of the rivers that run into the Northern seas, but nobody else could reach the city unless they were summoned.'

'Then how did you all end up in England?' James asked.

'When we crossed the Causeway that day, we reached this island.' Mr. Gray's voice shook. 'Who knows which of the magicians brought it here? We came in the middle of the War, in shock and grief. Not only for the loss of our families and our city but for the loss of our magic. We could no longer feel the presence of the Unseen in the air or draw on them to aid us in our troubles.

'Once we began to recover we sought for ways to win back the magic, but the more we tried, the less we achieved. At the beginning, a few among us conversed with the Spirits of this land, though never to any purpose. Then such encounters dwindled away to nothing. Since the Exiles' Club was founded, not all the labours of the surviving Clan Lords have moved a pin by magic.'

The wind dropped for a moment and all the birds were silent. A tang of salt drifted through the heavy scents of the garden, reminding Tilda of the seaside.

'Father talked about his friends at the Club,' James said. 'He meant to astonish them one day.'

Tears glinted on Beatrice Gray's face as her husband said, 'Friends who never did any good. You are missing my point, James. The magic died with Spellhaven, do you understand? Fine men and women have wasted their lives in their struggles to revive magic or somehow bring the city back to life. They have all failed.'

'Then a different kind of magic must be possible,' James said. 'I was trapped in that glass. It wasn't a trick. And what about what Father was trying to do with Nick?'

Mrs. Gray gasped. Her husband looked at her and stood up.

'I want an end to this nonsense. Nicholas, did your father ever show you any magic? Or teach you to work magic?'

Nicholas came to his feet and tipped his head up to look his grandfather in the eye. 'No he did not.'

'Then let us hear no more about it.' He stopped beside Tilda. 'I'll trace the man Lyulf for you. He has no right to your jewellery, whatever else.'

He strode away.

'But-' James said and Tilda interrupted, 'Help your grandmother back to the house.'

Mrs. Gray shook her head. 'Later,' she said. 'Just leave me here in peace for a little while.'

The next day, the sons of the local doctor called to invite Nicholas and James to play cricket, and Mrs. Gray took Tilda out on a round of local visits. None of this was much to their liking but all three acquiesced and maintained a careful politeness at mealtimes.

In the evening, Ivar Gray said, 'Let me show you something.'

The weather had cooled so they were gathered indoors, in the drawing room. He brought out a box of polished yew wood and they saw a device inlaid in silver on the lid, a gauntlet with long talons.

'That's the mark on the Gray cars,' James said.

'Look closer. This is the badge of the Graysteel Clan: the car mark has no cuff.'

The deep cuff was engraved in a diamond pattern.

'Did that use to be our name, Graysteel?'

Mr. Gray nodded. 'We cannot live here as the Clans lived in Spellhaven. I shortened the name and the device to mark the difference, but you boys should learn enough of the past to recognise truth from lies.'

'What is the Latin for Graysteel?' Nicholas asked. He had been so quiet all day that the others stared at him. Even his grandmother looked up from her embroidery. 'Didn't you all speak Latin?'

'Latin was the common tongue in the city,' Mr. Gray said, 'but Clan names were left as they were hundreds of years ago, when the founding fathers came from different places. Or they were the nicknames adopted in the early years. Our ancestors were from the Lowlands of Scotland and they had a fondness for tales of the giant Graysteel.'

He put the box down on a low table and Tilda knelt beside the boys to look at it. Inside was a pack of cards, which Mr. Gray spread out on the table. They looked hand painted, the designs intricate and bright, like the illuminations in medieval manuscripts. The backs bore a roundel of a white wall, topped by towers of red and gold on a ground of dark blue.

'Spellhaven City,' Mr. Gray said.

'Were the cards made there?' James asked.

'We brought nothing so futile away with us. These were made at the Club, to revive the craft as practised in the city.'

He showed them the four suits: golden cats; blue thistles; green theatre masks, comedy and tragedy together; and black crows with red beaks and legs. Then there was a bewildering array of court cards, portraits of men and women in elaborate costumes.

'These are beautiful,' Tilda said.

'There are too many for ordinary games,' James asked. 'Are they fortune telling cards?'

'I would not have them in the house if they were.' The answer came from Mrs. Gray. She sat apart from the others, by the open window so that she had the best of the fading light for her work, but she hardly touched her needle. The white silk roses stitched onto a cloud of white net must have strained her eyes even during the day.

'Even as a young girl, I never liked to look into the future. It would be worse now.'

James twisted round to gaze at her. 'Do you mean you could do it if you wanted? How-'

'James,' Tilda interrupted, 'let your grandfather tell you about the cards.'

He looked at her in reproach but he did not argue.

'Here are the seven Great Ladies of Spellhaven,' Mr. Gray continued. 'Duchess Ragnild was the first, the enchanter who laid the binding spells on the spirits of land and sea. And the next was Lady Virgil, who found out how to placate all the Unseen who gathered in the city when the Duchy was overthrown.'

The Duchess had a coronet of plaited red hair and wore a black cloak decorated with mountains and stars. The Lady wore breeches and a jacket in many shades of blue. Their faces were pale, with pointed chins and wide, dark eyes.

'I thought the magician lords were men,' James said.

Tilda's knees hurt. She rose to her feet before she became too stiff.

'There's a man.' Nicholas pointed at a card half-hidden among the others.

'Duke Ulfin, Ragnild's husband. He was no magician but a warrior and a strong ruler. He founded Spellhaven as a refuge, after he had quarrelled with half the war leaders of the Norse lands.'

'Are these lesson cards?' James spoke with distaste and his grandfather replied in much the same tone, 'They were made to play the traditional games of the city.'

Tilda backed away and sat down. She suspected the misunderstandings between the boys and their grandparents were about to increase but she could not think how to avoid them.

'Do you play them here?' James asked. 'You and grandmother by yourselves?'

'No. I bought them as a reminder of the treasures we have lost and all Spellhaven's long history. I keep them shut away so as not to remember too much.'

James turned his attention back to the cards. 'All those women have the same face.'

'Haven't you begun on iconography in your art lessons yet?' Mrs. Gray asked. 'All my children began on heraldic painting, as well as costume design and geometry, before they were of an age to choose their studies.'

It was a baffling list, nothing like the curriculum at the boys' school.

'Those arts would be of little use here,' Mr. Gray said.

'Aunt Rowan paints,' James said, 'but she uses different models for different faces.'

'The faces don't matter,' Mr. Gray said. 'Each personage has their own attributes, the symbols of their achievements. See the eternal knot hung on Ragnild's necklace, and the beehive brooch in Lady Virgil's hat.'

'I suppose there were no photographs to show what they really looked like,' James said. 'Did Father play with these cards?'

'He had no need,' Mrs. Gray answered. 'He had his own memories of Spellhaven. Before the downfall, he handled the Unseen Spirits with more promise than anyone else of his age in the Clan.'

'So Father was a magician.' James turned his back on the cards to look at his grandmother. 'What sort of things could he do?'

'Enough to make him discontented forever,' Mr. Gray said, 'once he had to live without magic.'

'Not forever,' Mrs. Gray said. 'It need not have been forever.'

'He was proud of both of you,' Tilda said, 'and of his sons.' Pride was not the same as contentment but never mind that for now. 'Maybe the boys could look at the cards another time. Then they could go for a run outside before bedtime.'

Nicholas and James were on their feet before she had finished, eager for release.

'Off you go.' Mr. Gray swept up the cards. Tilda would have liked to learn more about the pictures on them but she did not know what it would be safe to ask.

Thirteen

The oak tree was in the far corner of the school grounds, next to the road. Hugo Cole climbed into the tree on the day before his uncle was due to collect him for the holidays. School had been over for a week, and the last of the other pupils had already departed. So far, Hugo was moderately proud of the way he had kept himself cheerful. He hated the hour every morning when he listened to his ghosts, but once that was over they did not speak to him now, even when he was on his own, so he was a good deal better off than in the summer holidays last year. And he was to stay with Uncle Stephen for nearly a fortnight before he went down to the seaside with some second cousins. Whatever they were like, the seaside should be better than staying here all summer and he could not expect his uncle to look after him for the whole time. He could not help wondering what had become of Nicholas and James Gray. He did not think they had dropped him, despite the awkwardness over the exhibition he had not been taken to, which nobody had been willing to explain. Maybe he would see the Grays later on,

Uncle Stephen had said, and Hugo was determined not to bother them meanwhile.

He climbed the tree by way of distraction from his thoughts and to test himself. He scrambled onto the lowest branch by way of an abandoned lawn roller and a fence post, as he had seen other boys do. Then he pulled himself up to the next branch, where he rested, scratched and hot, but triumphant. He was not sure what to do next. He had a book in his pocket but he did not feel secure enough to read. He could see across the road onto the Heath in the distance, where boys flew kites and dogs chased one another. They looked remote, further away than a scene in a film. Nearby, birds fussed as they settled back after the disturbance he had caused and leaves rattled. Down on the ground he had scarcely noticed the wind, but up here gusts swooped through the tree and rocked the bough he sat on.

'Left you behind, have they?'

The voice startled him. He tightened his grip on a cross branch and looked down. Lyulf Lyulf stood outside the fence, almost directly beneath Hugo's perch.

'I won't listen to you,' Hugo said.

'Then you'll have to stuff leaves in your ears and push them in hard. I've got a loud voice when I need it.' Lyulf's forehead shone as he tilted his head to look at Hugo and his beard jerked up and down. 'What are you doing up there?'

'The caretaker's in school. He'll fetch the police.'

'If you want to jump, you ought to climb higher first. Else you will end up crippled, not dead.'

'I don't want to jump.' Hugo could not move out of reach of Lyulf's voice without climbing down and he could not climb down while Lyulf watched. 'I won't talk to you. Please go away.'

'You needn't be scared. I have no interest in cowards. All I want from you is a little information.'

'You tricked me. And J-. And my friend. I won't tell you anything.'

'James Gray,' Lyulf said, 'and his freak of a brother. Where have they gone?'

The wind tugged at Hugo's' shoulders and at the branch between his knees. He felt sick.

'Go away,' he whispered, without expecting any effect. 'Go away, go away.'

'You had better come down before you fall down. Here, catch this.'

The end of a rope flew upwards. Hugo flinched away and it caught among the twigs nearby.

'It's no trap,' Lyulf said. 'Ask the pals at your back if you don't believe me.'

'I won't,' Hugo said. 'I won't touch it.'

Lyulf pulled the rope back and threw it again. This time Hugo ducked and the branch dipped under him. He lay down on his stomach and clamped his arms and legs tight round the rough bark.

'Tell me about your friends and I'll get the caretaker to bring a ladder along to save you. Tell me who their teachers are.'

This was no secret. Hugo half sat up. 'The same teachers as the rest of us.'

'Not the teachers at school. Who teaches them magic? Who are their allies at the Exiles' Club?'

'Where?' Hugo stared at the cracked bark under his nose and tried to think straight. If he had none of the information Lyulf wanted, maybe he could answer questions without giving away his friends.

'Don't be a fool, boy. A score of pupils at that school must be from Spellhaven families.'

'I've never heard of Spellhaven.' Hugo sat up straighter.

'Why else were the ghosts on the Heath so quick to rouse to your summons?'

'The ghosts are nothing to do with the boys at school.'

'Are they not? And your friends have never spoken to you about their ancestors? Or the treasures of the Exiles' Club?'

'Never.'

Lyulf tugged his rope to the ground.

'Hardly worth calling them friends in that case. What do you know about them?'

Giving any answers had been a mistake. Hugo shut his mouth and shook his head. The rope flew upwards, now aimed as a lash. It struck Hugo's arm and he stretched out along the branch again.

'Where have they gone? Who are their real friends?' The rope burned across Hugo's thigh. 'When are they coming home?'

Hugo shut his eyes and tucked his head down among the leaves as best he could.

'Who is their mother's lover? Or their aunt's?'

Hugo said nothing. The questions stopped but the blows kept coming. Hugo clung on.

Rowan saw Stephen Cole as she came downstairs from her life class. He was taller than most of the people who milled around the entrance hall and he stood erect, disregarding all their chatter. His gaze was distant and severe. When Rowan headed towards him, he lifted his hat but his face hardly relaxed.

'Miss Gray, thank you for agreeing to see me. Do you know somewhere we can talk?'

Rowan steered him to the nearest café not frequented by her friends and warned him away from the buns. 'But their coffee is good.'

She lit a cigarette while they waited. Stephen's eyes were shadowed and the folds in his face had deepened since the last time she had seen him.

'Don't judges go on holiday in July?'

'The courts are in recess,' he said, 'but I have a mountain of paperwork to tackle. I had to put off some urgent matters while I took Hugo away.'

When he had telephoned, Rowan had wondered if he wanted to complain about her picture, but he had asked for Tilda first, so that seemed unlikely.

'Is Hugo all right?' Rowan asked.

'Not altogether.' The coffee arrived and Stephen waited until the waiter moved away. 'That's why I changed my plans. We had settled that he would stay with me for a few days and amuse himself while I was in Chambers, but when I collected him, he was in no fit state to be left alone.' He did not look at Rowan and she could not decide whether he was nerving himself to accuse her or brooding over something entirely different.

'Is this about Eyes in the Shadows?'

'About what?'

'My painting of Hugo and his ghosts?'

'No, not that. Hugo never saw it finished, did he?' He frowned again and then said, 'They told me you had decided not to sell it. If you ever change your mind-'

'I won't.' Rowan decided to clear the air. 'I'm not sorry I painted it but I won't sell it. Or exhibit it again.'

Stephen looked at her doubtfully. 'It's an important picture, I understood. You shouldn't let Hugo's troubles damage your career.'

Rowan was surprised as well as flattered. 'If I can paint another as good, people will forget about Eyes. If I can't, it doesn't matter anyway.'

Stephen continued to frown but at least he looked as though his mind was concentrated here, not a hundred miles away.

'That doesn't seem right,' he said.

'Never mind. Was it Hugo you wanted to talk about?'

'In a way. I wanted to warn your sister-in-law that Nicholas and James may be in danger.'

'What kind of danger?'

'Hugo was attacked by that man Lyulf. He has a collection of welts and bruises, and he is in a misery almost as bad as earlier in the year. I could hardly get him to speak to me or leave the school grounds.'

'Lyulf got at him at the school?'

'He was up a tree.'

Rowan stopped herself asking any more questions and listened to Stephen's account. At the end he said, 'Hugo wouldn't tell me everything that Lyulf said to him but the man was certainly most interested in your nephews. He promised to leave Hugo alone if he would answer questions about them.'

'Should we believe him?' Rowan asked.

'Hugo did. In fact, I might not have dug the story out of him at all if he had not been worried about Nicholas and James. He is afraid Lyulf plans to ambush them.'

'I dare say that's right. But does it follow that Hugo is safe from his attentions? Where is Hugo now?'

'Down in Hampshire, staying with cousins. I haven't told them the whole story: I thought it would be better if Hugo could leave his troubles behind. But they know he has not been well and they can see how he is marked. They'll keep an eye on him.'

'But they won't know what to watch out for,' Rowan said, as an observation, not a criticism. 'Not that we are much better off. What did you want to tell Tilda?'

'That Nicholas and James should be on their guard, and I am minded to report the attack to the police. I thought she should know, in case they want to speak to her again about what happened after the Fair.'

'And in the Park,' Rowan said. 'I suppose it all adds up, although they still won't know what to make of it.'

'What about the Park?'

'I forgot – you weren't in that.' Rowan sat back and looked at Stephen. 'This is harder to believe than Hugo's story, but remember, I was there.'

Stephen stared into his empty coffee cup while she talked and his frown sank deeper and deeper into his face.

'Did the police talk to the crowd?' he asked.

'I doubt it,' Rowan said. 'Why should they?'

'To find out what they saw.'

'The legal mind at work.' Rowan was more amused than offended. 'Everyone saw the legs sunk in the ground. Nobody could account for it. The Park Rangers have decided it is easier to drop the matter than to investigate it.'

'Hallucinations can be terrible things,' Stephen said.

'Hallucinations don't break stones.'

He shook his head. 'I don't mean to doubt you, Miss Gray. It's hard for me to make sense of all this, however much I try.'

'I wish you would call me Rowan. I agree nothing seems to make sense but that is because we don't know enough. And I doubt the police can find out anything useful.'

'What else can we do?'

'I mean to go back to the Exiles' Club. Somebody there must have run across Lyulf.' Rowan hesitated, 'I don't suppose you would care to come with me?'

'If you think I can be of any help.'

'They can hardly treat you like a child. I'll make the introductions and you can cross-examine anyone who seems shifty.'

'Not my kind of case,' Stephen muttered but he smiled. 'I should be honoured to accompany you, Rowan.'

Fourteen

Once or twice a year, Stephen Cole was invited to lunch at the Athenaeum, and from the talk in Chambers, he knew about the Soho clubs where refugees from all over Europe gathered to argue about poetry or politics. Some allowed women as well as men to become members. He expected Rowan's club to be more like the latter than the former, though he was not sure whereabouts in Europe these particular exiles came from. None of the Grays had said much about their background and until she proposed this expedition, Rowan had spoken of the Club only as a place to be avoided. Stephen was doubtful that much would be gained by going there but it was a place to start.

When Rowan led him to the four-storey building in Covent Garden, he thought at first that the Club rented rooms in someone else's factory, but the entrance, which opened into an array of small workshops, had only one nameplate, for Lost Causeway Enterprises. People greeted Rowan as she and Stephen went past on their way to the stairs.

'We'll start at the top,' Rowan said, 'that's where the real talking gets done.'

'But where's the Club?'

'Here. All of it.' Rowan clattered upwards in her high heels. 'The place was started to help people make a living when they first came to London, as well as to maintain the crafts of the old city. The social side is the third prong of the fork.'

Stephen's legs were longer but he was heavier than Rowan and had to exert himself to keep up. He was glad to pause on the third floor landing beside a stained glass window, a sea of blue and green waves, with white crests.

'Was this made here?'

'Of course.' Rowan looked back down. 'Pretty but retrograde.'

'More than pretty. Splendid,' Stephen said, but he moved onto the last flight of stairs.

They entered a big room, where an array of newspapers in a dozen languages hung on wooden batons near the door. Women as well as men, young and old, sat in little knots of conversation, and ceiling fans stirred the clouds of cigarette smoke.

'Rowan Gray, here to make our day!' A burly man, nearer to Stephen in age than Rowan, lifted her off her feet in a hug. As soon as he put her down, she pushed him away, not angrily but as a matter of routine.

'Hello, Piers. We'll talk to you later, if you like. Are any of the old Lords here this evening?'

Piers seemed unaware of any rebuff. He did not look at Stephen.

'They're too old to leave home much these days, but Domaldi might be in the Library, in his box. What do you want with him?'

'Later,' Rowan said.

She led Stephen briskly through the library, so that he only had a glimpse of the books and the complicated picture maps on display there. At the back was an open door to a small room, where an old man sat hunched over a puppet. He was trying to disentangle its strings but his fingers were clumsy. When he looked up, Stephen saw that his bowed shoulders were uneven and his neck twisted.

'Good evening, Lord Domaldi,' Rowan said. 'May I help you with that?'

'Ivar Gray's daughter?' Domaldi's voice was deep and slow. 'And who is with you?'

'A friend.' Rowan moved into the room and crouched down in front of the old man. Stephen followed though there was hardly space enough for him to stand between a model theatre and stacks of boxes.

'Stephen is helping me find things out.' She reached out for the puppet Domaldi held but he did not let it go.

'If you do this, I will take all the longer over the next one. What kind of things?'

'The knowledge to help three young boys.' Rowan straightened up. 'We're not here out of idle curiosity.'

'But you mean to ask questions I will not want to answer.' Domaldi glanced sharply at Stephen. 'Why should I speak to a stranger?'

'My name is Stephen Cole, sir. Maybe you could hear our questions before you refuse to answer them.'

Domaldi's head sank down onto his chest. 'Or maybe it would save trouble to send you away now. What gives you any claim on my good will, Rowena?'

'This is not for me,' Rowan said. 'We want to free my nephews from the attentions of Lyulf Lyulf. Do you know the man?'

'I do not.'

'Have you ever heard of him?'

'That question I will not answer.' Domaldi pulled himself out of his chair and Stephen saw that he had once been a tall man, but was now shrunken and twisted from bones which had broken and failed to set properly. 'I will not suffer that name to be spoken again in my hearing.'

'Then you must know something about him,' Stephen said. 'Will you tell us why you will not hear his name?'

'I will not. I will do nothing for you.'

'But what he is up to could matter to all the Exiles,' Rowan said. 'Let us tell you-'

'No.' Domaldi took hold of a walking stick and leaned on it. 'Will you leave me now or must I leave you?'

He could not outrun them but they could scarcely harass him down the stairs.

'Will you refer us to someone else we can speak to about the man?' Stephen asked.

'No.' As Domaldi stepped forward, Rowan and Stephen backed away. They found themselves outside the door and Domaldi shut it in their faces.

They looked at one another. Rowan shook her head.

'Let's try the smoking room,' she said.

Rowan introduced Stephen to several little groups scattered round the smoking room. They all seemed pleased to see her, though they did not know what to make of Stephen. He wondered if she ever brought her suitors here and how dull he appeared in comparison, but he let Rowan lead the talk, which ran along comfortably until she mentioned Lyulf. Then people shook their heads and said nothing, or else they jumped up and hurried away, muttering about forgotten appointments.

Eventually Rowan was cornered by Piers Marshall, the man who had greeted her earlier. Two others were with him, Frederick Burrows and Darius Fox. All three had been friends of her brother, well dressed and prosperous chaps, intent on welcoming Rowan and just about tolerant of her escort. They sat down and ordered iced tea, which Stephen had never tasted, but he welcomed the notion of a cold drink of any kind.

The conversation between the three men and Rowan was a fencing match. They asked her questions about her art classes and her acquaintances but did not listen to the answers. She asked them about the Club but did not mention Lyulf. Stephen could not decide whether she was preparing a circuitous approach or whether she did not want to rely on these men for information.

The black tea was refreshing, not too bitter and flavoured with ginger and apple. Stephen drank half his glass before Burrows sat forward to look at him.

'And what about you, Cole? Are you another painter?' He made it sound like a synonym for wastrel.

'I'm at the Bar,' Stephen said.

'Are you hoping Rowan will hanker after respectability when she grows up?'

'My nephew is a friend of her nephews. They go to the same school.'

'We know that school,' Marshall said. 'That school has been a disappointment to us, Rowan. Alick chose it because the Wulfing boys are there and half a dozen other sons of Exiles. But do they teach them about our history or let us give talks to the pupils? They fend us off every time we offer to go.'

'That wasn't what Alick wanted for them,' Rowan said.

Darius Fox had been the quietest of the group so far. Now he said, 'Which makes it unlikely that the school stirred you up to visit us here, Mr. Cole.' His smile was that of Counsel laying a trap in court.

Stephen looked at Rowan, who twirled the long string of beads she wore round her neck and did not return the look. He could not tell what she wanted but he was weary of stonewalling.

'I'm here to help Rowan find out about someone called Lyulf Lyulf,' he said.

The three men sat back and frowned at one another.

'Then you are wasting your time, I'm afraid,' Fox said.

'Was that why you wanted to speak to the Puppet Master, Rowan?' Marshall asked. 'You should know better than that.'

'How?' Rowan scowled at him. 'How am I supposed to know when nobody will explain anything?'

'Take our word for it, dear girl,' Burrows said. 'The less said on that subject the better.'

'It's too important for that. At least tell me why nobody will talk about him.'

'They can't,' a new voice spoke and they looked up at the waiter who had served their tea. He was clearing the table next to theirs but he paused and looked at Rowan. 'Six years ago, they all took an oath never to mention him or what he had done.'

In this place, it might have been less startling if the furniture had come to life.

'Don't they train the waiters here any more?' Burrows muttered.

'They are supposed to be from Exile families down on their luck,' Marshall said. 'Young man, have you no loyalty?'

The waiter flushed. 'I took no oath.'

Rowan leaned forward. 'But were you here six years ago? You must have been very young.'

'I worked in the kitchens as a lad, because my parents were down on their luck.' His voice was sardonic. 'I've been away since, trying to get a job abroad. Now I'm back and the place is crazier than ever.'

'Is that a reason for interfering in the affairs of your betters?' Marshall swelled where he sat, his face red and shiny.

'Just because you all panicked, you don't have to torment her as well,' the waiter said.

'But is that for you to judge?' Fox's voice was mild. 'Do you do this sort of thing often, young – what is your name?'

'Gavin Baker.' Now the waiter was pale but he stood up straight and looked at Rowan. 'I don't care if they report me. I'm sick of people who want to turn the clock back to a time that never was.'

'But I care,' Rowan said. 'You can't report him just because he wants to help me. What did Lyulf do, Gavin?'

He shrugged. 'Sold his soul to the devil, according to what was said in the kitchen.'

'But how exactly?'

'That's all I know.' He went back to piling up crockery.

'Then thank you for your help,' Rowan said.

'Forget it,' he said without looking up. They watched him go and Stephen said, 'I wonder if other servants from that time would know more. Maybe we could talk to them.'

Marshall groaned. Fox sighed and asked, 'You're not going to give up, are you? Suppose I tell you a story, Rowan, about a man whose name we need not specify.'

'Are you sure, Darius?' Burrows asked.

'Would you rather they turned the whole Club inside out?' Fox did not wait for an answer but settled himself deep into his armchair and steepled his hands together. 'Once upon a time, a student came to the Club, a youngster with no ties to Spellhaven or its people, so far as anybody could discover, but he had come across some garbled stories in his research into medieval European history and he wanted to learn more. Some of our senior members thought it was a mistake to take any stranger into our confidence unnecessarily, but others decided we would attract more unwelcome attention if we made a mystery of ourselves. Besides, the student was most beguiling and eager to please.'

Fox's voice was pleasant and well-paced. Now and then he glanced at Rowan but never at Stephen. 'This was a time when the first schemes for restoring our city had failed and likewise those for reviving our magic. So younger members were trying out new ideas, some more desperate than others. Did Alick ever talk to you about his experiments, Rowan?'

Burrows and Marshall drew in their breath.

'I wouldn't have listened. I wasn't interested,' Rowan said.

Fox nodded. 'How sensible of you. Now the student in question did listen, maybe not to your brother, but to Rhyming Kate, Harper Norval, and various others. The more keenly he listened, the more they told him. Eventually, he persuaded Norval to let him help in various trials. They huddled together in a corner of the library here for months and then they stopped coming. After a while Norval's old friends got a bit worried, so they went to call on him at home. He wasn't there.'

Fox came to a halt.

'Horrible business,' Burrows said.

'Don't spin it out,' Rowan said.

Fox grimaced. 'I've never told this story before. I doubt anyone has. Norval was missing for weeks and then one day he marched into the Club, jumping with rage like a true Berserker. Eventually, he calmed down enough to explain. He and the student had worked their way through all the devices for summoning magic they could find in old books of country legends, on the grounds that the truth might lie in them somewhere. I don't know what else they tried but the one that worked, after a fashion, involved skinning nine cats alive.'

'That's disgusting,' Rowan said.

'Just so,' Fox replied. 'The ritual got the attention of Unseen Spirits but not such as would ever let Norval bind them to his service. When he realised that, he tried to dismiss them. The student had other ideas. He took the Unseen for his masters and promised to carry out their bidding, whatever it might be. Norval objected and they laughed at him. They hunted him across Devon and Cornwall, so that he barely escaped with his life.'

Fox was not making fun of him, Stephen was sure of that much. Like his two friends, he had begun by ignoring Stephen deliberately and now had almost forgotten his presence. They believed in this story. Stephen was not sure he could do the same but he did not feel equipped to argue about it. Instead, he tried to think through the implications.

'What did the student get out of this?' he asked.

'Not being hunted.' Fox looked at him thoughtfully. 'And the commonplace rewards, wealth and power of a sort.'

'You mean he really did sell his soul to the devil?'

'No.' Fox raised an eyebrow and looked at Rowan, who said, 'But you could think of it that way, if it helps. I still don't understand about the oath.'

'Norval wanted to find the student and destroy him,' Fox said. He tried to persuade the Council of the Elders to put all the Club's resources into helping him. Before they could decide, Norval fell in front of a train and was killed, and the Club nearly split apart in the arguments about whether to take vengeance for his death. Eventually the Council decided that the student had done enough to bring about his own destruction, and that disaster would follow any attempt to meddle further with what Norval had stirred up. The oath was a means to put an end to the quarrels, as well as to signify their disapproval of what had been done.'

Fifteen

Ivar Gray's office at the motor factory was a small, utilitarian space, cluttered with old technical drawings and bits of machinery that no longer worked, but a visit there enabled Rowan to catch her father on his own, without the rest of the family. Tilda, at least, would have to be told the latest discoveries about Lyulf Lyulf, but Rowan wanted her father's opinion first.

He sat still, his hands flat on his desk, as he listened to her, and his face grew heavier with every word she spoke.

'There are worse fools at the Club than I suspected,' he said.

'You didn't know about the oath?'

'I'd stopped going there regularly long before then. Alick must have known but he dropped no hints.'

Rowan was not surprised. Alick enjoyed keeping secrets.

'I'm afraid James and Nick have stirred up this man's interest, and I made matters worse when I took Nick to meet him.'

'I owe Matilda an apology. I thought the boys were romancing,' Ivar spoke grimly, 'but Lyulf's powers don't explain what Nicholas did. How did he escape from the man?'

Rowan shook her head. 'He doesn't seem to know himself.'

'Is his mother afraid of what Alick may have taught him?'

Rowan shrugged. 'Tilda never saw Spellhaven. How can she understand that Alick would never do what Lyulf did?'

'Harper Norval grew up in Spellhaven. Exile can drive men to desperation when they will not give up impossible hopes.'

Rowan shivered, though the room was warm, then she pulled herself upright.

'You saw Alick every day, nearly. If he had submitted to a binding, or seen it done to Nick, you would have known something was wrong.'

'I hope so.' Ivar stared through her, deep into past unhappiness. Rowan leaned forward to catch his attention.

'How can we deal with Lyulf? We can't just wait for him to find the boys.'

'I'll come up to the Club,' Ivar said. 'People may be quicker to find ways round their oath for me than for you.'

'Some will be quickest to help Alick's sons.'

'And the boys will have more friends to keep them safe once they are known at the Club.' Ivar stood up. 'Come back to the cottage with me and I'll talk to Matilda tonight.'

'I'd rather not miss my class tomorrow morning,' Rowan said. If she went home, she would upset her mother, however hard she tried not to. 'I'll see you at the Club.'

On the day before the family returned to Highgate, Tilda and Nicholas went for a ramble. James had chosen to visit the motor works but Nicholas preferred to go out into the countryside. Once they were away from the house, Tilda said, 'You can go off on your own if you would rather,' and he shook his head. So they walked together through the beech wood behind the cottage and up the hill. On the move, Tilda felt her headache ease for the first time since she had left home. It had grown worse over the last few days, despite Ivar Gray's apology and his offer of help to tackle Lyulf. She accepted his arguments for taking the boys to the Exiles' Club, though his explanation of Lyulf's powers bewildered her. Maybe Rowan would help her make sense of it. Meanwhile, her dislike of the Club grew with everything she learned and this had become hard to conceal from her parents-in-law. She did not want to go there, but letting the boys go without her would be worse.

Out here, nothing seemed to matter as much. The morning was cloudy and mild, damp under the trees. Tilda welcomed the protection of her long skirt and her cardigan, though Nicholas wore his sleeves rolled up and his knees were bare. He matched Tilda's pace, except when he halted to track the drumming of a woodpecker or to stare at the pattern of a fungus. Sometimes Tilda waited for him; sometimes she wandered onwards and he ran to catch her up.

By the time they came out of the trees, the sky had cleared and the sun was hot. The pebbles in the path shone in the glare and the turf smelled dry.

'This way,' Nicholas said. Before Tilda could object, he plunged down a steep track through gorse bushes. She would have preferred to stay in the sun but she followed him back into the woods. The undergrowth was thicker here, tangled under trees of oak and hazel. The path was narrow, beset with knobbly roots and hidden hollows of mud. Tilda expected it to peter out any moment but Nicholas moved purposefully, pushing past brambles and clumps of nettle. Tilda picked her way more carefully and was about to call out to Nicholas to wait when the path levelled out and widened. Nicholas stood still, beside a moss-coated lump, taller than he was. He looked round and smiled at her.

The lump was the broken edge of a wall. Through the gap beside it they could see a neglected garden. Mounds of bindweed and honeysuckle bordered rough grass sprinkled with vetch and buttercups. Across the grass was another gap in a box hedge. Nicholas ran across, and Tilda followed him through the second gap and down into a circular space. On the inside, the hedge was lined with a ring of stone benches and the middle of the circle was filled by a many-stemmed willow tree. Maybe it had once been surrounded by a pond but the tree had taken over. Its roots rose from a patch of mud, clotted with broken branches and old leaves.

Nicholas circled the tree, keeping his face towards it. Tilda stood and watched him. As he came towards her, she asked, 'What is this place?'

He frowned and put his finger to his lips. He went round twice more and then took Tilda's hand to pull her over to sit on a bench in the shade.

'There was a house once but now it's a ruin,' he said.

'Have you been here before?'

'With Father.' Nicholas settled into stillness. 'It's a good place.'

Tilda drew in her breath to ask more questions, saw his face, and changed her mind. He was not quite smiling but his mouth was soft and his eyes at ease. She sat beside him, accepting his silence. The willow tree was busy with birds and dragonflies flashed over the roots, while a breeze blew in the scent of honeysuckle from the outer garden.

'Friendling, well met!' The willow branches parted and a girl stepped out from the middle of the tree.

'Sallikin, you're here!' Nicholas stood up and now his smile was broad. 'Please will you meet my mother?'

Tilda stood up and faced Sallikin in bewilderment. She had a girl's voice and a long, slender shape, but her narrow face was older, lean and weathered. Her grey eyes were stern as she gazed at Tilda. Then she nodded.

'There's no guile in you. Welcome, mother of Nicholas.'

Tilda reached out to her son in alarm, though she did not know what frightened her. The woman was dressed like nobody Tilda had ever met, in trousers and jacket of a silvery cloth, faded and stained with green. The buttons were black pearls, misshapen but lustrous. Her dark hair was cut into ragged points and her feet were bare. Tilda was reminded of an aristocratic acquaintance of her grandmother, a dowager who had taken to gardening in her best clothes because she was determined nobody else should ever wear them, but this stranger looked comfortable in her clothes, as though it would never occur to her to wear others.

'Don't worry.' For once Nicholas allowed Tilda to hold his shoulder. 'Father made a mistake, but he told me it was all right afterwards.'

'After what?' Tilda's alarm increased. 'Please, Miss Sal- please ma'am, what did Alick do?'

'Call me Sallikin.' The woman laughed and Tilda was comforted. 'What did the man tell you?'

'Alick's dead.' Tilda's knees were wobbly and she sat down on the bench. 'I never knew he had been here.'

'You did not share his quest?'

'I did not believe in it.' She wanted to explain the muddle of her feelings to this stranger so much that she almost forgot about Nicholas. 'I would have hated the way he lived, in the city that was drowned.'

'Spellhaven was a wondrous place.' Sallikin sat down on the grass. 'I was never there but I have heard about it from many people.'

'We could never have gone there. Father knew that,' Nicholas said. He stayed on his feet, his look earnest but not unhappy.

'But he set an ambush, in the hope that he could gain power over me such as the Lords Magician wielded in Spellhaven,' Sallikin said.

'The Exiles talk about the Unseen who filled their city,' Tilda said.

Sallikin nodded. 'This land has many Spirits, native and wandering, though we are not crammed together like the Unseen of Spellhaven. Sometimes we manifest ourselves, as we please or as we must. In this place, I am often as you see me now. I do not know how your man knew that.' She glanced at Nicholas, who shook his head. His frown had returned but it eased when Sallikin patted his foot.

'Maybe he came by chance but I do not think so. He brought Nicholas into this garden one afternoon in spring. I was curious, for I had not seen men here since they stopped scything the grass. They carried in a board, which unfolded, and a box of gaming pieces. I watched the man teach the boy to play and I was more curious still. The game was not chess, which is a battle game, nor Fox and Geese, which is a hunt, but one I had never seen before.'

'It was Carthago, a siege game from Spellhaven,' Nicholas said. 'Father was teaching me to play.'

'I have a weakness for games of skill. I watched for a while and then I let myself be seen.'

There was a coil of ivy round Sallikin's wrist. Tilda thought it was a bracelet until Sallikin turned over her hand. The stem went through the skin and grew out of her vein.

'I asked to play and Nicholas gave up his place to me. After a trial, the man from Spellhaven suggested a wager and I agreed. Nicholas had wandered off but he came back in time to protest,

"You told me the besiegers must always have first move, Father. Or it is mathematically impossible for the besieged to win." '

'I thought Father had forgotten,' Nicholas said as he stared at the ground. 'I did not mean to give him away.'

'What was the wager?' Tilda asked.

'Small enough in seeming,' Sallikin said, 'his belt buckle against a button from my jacket. But of course I would not have left anything of mine in his hands without trying to win it back.'

Tilda was furious with Alick all over again, but consoling Nicholas was more important. 'Your father must have been glad you were there, Nick. He was no cheat, not in his true self.'

'He was angry,' Nicholas said, bleakly. 'He walked away so as not to hit me.'

'He left you here by yourself?' Tilda's hands gripped the stone edge of the bench until they hurt.

'I was with him,' Sallikin said. 'He had my gratitude, so I offered to show him some of my treasures. His courage and courtesy in facing what he did not understand turned gratitude into friendship.'

'I was interested in it all,' Nicholas said. He looked at Tilda. 'Father did come back, and he said what's done is done. He didn't blame me.'

'Good,' Tilda spoke gently, as much for Nick's sake as out of loyalty to her dead husband. She wondered what Sallikin regarded as treasure but decided not to ask. 'Nicholas, when you broke the glass balls, did Sallikin help you?'

'What glass balls?' Sallikin asked. When they told her, she laughed. 'I was not there, but wherever Nicholas goes, the Spirits recognise him as my friend. They watch him and play with him, as the humour takes them.'

'I felt the glass,' Nicholas said. 'I felt where it wanted to break.'

Sallikin nodded. 'You are learning how to speak to the creatures of the earth and the stuff of which things are made.'

'It's not magic,' he said. 'I don't cast spells.'

The difference mattered to him. Tilda could see that, though she did not understand it. 'Is that what happened in the Park?' she asked.

'Sort of.'

'I heard that news,' Sallikin said. 'The stones and the ground below them felt your determination to root yourself down and came to your aid. They were sad when you left them.'

'Ought I to thank them?' Nicholas asked. 'Mother, can I go back there?'

'I'll take you,' Tilda said, though she did not relish the prospect. 'Why didn't you explain all this to your grandfather?'

Nicholas's chin sank down. 'I promised Father not to tell anyone. I haven't told you.'

But he had brought her here. Tilda looked at Sallikin, whose glance was bright and strong.

'We think this Lyulf is a danger to Nicholas and his brother,' Tilda said.

'The man has powerful Masters,' Sallikin said. 'Too powerful for me to confront, but Nicholas will be safe here with me.

'What about Mother?' Nicholas asked. 'And James?'

Sallikin looked searchingly at Tilda and smiled. 'Your mother would never be contented here for long. I would need to meet James before I could judge about him.'

'He is too young to withdraw from the world,' Tilda said. 'So is Nicholas.'

Nicholas nodded. 'Then need we explain anything to anybody? They'll ask too many questions.'

They would badger him to show what he could do. Tilda did not want that.

'I will not be so easily taken in again by anyone from the drowned city,' Sallikin said. 'Nevertheless, I would prefer not to be disturbed by foolish desires and futile endeavours.'

'I won't say anything if you would rather I didn't, Nicholas,' Tilda said.

They both smiled at her in reply, smiles that cheered her like a flourish of music.

'Drink with me before you go,' Sallikin said. 'Nicholas, find a cup for your mother.'

Nicholas went across to the willow tree. He scooped a handful of dead leaves out of the puddle round the roots and plaited them into a saucer, which he dipped into the water. He grinned at Tilda as he came back towards her. Her lips puckered when she saw the trickle of muddy water but she did not mean to offend her son or his friend. She would not need to swallow more than a spoonful.

Nicholas gave the willow saucer to Sallikin, who took it in her two hands and breathed on it, singing a wordless melody so low that

Tilda could only just hear her. The saucer grew into a cup and the water cleared. Sallikin tasted it and nodded.

'Drink now,' she said, and handed the cup to Tilda.

The taste sparkled in her mouth like the water Tilda remembered from her childhood, from hill streams cold and deep. She would have liked to drink more but it did not seem right.

'Thank you,' she said and handed the cup to Nicholas.

Sixteen

James eased open the door to the garden and slipped outside, a saucer of milk in his hand. The moon was bright tonight but he found a patch of shadow round the corner where he could settle down. The family had been back in Highgate for three days and he was anxious for news of the cat released from Lyulf's trap. Nobody had seen the creature since its escape but James was not convinced it was in a condition to fend for itself. He had worried about it every day in Hertfordshire, despite promises from Rowan and Cook that they would continue to put out milk at night.

On their return, Cook said, 'I did what I promised for a week, Master James, but I couldn't go on. I didn't grudge the milk but I won't have nastiness on the kitchen doorstep to turn my stomach in the mornings.'

'Nastiness?'

'Dead birds, baby ones. And once it was a mouse.'

'Then there's something in the garden besides hedgehogs.' James was too pleased about this to be reproachful. 'But it might be a different cat.'

'Whatever it is, it gets no more milk from me.'

James was not satisfied. By now, he had crawled all over the garden, hunting for cat hairs, not that he could remember clearly what colour the escaped cat was. Inside the glass, its eyes and mouth had taken all his attention. Once out, it had moved so fast that he had only a vague impression of dark, uneven fur. But in any case, his hunt turned up nothing.

'Can you call the cat?' he had asked when Nick came up to bed.

'Better not.'

James was aggrieved. 'I only want to be sure it's safe.'

'Lyulf must have called it into his trap.' Nick did not look up from his book. 'How is the cat to tell the difference?'

So James had decided to come out on his own to watch. The milk was not Cook's because he had saved it from his own bedtime portion. He did not mean to touch the cat but only to see whether its injuries had healed and its fur had grown back. If it was still in a mess, Nicholas would have to help.

He changed position more than once. He backed away from the saucer, so as not to scare any creature from approaching it. Then he worried he would not be close enough to see and inched forward again. Eventually he put the saucer in the moonlight and perched on the corner of the rockery in the shadow of the house. He had a wider view from here than from the ground, though the stone dug into his buttocks through the thin cotton of his pyjamas.

He was glad to be home, even though everyone said that London was grimy and deserted in August. For the last few years he and Nicholas had spent the month down in Gloucestershire, in the place where his mother had grown up, and visited their Gray grandparents on the way back. James did not mind joining in his cousins' games or exploring the countryside for prehistoric remains. He did not even mind being with his grandparents, though he was usually baffled by Ivar's reminiscences and his attempts to cheer up Beatrice were seldom a success, but this year, he was sure they had been taken to Elephant Cottage chiefly to get them out of the way while more exciting things happened in London. James had not yet made a plan of his own for dealing with Lyulf Lyulf but he did not mean to be left out. Whatever was to happen, Nicholas would naturally be in the middle of it, but James suspected he might have to fight for his place. Meanwhile, he wanted to check up on Hugo Cole as well as the cat.

He was too uncomfortable to doze, and not very warm. The day had been hot, so at first he was grateful for the cool night air, but later a chill crept up his legs and tweaked his nose. He thought about fetching a scarf but he did not want to leave his post. He tried to make sense of the night noises: the cries of owls over the heath, the rustle of the trees, and faint rumbles that might be trains or lorries far away. Then there were small scurries close at hand, which made him strain forward to catch sight of their cause. He saw the leaves shake on the hollyhocks, bright-edged in the moonlight but he could not tell what had disturbed them.

He went back to thinking about Lyulf. If they could find his new premises and break in, how many captives would Nicholas be able to free from the glass balls before they wore him out?

The scream knocked him sideways and for a moment he did not know where he was. He braced himself on his hands. He must have been closer to sleep than he had thought possible, but now he was wide awake, his heart thudding, his mouth dry. Nose to nose with him was a lithe blackness with yellow eyes and gleaming teeth. The hairs on its tail caught the light as they switched back and forth. Before James could notice anything else, the creature yowled again. Its paw stabbed at James's leg. Then it skirled away, upset the saucer of milk and leaped into the shadows.

'Come back,' James shouted, though he knew it was useless. 'I won't hurt you.'

He was bleeding. The cat's claws must have pierced his pyjama leg. When he looked down to examine the damage, he saw a small broken lump by his feet. He prodded it gingerly into the light and found it was a dead bird, a sparrow.

'I don't want your prey,' he called. 'Come back and take it.'

Nothing moved until a light went on in the house and the garden door opened.

'James?' It was his mother's voice.

The cylinders, about the width of fat cigars, were wrapped in blue paper printed with zigzags. The box must hold a dozen.

'You make fireworks here, in the middle of London?' Tilda asked.

'We only keep a few on the premises,' Piers Marshall answered. 'For demonstration purposes.' He sounded politely dismissive. Tilda looked round to see whether anyone else shared her opinion of this folly, but Ivar Gray had gone up to the top floor of the Club, leaving her and the boys to get acquainted with Marshall and Fred Burrows. It had been Burrows's idea to show them this laboratory cum showroom and his face was even less responsive than Marshall's. Burrows was the inventor and chief designer of the materials which kept the enterprise busy and profitable. As well as the fireworks, they produced inks of different colours, varnishes, and coated papers. The experiments were done here and prototypes made. The successful products were then manufactured on a site in South London, managed by Marshall.

'But you can't let off fireworks indoors, can you?' James asked.

'We go up on the roof,' Marshall replied. 'We'll take you chaps up for a show if you like, but it has to be after dark, or there's no point.'

James glanced at Nicholas, who stood in the middle of the floor, withdrawn deep into his own thoughts, so he looked at Tilda, who said, 'Maybe later in the summer.'

'Maybe Howler could come too,' James said. He did not wait for an answer but sniffed at a jar full of a murky green liquid. 'Ugh! How do you stop the inks smelling beastly when you sell them?'

'Chemistry,' Burrows said. His assistants, who had not been introduced, were busy at long benches, set under the windows. The depths of the room were filled with more jars and bottles, coated with dust and cobwebs. Burrows picked up a small flask and added a few drops from it into the jar, which fizzed. 'Don't they teach chemistry at your school?'

'They don't let us muck about with the equipment much.'

'In Spellhaven, you would have started an apprenticeship by now,' Marshall said. 'Did your father tell you the kind of things we used to get up to there, the three of us?'

For a moment James's face was almost as blank as his brother's. 'He said there were no motors in Spellhaven. We liked him to tell us about his motor races.'

'Young brats.' Maybe Marshall meant this to be jovial. 'But you're older now. Aren't you keen to try your hand at what we do here, young Jimmy?'

'Mr. Marshall,' Tilda said and Burrows interrupted her.

'We were Alick's friends since we were five years old. Maybe we can guess what he would have wanted for his sons better than you can.' He loomed over her, his face white, his cheek twitching. He was not as big a man as Marshall but lean and intense, with too many teeth.

'You evidently don't know he disliked hearing his son called Jimmy.' Tilda regretted these words as soon as she had spoken them. She was determined not to enter into competition over her husband's memory. She had come here to let these men befriend the boys. James did not care for the diminutive and that was what mattered now.

'I was never any good at names.' Marshall's face was red but he did not sound apologetic.

'And we had more important things to think about in those days,' Burrows said. 'Plans that were important to Alick, Mrs. Gray, that he would have wanted his sons to play a part in.'

'They have only just been introduced to you,' Tilda said. 'Shouldn't you take some time to get acquainted?'

'We would have been acquainted for the last five years if you would have let us.'

James looked from one adult to the others and then went to stand beside his brother. 'We can't be apprentices,' he said. 'We have to go back to school in September.'

'You shouldn't interrupt, James, when grown ups are talking,' Marshall said.

'Perhaps we should continue this discussion somewhere else, without the boys,' Tilda said.

'It's time you let them grow up,' Burrows said. 'They will have to live in a man's world soon.'

'So they will,' Tilda said. 'The world where families still mourn their losses from the War and nobody knows how to stop the Great Powers preparing for another. How will learning the ways of Spellhaven help them in this world?'

Marshall's face went from scarlet to crimson. 'We fought in the War,' he said. 'While we were still mourning our dead from the drowning of our city, we went out to the Front and stood by Alick's side before you ever met him.'

Someone rapped on the open door of the laboratory. Tilda turned, glad of any interruption.

'The windows are rattling from your noise,' the newcomer said. 'Whatever this is about, why shout it to the world?'

'Come in, Darius,' Burrows said. 'Help make her understand.'

Tilda had been introduced to Darius Fox upstairs as another of Alick's friends but had not paid him any attention until now. He looked younger than the other two, or perhaps he took more care of his appearance. He was medium tall and slim, fashionably turned out in a light summer jacket, with a silk scarf in place of a tie. He smiled at Tilda as he walked forward and then grimaced.

'Another noxious brew. Can't you open the windows?'

'Couldn't we go outside, please?' Nicholas asked. His face was pale and clammy.

'I believe there's a game of roof cricket going on,' Fox said. 'Why don't you two take a look, while we find your mother a cup of tea?'

This sounded even more improbable than the fireworks.

'What happens if you hit a six?' James asked.

'The nets knock the ball down,' Fox replied. 'The rules are a bit different from ordinary cricket but you'll soon get the hang of them.'

Tilda did not want tea but she could see that Marshall and Burrows would not relinquish their argument. She would have agreed to anything which meant the boys did not have to listen to any more of it.

The Strangers' Room was stylish and modern, with pale geometric prints on the curtains and low slung, angular chairs. Nobody else was about and the air smelled empty.

'We'll be more comfortable in here,' Fox said, after their tea had been served. 'Not that we think of you as a stranger, of course, Mrs. Gray, but the Smoking Room is baking hot this afternoon.'

'Thank you.' Tilda looked at Marshall, who blew out his cheeks and said nothing. Burrows had stayed downstairs, to work on a formula, he said. Tilda guessed that Marshall was considered between them to have the greater skill in handling women. She did not mean to be persuaded into supporting any of their schemes, but she had come here to make amends for cutting off Alick's sons from connecting with their past.

'Tell me about your business, Mr. Marshall,' she said. 'Did your family start it up when they first came here?'

He looked surprised. 'We weren't scrabbling to make a living, if that's what you mean. The Clans had investments in England from long before the Drowning.'

'Then it's your show?'

'I wanted something to do after the War and Fred needed a partner. His stuff is better than anyone else can make, but he would mess about pointlessly in the lab if he didn't have someone to manage the practical side.' He sounded a little more at ease now. 'We supply varnishes for the interiors of Gray Motors, you know.'

'Then they must be very good.' Tilda was sure Ivar would not accept inferior quality, even from friends of Alick. 'And the inks? Who buys those?'

'Fancy shops.' Marshall leaned forward, 'Listen, Mrs. Gray-'

'Map makers,' Fox interrupted. 'Duchesses with invitations to write, calligraphers, and miniaturists. London contains more such folk than you might suppose and not all of them are members here.'

Marshall grunted and sat back. Tilda looked at Fox. 'But some are. Are you one of them?'

'Not I.' He was amused, whether at her question or Marshall's irritation, but his light voice was kind. 'I write for the newspapers. You ought to meet some of our fine craftsmen, though, and see their work on display in the library.'

'I'd like that,' Tilda said.

'Your sons ought to see such work,' Marshall said. 'And read the books and learn Spellhaven Latin.'

'Plenty of time for that,' Fox said.

'I have no wish to prevent them,' Tilda said, 'but it mustn't interfere with their education, or involve them in experiments beyond their years.'

Marshall's face reddened once more. 'Don't you trust us to look after Alick's sons?'

Fox answered before Tilda could speak, 'Why not take matters one step at a time? Let's not rush things.'

Back at home, Tilda walked out into her garden before supper. The sky was still light but a breeze cooled the air and brought out the scent of the roses. She was glad to be on her own for a few minutes but the garden disappointed her. The leaves on the trees were dull and the lawn was dry. Her gardener took great pride in the flowerbeds, which were bright and tidy but not restful. Tilda thought of Sallikin's garden, not so many miles away, but it would not be fair to the gardener, or her neighbours, to make a ruin here.

Ivar Gray came out of the house.

'I'm going back to the cottage,' he said. He had been staying at the Club, as always when he was in London on his own. 'I've done all I can for now and I'd rather not leave Beatrice on her own any longer.'

Tilda would have liked to protest, even though she would breathe a little easier in his absence. She would have felt less nervous about Lyulf with Ivar near at hand, but she would not make more demands on him than she must.

'Thank you for coming,' she said.

'You can telephone the Works if ever you need me and I'll come at once.'

Seventeen

R owan dragged the flat of the paint brush across the canvas and stepped back to consider the effect. She tried a few more strokes and then stopped. She had not settled down to a major painting since the success of the exhibition earlier in the summer. She did not want to turn out weaker versions of Eyes in the Shadows but she could not decide which direction to go in next. The present exercise was intended as a corrective, to clear her head. She had grouped some of her basic equipment together in a still life: jars, old canvases, a discarded palette, and a heap of brushes. And she had set out to paint them, not as objects with a character of their own, but as an arrangement of lines and shadows. The result was dreary, so she had added more paint in stronger tones. It was not an improvement. She chewed the end of her brush, while she wondered what to try next.

The opening of the door was almost welcome, but she discouraged visits from strangers while she was working as a matter of principle. Tilda and the boys were out, so she did not turn her head.

'Whoever it is, tell them I'm busy, please, Molly.'

'She said to come on up,' a male voice answered. 'I expect she mistook me for an art student.'

Rowan swung round. At a second glance, she recognised the young waiter from the Exiles' Club.

'Hello, Gavin. I didn't realise it was you. Come in.'

'I'm sorry to disturb you, Miss Rowan. I looked for you at the School yesterday but they said you hadn't been in this week.'

'Is something wrong?'

After the encounter in the Smoking Room, Rowan had spoken to the Club Secretary, to make sure that the boy's indiscretions were not held against him. When she was told he had left of his own accord, she had taken the trouble to track him down. He did not mind being a waiter, he said, while he tried to establish himself as a political playwright, but not at the Club, if he could help it. The place reminded him too much of his childhood. Rowan had given him an introduction to her Art School, for work as a life model.

'I'm doing fine,' he said now. 'I'm waiting tables three nights a week at a dive in Soho and I model for those classes in the mornings. I don't have to see people who knew my mother when she was a girl and I can plan out my dialogue while I pose.'

He looked well, dressed in a black jumper with a red scarf, much like the younger students at the School but neater and with shorter hair. Rowan offered him a cigarette and nodded him to a seat.

'What did you want to see me about?'

He perched on the edge of the couch and turned the cigarette over and over the backs of his fingers.

'You went to all that trouble to help me. I've been wondering what I could do to thank you.'

'You did most of it yourself,' Rowan said, 'and the school is always short of models.' They were especially short of good-looking young men capable of standing still and willing to pose in the nude, but he was too young to be teased about that.

'All the same, you asked after me. I didn't expect that.' He kept his gaze on the cigarette, which he seemed to have no intention of lighting. 'I don't mean to make a nuisance of myself but I would like to do something for you. But most likely you have talked to Dr. Hunter already.'

With a little encouragement, Rowan thought, the boy would be carrying her easel and inviting her to play readings, but he was much too young and she hated politics.

'Who is he?'

'It's a woman. Not a medical doctor but a don at the University. At the Club, they call her Rhyming Kate.'

Darius Fox had mentioned her and Rowan had a vague memory of the woman who had been the first among the Exiles to graduate from Oxford.

'I never had much to do with her,' Rowan said. 'Should I speak to her?'

'She knew Lyulf Lyulf better than anybody in the early days.' Gavin looked up, his face earnest. 'I asked around, to make sure I'd remembered this right. The gossip was that those two were very close, maybe more than friends, which made the others feel even more like fools when he went off with Harper Norval.'

After all, the boy deserved to be taken seriously.

'She'll hardly be in touch with him now.'

'But she might remember something about him that would help you, and she might be able to help with the magic as well.'

'You don't mean she has done what Lyulf did? If anyone suspected that-'

'No, she's all right, Dr. Hunter,' Gavin said. 'Crotchety but a good egg.'

'Then she can't work any magic or the whole Club would be shouting the news.'

'Maybe not but she's different from the others,' Gavin said. 'Even the Puppet Master is interested in her research.'

The Puppet Master was Domaldi, the last survivor among the great Magician Lords of Spellhaven. Like all the rest, he had lost his magic in the Drowning. Domaldi had broken so many bones in his struggle to regain his powers that he could not walk unaided or sit up straight. His mind remained sharp, however, and his puppet shows were terrifying. He embodied that essence of the Exile which Rowan was determined to leave behind her, more than ever now that she had asked him for help and been refused.

'What kind of research?'

'English plays of the Seventeenth Century,' Gavin said and grinned at Rowan's surprise. 'She gets her post delivered to the Club. I used to take it up to her sometimes.'

'What has that to do with Spellhaven magic?'

'That's what she told the librarians she was working on. Maybe the real research is something else, but she reads minds and uncovers secrets. Nobody can lie to her.'

'Is that more kitchen gossip?'

'Backstairs gossip.' Now he sounded defensive. 'But the staff at the Club aren't bamboozled easily. I've seen people run away from her smile.'

'And she was once Lyulf's friend,' Rowan said, mostly to herself. 'Thank you, Gavin. That is a help.'

Rowan sent a note to Dr. Hunter and was invited to a meeting in one of the cubby holes partitioned off from the Club Library. When she arrived, the Doctor was studying a spread of drawings, mostly portrait sketches in charcoal.

'Did you do these?'

Rowan recoiled as she looked at them. 'Years ago. I thought I had torn them up.'

When she was first in London, Rowan taken lesson at the Club and had sketched anyone who would sit still for her. Later, she had made her escape as much from the artistic traditions as from the social side of the Club. She had collected all her work together for her move to the studio in Tilda's house and had weeded it out ruthlessly. Or so she had thought.

'They were in the stacks,' Dr. Hunter said. 'I dug them out after I heard about your big picture.'

Rowan could not tell whether this was polite interest or a sinister curiosity. Not that Dr. Hunter looked sinister. She was a short, stocky woman, dressed, despite the heat, in a mulberry velvet jacket over a divided tweed skirt. A blue beret was squashed onto bushy, white hair and pinned with an enamel butterfly in green and scarlet. Anywhere else in London, this outfit would have looked like fancy dress, but a good few of the Exiles dressed even more flamboyantly. The skirt and stubby, ringless hands with short nails suggested that Dr. Hunter chose practicality over style when it mattered. She must be about the same age as Rowan's mother but she looked younger.

The lines on her round face marked her with determination, not anxiety, and her glance was lively as well as shrewd.

'Sit down,' she said. She swept the sketches into a bundle, which she put under her elbow. 'What do you want with me, Rowena of the Graysteels?'

Retrieving the sketches would have to wait, Rowan decided. 'I want to tell you about my nephews.' She avoided Lyulf's name, as she told of his escapades.

Dr. Hunter listened without interruption, though her mouth drew deep trenches down towards her chin. At the end, she said, 'You know about the oath I swore, or you would not have known enough to tell me all this. Do you expect me to break it?'

'Only if you want to,' Rowan said and saw Dr. Hunter's face go cold. 'I mean, it's in a good cause. The man's a danger and not just to my nephews. The cat Nicholas released was in a horrible state and who knows who or what else are in similar traps.'

This argument made no impact and Rowena tugged at the back of her hair to clear her mind. Half a dozen of her friends would happily have explained the unhealthy effects on the Doctor's psyche of sticking to irrational promises, but Rowan suspected that direction would lead only to disaster.

'Or keep the oath,' she said. 'You're a woman of ability, you teach at a University. Maybe you can help us face up to the man now without talking about what he did then.'

Dr. Hunter's gaze warmed a little. 'I teach and research English literature. Is that why you picked me to ask for help?'

Rowan let go of her hair and reached for her necklace while she thought some more. Today she had put on a new string of cultured pearls, not as satisfying to twist as her wooden beads but better than nothing. She could not light up a cigarette here, because relays of librarians would pounce in to extinguish it.

'You knew him better than most, I'm told. I thought you might want to help. And they say-' she stopped.

'What do they say?' Dr. Hunter bit out the words.

'That you can uncover secrets. Maybe even predict the future.'

Dr. Hunter snorted. 'Nonsense. Who told you that?'

'No end of folk.' Rowan had sounded out an assortment of Club acquaintances about what Gavin Baker had told her. If anything, he had underplayed Dr. Hunter's reputation. 'You put an end to the split in the Wulfing Clan, I hear, and you filled in two inches on the Great Map.'

'The map deals with the past, not the future.' Dr. Hunter's voice eased. 'And the rest of it is a matter of painstaking common sense.'

Rowan sighed and sat back. 'Then you must have more common sense than anyone else among the Exiles. Won't you use it to help us?'

Dr. Hunter took her time. She studied Rowan's face and then the rest of her, while Rowan pressed her lips together and tried not to fidget.

'You can hardly be as flighty as you look,' Dr. Hunter said. 'If I help you, what will you do for me?'

Rowan had not thought of this possibility. 'What do you want?'

Dr. Hunter patted the sheaf of Rowan's drawings. 'For you to paint me some pictures. Subjects and treatments of my choosing.'

'You want me to paint to order?' Rowan's dislike was immediate. 'I don't do that kind of commission.'

'Prouder than Michelangelo, are you?'

'Those days were different.' Rowan tried to sound reasonable. 'Why? What are you after that I would be any good at? Those sketches are feeble.'

'They are over-hasty and muddled, but they show observation and the glimmerings of imagination. And now and then, you catch a likeness remarkably well.'

'Photographs do that,' Rowan said.

'Not for what I want.' Dr. Hunter leaned forward. 'You can help me bring the plays back to life.'

'Which plays?'

'The lost plays of Spellhaven. Especially the ones from the great Jacobean playwrights. Maybe some medieval pageants too, though they would take more effort to stage.'

The senior Exiles had a gift for making Rowan confused and vaguely guilty. 'If the plays are lost, how can they be brought to life?' she asked.

'By observation and imagination.' Dr. Hunter's eyes gleamed. 'There is no end to the treasures in the Club archives. Some complete scripts but many more plays where we have only descriptions of performances or notes from rehearsals. I've been putting them together bit by bit.'

'Is that your University research?' Rowan was startled. For hundreds of years, playwrights and poets from all over Europe had been lured to Spellhaven and made to work on the city's stages for three or five years to earn their freedom. So it was no surprise that the archives might hold treasures but the Exiles were usually wary about revealing much of their history to the outside world.

'Most of it will never be published,' Dr. Hunter said. 'That's not my purpose.'

'Which is?'

'The Spirits.' Now Dr. Hunter was impatient. 'The Unseen Audience. You young people forget too easily.'

In her memory, Rowan could taste the salty sparkle in the air of the old city. She had stood among the audience for the great shows as a child, aware of the pressure all round from the Unseen, at whom the performances were chiefly aimed, but that had been before the Drowning and the nightmare of escape across the Causeway.

'The bindings were destroyed. There is no Unseen Audience any more,' Rowan said.

'A non-sequitur of the most blatant.' Dr. Hunter seemed to take Rowan for one of her students. 'The Spirits can be anywhere in this country, where no wards are set against them. Because they are not bound, the necessity to entertain them is not pressing. In Spellhaven, they could poison the air and drive us all to madness if they were not humoured. Here they just go away. But if we could find the right shows, maybe they would recall the pleasure of their lives in Spellhaven. Maybe they would work with us to make magic once more.'

Rowan had heard other versions of this theory, from the puppet players and others. It never seemed promising. 'But how will paintings help?'

'When I work with a troupe of actors, I tell them what I have gleaned about plot and character from one of the old plays and set them to improvise. So far, the results are not impressive. Maybe pictures would rouse them to something better.'

Rowan had friends who worked in the theatre as set or costume designers. From that perspective, painting to commission seemed less objectionable, but it would be a distraction from her serious work.

'The Club has dozens of skilful painters,' she said.

'I want to try out your work,' Dr. Hunter answered, 'and you are the one who asked me for help.'

Must true artists renounce their families? Rowan had sat through many earnest discussions about the need to sacrifice everything for one's art. Most of the participants wanted an excuse for not writing thank you letters or visiting their parents except when it suited them, but they had not survived death and destruction as Rowan had. She could not turn her back so easily on her family and Lyulf's exploits filled her with outrage. She would hate to be left out of the fight against him. Maybe serious work could be combined with other kinds, after all.

'What exactly do you want me to do?'

Eighteen

Net curtains hung in the windows of the houses either side of Lyulf's abandoned shop. When Stephen knocked at the doors, nobody answered. He tried houses further away with the same result. The doorsteps shone in the sun and the air was still. Did people who lived in places like this go on holiday in August? Stephen was not sure. Noise boiled away in the distance; voices, bangs, and rumbles, but nothing close by. He went on knocking at doors until he came to one that was open. A woman sat on the threshold, knitting at a furious pace. She did not look up when Stephen greeted her and would not listen to his questions.

'Market's round the corner,' she told him. 'I'm busy.' And repeated the same words, louder and faster, whatever he said.

There were plenty of people in the market, a jostle of children, men, and women, who shouted, bargained, pushed past one another, squabbled, and laughed together. Now the noise combined with the smells of sweat and rotten fruit to build a wall against Stephen's advance. He took a deep breath, buttoned his jacket to protect his wallet, and pushed forwards.

He decided that the stall holders were the most likely to have useful intelligence and that they would be more likely to part with it to a stranger if he was prepared to buy. Soon he had acquired a jumble of oddments he did not want, including a scrubbing brush, a pair of shoe laces, and a net of cabbage. He asked his question in the moments after he had chosen his goods and before he paid, but the answers were not helpful. Mostly variations on 'Never heard of him', and in the bustle, he had no way of judging whether these were evasions or the simple truth.

He could not carry much more. His eye was caught by the children who gazed at a rainbow display of sweets, sticky in the heat. They swayed to and fro with the crowd but made no move to buy. Stephen decided to change tactics. He bought a mixture of the sweets in a cone of paper and squeezed into the space between the stall and a shop front behind. He put his other purchases down by his feet and held out the sweets at knee level.

'Would you like to share these out?'

The children stared at him but made no move towards him. He leaned down and pitched his voice low, to cut through the din. 'I need some help,' he said. 'Do you children live round here?'

They were round him now, half a dozen children, wide-eyed and grubby, but their hands were behind their backs and they did not say a word.

'The sweets are for you, whether you can help me or not, but if you can answer-'

'Get out of here!' A woman surged through the crowd and batted the children away from him. As she swiped at their heads, they ducked and ran away without a word. The woman set her hands on her hips and swore at Stephen, who flushed cold when he realised what she was accusing him of.

'You misunderstand me,' he straightened up and said. 'All I want is to ask some questions.'

'And I'm the Queen of Sheba. Get out of here before I fetch the lads to make you.'

Other people were turning round to see what the fuss was about. If he moved, Stephen thought, they would mob him. In his courtroom voice, he said, 'I mean no harm. I'm merely in search of a man called Lyulf.'

The name broke the pressure around him. People glanced at one another or took a step back. A man with red braces said, 'Nothing to do with us.'

'But you recognised his name,' Stephen said. The crowd began to turn away and he said, 'Please! I know he used to live near here.'

'Count yourself lucky if that's all you know,' Red Braces said. 'Give it up, Mister, and leave us alone.'

'I know he is a nasty piece of work. What has he done to frighten you?'

They turned back and another man asked, 'Who says we're frightened?'

Stephen took a deep breath. 'He's plainly not a friend of yours. Why won't you tell me about him?'

'We don't know you. Why should we help you?'

Stephen thought about offering them money, but that might be a worse mistake than the sweets. 'Lyulf hurt a youngster, my nephew, and he is making trouble for friends of mine.'

'Then get them out of his way,' Red Braces said. 'Ordinary superstition's one thing. He is another.'

'What did he do?'

Now there was an empty space around Stephen. As it widened, he raised his voice. 'Just tell me where to find him.'

'How would we know?' Red Braces asked. 'We're glad to be rid of him.'

'Didn't he leave a forwarding address? Is anyone still in touch with him?'

'You're not listening, Mister. We kept out of his way, took no messages from him, and received none for him. He had no friends here.'

There were no toy fairs in August, but maybe Lyulf had dealings with toyshops. To prevent further misunderstandings, Stephen asked Tilda to accompany him on his inquiries. She agreed, though when he arrived to collect her, she said, 'I hope this isn't keeping you away from your holiday. That man said his sales were to connoisseurs, not children.'

'But the man is a liar.' Tilda looked tired, Stephen thought, her face thin and strained, but she was an encouraging companion, nevertheless, calm and elegant. When they were settled in the taxi, he said, 'He went to the Toy Fair to lure children into his traps. What if he is looking for more?'

'I agree we ought to check. Mind you, his shop was more like an antique dealer's.'

Stephen thought about this. 'Like a junk shop? With bric a brac and jumble sale bargains?'

'Grander than that. A place where hardly anything is on display and the owner writes learned articles for the British Museum.'

'Those people all know one another. I doubt Lyulf could have remained so secretive if he had secured a foothold in that world. Let's try the toyshops first anyhow.'

The toy department was almost as bewildering as the street market, though much quieter. The perfumed air was hot and the outside world seemed far away. Tilda did not chatter as Rowan would have done, but walked steadily beside Stephen, her gaze alert. Few children were about here and those few seemed dazed by the soft toys, bigger than they were, the shiny cars with real engines, and the 3D jigsaw puzzles.

'You were right,' Stephen said. 'This would not have been much fun for Nicholas and James. I hope you didn't mind deserting them for the day.'

'I'm glad to do something to help, and the boys will have a better visit at the Exiles' Club without me.'

'It's a strange place,' Stephen said.

'But one they need to learn about.' Tilda sounded determined rather than convinced. She looked up at Stephen. 'James would like to take Hugo there. Would you object?'

Stephen hesitated. His cousins' reports about Hugo were unhelpfully bland: he slept and ate, though not heartily, and gave no trouble. Hugo's own letters were polite but unenthusiastic. They might have been copied from a book of samples: 'how to write to a busy uncle without adding to his burdens'. They gave Stephen no assurance that Hugo had recovered from Lyulf's onslaught, even if his bruises had faded.

'I don't want him frightened again,' he said, 'but he is lonely. He would like to be with your boys again, before they all go back to school.'

'They will be pleased to see him. He can stay with us in Highgate, if you think it would be safe.'

'That's very kind,' Stephen said. 'Wouldn't it be a worry to you?'

'It would cheer up Nicholas and James,' Tilda answered. 'I'm not sure how well I can protect any of them but maybe they will be better together than apart.'

'I wish you could all move away from the danger. You don't mean to go out of town again yourselves?'

'Not this summer,' Tilda said. 'How could we stop Lyulf from following us?' I'd rather be near the Exiles when we meet him again, whether we find him or he finds us.'

'Very well.'

Stephen had lost his bearings but he thought they had walked round in a circle. They had passed countless displays without seeing anything made of glass. He beckoned to a sales assistant, who said that snow globes would be imported from Austria but not until the autumn. He refused to acknowledge the possibility of globes with any other contents and rebuffed Tilda's questions about the secrets of their manufacture.

At Selfridges, they wasted no time looking but spoke directly to a sales assistant who could tell them nothing more. After that, they tried big shops and small ones, with no better results.

For Stephen, one of the chief advantages of a service flat was that he could do without live-in servants. A cleaner came in daily while he was busy elsewhere and he could order in meals or eat out, as he often did. His sitting room was large and high-ceilinged, more or less unchanged since he had taken the flat, with parchment-coloured walls and lumpy, mismatched furniture, but the bookshelves were crowded and the surfaces uncluttered, as he liked them. Often, when he let himself in after a long day in Chambers, he did not switch on the lamps. Instead, he used the illumination from the windows across the street to pour himself a whisky and sit down. Then he could rest his eyes as well as his mind, while he let the day sink into the past.

His practice at the Bar had begun to flourish too recently for him to take much time off while he was in London. He planned to go for a week's fishing near the seaside village where Hugo was staying, before he brought the boy back to visit the Grays. Meanwhile he had wasted many hours on the search for Lyulf, so he needed to catch up with his briefs before his instructing solicitors returned from their holidays. He carried a bundle of papers with him when he entered his sitting room one evening late in August. He reached for the light switch, meaning to do some work. At the same moment, he saw a bulk, a dark mound across the room where nothing should be. His heart pounded, even as he flicked the switch. He stared at a solid, unwashed body, a man who sat in Stephen's own seat, with Stephen's glass in his hand.

'Who the devil are you?' Stephen dropped his papers and his fists clenched at his sides.

'You must be able to work that out. I'm the man you've been looking for.' The stranger's appearance fitted Rowan's description well enough, although his smock was grimy and his beard untrimmed. His voice was loud and sardonic.

'Who let you in?'

'The door was on the latch.'

Stephen did not believe him. He was surprised by the strength of his desire to seize Lyulf, run him out of the flat, and fling him down the stairs. He could do it, he thought. He was bigger and in fair condition, though he had not been in a real scrap for years, but it would be ridiculous to throw the man out now after trying so hard to find him.

'Did you steal a key? Or deceive the porter?'

'What does it matter? You wanted me. I'm here.'

The locks would have to be changed. Stephen walked forward. None of the chairs in the room were a comfortable fit for him, except the old fashioned wing armchair he had installed himself, the one Lyulf occupied, but Stephen did not care to sit down with the man in any case.

'Why have you come?'

'To take a look at the ghost mare's uncle.'

'The what?'

'Whatsisname's uncle, the boy the ghosts ride like a pony. Have the rest of the family cast you out as well as him?'

Stephen's anger slowed down as it grew. If Lyulf meant to goad him into haste, he would be as patient as a crocodile waiting for its prey.

'You attacked my nephew. You could do time for assault and battery.'

'Only if you went to the police, which you didn't.'

'Maybe you're not frightened of the police.' As Stephen spoke, he recognised the taint in the air, which intensified as he drew nearer to Lyulf. 'But you are frightened of something. Is someone else looking for you, someone you can't bewilder so easily?'

'Naah, they know where I am,' Lyulf said. 'They always know. I'm not such a fool as to hide from them.'

'From whom?' Stephen softened his voice.

'If you expect me to talk about them, you'll have to give me another drink. You've plenty to share.'

The whisky decanter was in its usual place on the sideboard and the glass in Lyulf's hand was empty.'

'I'll have to throw that glass away,' Stephen said. 'You get no more of my whisky. You came here to talk or you would have left by now.''

Lyulf grunted. 'You wouldn't sneer at their servant if you had ever met my Masters, the Connoisseurs of fear and hate.'

'Why do you serve them?'

'I had no choice, once they sprang their ambush. Fifteen hundred years they were in servitude in Spellhaven, so they say. Plenty of time to work out their vengeance. They showed me what it would be like, held inside glass for them to gloat over.'

'So you catch other people for them.' Stephen decided he must sit down after all and dropped into the chair that faced Lyulf. 'You trap children!'

'Children are easier to lure inside the glass bubbles, and they last longer before they give up. The Connoisseurs don't like it if the inmates die too quickly.'

Lyulf was a liar, but this story fitted horribly well with the tale told at the Exiles' Club and with everything else Stephen knew. Except for one point.

'You offered to sell one of the glass balls to – to an inmate's mother. Was that part of your Masters' plan?'

'They don't maintain such a close watch on me, not every moment.'

'So you arrange a little extortion for your own benefit?'

'You can't blame me if I have a weak moment when a beautiful woman weeps at my feet. Consolation for her, a little money to keep me in whisky, and the Connoisseurs none the wiser, until that freak boy interfered.'

Nicholas. 'What did he do?'

'The Connoisseurs felt the disturbance when the glass shattered.'

'They were there, in that little shop?'

'Not then. They felt the break in the magic, wherever they were. They came that night, all seven of them, to torture me.' Lyulf was sweating and his voice had dulled.

'You survived well enough,' Stephen said and Lyulf glared at him.

'You can't imagine. Whatever you've dealt with in your tidy, well-fed, silver-spoon life, they would have you whimpering worse than your little nephew if you ever had to face them.'

Stephen thought of the mud on the Western Front but he said nothing.

'They gave me another chance when I told them about those two Spellhaven boys,' Lyulf said. 'They want both of them but the dark one especially.'

'That's why you tried to trap him in the Park and failed,' Stephen said, 'and you failed to bully my nephew into helping you.'

'I failed then,' Lyulf said, 'but your nephew I can trap if I please. He doesn't know how to protect himself and neither do you.'

'What good will that do you?'

'The Connoisseurs are losing faith in me. I need to offer them something before they decide to replace me, but I wouldn't take your nephew if I could have the other boy instead.'

Stephen could hardly speak. 'What do you mean?'

'You've made friends with the mother. You could invite the boy here. Or somewhere else, anywhere I can knock him unconscious before he sees me. Then I can put him into a trance before he's properly awake and he may not find it so easy to escape.'

'Get out!' Stephen surged to his feet.

Lyulf did not move. 'Don't you want to keep your nephew safe? Nobody else would know, I promise you.'

'Get out!' Stephen flexed his hands. 'Or I will break that glass in your face before I throw you out.'

'Don't be a fool.' But Lyulf stood up and edged round Stephen to the door. 'Think about it.'

'I'll count to three.'

'If you change your mind, look for me at the Puppet Theatre.'

Stephen swung round with a roar and Lyulf ran.

Nineteen

The curtains in Tilda's sitting room were closed for the night. Earlier on, the flowers in the fireplace had been enough to cheer the eye, but as Stephen told of his meeting with Lyulf, Tilda's skin shrank with cold and she saw the same chill on the face of the other two listeners.

'I should have held onto him,' Stephen said, 'but I'm afraid I was too angry to think straight. I'm sorry.'

'You mustn't apologise,' Tilda said. 'I never meant to involve you in our affairs.'

'You helped my nephew,' Stephen said and Rowan looked up at him.

'We're all in it now, aren't we? I thought I was wrong to take you to the Club, Stephen, but Hugo needs protection as much as Nicholas and James.'

Tilda looked from one to the other and then turned to Dr. Hunter, invited here at Rowan's request. She was an oddity, in clothes so resolutely unfashionable they must be homemade, but with the swagger of an actress. Tilda felt no pressure from her of unspoken demands, as she did in the presence of the other Spellhaven exiles she had met. All the same, her reputation, as reported by Rowan, increased Tilda's unease.

'If we can protect anyone,' Dr. Hunter said. 'The sooner we can get Lyulf to talk to us, the better.'

'How can we?' Rowan asked. 'We can't frighten him. Not the way his Masters do.'

'He may be frightened enough to want to escape from them,' Dr. Hunter said. 'We can offer to help him.'

'How?' Stephen asked.

'I'll have to find out more about them before I can answer that, but from his point of view, it ought to be worth a try.'

'But how do we find the man again?' Stephen asked. 'How many Punch and Judy shows come into London at this time of year?'

'Puppet Theatre, you told us, not Punch and Judy,' Rowan said.

'Is there any other kind?'

'The Varangians,' Dr. Hunter answered and Rowan said, 'That's where the Puppet Master and his disciples put on their shows. Although I wonder how Lyulf wormed his way in there and why Domaldi hasn't thrown him out.'

'Himself is not often there, these days,' Dr. Hunter answered, 'and he never knew the man well. I dare say a false nose and lurking out of the way would do the trick.'

'Then you can show me where to find him again,' Stephen said. 'But what shall I do when I face him this time?'

'We'll face him,' Rowan said.

Dr. Hunter nodded and said, 'But it might be as well for you to come with us, Mr. Cole, to draw him out.'

Not for the first time that evening, Tilda checked that the door to the hall was firmly shut. Nicholas and James were in their room upstairs and she hoped they were asleep by now. As far as she knew they had no reason to be wandering about, but she never expected to be aware of all their enterprises. Ordinarily, she would have trusted them not to eavesdrop, even if they did come downstairs, but in this case she would rather take no chances.

'I should be there,' she said. 'Won't you stay with the boys, Rowan?'

'You can't go, Tilda,' Rowan said. 'You hate the very notion of magic.'

Tilda hated what the Exiles wanted, which was not the same thing, but this was not a moment for complicated explanations. 'What difference does that make?'

'You don't understand how to tackle Lyulf,' Rowan answered.

'Do you?' Tilda looked at Dr. Hunter. 'Either of you?'

'Not completely,' Dr. Hunter said, 'but I've always done my best work when I improvise.'

'Then I can help you instead of Rowan.'

Dr. Hunter shook her head. 'Rowan grew up in Spellhaven. I'd rather she came.'

'They are my sons,' Tilda said. 'I ought to be there.'

'The rest of us will set about this business with easier minds if you stay with the boys,' Stephen said. He looked anxious, leaning forward in his chair, his hands clasped between his knees. Dr. Hunter and Rowan, by contrast, had both cheered up at the prospect of action and sat tall, bright-eyed and brisk.

'Are you sure this is the right thing to do, Stephen?' Tilda asked.

'Not really.' He sat back and smiled at her. 'But it's better than waiting for Lyulf's next move.'

The smile made Tilda feel worse. 'I suppose I could send the boys to their grandparents.'

The other three began speaking at the same time. Dr. Hunter's voice was the crispest.

'Nonsense. You cannot help by coming with us. If we make a mess of things, which is entirely possible, then you can take your turn later.'

The wall lights in the restaurant were sparse and dim. The candles on the tables were extinguished one by one as the late-night diners left. Stephen sat with Rowan and Dr. Hunter while they ate. He was not hungry, though he ordered to keep them company. The pasta stuck to the roof of his mouth and he gave up after a few forkfuls. They were in no hurry. The waiters left their table alone, as agreed earlier with the proprietor, and they could not make their move until the restaurant had shut down for the night.

The Puppet Theatre was in the basement. Rowan and Dr. Hunter had arranged this meeting after they discovered someone spent his nights down there.

'Why does a Puppet Theatre need a night watchman?' Stephen had asked.

'He's more of an odd job man,' Rowan had answered. 'A down and out who scrubs floors and unblocks drains. He told them he slept in the doorway and they felt sorry for him.'

'That doesn't sound like the man I met.'

'There is nobody else he can be. Dr. Kate and I have accounted for the others.'

Even Rowan, Stephen noticed, avoided calling Dr. Hunter by her first name on its own. Not that she was a pompous woman, or one to take offence at trivialities, but her presence had a strength which made a degree of formality natural. Whether she could deal with Lyulf was another question. Stephen would have preferred a battle plan he could understand but he had nothing useful to propose. He did not even know how much he believed of what he had been told. He trusted Tilda, at any rate, and he would not let the women face Lyulf by themselves.

Over coffee, Rowan and Dr. Hunter sustained an intense argument about the use of scenery on the Elizabethan stage. Stephen listened for long enough to decide that they were enjoying themselves, however exasperated they sounded, then he let his mind drift back to the legal analysis he had started to draft that afternoon. He was almost asleep when a silence made him glance up. The argument had stopped and the room was empty. Light no longer shone from under the door to the kitchens.

'Time to go?' Stephen asked. The others nodded and Dr. Hunter wrapped a shawl over her head and shoulders to obscure her features.

The auditorium was tiny and the only light shone from a single lamp, low down on the stage. Stephen walked ahead of the women past the rows of seats, until he could see the face of the man beside the lamp. Lyulf wore a drab coat and a cap was pulled down over his forehead. He sat on the floor with a circle of puppets around him, large marionettes of beasts and monsters. The whites of their eyes glared in the lamp light but their shapes were not easy to make out. Stephen spotted a bear, a lion, a minotaur, and a woman with a cat's head. He decided to fix his eyes on Lyulf and not allow himself to be distracted. As Stephen approached, Lyulf looked up from the head of a dragon in his lap.

'Who's that with you?' he asked. 'I gave you no permission to bring anyone.'

Stephen could rest his elbows on the rim of the stage, which meant he was at eye level with Lyulf. The women on either side of him had to look upwards.

'Did the Varangians give you permission to take those creatures out of their boxes?' Rowan asked.

'The nightmare painter,' Lyulf said. 'Which of your nephews do you want to sell to me?'

Dr. Hunter pushed her shawl away from her face and said, 'We have come to help you, you wretch, not to trade insults.'

Lyulf jerked as though a wasp had stung him. 'Rhyming Kate?' he asked, his voice low and sharp. 'Insults were all I was ever good for, remember?'

'Reminiscing is overrated,' Dr. Hunter said. 'Let's not waste time.'

Lyulf put the dragon puppet down and craned forward to peer at her. 'You are not as scraggy as I expected. Did you find another lover to keep you plump for so long?'

'Mind your manners,' Stephen said, though he knew it was futile. Dr. Hunter patted his arm.

'The man's frightened,' she said.

'Of you?' Lyulf put his hands on his knees and grinned. 'Can you draw me into a maze I will never escape? Or summon a wind to hound me to the World's End?'

'Not of me,' Dr. Hunter said. 'You're frightened of the Masters you are stupid enough to serve. Are you hoping the puppets can protect you?'

'There's no life in them, not even when Domaldi pulls their strings,' Rowan said.

Lyulf picked up the dragon and pointed it at Stephen. 'Why did you bring them here, the old hag and the young termagant? I only invited you.'

The dragon's eyes wobbled in their sockets and the dagger of its tongue quivered between pointed teeth. Stephen forced his gaze back to Lyulf and said, 'They are friends of mine. I brought them to help me persuade you to change sides.'

'Your nephew would know better than that.' The dragon dropped down into Lyulf's lap. 'He had the wit to run away, the first time he met me.'

'You told me you can't run away, that your Masters can always find you,' Stephen said. 'So why hide in here? Have all your powers earned you nowhere more comfortable to sleep?'

'The Masters like some places more than others,' Lyulf said. 'The puppets remind them of Spellhaven, so they would rather be somewhere else, but they will come if they see a need, or if I call them.'

'Is it Spellhaven they want to avoid or Domaldi?' Dr. Hunter asked. 'How sure are they that he is a magician no longer?'

'They heard Norval scream to him for help and get none,' Lyulf said. 'They sent me to taunt him when the Exiles' Council threatened to hunt me down, and they watched him fall flatling when he tried to hit me.'

The air was dank down here and stale, drained by the breath of a thousand audiences and the exertions of the puppeteers. Stephen did not know whether the cramp in his gut was caused by lack of food or by Lyulf's words.

'What took you so long, then?' Rowan asked. 'If you have been luring children into glass bubbles for years, why haven't you snatched children from the Exile Clans before now?'

'Until now the Masters have cared about quantity, not quality. Why should I bother with the children most likely to recognise magical traps? There were plenty of the other kind. If your nephews had been properly educated, they would never have got me into this trouble.'

'Blaming others won't help you,' Dr. Hunter said. 'When you cheated your Masters, you must have known you would lose their trust, sooner or later.'

'Is that what you came to tell me? You never were any fun, Kate, but at least your lectures used to give me information I didn't already possess.'

'When I knew more than you did about magic.' Dr. Hunter's voice was steady. 'Maybe I still do.'

'You haven't seen what I've seen,' Lyulf began with a mutter which rose into a shout. 'You never faced up to the real stuff. You were nowhere near when your friend Norval skinned the cat, the ninth cat, when it came back to life and licked his throat, and I felt a giant claw, cold as ice, scratch the back of my neck.'

'I wasn't there,' Dr. Hunter agreed, 'so I haven't been scared out of my wits by your Masters. If there is a way to escape them, I'll help you find it.'

'I don't need to escape them.' Lyulf folded his arms and hunched inwards. 'I only need to trap the freak boy and his brother.'

'Nobody will help you do that,' Stephen said.

'The boys are catching up with their education at the Club every day now,' Rowan added, 'and they are watched over by their fathers' friends, who don't need to name you to fight you.'

'Even if you succeed,' Dr. Hunter said, 'how long before you make your next mistake? How long before your Masters demand a service you cannot deliver?'

Lyulf pushed himself up onto his knees. His shadow jumped up high behind him and his eyes glared at Dr. Hunter.

'What do you care? Maybe you'd like to buy a ticket to watch them destroy me.'

'Don't you want to get free of them?' Dr. Hunter asked. 'Or are you too afraid to try?'

Lyulf grinned. 'Aren't you jealous, Kate, of the magic the Connoisseurs have given me, magic dancing at my fingertips as it did for you, long ago?'

'Better not be too ambitious,' Rowan said. 'Your last attempt to snare my nephew did not go so well.'

She was close enough for Stephen to feel her quivering, though it did not show in her voice. On his other side, Dr. Hunter stood strong and solid. Stephen had to breathe slowly and harden his muscles to stop himself shaking, as much from fatigue as anger.

'If you were free again, you could sleep in a proper bed,' Dr. Hunter said.

'And write your reminiscences,' Rowan said. 'Nobody would believe them but they'd pay to read them all the same. You could enjoy shocking people without the trouble of hiding from the police. And your Masters.'

'If I could get free.' Lyulf's voice dropped to a murmur. 'You have said nothing to show me that's possible.'

'You'll need to work at it as much as I will.' Dr. Hunter's answer was prompt and mildly impatient. 'I want to know the terms they laid upon you, and everything else you have learned about them.'

'You want to argue me out of their grasp!' Lyulf sat back on his heels and howled out a laugh. 'What kind of a fool do you take me for?'

'One with no other choices left,' Dr. Hunter said, 'or you would have walked out on us before now.' She turned to Stephen and Rowan. 'I'm going up to sit with him. You two don't need to stay.'

'I think we do,' Stephen said. 'He hasn't promised you safety.'

'And if he did, we wouldn't believe him,' Rowan said.

'Wait here, then,' Dr. Hunter said. 'Sit down.'

She stumped up the stairs at the side of the stage and went across to Lyulf. He watched her come in silence. Stephen glanced at Rowan. He would have preferred to stick more closely to Dr. Hunter, but she was an expert of a sort and he did not trust his judgement over hers.

Rowan sighed and backed away to sit down in the front row of the stalls.

'This had better be near enough,' she muttered. Stephen took a seat beside her.

'Let's clear the ground.' Dr. Hunter picked up the puppets, one after the other, and tumbled them into their boxes. 'You need to think, not dream.'

Lyulf made no move to help but he did not stop her.

'Now,' she said, 'tell me about the cats.'

Lyulf went from kneeling to sitting and put his hands on his knees. 'The cats are dead. The cats never mattered.'

'Do your Masters always take the form of cats?'

'They take whatever form they bloody well please, which is whatever will disturb me most when they appear.'

'Such as?'

'The more we talk about them, the more likely we are to attract their attention. Is that what you want?'

'Not yet,' Dr. Hunter said. 'At least tell me what promises you made them. Can you do that without summoning them?'

'What good will it do?' Lyulf's voice rose into a howl again. 'Norval couldn't fight them with words. Neither can you.'

'Help me to try,' Dr. Hunter said, 'or run away now. I've no patience with this whining.'

'If the Connoisseurs come,' Lyulf began softly and she interrupted, 'If they come now, they will punish you for cheating them. The rest of us have made no sacrifices to them nor trespassed within their sphere.'

Lyulf stared at her. She did not falter or even blink but said, 'Let's start with something easier. Who was the first captive you lured into glass?'

After another pause, Lyulf said, 'I caught three at once. Three rowdy boys out on Mischief Night begging with a Guy and threatening people who would not give them any pennies. I said I would show then a good place to gather firewood and sent them one by one into the maze.'

'What were their names?'

He shrugged. 'I never remember the names.'

'How far have you travelled in search of your prey?'

Two hours later, by Stephen's watch, the questions continued. Dr. Hunter would have done well as a cross-examiner, he thought. She had the persistence and the invention to probe all round a subject. She was not distracted by irrelevancies and she did not reveal which were the answers she wanted, but in court, she would have had water to drink and a judge to stop her before everyone's concentration failed. Tonight, her voice grew hoarse while Stephen slipped into a daze, unable to keep track of the ever more peculiar information extracted from Lyulf.

'What happened in the Park?' Dr. Hunter asked and Rowan grew tense at Stephen's side.

'The boy had help,' Lyulf said.

'He must have done,' Dr. Hunter said. 'Help from someone not afraid of your Masters. Who was it?'

'Ask him.' Lyulf was more weary than sullen by now.

'Did it hurt you, whatever it was?'

'No,' Lyulf said and then more slowly, 'no. I was held like a mouse in a bear's paw but I was not hurt.'

'Could your Masters match that strength?'

Lyulf thought for a long time and said, 'I don't know.'

'Maybe we should try to find out.'

Twenty

The beach was a small one, more pebbles than sand, but relatively free from crowds. Hugo's cousins ran into the sea and he followed more gingerly. They had taught him to swim soon after he arrived to stay with them and he was pleased that they now left him to move at his own pace. The pebbles were sharp under the soles of his feet and he went as fast as he could. Once he began to swim, the cold salt water searched out the remains of the bruises and cuts inflicted by Lyulf, but they hurt less every day and the sting helped him battle against the waves and against his own thoughts.

His cousins milled around, splashing and ducking one another under water. Hugo veered away from them and headed out towards the horizon. They were far gentler with him than with one another. At first he had been grateful that they did not tease him, but he was fed up with being grateful now. If he joined the others, he would spoil their sport, though they would pretend otherwise and he would have to pretend to like it. His solitary summers at school had been less burdensome than he had realised at the time. At least nobody there had been hovering around, expecting him to enjoy himself. He would be glad when term started and he could go back to the tolerant contempt of his classmates, but he had an ordeal to face before then.

His latest letter from his uncle apologised that he would not be coming down to take Hugo fishing after all.

'I'm taking longer to catch up with my paperwork than I expected,' Stephen had written. 'Mrs. Gray has very kindly invited you to stay from the beginning of September and I will be able to see you there. Nicholas and James are looking forward to your visit.'

Nicholas and James knew about Hugo's beating. He had been determined that they should be told, as a warning, but he was not sure how to face them now. They had already seen his cowardice at the Toy Fair but this would be worse. James would be full of questions and Nicholas would say nothing, so that Hugo would have no idea what he was thinking.

At least he could swim all right, through the surge and swell of the water. He practised breast stroke for a while and then changed to crawl. His arms lost their rhythm and his head went under a wave. He tried to turn round, to float on his back, and heard a shout.

'Hugo! Hugo, no!'

He tried to turn again, but someone grabbed his arm and he floundered downwards. Water went up his nose and into his eyes. Then he was tugged upright and set on his feet, up to his armpits in water. He was surrounded and thumped on the back as he choked.

'What the devil, Hugo?' That was seventeen year old Richard, usually a humorous and imperturbable fellow. 'What were you playing at?'

'Nothing.' Hugo rubbed his face and looked round in bewilderment. Two more cousins stood by him, their faces blank with alarm. 'I wasn't out of my depth.'

'You went under, though,' Richard said, 'and you were heading for France, by the look of you.'

'I was all right,' Hugo said. 'I went under when someone grabbed me.'

'You didn't look all right.' Richard's face did not relax. 'And now you're shivering. We'd better go in.'

Halfway up the beach, Richard's clasp on Hugo's shoulder softened. 'You're not a strong swimmer yet, you know. You have to be more careful.'

'I like swimming,' was all Hugo could bring himself to reply. Of course he would have to be careful if someone was liable to grab him at any moment but he did not mean to thank them for it.

The room was grand for a basement, with a marble floor and pictures painted on the walls. With Nicholas at his side, James looked for the other boys Marshall had told him about, but saw only a collection of drums and a thin little man.

'Meet Mr. Grimble,' Marshall had said. 'He will tell you about the Grand Melee. It's not a free for all, whatever it looks like.'

So far Grimble did not seem eager to tell them anything. He sat on a stool beside the drums and tinkered with them. He polished the sides, adjusted screws, stroked the tops, and leaned down to listen.

'Are those army drums?' James asked. They were wider than he was, painted in scarlet and silver.

'Spellhaven had no armies. We never needed them.'

'Are they from the old city?' The drums did not look that old but they could have been repainted.

'They are copies of the Causeway drums. The originals are upstairs, never been played since the Drowning.'

The Club contained many objects made from memory of their equivalents in Spellhaven, or at least developed in the old styles. James had not been shown direct copies before.

'Were you there? Did you play the real drums on the March?' he asked.

'Nothing pretend about these.' Grimble picked up a drumstick and tapped once. The boom was not loud but James felt it in the soles of his feet. When Grimble said nothing more, James asked, 'But what about the March across the Causeway? Father told us there was music.'

'Pipes and drums and singing. That's how they drew us down the hill and out of the city. Might've been better if they hadn't bothered.'

Nicholas shifted his feet but he did not speak.

'But you would all have drowned,' James said. 'Father would have drowned.'

'And you would never have been born.' Grimble tapped the drum again, as though in satisfaction at this prospect.

'How are you getting on down here?' Marshall returned, jovial and hasty as usual. 'Have you shown them what to do?'

'I'm not a teacher.' Grimble did not look up.

'But you know the dance as well as anyone,' Marshall said.

Grimble bent down over his drums.

'Do you want us to dance?' Nicholas asked.

He sounded more puzzled than disapproving, so James hurried to make their position clear. 'We don't do dancing. Not any kind. You said it was a game.'

Marshall smiled. 'A game and a dance, and a matter of life and death. Think of it as a war dance, if you like.'

'But?' James frowned at Grimble, who nodded.

'Spellhaven fought no wars. I've told them that.'

'A tournament, then.' Marshall's voice thinned. 'A training exercise. Every child from the Lordly Clans played this game. Your father was one of the best.'

'What do we have to do?' James could not feel much enthusiasm but he was willing to try.

'I'll show you. We need a crowd to play properly, but you can have a quick try out on your own first. Take off your shoes and socks and go into the middle of the Ground.'

The Ground was a circle inlaid with rings of different colours, yellow, red, green, and black. James took up position beside Nicholas, who wore one of his medium frowns, not mountainous but solid. The marble felt cold and slippery under James's bare feet.

'Now,' Marshall said, 'listen to the drums. They'll tell you when the boules are aimed at your ankles and you have to jump above them.'

The boules were as big as apples and made of polished wood. Marshall set them skimming one at a time along the floor. James could not predict their trajectories by watching them and was rapped painfully on the ankles more than once.

'Listen to the drums,' Marshall called out again. Grimble beat out a tune which repeated itself and went into reverse or shifted sideways. James could not hold it in his mind but he could let his feet move in the rhythm. If he did not focus his gaze or try to time his moves, but let the music flow through him, he could jump clear of the boules as they came.

'Not bad.' Marshall stopped to mop his face. 'Now you, Nicky.'

Nicholas had made no attempt to jump or dodge so far. The boules knocked into him and he curled his toes but otherwise took no notice.

'Come on, boy,' Marshall called. 'If your brother can do it, so can you.'

A door banged and he turned round. Six boys and three girls came in. James recognised two from school and a couple more from upstairs at the Club.

'We're just warming up,' Marshall said. 'Join in when you are ready.'

Nobody explained the rules. The players used their hands to push the boules at one another, spun out of the way with hands on one another's shoulders, turned cartwheels, and jumped higher as the drums grew louder and faster. Marshall ran round the outside of the Ground and pushed the boules back in when they slid across the boundary.

'Get moving, Nicholas,' he shouted.

'No,' Nicholas said and everybody turned to look at him. He sat down in the middle of the Ground, while boules thudded into him. The other players came to a standstill. The drums stopped.

'Are you all right?' asked one of the girls.

'I'm not playing this game,' Nicholas said.

'You haven't even tried,' Marshall said. 'What's the matter with you?'

'This isn't Spellhaven,' Nicholas said. 'We are not apprentice magicians.'

'Of course not,' Marshall said, 'but your father would have wanted you to prepare yourselves, both of you.'

James's legs hurt worse now than when they had been hit. And the floor was colder than ever. 'Prepare for what?' he asked.

'They know.' Marshall looked at the other children, who shuffled their feet and avoided his gaze. 'Learning to be a magician begins with alertness of mind and training the body to obey what it cannot understand.'

'But what good is that, if we can't be magicians?' James asked.

'You can be ready to seize any chance that is offered to you.' Marshall said. 'You can search for any glimpse of magic renewed and never give up. You father never did.'

Nicholas walked off the Ground and sat down to put on his socks and shoes. 'Not me,' he said. 'Do you want to play, James?'

'I want to find out how it works.' James realised this was true as he said it. 'Can I have a go on the drums?'

'Not fair,' and 'Not likely,'; complaints from the other children fell away when Grimble spoke. 'You're wasting my prowess with this pair, Marshall. Take them away.'

Fred Burrows poured liquid into a bowl and began to stir. The surface was a dirty brown, with yellow streaks and grey bubbles.

'What is that?' James asked.

'Wait and see.'

They were in a dusty corner of Burrows's workshop, where the air was soaked in the smells of a thousand experiments. Burrows's hands were scarred and stained, much worse than the Science Master at school. His attitude to James was one of grudging tolerance, easier to deal with than Marshall's eagerness.

'Where's your brother?' he asked and grunted without disapproval at the answer.

'Up on the roof.'

Marshall would have wanted to know what Nick was up to. James had left him flat on his back, staring at the clouds. Since the row over the Grand Melee, the men at the Club had given up trying to badger Nicholas, but they continued to watch him and question him. He took refuge in doing nothing and the roof was where he liked to do it. James could see his point but for his own part, he was interested in finding out more about the Exiles, despite their oddity.

Burrows stirred the bowl with a regular, sweeping action. The liquid did not fizz or smoke, though its colour paled and spread more evenly.

'Were you a Lord Magician, in the old city?' James asked.

Burrows gripped the copper bowl more tightly in the crook of his elbow. 'On my way to it, maybe.'

'An apprentice magician?'

'And lucky to have got that far. I wasn't from one of the Lordly Clans like your father. I earned my apprenticeship the hard way.'

'How was that?'

'Scouring the pots in my mother's soap boiling business and turning the scum red to amuse myself. I got thrashed for it often enough before the old woman realised I might have a talent worth investing in.'

James sniffed at the bowl but could not separate out the smell from the miasma around him. 'Are you making soap now?'

'No.'

'What did you do when you were an apprentice?'

'Scrub my master's pots, and help him keep the Unseen Spirits in good humour, the few who ever condescended to listen to him. He was only a minor magician, frightened of losing his powers over them.'

Burrows's voice grew sourer than usual and his face was grim, but James was too interested to be warned off.

'But if the Spirits were held in slavery, didn't they have to obey orders?'

'Who told you they were slaves?' Burrows put the bowl down and glared at James. 'The Spirits who filled the air of Spellhaven were capable of sending a man mad or poisoning the air we breathed unless we humoured them. Duchess Ragnild's spells protected the city and lulled the Great Powers to sleep below our feet, but the rest we had to accomplish on our own.'

'Then if the Spirits were not slaves, why did they obey the Magicians there and not here?'

'Because the Binding Spells have been broken.' Burrows's voice slowed down as though he had more to say than he meant to put into words. 'Or so the Council of Elders maintain, but some of us believe it's not too late.'

'Too late for what?'

'Is the mixture ready?' Marshall came towards them. 'I've brought some bread.'

'Curdled, most likely.' Burrows looked into his bowl with disapproval. 'The boy distracted me.'

'It doesn't look too bad.' Marshall dipped a finger into the mixture and licked it. 'Just needs hotting up. Can you find your brother, James? You should both taste this.'

'You didn't say it was to eat.' James tried not to pull a face.

'Everyone in the Club enjoys Mouse Porridge,' Marshall said. 'Fred's recipe is one of the best.'

James could not tell if this was meant as a joke but it seemed pointless to ask. 'I'll fetch Nick,' he said.

'The Spirits of Spellhaven never obeyed us, James,' Burrows called after him. 'The magic worked when we pleased them. Some of us think the Spirits of England must be ripe for pleasing, if only we could work out how.'

Twenty-one

Daylight never reached into the auditorium of the Varangian Puppet Theatre, which had no windows. When she entered one morning, Rowan blinked at the bright yellow light from the electric chandeliers. Then she blinked again at the crowd of faces in the stalls, faces with glass eyes and red mouths. Dr. Hunter was working her way along the rows, filling the seats with puppets.

'What are you doing?'

Dr. Hunter turned and saw her. 'Is that the cloak? Let's have a look.'

Rowan put down the bundle of cloth and said, 'We can't take the puppets into the Park.'

'We're not ready for the Park.' Dr. Hunter came towards her. 'The puppets will help us get used to an audience, don't you think?'

'Or terrify us,' Rowan said, 'and the puppeteers will roast us, when they find out.'

'They gave us permission. I told you: the space is ours every morning this week.'

'The space, not their precious creations.'

'We'll do them no harm.'

Dr. Hunter shook out the cloak and spread it across the back of a chair. She and Rowan studied it together.

The play they were preparing was a romantical tragic-comedy about the Man in the Moon. Rowan did not think much of it but Dr. Hunter insisted it was the right kind of entertainment to engage the Spirits of Hyde Park. According to her research, the Lords of Spellhaven had first pacified the Spirits of the old city with shows like this, after the downfall of the Dukes. Nobody these days knew how the Duchess Ragnild had bound the Great Spirits to her will, but once the Duchy was overthrown, the Spirits had been prevented from poisoning the air of the city through the shows of all kinds that were performed day and night. And so, Dr. Hunter reasoned, if Rowan and her allies could pick the right show, they could please the unbound Spirits of this land. In this way, they could attract their attention long enough to ask for their help.

The text of the play came from an anonymous seventeenth century manuscript, full of grandiloquent verse, which was at least fun to speak. Dr. Hunter had adapted it for performance by four players and had woven in an appeal for aid and sanctuary. This was to be spoken by Lyulf, in the person of a stray shepherd, persecuted by jealous rivals. The cloak was for the Man in the Moon, as played by Stephen Cole. Rowan had struggled to master the knack of painting on cloth until, with help from theatrical friends and several tries, she had achieved a result that half satisfied her. Mountains in silver and gold spread across the black silk, below white clouds and skeins of silver grey geese.

'Not half bad,' Dr. Hunter said. 'We might get somewhere with this.'

The other costumes were plainer. Rowan and Dr. Hunter played several parts each, as mischief making nymphs and quarrelsome gods, so they wore white tunics with different headdresses to change from role to role. Things would have been easier with more performers, but Rowan and Stephen were both anxious not to involve Tilda. Nor could they call on anyone else without providing explanations they did not want to make. Lyulf's participation remained grudging and he insisted on wearing one of his own smocks, which suited his part well enough. Rowan was not sure whether he believed in Dr. Hunter's plan or hoped to use it to gain access to Nicholas in some roundabout way.

Stephen's tread on the stairs was heavy and deliberate.

'There you are, Stephen,' Dr. Hunter called. 'Have you learned your lines?'

'I think so.' He came up onto the stage without shying at the puppet audience. Rowan suspected that he had gone beyond surprise at anything he saw here. She draped the cloak over his shoulders.

'Splendid,' Dr. Hunter said. 'You could play King Arthur or Charlemagne in that.'

For a moment, with his back straight and his head erect, Stephen wore an invisible crown. Then he squinted down at his flanks and the effect was lost.

'So long as none of my instructing solicitors wander past,' he said.

They planned to perform outdoors, because the Spirits congregated more freely in the open air. At first Rowan had argued for a midnight show, but that would have risked interference from the Park authorities and anyhow, Dr. Hunter wanted to copy the conditions of the earlier visit so far as possible. By day, they could claim to be amateurs performing for their own amusement and it would not matter of they attracted a crowd. The Spellhaven shows had traditionally been watched by a human audience as well as the Unseen.

Rowan did not mind making a fool of herself in public. She had joined her wilder friends in a few absurd stunts before now, but things must have been different for Stephen.

'I suppose we could wear masks,' she said, looking at Dr. Hunter. 'Would masks add a touch to our style?'

Dr. Hunter looked tempted but she said, 'We haven't time to get used to masks. If anybody sees you, Stephen, tell them you are humouring an old woman.'

'Or say it's a version of Siberian cricket and offer to explain the rules,' Rowan suggested.

'I'd rather not have any more complications.' Stephen drew himself up. 'I don't need to explain to anybody.'

'Bloody right you don't.' Lyulf's arrival was noiseless. He swore because Stephen hated him to do it in the presence of ladies, though Rowan did not care and Dr. Hunter hardly noticed. 'Never give your secrets away to a woman, however cunningly she asks you.'

Dr. Hunter frowned. 'Your banter used to be so charming, or did I only think so because you flattered me?'

Lyulf came up beside her and scowled down at the puppets in their seats. 'You made me put them away, the other night. What are you doing with them now?'

'Remembering Spellhaven,' Dr. Hunter said. 'We must get more life into our performance somehow.'

They had visited Dr. Hunter's house for a couple of read-throughs, which had been pretty stiff. Dr. Hunter was convinced that they did not need professional actors to gain the goodwill of the Spirits, but they must show passion and energy. She had borrowed the stage for rehearsals so that they could move about freely, and she had urged them to learn their lines by heart. This was to be the final run through before a performance in the Park tomorrow.

They began slowly. Stephen spoke the Man in the Moon's triumph at the banishment of his nagging wife and his determination to admit no strangers to his domain, followed by his collapse into melancholy and loneliness. Stephen's recital was fluent, so long as he could stand still, but when he made his escape from the moon and came to Earth, to try his luck among the nymphs, he had to move around. Not only did he falter when he tried to move and speak at the same time, he had a tendency to stop whenever he caught sight of Rowan or Dr. Hunter. In this scene, they were gods determined to punish him for his unkindness to the wife they had given him.

'Don't watch us,' Dr. Hunter hissed. 'Forget we're here.'

She and Rowan began their quarrel at a fast patter but mixed up their lines and had to start again.

Through all this, Lyulf lounged at the side of the stage and stared at the puppets in the stalls. Rowan would not have been surprised if he had walked out or refused to join in, but he responded promptly to the cue for the shepherd's first entrance and uttered his first lament with vigour. All the nymphs were in love with him and his friends were furious that he would not choose one, so that they would have a better chance with the rest. For the first time, as he spoke, Rowan glimpsed what Lyulf had been like as a young man, before his troubles soured him. He made the shepherd a nimble, bustling lad with a quick grin and a warm, eager voice. If that had been Lyulf in his student days, maybe Dr. Hunter and other Exiles had been half in love with him, as he claimed.

Lyulf's entry brought the play to life. Rowan spoke her lines as they came, focused on each moment. Stephen lost his self-consciousness and Kate Hunter her directorial anxiety. Nothing like this had happened at their earlier rehearsals.

The gods inveigled the Man in the Moon into changing places with the shepherd, to the bewilderment of both and the distress of the nymphs. The mood darkened when the shepherd learned to fly in the Moon cloak and decided that he wanted the Sun for his lover. His flight ended in a crash and the cloak was ruined. When he tried to give it back, the Man in the Moon refused to take it.

The play needed music. Rowan had thought that when she first read it, but they had no musicians and a gramophone would be all wrong in the Park, so they had decided to do without and she had forgotten the problem until now. Stephen and Lyulf stood with the cloak between them, its damage invisible except through their words as they accused one another of spoiling it. As they spoke, she heard a tune, so dim and tentative she thought her mind was playing a trick on her. Then the music grew louder, a whistling of a tune she half recognised, though she doubted she had ever heard it before. It was not "The Miller of Dee" nor yet "The Graysteel Ride" she remembered from her childhood but something like them both.

Rowan glanced at the other three. Dr. Hunter's frown was uneasy but the men seemed unaware of anything outside their roles. Rowan did not see how any of them could whistle and speak with full, rounded voices simultaneously. She looked out into the auditorium, where the puppets no longer lolled in their seats. They sat upright, with heads that swayed to and fro and some of them beat time to the music with their hands.

Rowan caught her breath. As she hesitated over her next entrance, Dr. Hunter gripped her arm and muttered, 'Don't say anything. Don't stop.'

'But this is meant to be a rehearsal,' Rowan muttered back. 'We're in the wrong place.'

'We can't afford to lose this chance. Come on!'

The gods in the play rebuked both the Man in the Moon and the shepherd for their presumption. As Rowan and Dr. Hunter spoke their lines, the music flourished round them, with a violin joined to the whistle. It bestowed a baroque flavour on the scene, both cheerful and threatening.

This was the moment for Lyulf as the shepherd to utter the appeal for clemency and protection written by Dr. Hunter. Instead, he spoke lines of his own, just as cleverly moulded to fit the play. He flattered the gods, as Dr. Hunter had intended, though in different words, and declared himself a feeble creature in comparison, but then he called on any old friends who could hear him to come and join the fun.

'Plenty to amuse you here,' he said. 'Time for you to help instead of letting me do the work.'

'No you don't,' Rowan said, as the words caught up with her. She swept up the cloak and tried to smother Lyulf in it.

'Wait,' Dr. Hunter said. 'Keep the play going.'

Lyulf dodged Rowan and Stephen grabbed his arm.

'Hit him, Kate,' Lyulf said. 'And her. And we'll give them both to the Masters.'

The music stopped and the puppets flopped back, lifeless in their seats. Two newcomers stood in the auditorium and voices said, 'Not now. Not here.'

Everyone stood still.

'Don't you want them?' Lyulf asked.

'We don't want to be here,' the voices sounded in unison, rich and dark, but they dragged at the words as though it hurt them to speak. 'We have come for you, cheat and traitor.'

The newcomers approached. They were beautiful. The woman was tall and stately, with red hair. Luminous, golden skin shone through her mantle of white, embroidered with white spiders' webs. The white haired man beside her was taller still and covered in iridescent mail, supple as fish skin.

'Lord Thurlin, Lady Siriol. How am I a traitor?' Lyulf kept his voice light but Rowan felt his body clench beside her.

'The first command we laid on you, above all others, was to summon no more of our kind, never to charm or beguile any such, by any manner of means,' Lady Siriol said.

'I never have,' Lyulf said. 'They did this, these three would-be magicians, not I.'

'You helped them,' Lord Thurlin said, 'and you called us here, where the grime befouls the fair bodies we chose to console us for our years of captivity. You have cheated us and mocked our vengeance'

'I helped them so that I could give them to you.'

'Don't turn it all to misery, Great Ones,' Dr. Hunter said. 'The play was for delight and the sharing of pleasure, not pain.'

'Not our delight,' Lady Siriol said. 'You did not mean for us to come.'

'But you are welcome.' Dr. Hunter sounded amazed and more pleased than afraid. 'Why ever you have come, you are welcome. The company of your kind has been sorely missed by those of us who remember Spellhaven.'

The air turned biting cold. Rowan looked but did not say, 'Shut up, Kate,' and took a step forward. 'We have absolutely no plans to beguile anyone or bind them to our will,' she said.

'Easy to say now.' Lord Thurlin's eyes were dark with pain. 'What would you have done with the musicians if we had not interrupted?'

'We did not expect the musicians,' Rowan said.

'They wanted me to betray you and escape from your control,' Lyulf said.

Rowan stepped back. She was worried about Stephen, whose frown was harsh, his breathing thick and unsteady. Dr. Hunter looked so transported by success it would be dangerous to let her speak, and one thing Rowan remembered from her childhood was the unwisdom of lying to the Unseen.

'So we did,' Rowan said, 'but only to protect our families. We mean you no harm.'

'You would say that now.' Lyulf folded his arms and backed upstage, away from the Masters as well as from the others.

'Hold still,' Lord Thurlin said. He raised his hand and cracked a long, silver whip, which landed on Lyulf's shoulder and stuck there.

Rowan felt the chill as the whip passed by, though there was no substance to it, only a shifting in the air. She flinched but did not move.

'We would never have hurt the musicians,' Dr. Hunter said. 'We don't mean to hurt anyone, not even him. My dearest wish is to talk to you and your kind, not to trick you.'

'Pious Kate,' Lyulf said, 'of course you wouldn't have hurt me. I'm your last hope for the magic you long for more than love.'

'I hope for nothing from you,' Dr. Hunter said. 'I wish I had never taught you any of Spellhaven's lore.'

'You called us here, Lyulf,' Lady Siriol said. 'You have cheated us and concealed our prizes from us. Why should we make your quarrel ours?'

'Because you need me. You will have nobody to set traps without me.'

'Better no servant than a traitor.' Thurlin's whip twisted and threw out sparks. 'Come with us now.'

Lyulf screamed as the whip dragged him forward. He wrenched himself round and tried to run but more whips reached out and laid hold of him. He screamed again and writhed as they dragged him off the stage, down towards the Masters.

'Don't!' Dr. Hunter whispered.

'He is ours,' Lady Siriol said. Silver flashed from her hair and she nodded to Thurlin.

'Meddle no more with us or our kind and we may be generous enough to leave you alone,' he said.

The screams stopped. The whips coiled into a fiery bundle round Lyulf's body, which writhed until Rowan could watch no more. She sat down on the floor and put her head in her hands.

When she looked up again, Stephen and Dr. Hunter sat nearby, their heads bowed. The Masters had gone and so had Lyulf.

The next day, a man's body was found in the Thames. According to the police reports, the face was so broken as to be unrecognisable, but from a card inside a wallet, the body was identified as that of Lyulf Lyulf, Purveyor of the Unexpected.

Twenty-two

Hugo sat up in bed, tired from his train journey but not sleepy. He folded back the cuffs of the pyjama jacket, which were too long. Mrs. Gray had lent him a pair belonging to Nicholas, after condemning what he had brought with him. She had promised to take him shopping before he went back to school, which was kind, because nobody had bothered about his outfits for ages, but the kindness only intensified the pressure which seemed to have filled the house since Lyulf's death. Hugo had felt it as soon as he arrived, even before he was told the news by James and Aunt Rowan, with interpolations from his uncle. Mrs. Gray had listened in silence, while the others avoided her eye and twitched when she moved. James had complained that he and Nicholas had been left out of the fun.

'And you too, Howler,' he added.

'I can't imagine anything less like fun,' Mrs. Gray had said. 'Irresponsible antics inviting trouble are not fun. Hugo knows that if nobody else does.'

Stephen and Rowan had both stared at the floor. James had started to argue, looked at his mother, and stopped. She was furious, Hugo could see, at the risks the others had taken without telling her. And maybe, like Hugo, she was frightened about Lyulf's Masters, who sounded even more dangerous than Lyulf.

James lay on the bed opposite, his hands behind his head, his eyes open. Nicholas's side of the room was tidier than the other, with nothing on the walls except drawings of trees. The bedside table had books about birds and prehistoric mounds, but none of the paraphernalia which surrounded James. The boys had been allowed to choose their own sleeping arrangements. Nicholas had gone to occupy the guest bedroom in solitary splendour while Hugo shared with James. Nicholas might be in Hugo's class but it was James who wanted to talk and Hugo did not mind the switch. He was glad not to have to sleep alone.

'Do you think he really is dead?' James asked.

'His name was in the papers.'

'But it could have been a trick.' James sat up and hugged his knees. 'Wouldn't he be more use to his Masters alive than dead?'

'I don't want to talk about them,' Hugo said.

'Neither does Nick.' James sounded more resigned than reproachful. 'But we don't know how many other people he lured into glass balls. Or where he put them. Or cats.'

Hugo passionately did not want any more adventures. 'Even if we did know, there's nothing we could do about it,' he said.

'Not if we don't try.' James stuck his legs out straight and wiggled his ankles. 'I tried to tell the chaps at the Club about Lyulf but they shut me up.'

'I don't understand about the Club,' Hugo said.

'It's not an understandable place,' James said. 'They tell us all this stuff about the old days but they don't answer questions properly. And the boys aren't much use, even the ones from school.'

Answering questions to James's satisfaction was not easy but Hugo was not going to tell him so. 'What do you do there?'

James shrugged and turned over to prop his head on his hands. 'Play silly games. One can see for miles from the roof, though. And listen to old stories. Your ghosts might like it there.'

'Then I would not.'

'You might.' James bounced round and sat up to look at Hugo. 'The men there would believe you, not like at school. Some of them used to live with ghosts and such all the time in the city my family came from. They might know things that you could use.'

'Did you tell them about me?' Hugo tried not to whimper.

'Course not.' James lay back, offended. 'I thought you could come there with me and see if you wanted to tell them.'

'Decent of you.' Hugo did not know what else to say.

'Nick turns into a black lump while we're there. I'll be glad to have someone else to talk to.'

Rowan's studio needed cleaning up. That was its permanent state, in fact, but this morning the clutter of discarded props, unemptied ashtrays, piles of magazines, and cobwebbed layers of canvases seemed more difficult to navigate than usual. The daily cleaner had orders not to come in here, so the job was up to Rowan. Maybe getting on with it would improve her mood. She opened the window wide and rolled up some overalls to use as a duster.

She had not achieved much when she was interrupted by a visit from Darius Fox.

'Can I help?' he asked, when she explained what she was doing.

Rowan shuddered. 'Don't touch or I'll never find anything again. If you want to talk to me, stand over there, by the window, and don't move.'

He leaned against the window ledge and looked at the pictures on the walls and stacked along the floor.

'I never realised how busy you've been,' he said. 'Realism, Fauvism, Expressionism – is there a style you haven't tried out?'

'Old Spellhavenism,' Rowan said. 'You don't paint, do you?'

'I write, dear girl, you know that. You'll see my essays in all the best literary papers, if you look for 'em.'

Rowan knew Darius least well of her brother's friends. He was a few years younger than the rest, though old enough to have more memories of Spellhaven than she did. He was less inclined to treat her as a child than Marshall or Burrows, though harder to fathom. This was his first visit to the house.

'Tilda's at one of her meetings,' Rowan said. 'She won't be back for hours.'

'It's all right.' Fox smiled. 'I haven't come to cadge an invitation to lunch. Rhyming Kate has been telling me a remarkable story and I'd rather like to hear your version, that's all.'

Rowan could not tidy up and think at the same time. She shifted a pile of half-sorted papers and sat down on her couch. Instinctively, she reached for a sketchpad and pencil.

'Lyulf Lyulf is dead and the puppeteers are unhappy with us for tangling up their precious creations. That's all I know for certain.'

'Did your gallant friend kill him?'

'Stephen?' Rowan stared at Darius but he did not appear to be joking. 'Dr. Hunter never told you that.'

'She told me you summoned an Unseen Audience for a muddle of a play. She wants me to help her do it again.'

That almost explained why Dr. Hunter had spoken to him. Rowan drew a hedgehog and surrounded it with cats' heads.

'Do you think she would make a mistake about that?'

Darius wandered away from the window. Rowan glanced up but his hands were in his pockets, so she did not protest.

'Nobody else has managed it,' he said. 'Not even Domaldi, since the Drowning.'

'I don't know what we did,' Rowan said, 'but we were not in control of it, even before Lyulf made it worse.'

'We're bound to have a lot to relearn,' Darius said. 'We've always realised that.'

'What does Dr. Hunter want you to do?'

'She has a list of plays to try out and she is scouting for more actors. She has hopes of your nephews but I gather Mrs. Gray is not keen.'

Rowan added whiskers to the cats' mouths and made the tips of their tongues stick out. Tilda had thawed over the last few days, but only up to a point, and Rowan would not discuss Tilda with other people.

'The Club is full of amateur actors,' she said.

'Some better than others.' Darius's voice quickened. 'Is this the picture all the fuss was about?'

Rowan looked up. He had tipped some canvases away from the wall and discovered Eyes in the Shadows, set there with its back to the room. She jumped to her feet.

'I asked you not to touch anything.'

'Sorry,' he said, but he twisted the painting round for a better look. Rowan took it away and put it back in its place.

'If you are really interested in my painting,' she said, 'I'll send you a card for the next exhibition.'

He smiled. 'I'll see your work before then. Kate said you'll be helping with the plays.'

'That's different.' Rowan went back to the couch. 'Go away. You're distracting me.'

The picnic on Hampstead Heath was held on the Saturday before the boys went back to school. Tilda felt obliged to offer some hospitality to Burrows and Marshall in return for their kindness to her sons, but she could not bring herself to arrange a dinner party, which she suspected they would find as awkward as she would. A picnic lunch meant that everyone would be free to wander about as they pleased. In consultation with Cook, Tilda made sure the catering was splendid. She invited Stephen Cole as well as Hugo, partly in apology for her anger the last time they had met. He had been deep in shock at Lyulf's death and she had been unfair, even if she continued to resent the way she had been kept in ignorance of what was being planned.

Tilda had not entirely forgiven Rowan, for that matter, but they had settled into an undeclared truce. Tilda was grateful for Rowan's help with the picnic, given her dislike of outdoors and weather. Dr. Hunter was invited at Rowan's suggestion, to talk to the men. Tilda had not much wanted to meet her again but saw no sense in bearing a grudge. A couple of James's school friends were invited to dilute the mix and at the last moment Darius Fox was added to the guest list. When she sat on her tartan rug and surveyed the gathering, Tilda could not quite remember how Fox came to be there but he was an obliging guest, cheerful and at his ease with all the others.

They were lucky with the weather. The sun was warm for September but the hill was cooled by a breeze. The vista across London was hazy with fumes, so that you could only just make out the dome of St. Paul's if you knew where to look, but the sky was wide and blue above them. Other parties out on the Heath had chosen spots nearer the village or the Round Pond, which meant that Tilda's party could spread themselves out in peace.

The game pies, cold beef, home-baked bread, and the relishes and mustards were admired as they were unpacked, but when they settled down, none of the guests ate as heartily as Tilda would have liked. Even the boys picked at their food, between uneasy glances at one another and brief, random scuffles. They drank lemonade but the grownups had white wine, chilled in an ice bucket, which they sipped more cautiously than it deserved.

'Do your students invite you to their picnics, Kate, or do you scare them too much?' Darius Fox asked.

'What picnics?' Dr. Hunter's eyes glinted. 'My students study.'

Rowan looked up. 'Surely term hasn't started yet.'

'True. What they get up to in the summer, I don't know, but when they're in college we expect them to work. The idlers can go to Oxford or Cambridge: we've no patience with them.'

'I bet you scare them,' Fox said. 'Where did you do your idling, Cole?'

'Oxford,' Stephen answered, 'soon after the War.' He looked tired, his eye sockets dark, his cheeks sunken, but he had smiled at Tilda when he arrived and his hands were relaxed on his knees, even if he was not eating.

'I don't suppose much idling was done then,' Tilda said.

'We hadn't the strength for it,' Stephen agreed.

'What about when you were reading for the Bar?' Fox looked from Stephen to Dr. Hunter. 'Any wild parties? Any amateur acting or masquerades?'

'No.'

'What about your student days, Darius?' Rowan asked. 'You were up not so long after the War, weren't you?'

'At the other place.' Fox smiled. 'That's where I learned to idle.'

Marshall looked up from his plate, his face flushed. 'The Clan wasted their money on you, then, while the rest of us sweated to find our footing in this new country.'

I must have been mad, Tilda thought, to bring these people together here. I should have invited them all to the circus or James's choir concert. Then no conversation would have been necessary.

'Have some more pie, Mr. Marshall,' she said. 'Didn't you and Mr. Burrows start up your business while you were still in the army? Alick told me you wanted him to join.'

'He'd have been an ace salesman.' Marshall's flush turned into a mournful scowl. 'But he was too fond of showing off those cars.'

James was fidgeting. Stephen looked at him and said, 'The other place is Cambridge, James. Or Oxford, depending.'

After lunch was easier. Marshall and Burrows organised the boys into a game of outlaws and they were glad of the excuse to scatter. Tilda wondered if any of them would stick to the game once they were out of sight, but provided the men were occupied, she did not much care. She promised to make tea when they returned. Fox went into a huddle with Rowan and Dr. Hunter over a sheaf of papers. They shifted to a polite distance, plainly reluctant to be overheard. That left Tilda with Stephen.

'What about moving into the shade under that tree?' he asked. 'The others will want to cool down a bit when they come back.

The cedar tree was a few feet across the slope. Stephen and Tilda carried the hampers, rugs, spirit kettle, and tea things over in relays, hardly speaking. When they were settled again, Stephen stretched out sidelong, his face tilted into the breeze.

'That's good,' he said.

The plunge out of the sunlight was as invigorating as cold water against the skin,but Tilda could hear the strain in his voice.

'Are you going to escape from London at all, this summer?' she asked.

He shook his head. 'Not worth it now. And I'd rather stay near Hugo, for the time being.'

'In case of more trouble?' Tilda kept her voice steady.

Stephen did not answer directly but said, 'I wish I understood all this better. I wish I knew what to do.'

The words might have come out of her own mind. Tilda wanted to echo them but after a moment she said, 'If I had listened to Alick properly when he told me about his own life, if I had believed him about the magic, I would never have married him.'

Stephen held himself still. 'But then you wouldn't have Nicholas and James.'

'I know. That's what makes it hard.'

Hugo slipped away from the game as soon as he could. The other boys did not want him and he would feel safer near his uncle and Mrs. Gray. He saw them as he came back up the hill. She sat propped against a hamper, her head bent over some sewing. He was stretched out full length and looked asleep. Not far away, Rowan Gray sat with her sketchbook beside Dr. Hunter, who also lay asleep. Hugo wondered how close he could creep without disturbing them. Then he saw Darius Fox under the light shade of a hawthorn bush, with a chess board at his side. He beckoned Hugo over.

'Want a game?'

Hugo nodded. He was not much of a player but this was better than being shooed away. After a few moves, Fox said, 'You're the boy with the ghosts, aren't you?'

'Who told you that?' Hugo was furious as well as miserable.

'I saw Miss Gray's painting.' Fox sounded amused. 'I don't blame you for not wanting to share your secrets.'

James had not split on him. Hugo was a little comforted by that.

'It's not secrets,' he said. 'I don't want to talk about the ghosts.'

'Quite so.' Fox moved a pawn and smiled down at the chess board. 'You have an opportunity grown men have struggled for in vain. In your shoes, I daresay I would keep it to myself.'

Hugo wanted to run away but he was so tired of making a fool of himself. 'I don't understand what you mean.'

'Have you decided what you will do with your ghosts?' Fox's glance up was friendly but impersonal. His schoolmasters looked at him like that when they told him to think and not just learn something by heart, as he preferred. 'The Spellhaven Exiles could give you some tips, if you're not too proud to take them.'

'I won't do anything with the ghosts,' Hugo said. 'All I want is for them to leave me alone.

Fox's eyebrows rose. 'You don't need to be that Machiavellian, young Hugo. If you are determined to do without help, just say so.'

'That's not it.' Hugo put down the chess pieces and drew himself up into a ball. 'I never meant to summon the ghosts. I've tried and tried to make then go away.'

'Then you are even more surprising than I thought. Tell me what happened.'

In Tilda's drawing room that evening before supper, Hugo said, 'Please, Miss Gray, may I see the picture?'

Rowan frowned at him. She had just begun to relax, now that the troublesome guests had departed. Only Stephen was staying on, to spend a little time with his nephew. She had hoped to forget what had brought them all together for now and she was sure Tilda did not want to discuss the picture, but Hugo said, 'Mr. Fox told me about it.'

'I might have guessed.' Rowan looked at Stephen. 'It doesn't seem fair for Hugo only to hear about it from other people.'

'And us,' James put in. 'We haven't seen it either.'

Rowan looked at Tilda, who was slow to speak. Then she said, 'Very well. Let's not make a bogey of it.'

Up in the studio, Rowan pulled Eyes out of its corner and turned it round. The three boys stared, their faces solemn and puzzled.

'Those aren't real ghosts,' Hugo said, sounding relieved.

'What are the real ones like?' James asked.

Hugo shook his head.

'You should never try to paint the real ones, Aunt Rowan,' Nicholas said.

He was right, Rowan thought, but how did he know? 'What makes you say that?'

He shrugged. 'I just know.'

Twenty-three

The wooden banisters were curved into waves and the stair treads were inset with little brass figures, stars and animals. Hugo had not expected such a grand staircase, especially as the entrance to the Exiles' Club seemed more like a factory. He followed Piers Marshall warily upwards, with James at his side.

They had been back at school for three weeks and this Saturday afternoon was Hugo's first opportunity to come here, at Marshall's invitation. Tilda had taken Nicholas to a meeting. Stephen had dropped the boys at the Club and was to call for them later.

The workshop on the third floor was ramshackle by comparison with the areas through which they had walked below. Hugo could not work out how the space was arranged. Rolls of paper leaned against enormous glass jars filled with murky oils. Planks stretched across copper tubs and wooden crates were stacked in uneven towers with lists and diagrams pinned to their sides. The afternoon light from the tall windows was thick with dust. In all the muddle, it was difficult to be sure who might be present but the workbenches were unattended. Fred Burrows stood by a desk in the depths of the room and nodded as they approached.

'How long have we got?' he asked.

'A couple of hours,' Marshall answered. 'Sit down, boys. We want to have a serious talk with you.'

Hugo stood still and glanced towards the door.

'We have to be serious all week, at school,' James said.

'This is different. Sit down.' Marshall pushed long-legged stools towards them. James looked at Hugo and Marshall said, 'We want to help. You can listen to us, at the least, surely.'

It would be ridiculous to run away so soon. Hugo sat down and James followed his example. The two men stayed on their feet, two solid bulks, their faces intent on Hugo.

'We hear you have uninvited company, young Cole,' Marshall said. 'Is that true?'

Hugo drew in his breath. 'I don't want to talk about that.'

'You don't have to go into it all,' Marshall said. 'Just confirm what you said to Mr. Fox. You are haunted by ghosts and you want to be rid of them.'

Darius Fox had made no promise of secrecy but Hugo felt betrayed all the same. He nodded.

'Good.' That was Burrows. Hugo winced and James kicked his stool, but before they could speak, Burrows said, 'This isn't just gossip. We have a reason for asking.'

They waited. Marshall looked from James to Hugo and said, 'The fact is, we would like to take over your ghosts, to transfer the haunting from you to us.'

Hugo's lungs squeezed shut.

'Is that possible?' James asked.

'We've worked out a plan,' Burrows said, 'provided your friend means what he says-'

'You don't understand,' Hugo said, as he had so often lately. 'You wouldn't want anything to do with them if you knew what they were like.'

'Now that's a natural mistake.' Marshall smiled. 'But you're the one who doesn't understand. We grew up with ghosts, Fred and I, as well as all kinds of Spirits filling the air around us. Your ghosts will be much less trouble to us than they are to you.'

'That makes sense, sort of,' James said, 'but can you be sure these are the same kind of Spirits as you were used to in the old city?'

'We'll take our chances on that.' Burrows's answer was fierce.

'Why do you think the ghosts on the Heath were so stirred up, ready to fasten on young Cole here when he gave them the chance?' Marshall asked.

'I've wondered about that,' James said. 'If it has happened before to other boys, one would expect to find some evidence somewhere, but maybe they wouldn't have wanted to talk, any more than Howler.'

'Or maybe the little cluster of Exiles at your school had something to do with it,' Marshall said. 'Maybe their presence has stirred things up on the Heath, with longings and knowledge that have come together as never before. Could that be what happened?'

'The ghosts never talk to me about the Exiles,' Hugo said.

'They might not know themselves,' Burrows said and Marshall added, 'But if we are right, the ghosts are much more our responsibility than yours. Do you see that, boy?'

'They have sworn never to leave me,' Hugo said.

'But they know you don't want them,' Marshall said. 'They will have a much more interesting time with us.'

The last person who had offered to help was Lyulf Lyulf, but he had never promised to set Hugo free. This time it was hard to see any trap in what they wanted to do, if they could do it.

'Will it hurt?' James asked.

Burrows and Marshall looked at one another.

'Don't see why it should,' Marshall said.

Hugo could bear pain if it would set him free. Marshall and Burrows made him uneasy, but they did not frighten him as Lyulf had.

'Are you sure you know what to do?' he asked.

'Fred and I are used to making experiments, remember,' Marshall said, 'and rescuing them if they don't go to plan.'

Hugo wanted to get out of this room, out of the building, away somewhere nobody would stare at him with greedy eyes.

'I don't know,' he said.

'Maybe you ought to ask your uncle?' James asked.

Nicholas was the person Hugo wanted to consult but he did not suppose Marshall and Burrows would take that seriously. As it was,

Burrows said, 'We've had enough trouble making the arrangements for today. Surely you don't expect us to do it all again?'

'You want to do it today?' Hugo froze. 'I'm not ready today.'

'Come on, boy!' Burrows leaned towards him and was pulled back by Marshall, who said, 'The trouble is, our Saturdays are mostly full. If we don't act today, there may not be another chance before Christmas.'

Hugo looked at James, who made a face. 'I suppose the sooner the better.'

'Think of it like a visit to the dentist,' Marshall said. 'The waiting would be the worst part.'

'But if it doesn't work-' Hugo said.

'You'll be no worse off than you are now,' Marshall said.

'Don't you trust us not to hurt you?' Burrows asked.

Hugo did not mind so much about being hurt, though he would rather they did not think he was a coward. Their plan troubled him, but he did not know why and he could not argue any more.

'All right,' he said.

'Well done, old chap,' Marshall said and Burrows grinned at him.

Marshall looked at James.

'Why don't you wait up in the library? You can look at the maps of the old city.'

James did not move. 'I want to see what happens.'

'Better not,' Marshall said. 'We will need all our concentration for Cole. We don't want to have you to worry about as well.'

James stiffened. 'I'll keep out of your way.'

'You'll fidget,' Burrows said. 'You'll twitch and wriggle, just like you always do.'

'I won't,' James glared at him. 'I'll be as quiet as a tracker in the woods, I promise.'

'Sorry, James,' Marshall said. 'It wouldn't be fair to your friend to take the risk.'

James looked at Hugo, who shook his head. He did not want to be alone with the men, but James had ended up in Lyulf's trap because of Hugo. That must not happen again.

'Off you go,' Marshall said. 'When we've finished, we'll buy the pair of you the most slap up tea the Club can provide.'

Now James's grimace was one of disgust, but he slid down from his stool and walked away.

The workshop was so crowded that there was no clear line of sight from one end to the other. When he reached the door, James opened and shut it from the inside. Then he waited. Nobody came to check up on him. He slid sideways and crouched down in a corner. He did not see how he could spoil the experiment from here and he was fed up with being left out. He had not promised to leave the room and Howler needed looking after, anyhow.

The floor creaked and furniture thudded, to the accompaniment of grunts from Marshall and Burrows. James crept nearer, until he found a spot under a big desk from which he could watch them. They had cleared a space round a trolley, which was covered with a rug and a cushion at one end. They lifted Hugo up there and Burrows handed him a beaker.

'Drink this,' he said.

'What is it?' Hugo peered down and sniffed.

'Just a cordial to relax you.'

James was too far away to separate out the drink's aroma from the usual acrid chemical smells in here. Hugo's eyes looked enormous, dark holes in the white scrap of his face. After a brief hesitation, he gulped the cordial down and shuddered.

'That's it,' Marshall said. 'Lie down now and don't be afraid.'

He and Burrows stepped back into the shadows. When they reappeared, they had taken off their brown suit jackets and their ties. Now they wore embroidered coats in red and black, along with baggy black hats, decorated with dozens of shiny brooches. They looked like actors who had forgotten to change their trousers. Marshall drew down the blinds on the window and the room was filled with a deep twilight. Burrows set light to the biggest candles James had ever seen, five of them set in a circle round the trolley, each bedded in an enormous flower pot.

Hugo lay face up on the trolley. The men took up position inside the circle on either side of him. Each had a mug in his hand, from which he drank.

'Are you awake, Cole?' Marshall asked.

'Your hats look funny,' Hugo said, 'and the shadows are too big.'

'You mustn't go to sleep but you can shut your eyes,' Marshall said. 'The hats are to honour your companions. The Unseen audiences in our city loved fine costumes and extravagant styles.'

'The ghosts are not unseen, not by me.' Hugo's voice was slow and dull, as though it had to force its way out from under a pile of blankets.

'Can you see them now?' Burrows asked.

'I don't want to look at them. This isn't their hour.'

'But we need to talk to them.' Burrows's voice sharpened. 'Call them for us.'

Hugo shook his head without raising it. 'They'll laugh at your hats.'

'Forget the hats,' Burrows said but Marshall took over.

'Let's see what we can do. Fred, do you remember how we used to feed the ghosts in the old city?'

Burrows took another swallow of drink. 'We used to entertain the Unseen,' he said, 'and the great Clans had their special ceremonies and festivities. Did we feed the ghosts?'

'That's what we called it,' Marshall answered. 'On the longest night of the year, my family danced through the streets until dawn along with everyone else, but we left gingerbread and spiced wine in the hall, so that the ghosts could help themselves while we were out. Have you ever offered wine to your ghosts, Hugo?'

Hugo tossed from side to side. 'They can't eat or drink. They hate me because I can.'

'You're a boy.' Burrows sounded irritated. 'A mere snip of a brat, who has been nowhere but school. What can you know about hate?'

'They know.' Hugo went rigid. 'They make me listen every day.'

'They would not bother with you if they had real strength,' Burrows said. 'The ghosts we remember fought battles with the Lords Magician and wrestled the skin off the bears of the mountains. They would never have paid any attention to you.'

'You don't understand!' Hugo's head jerked up and then fell back again.

'Maybe not,' Marshall said. 'Won't they talk to us directly, your ghosts? Then we'll see what they are really like.'

'They are not my ghosts.' Hugo's head rolled round and round.

'Call them,' Burrows said. 'Let them speak for themselves.'

'They're already here.' Hugo's voice rose in a howl James had not heard for months. 'They are always with me.'

Marshall picked up a bucket and beat on it with a ladle in a slow, steady rhythm. Burrows scattered powder into the candle flames and splashed drops of cordial over them before he replenished his mug and Marshall's. The candles flared up and then steadied, but now they burned as green as grass.

'Show us, show us,' Burrows chanted and the drumming quickened. James could smell the cordial now, musty and rich, like ancient fruit cake.

'We can humour you,' Marshall sang out, 'befriend you, please you, much better than this boy.'

'You are a pair of fools.' The hoarse, grating voice came out of nowhere and then James saw them; bloated bodies, some naked, some in filthy rags, and heads of matted hair. They were solid and they jostled round the circle of candles but did not enter it. The faces were not turned his way, but he caught a glimpse of one where bone showed through skin crusted with blood and another crawling with maggots.

'The boy is ours,' the hoarse voice said. 'Keep away from him.'

James's view of Marshall and Burrows was blocked but he felt their shock. The drumming ended and Marshall whispered, 'Great Phantoms, you are more remarkable than we dreamed.'

'We don't care about the boy,' Burrows said. 'We want your company.'

More voices spoke, overlapping one another, 'We can't taste your drink. We won't dance to your music. We don't want you.'

'We'll find ways,' Burrows said. 'Now you have manifested yourselves to our sight and hearing, we'll help you to the other senses as well.'

And smell, James thought. A cold stink of rotten meat and earth swamped all the other smells in the room.

'So that you can cozen us into doing your bidding,' the voices said.

'We could do as much for you as you would for us,' Marshall said.

The ghosts' laughter made James's stomach shrivel, though it was not aimed at him.

'What could you do for us?'

'Tell us what you desire? What about names?' Marshall began to sound desperate. 'We could give you fine new names, epithets to celebrate your deeds, fires to warm you, and handsome women for you to admire.'

A single voice spoke, thin and cold. 'Do you suppose we don't know what happened in your city?'

'None of you were there,' Burrows said. 'The boy told us you died on the Heath.'

'But we have heard the stories.' This was the harsh voice which had spoken first. 'Not the lies you repeat but the tales of the escaped Spirits, as they spread out across the world. You can't fool us.'

'We've tempted you, though.' Burrows sounded angry. 'Or you would never have let us see you.'

'That's to put an end to your antics.' The voices all spoke together and their bodies pushed inwards. 'And to punish the boy for bringing us to your den.'

Stiff with cramp and fear for Hugo, James could not stand up but he staggered out of his hiding place and crawled towards the circle of candles.

'Forget the boy,' Marshall said. 'What good is he to you?'

'He is ours. Ours to plague day and night.'

'No!' Hugo sat up like a jack in the box. 'You promised to leave me alone except for your hour.'

'You should not have brought us here.' At the gloat in the voices, James rose to his feet, though he did not know what to do. 'You deserve worse torment for trying to shake us off,' they said.

'You never forbade me,' Hugo said, on the edge of a scream. 'I haven't broken my promise.'

'As good as,' they answered, 'and what's one more broken oath to the likes of us.'

'That's not fair,' James shouted as he ran forward and tried to push his way through the ghosts to get to Hugo. He could not touch them but he made no headway and their stench choked him.

'What the devil?' Marshall roared and Hugo shouted, 'Leave him alone!'

Someone knocked over one of the candles and liquid spilled from a mug on top of it. The ghosts vanished. Everyone stared at a patch of wild flames on the floor. Then Burrows said in a new voice, 'Get the boys out of here! Now!'

Marshall dragged Hugo off the trolley, seized James by the shoulder, and thrust them to the door. James twisted round to see Burrows heave over one of the giant flowerpots. Sand poured out and smothered the flames.

The boys refused tea and sat in the Strangers' Room in a miserable silence. Marshall sat beside them, his face hidden behind a newspaper.

When Stephen Cole arrived to collect them, he took one look and said, 'Are you all right, you two?'

'We've had a bit of a scare,' Marshall said. 'Nearly set fire to the workshop, but no real harm done in the end. Fred's clearing up now.'

Twenty-four

Rowan sat in the café opposite the doors of the Exiles' Club and looked out at the rain. The spindly chairs here were nothing like as comfortable as the armchairs in the Club, but Rowan was early for her appointment with Dr. Hunter and she had decided to smoke a cigarette in her own company before she went across the road. She had a portfolio of sketches by her side, a mixture of set designs and character studies for Dr. Hunter's plays. Rowan was happy with none of them and increasingly reluctant to be further involved in Dr. Hunter's plans.

To Rowan, the moment in the Puppet Theatre when she had felt the presence of the Unseen Audience had been at least as terrifying as inspiring. She was not sure she wanted to make it happen again and she was afraid of attracting the attention of the Spirits which had destroyed Lyulf, not just for herself but for her nephews. The boys were back at school, apparently unmarked by the events of the summer. Admittedly, James had seemed unusually subdued by his visit with Hugo to the Club last weekend. Both boys had been quiet at supper and had given no more than vague answers to questions about the fire in the workshop. Burrows and Marshall were not much better, which suggested that whatever had happened had not been entirely the fault of the boys. Maybe it would be healthier for the boys to spend less time at the Club from now on. Maybe Rowan could do the same and go back to the life she had led before this summer. She had promised to help Dr. Hunter but for how long? Could she hand over the portfolio and stop there?

'Rowan, old girl!' Vernon Swift loomed out of the dim afternoon to stand by her table. 'Someone said they had seen you round these parts.'

'Hello Vernon.' Rowan put out her cigarette and tried to remember her manners. 'Have you been looking for me?'

'Only wondering, you know, is everything all right? We've hardly seen you since that – erm – that little bit of trouble in the Park. Did that turn out all right in the end?'

'In its way,' Rowan said. 'I was grateful for your help. So was my sister-in-law.'

'Least we could do. We weren't really sure what to make of it all.'

He and Henry Bailes must still be brooding over what they had seen, but Rowan had no intention of trying to explain.

'You were both splendid,' she said, 'and the whole thing is over with now.'

'Good, good. Only you haven't been coming to the usual watering holes since then, or Joanie's afternoons and such.'

Rowan had meant to go to something or the other most weeks. She had not noticed how long it was since she had actually turned up.

'I've had a busy summer,' she said.

'We've missed you.' Vernon turned his hat round in his hands and stared at it. 'Especially in class. Your wild anarchist is getting restless.'

'My – who?'

'The young man you sent along to model. He keeps asking after you. We're afraid he'll stop coming if you don't turn up soon.'

'Gavin Baker has more sense that that,' Rowan said. 'I've been helping out with a big stage project.'

'And when it's over you'll come back?'

'I expect so.' It was what she had been planning, just a few minutes ago, but when she imagined herself in the depths of another debate about the subject of her next important painting or a fret over technique in class, she could feel no enthusiasm. She gathered her belongings together and stood up.

'I must go. I'm on my way to a meeting now,' she said.

'You can do better work than this.' Dr. Hunter riffled through Rowan's new sketches without lingering over any of them.

'Not lately, I can't.' Rowan sat across the desk in the library cubby hole. 'It might help if you made up your mind which play to work on.'

'I need the pictures to help me decide. And a few more actors. Are you sure Stephen Cole can't be persuaded?'

Rowan did not care to ask him.

'He's too busy,' she said, 'What about Darius and his friends?'

'They're not serious enough.' Dr. Hunter sat back and folded her arms. With the top window open, the room was chilly, small as it was. Dr. Hunter had taken to wearing the Moon cloak as an outsize shawl and her sea blue beret was pinned with a parrot enamelled in green and scarlet. Her stare was fierce enough to daunt an army of actors. 'They don't believe anything can happen.'

'Pick the likeliest and start them rehearsing,' Rowan said. 'That worked last time.'

'We minded about what we were doing,' Dr. Hunter said. 'Even if each of us had a different reason.' She picked up the sketches again and went through them more slowly. 'Didn't any of the plays appeal to you?'

Her expression was gloomy and eager at the same time, ready to be set alight if only she could strike the right spark.

'Hold still,' Rowan said. She turned over one of the rejected sketches and took a pencil from the litter on the desk. 'Go on talking.'

'What for?' Dr. Hunter frowned as Rowan outlined the shape of her head on the paper. 'My portrait's no use to us.'

'It won't be a portrait. It will be whatever you want to turn it into. How about a Titania who doesn't give in to Oberon?'

'There's no such play.'

'Or a female Dr. Faustus? Take Marlowe's play and tweak it. You could do that.'

'Maybe.' Dr. Hunter shifted in her seat but held her pose well enough. 'It doesn't follow the Unseen would be interested.'

'They might.' Rowan carried on sketching. 'I made a mistake over those scripts,' she said, as much to herself as to Dr. Hunter. 'What I need are live faces, the more peculiar the better: squashy, twisty, folded into layers all alive-o.'

'Like a bag of buns?' Dr. Hunter said. 'People used to compliment me on my looks, now and then.'

She did not sound offended. Rowan grinned at her.

'Just a few minutes more. Then I'll take this away and work at it. And you can see if it won't inspire something useful.'

Two days later, Rowan stood in her studio and considered the painting that had grown from her sketch of Dr. Hunter. Portrait painting was for society painters and amateurs, but the shapes on the canvas now were just beginning to catch the whole world inside Dr. Hunter's head and Rowan was more excited than she had been over her work for months. She would have liked another sitting but doubted she could talk Dr. Hunter into one. Maybe some of what she wanted to express could be put into things as well as faces. She marked out the line of a desk and considered what to put on it, to hint at Dr. Hunter's past enthusiasms or inspire her to new ones.

'That concludes the meeting. Before you all go off to your busy lives, who would like a walk round my gardens?'

The question was asked with a polite desperation that Tilda had heard before. The unspoken assumption among the members of this Committee was that Mrs. Mandeville agreed to host meetings principally for the chance to show off her extensive grounds, but the other members were serious-minded women, reluctant to indulge her. Tilda herself had a pile of overdue correspondence waiting at home, but these days she could not immerse herself in other people's troubles as easily as she had before. The meeting had turned into a prolonged squabble about fundraising and many of her unanswered letters were requests for her to take sides in other quarrels.

'That would be very kind,' she said to Mrs. Mandeville, who looked startled. Everyone else glowered at Tilda and broke into excuses for leaving at once.

The day was fine but not warm. Tilda walked at Mrs. Mandeville's side on a path between tidy flower beds.

'Not the best time of year,' Mrs. Mandeville said. 'The spring bulbs will go in soon, but for now it's mainly chrysanthemums and one has to be so careful with those. Let me show you the shrubbery first.'

The path went past evergreen bushes and some curious hollies with double prickles. Mrs. Mandeville continued to talk but Tilda listened only just enough to make appropriate responses. The rest of her mind compared what she could see with the layout of her smaller garden at home. The outlook here was quieter, less fussy but still formal. Leaves were swept into piles, stems were tied to stakes, and the gravel was free from moss.

'Maybe I should dig out the lupins,' Mrs. Mandeville said. 'They make such a mess every year.'

'Do you do your own digging?'

'My dear, where would I find the time?' Mrs. Mandeville was startled again. 'A wonderful chap does all the hard work for me. Are you a great gardener, Mrs. Gray?'

'Not yet,' Tilda said.

She walked home, an uphill walk at a brisk stride which nevertheless allowed her to notice the front gardens of the houses she passed. Even the wisterias looked drab this month and the ivies were clipped into neat edges. She stopped for a while at a house which looked empty, its windows dark and curtainless. The branches of a little tree had spread over the whole of the front garden. Tilda thought it was a crab apple, its leaves yellow and its fruit red in the bright sunlight. It would be impossible to live in that house without having the tree cut back but for now, until the leaves fell, it made a magnificent show.

In the house, she found Rowan, sitting at the foot of the stairs in the hall.

'There you are.' Rowan jumped to her feet. 'Tilda, will you sit for me?'

'For a portrait?' Tilda frowned. 'I don't know-'

'Not a portrait. I need faces, that's all. Interesting faces.'

'Is that a compliment?' Tilda pulled off her gloves. 'I really ought to write some letters.'

'That's fine, just let me sit in the corner and draw while you write.' Rowan sounded more cheerful than she had for weeks. Tilda welcomed the change but it made her nervous.

'Is this anything to do with Dr. Hunter?'

'I've promised her some pictures. I won't involve the boys.'

'I'd rather you didn't come to any harm either.' Tilda did not want to sound interfering. 'What is she up to, exactly?'

'She wants to revive some old plays. She hopes to attract an Unseen Audience but I'm not expecting that to happen.'

'But if it does?' Tilda hesitated. 'Are you trying to paint the Unseen?'

'The way I painted Eyes?' Rowan shook her head. 'That was all wrong. I won't try that again.'

If Stephen had been on his own, he might have turned tail halfway down the stairs to the Puppet Theatre. Whenever he recalled what had happened there, he reverted to the cold misery which had held him prisoner for too long after the War. He did not think Rowan had understood this when she had invited him to come with Tilda this evening. They were to see one of the Varangian Company's shows.

'You will feel better about the place when you see it put to its proper use,' she had said, 'and maybe it will help you make sense of the Exiles you've met.'

Stephen had little inclination towards either of these possibilities, but he did not want Rowan to feel that he blamed her for what she had let him in for, and he was glad to spend the evening with Tilda.

Tilda was at his side now, elegant in dark red and russet brown.

'Have you been here before?' he asked.

'No. This wasn't Alick's kind of thing.'

'Or yours?'

'James wants to come. I decided to see for myself first.'

'I hadn't thought about the boys.' Stephen was worried about the look on Hugo's face the last time he had seen him, but he doubted this was the way to cheer him up. 'I wish Hugo's parents would pay attention to my letters.' He had not quite meant to say that aloud.

Tilda put her hand on his arm but she only said, 'I don't suppose Nicholas will be interested. Hugo can stick with him.'

Rowan met them at the foot of the stairs. 'Splendid,' she said. 'Stephen, may I come and watch, next time you are in court?'

He was more puzzled than horrified. 'My cases are very dull,' he said.

'I won't care about that. I want to study the faces. Men's faces.'

Rowan looked cheerful tonight, the dazzle of her glass beads and harlequin jacket matched by the gleam in her eyes. Stephen was reluctant to squash her élan but he did not want the responsibility of taking her into court.

'Don't the wigs make everyone look alike?' Tilda asked.

'They do, rather,' Stephen said. 'What about your artist friends?'

'Too young,' Rowan said. 'Will you sit for me, Stephen? Just let me draw you while you read your briefs.'

'In Chambers?' That would be even worse.

'Don't let her, Stephen,' Tilda said. 'She'll complain if you twitch or pause for thought.'

'Of course, the courts are open to the public,' Stephen said.

'What a pressing invitation.' Rowan grinned. 'Never mind. I'll try something else.'

Darius Fox joined them then and they took their seats.

The first play was a farce about a wealthy woman determined to find husbands for her three daughters, who were equally determined to make their own choice. They were visited by a sequence of suitors, whose wooings were interrupted by a Punchlike figure. He caused mayhem in each scene and escaped before he could be caught every time.

After half an hour, Stephen began to relax. The puppeteers were visible, dressed in black and so skilful that it was easy to disregard their presence, but the movements of their marionettes had none of the eerie quality he had feared. The music played by a trio in plain sight was jazzy and complicated, but not disturbing.

The three daughters ran off with their lovers and the Punch married the mother. The audience applauded and Stephen saw that Tilda was smiling.

'They are good,' she said.

'But hardly suitable for James.'

'Not that play, anyhow.'

In the interval, a tall young man came up to their party. 'Good evening, Miss Gray.'

'Hello, Gavin.' Rowan's greeting was friendly but not warm.

Stephen was trying to remember where he had seen the fellow before when Darius Fox said, 'By Jove, it's the anarchist waiter. Have you come to cause a riot?'

'I don't work for the Club any more. I can go where I like.'

'And you write plays,' Rowan said. 'Have you tried your hand at writing for the Varangians?'

Baker shook his head. 'Not my scene. I wondered, Miss Gray, Rowan – are you ever coming back to classes?'

'Any day now.'

'Your friends miss you.'

'So they tell me.' Rowan handed her empty glass to Fox and smiled at Baker. 'Are your friends here? Will you introduce me?'

She came back as they returned to the auditorium.

'He would sit for you,' Stephen said.

'Too pretty,' Rowan answered.

The second play was darker, the tale of Cupid and Psyche and the ordeals she suffered. Stephen was surprised to be brought close to tears by a wooden doll, her head bowed in despair over her task of sorting peas from beans. Her wavering, lonely music lingered in his mind, even after the rollicking dance which ended the show. When the musician took his bow, Stephen recognised the old man, Lord Domaldi, whom Rowan had taken him to see on his first visit to the Exiles' Club.

'How can he play with his hands so crippled?' he asked her.

'He doesn't play much these days,' she answered, 'but he wrote that tune. I suppose it's soaked into him.'

Twenty-five

Tilda stood in her garden and considered how she might change it. The rose bushes had been pruned into stumps jagged with black spikes and the earth between them was bare. Even back in June, Tilda had found these roses a disappointment, their colours gaudy and their scent overpowering. Lupins would be better, she decided, even if they were untidy. Or a crab tree, with daisies and dandelions among the roots.

She had no time to garden. This morning, with the boys at school, she ought to be making notes for her afternoon meeting. People were depending on her to draft letters to MPs about the League of Nations, although she had begun to doubt that they could do any good. She had not yet thought of a sensible way to tackle the gardener, but the breeze curled pleasantly round her ears and the blackbird on the lawn was a cheering sight.

The door opened behind her and she turned round. James and Nicholas came towards her, their faces solemn.

'Boys, what's wrong? Have you been sent home from school?'

'Not exactly,' James answered. 'We need to talk to you.'

This made no sense. Tilda felt their foreheads, which were warm but not hot. They ducked away from her and Nicholas said, 'James is on a cross country run. I had to bunk off French but it doesn't matter.'

'Certainly it matters,' Tilda said. 'Do you mean you ran away?'

'We'll go back,' James assured her.

'I'll get detention,' Nicholas said. 'Lots of boys get detentions.'

'But why are you here? What's wrong?'

'We had to see you,' James said. 'Howler needs help.'

'Hugo? But he was here with you at the weekend.'

'We couldn't talk in front of him,' James said, 'and we didn't realise how bad he was then.'

'He gets worse every day,' Nicholas said. 'That's why we couldn't wait any longer.'

They were serious, Tilda realised. This wasn't a stunt or an excuse for mischief but a considered judgement about the right thing to do.

'Come inside,' she said.

In the drawing room, she sat down with them and said, 'First of all, in half an hour, I'm taking you back to school. You must both give me your word not to do this again, and then I'll listen to what you want to tell me.'

The boys looked at one another.

'I can't,' Nicholas said.

Anger would be useless against Nicholas.

'It isn't fair to the school, otherwise,' Tilda said. 'They can't be responsible for you if you won't stay there.'

'I will if I can,' Nicholas said. 'I just can't promise.'

'You have to listen to us about Howler,' James said. 'He's going to die and it's my fault.'

'Nonsense,' Tilda said. James did not argue but stared at her, his mouth open and round as his eyes. If he had run out of words, matters were serious. Tilda sat back. 'What do you mean?'

'He won't eat or speak, and he tries not to wake up in the mornings,' Nicholas said.

'He's shrunk,' James said. 'This morning he looked like one of the infants beside the rest of his class.'

Nicholas had grown in the last six months, more upwards than sideways. Hugo had not, but boys did grow at different rates.

'What are your schoolmasters doing about all this?' Tilda asked.

'They don't notice because he's stopped howling,' James said. 'They think that's a good sign but they are wrong.'

Tilda looked at Nicholas. 'If he never speaks, surely they notice.'

'He does as he's told,' Nicholas said, 'and he mutters in class if he has to. Nobody bothers him much.'

Tilda thought back to the weekend. Hugo had spent Saturday with his uncle and they had both come to Sunday lunch. She could not remember if Hugo had said a word or what he had eaten. He was alarmingly easy to overlook.

'How can any of this be your fault, James?'

'Because of the ghosts,' James said. 'They won't stick to their bargain any more. They jeer at Howler day and night because I took him to the Exiles' Club.'

'What happened at the Club?'

James and Hugo had both been subdued when they had come back from their visit, but Tilda had asked no questions at the time. She was determined to let her sons engage with their father's world as much as they chose. The less she was told, the easier she found it to suppress her own dislike of the Club. When James described what had happened in Burrows's workshop, for a moment she wished she did not believe him. Then she was ashamed. She had seen enough to know such things were possible. If she could not keep her boys away from them, she had to be able to face them herself.

'Mr. Marshall invited Hugo to go with you,' she said. 'Hugo agreed to what they tried to do. None of that was your doing.'

'I told Howler beforehand that they might be able to help him,' James said. 'He wouldn't have been there but for me.'

'Whoever's fault it is, Howler needs help,' Nicholas said.

Tilda thought about this and nodded. 'What do you want me to do?'

The boys looked at one another again.

'We thought you'd find a way,' James said. 'You did before, when Howler came to see you.'

She had been working from false premises then. Now she felt even less qualified to help but she did not want to let her sons down. 'I ought to talk to Hugo's uncle, and then maybe to Mr. Marshall and Mr. Burrows.'

Nicholas frowned. 'They don't know as much as they think they do.'

'Very likely, but you say they made the ghosts speak. If they're given the chance, perhaps they'll come with some better ideas about what to do next.'

'Will you talk to them quickly?' James asked. 'Not fitted in between meetings.'

'As soon as you are back at school.' Tilda stood up. She decided not to ask for their promises again. Maybe Stephen Cole would know what to say to keep them there.

Stephen and Tilda sat in the Strangers' Room of the Exiles' Club and waited for Piers Marshall to arrive. Nobody else was there. Tilda's dislike of the Club grew every time she entered it, but she did her best to shut her feelings away where they would not show.

Stephen said, not for the first time, 'I'm sorry your boys are in trouble at school on Hugo's account.'

'Apologies and detentions,' Tilda said. 'Not too savage, which is just as well. I would rather they didn't develop a taste for martyrdom.'

'You should be proud of them.'

'That doesn't stop me worrying.' Tilda looked at Stephen's frown and said, 'Hugo's had worse to endure. You should be proud of him too.'

Stephen's smile was unexpected and painful. 'You're right. It doesn't help.'

Marshall arrived in a rush. 'Have I kept you waiting? Things are so busy downstairs. Will you have some tea?'

'No, don't worry,' Tilda said. 'We won't keep you long.'

'Well then.' Marshall sat down opposite her. 'What is this about?'

'About my nephew, Hugo,' Stephen said. 'Would you mind telling us what happened, from your point of view, when he and James visited you here?'

'Oh dear!' Marshall settled himself foursquare in his seat. 'We've been hoping to draw a veil over that, Fred and I. The boys did no real damage in the end.'

Tilda felt Stephen grow tense beside her. 'Draw a veil over what?' she asked.

Marshall shrugged. 'It was a game, Mrs. Gray, based on our memories of Spellhaven. Not the sort of thing you care for, I appreciate, but you agreed your sons should learn about their history.'

'What happened exactly in this game?' Stephen asked.

'I doubt it would mean much to you. You have no connections to the old city that I know of.'

'Neither has my nephew.'

'James was so eager to have him along, and at that age we thought the romance of the story would be enough.'

'Have you seen my nephew since that day, Marshall?'

'Upset, is he?' Marshall grimaced. 'If we'd realised what an imaginative chap he is, we wouldn't have let the game go so far.'

'I understood that the Exiles believed in ghosts, Mr. Marshall,' Tilda said.

'On the island, certainly.'

'And the possibility of them here. I remember what you said to me when Alick died.'

'Maybe we said more than we meant.' Marshall looked at her earnestly. 'His death was a terrible shock, after all. We were scarcely thinking straight.'

'Are you implying that my nephew's ghosts are not real, Marshall?' Stephen asked.

Marshall shrugged. 'Each to his own beliefs, when it comes to that sort of thing, old boy.'

'But James saw them that afternoon,' Tilda said, 'and he told us that you and Mr. Burrows spoke to them. You must have seen them too.'

Marshall's face turned red but his gaze was steady, almost a glare. 'I admit the game got out of hand, otherwise the candles wouldn't have been knocked over, but I hardly think you can complain. The boys-'

'We're not here to complain,' Stephen interrupted. 'We've come to ask for your help.'

Marshall looked no happier. 'Help with what?'

'With Hugo's ghosts.'

Stephen turned to Tilda, who said, 'James tells us they torment him constantly now, worse than before. You found a way to speak to them. Can you not suggest a way to pacify them, if not to banish them?'

Marshall shook his head. 'We're simple, clumsy fellows, Fred and I. I wonder, has the boy seen an alienist?'

'We want help to stop Hugo from going mad, Mr. Marshall,' Tilda said, 'not encouragement to pretend that he is.'

'All we did was entertain the lads for an afternoon, Mrs. Gray. Maybe they just need time to calm down.'

Tilda stared at him. She and Stephen had decided not to draw attention to Hugo's plight by visiting him at school, so they only had James's account of events to rely on. Nevertheless, she was in no doubt who to believe.

'May we bring James and Hugo to see you?' Stephen asked. 'Then you can explain your position to them.'

'We really are very busy just now.' Marshall looked at his watch and jumped to his feet. 'I'm afraid I must be on my way. Perhaps some time after Christmas…'

He left without finishing the sentence.

Rowan knocked at the door of the workshop and entered without waiting for a response. A white-coated youngster came towards her and she said, 'Hello, Bobbie. Are Fred and Piers inside? We won't keep them long.'

She swept onwards, disregarding Bobbie's anxiety. James and Hugo followed her, with Stephen at the back to make up the sortie. As usual for a Saturday afternoon, the place was quiet but Rowan was confident of finding her prey. One of her friends had been on watch all day.

She headed past the filing cabinets towards the benches under the window. Fred Burrows glanced round and scowled. 'Piers! Come and deal with these people.'

'I knew you'd be pleased to see us,' Rowan said.

'Of course we are.' Marshall emerged from the depths of the room. 'But we both have the dickens of a lot to do today. No spare time, I'm afraid.'

'This won't take long.' Rowan beckoned James and Hugo forward. 'We just need to clear up a misunderstanding. Explain to the boys, please, what happened the last time they were here.'

Warned in advance, neither of the boys protested. Rowan had been shocked when she had taken a good look at Hugo. He had shrunk over the last few weeks and his skin was a pallid grey. She could not understand why she had not noticed sooner. James was merely rigid with anger.

Burrows glared at her, not at the boys.

'This isn't going to do any good, Rowan,' Marshall said. 'What's the use of upsetting them again?'

'Tell the truth and we won't be upset,' James said.

'Please don't interrupt, James,' Marshall said. 'Cole, I explained all this before.'

'Not well enough.' Stephen's voice was mild. 'Explain again.'

'There's nothing we can do for you,' Burrows said. 'Go away.'

He turned his back and James took a step towards him. 'You forced Hugo to summon the ghosts. You can't abandon him now.'

'Nonsense.' Burrows did not look round.

'Suppose we take the matter to the Council of the Elders?' Rowan asked. 'Will they approve of what you did?'

'Now, Rowan, let's not get worked up about this,' Marshall said.

'The Elders won't listen to her.' Burrows never looked round but stared out of the window. 'They haven't seen her for years.'

'They'll listen to my father.' Rowan lowered her voice to keep from shouting.

'You'll do no good,' Marshall said. 'When some things go wrong, you only make matters worse by trying to fix them. Maybe we should not have let the game go so far-'

'It wasn't a game,' James cut in.

Marshall shook his head. 'Let's not argue about that.'

'Get them out of here, Piers,' Burrows said.

'You really do have to go.' Marshall lumbered towards them and Rowan instinctively backed away. Marshall faced up to Stephen, who looked as though he might swing a punch, but then he shrugged and stepped aside. 'Come on, boys,' he said.

They regrouped in the café across the street. Without consultation, Rowan ordered hot chocolate for everyone and then turned her attention to James and Hugo. Both were perched on the edges of their chairs, their eyes wide with shock.

'We don't doubt your word,' she said. 'We believe what you told us.'

Hugo was as bloodless as a paper cut-out. James looked hollow, his energy sucked away by rage.

'But you let them send us away,' James said.

'Mainly because we could see they would be useless. They were too frightened to make sense.'

She looked at Stephen, who nodded. 'I'm afraid that's right,' he said. 'I don't believe they have any idea what to do next.'

'But they lied,' James said. 'If Nick had come, he would have made them confess.'

'He didn't think so,' Rowan said. In fact, Nicholas had said the two men would be harder to tackle in his presence and Rowan had trusted his instinct. Tilda had stayed away for the same reason.

The hot chocolate arrived and Rowan stirred hers briskly. The others stared into their cups without touching them.

'Drink,' Rowan said. 'It'll put strength into you.'

Hugo shuddered and pushed his cup away. Rowan reached out and clasped his hand.

'You mustn't give up, Hugo. We'll find someone who knows how to help you. There are plenty of Exiles with better wits and greater learning than those two buffoons.'

Hugo stared at her and muttered something. He spoke too quickly and shakily to be intelligible but Rowan caught a mention of Darius Fox.

'We'll speak to Darius,' she said, 'and to my father and maybe Lord Domaldi. We'll keep on until we find the answer, but in the meantime you have to eat, or we'll be too worried to think straight.'

She glanced up at Stephen, who said, 'There must be another way to deal with the ghosts. Can you hang on while we look for it?'

He made it a real question, not a command. Hugo looked at him for a long time. Then he picked up his hot chocolate and took a sip.

Twenty-six

James stood at his grandmother's side while she looked at the map of Spellhaven hanging on the wall. It was headed Ab Urbe Condita 200. He had enough Latin to know that the map was supposed to show the city two hundred years after its foundation, the earliest of six painted maps on the walls of the library in the Exiles' Club. James had been glad when Beatrice Gray had offered to bring him here with Nicholas as a half-term treat, but not because of the maps. He had not been in the Club since the confrontation with Marshall and Burrows and he wanted nothing more to do with them, but maybe if he could learn more about the old city and its magic, he would find a better way to do battle with Hugo's ghosts. He trusted Rowan's promise but her endeavours to find help had come to nothing so far. James did not see why he should not carry out his own researches as well.

Beatrice Gray came up to town every October to plan her Christmas orders. In previous years, she had taken her grandsons to tea at Selfridges, a sticky and solemn occasion. Now that they had been introduced to the Club, she had proposed to bring them here instead. When Tilda consulted the boys, Nicholas had been silently unenthusiastic but James said yes. James had asked to come up to the Treasure Room, as this part of the library was called. As well as the maps, it contained all manner of things made by the Exiles to preserve the crafts of their old home and a few relics brought out of the Drowning. Drums, models of houses and towers, cloths embroidered with trees and flowers, chess sets, paintings of dragons and bears: James would have liked to test them all for traces of magic, but he did not know how to set about it and he would frighten his grandmother if he asked her. Nick might know but Nick had withdrawn deep inside himself, as he always did in this place.

They had the room to themselves, apart from a librarian working in the distance.

'Did you learn magic when you were a girl, Grandmother?' James asked.

'The Citadel was built of golden stone,' she said. 'Not this dingy yellow. I used to see the ruins from my bedroom window, even though nobody could enter them.'

'But Grandmother-'

They were interrupted by Darius Fox, who greeted them and said, 'My mother and Dame Alicia are down in the sewing room, Mrs. Gray. Wouldn't you like to see their latest designs?'

'I might,' Mrs. Gray sounded wistful, 'but I'm here to have tea with the boys.'

'They can spare you for a while. I'll look after them, if you like, and meet you for tea in the Strangers' Room.'

James hated being made to feel like a parcel. On the other hand, Fox might be a good person to talk to. They had not seen as much of him as of Burrows and Marshall, but when he talked to the boys he did not huff and puff like the others. Hugo was wary of him, so James did not mean to trust him, only to ask him questions.

When Mrs. Gray had departed, Fox asked, 'Have you seen the masks? They're over here.'

Inside a cupboard, masks were displayed in rows. Some were porcelain, painted with stars or butterflies; some made of feathers, with bronze eye ridges and curved beaks; others of leather, engraved with tiger snarls or shaped into dragon heads.

'I say!' For a moment, James was distracted from his plans.

'Lots more here.' The bottom half of the cupboard was fitted with deep drawers. Fox pulled out one which contained layers of masks heaped together. 'Would you like to try some on?' He picked up a golden sunburst and handed it to James.

'What does it do?' James held the thing away from his head to examine the cracked paint and shaky curves.

'Helps you play out your dreams.' Fox rummaged in the drawer and pulled out a silver face of twisted tree roots. 'What about you, Nicholas?'

Nick put his hands behind his back.

'Did any of these belong to magicians?' James asked.

'These were all made in England,' Fox put back the tree mask and sorted through others, 'where we have to rely on our imaginations for magic. And that reminds me, how is your friend Cole?'

'He doesn't imagine his ghosts,' James said. 'I saw them.'

Fox did not look up from the masks.

'I understand from your aunt that he would like to be rid of them.' He sounded entirely matter of fact, to James's relief.

'Desperately,' James said. 'Do you know what to do? Is it something to do with the masks, something we can help with?'

'Steady on.' Fox reached out and patted James lightly on the shoulder. 'These are just make believe. I told you that.'

'But-'

Fox turned and leaned against the door jamb of the cupboard. 'I never acquired much magic in Spellhaven, not like poor Fred or your father. Lucky for me, I dare say, because doing without, after the Drowning, didn't come so hard. Just the same, I couldn't resist when Alick began flying his kites.' He glanced across at Nick. 'How well do your remember your father, boys?'

Nick might have turned into a tree, one that used a human mask to hide its face.

'Father never played at kites with us,' James said stiffly.

'Not the kind with string.' Fox smiled. 'The kind in your head which reach for the moon and fall back to earth crusted with diamonds. Did Alick ever talk to you about those, Nicholas?'

Nick went further away inside himself. 'Father never met Howler Cole,' he said.

'Didn't he?' Fox delved back into the cupboard. 'But mightn't his schemes hold a clue to solving Cole's problems, nevertheless?'

He picked up a black, circular disc, marbled in white and grey, its eyes and mouth small round holes. 'Try this one?'

He held it out but Nicholas did not take it.

'I don't want one.'

Fox raised an eyebrow and held out a different mask to James, one with leopard spots and grinning teeth. James barely glanced at it.

'What schemes?' he asked. 'What do you mean?'

'I'm hoping your brother can tell me.' Fox put down the masks and turned his full attention to James. 'I'd like to help your friend but it's not easy. I'd have a much better notion where to start if I knew what Alick taught Nicholas about magic.'

James frowned. 'Why? The ghosts have nothing to do with Spellhaven.'

'Then what a remarkable coincidence that young Hugo is a friend of yours.'

This was turning into another pointless argument. 'Mr. Marshall thought the ghosts were restless because of all the Exile boys at school, not just us,' James said.

'Maybe,' Fox was looking at James but his words were obviously aimed at Nicholas, 'but what if Alick's magic is the only way of banishing them? Nobody else has made any headway.'

'Father had no magic.' Nick's voice was so flat it might have emanated from one of the masks or the air around them.

Fox's face lost its good humour. 'That doesn't make sense, Nicholas,' he said. 'You have done things nobody has been able to do since the Drowning. Whatever Alick taught you, why won't you let the rest of us help you learn more?'

'Lyulf wanted to teach me,' Nick said.

'And you were right not to trust him.' Fox grimaced. 'Is that the trouble? I've never trapped anyone in glass or tortured a cat. If your Aunt Rowan will vouch for me, will you answer my questions?'

'No.'

Fox looked at James. 'Has he told you anything?'

James was indignant and afraid, both at once. 'Aunt Rowan would not ask me that,' he said.

'An ungentlemanly question, is it? Do you realise how serious this business is?' Fox looked from James to Nicholas and back again. Then he shrugged. 'We had better go and find your grandmother.'

At the far end of the Grays' garden was a cherry tree with low spreading branches. Nicholas liked to spend hours wedged up there, even in the winter. James preferred more activity, but he could run around the tree while he talked to Nicholas or put bits of equipment together in a nook between the tree roots. The day after their encounter with Fox, James had choir practice in the morning and both boys lunched with a school friend. When they reached home, they had only an hour to spend in the garden before tea. Nicholas went straight to his tree and climbed into it. James sat down at the base and tied knots in a rope he hoped to turn into a hammock.

For a while, neither spoke and then James said, 'I wish I knew whether that cat ever comes here anymore.'

Nicholas did not answer.

'Mr Fox asked you the wrong questions, didn't he?'

No answer. James abandoned the rope and scrambled into the tree himself, to a perch where he could watch Nick's face.

'Mother told me Grandfather will talk to Howler next time he is in town, but she's not sure when he can come.'

Nick's expression was hard to make out in the fading light. 'If I could banish Howler's ghosts, I would,' he said.

'I know that,' James said, 'but there must be things you're not telling. Secrets you're keeping.'

Nick's eyes flickered in the shadows. 'Not my secrets.'

'No.' James dug his fingernails into the tree bark. 'Father promised me he would let me go with the two of you when I was old enough. I'm older now than you were then.'

'Not Father's secrets.'

'You don't have to tell me anything.' James hated whining at Nick, because he invariably ended up feeling a fool, but this mattered more than his dignity. 'I don't even want to do any magic, if it's like what Lyulf did. But suppose Fox is right. Suppose he could work out how to banish the ghosts if you talked to him.'

Nick turned his head away. The branches were black against the gloom of the sky and Nick nestled into them until he could hardly be seen.

'Fox is wrong,' he said.

'How can you be so sure?' James leaned forward to recapture his brother's attention. 'You can make mistakes like other people.'

'Not about him.' Every time he spoke, Nick sounded as if he had climbed further away, though he had not moved. As James scowled at him, he swung out of his branch and jumped to the ground. 'Time for tea,' he said.

That evening, the boys did not speak while they prepared for bed. Once the lights were out, James said, 'If nobody knows the right way to help, we have to experiment. Fox is the only one who has offered to try.'

'Marshall and Burrows experimented,' Nick said and James sat up in the darkness.

'I admitted that was my fault. I know I should have stopped them.'

'I didn't mean that.'

'Just because one experiment went wrong isn't a reason never to try again.'

'I don't want to talk about it anymore.' Nick's sheets rustled as he turned to face the wall. 'Go to sleep, James.'

Every November since her husband's death, Tilda had helped out at the local Christmas Bazaar. She was not comfortable persuading people to spend money but the organisers had quickly spotted an opportunity in her skills at wrapping presents. They set her up with a separate stall stocked with ribbons and tissue paper, where she could admire what people had already bought and turn awkward shapes into elegant packages. In previous years, she had enjoyed the chatter and the glimpses into her neighbours' lives. This year, she found it hard to pay attention to her customers while she worked, but she smiled at them and they did not seem to notice how little she spoke.

Darius Fox arrived, dapper and energetic, with a bundle of jam pots and boxes of fudge. He looked exotic in this setting, among all the women and much older men.

'I thought I'd find you here somewhere,' he said.

'What a lot you've bought!' Tilda spread out his purchases on her table.

'All in a good cause, I'm told.' He smiled at her and stood at his ease, seeming oblivious of the people queuing up behind.

'Decent of you to come,' Tilda said. 'Do you want these wrapped together or separately?'

'One at a time, please.'

'That will take me awhile. Would you mind leaving them here, so that I can fit them in between parcels for other people?'

Fox blinked. 'I was hoping you'd have time for a chat. Aren't you entitled to a tea break or something?'

'I like to keep busy. Gold ribbon or silver?'

'You choose. And tell me what you thought about the Puppet Show the other night?'

Tilda paused in measuring out the tissue paper. 'Has something happened?'

'Nothing sinister.' Fox smiled again. 'No, it just occurred to me that you might like to come with me to a proper play one evening.'

Tilda looked away in disappointment. She had thought Fox was a man of sense, even if she was wary of his friends.

'I'm afraid I don't really have the time,' she said.

'Not for an evening out once in a while?' He sounded amused and when she met his gaze he raised an eyebrow at her.

'I'm afraid not, she said, 'and I really ought not to make these people wait any longer.'

'I'll be back,' he said and wandered away.

At school, James saw little of Nicholas or Hugo, unless they sought him out. Because they were in the senior form, the initiative had to be theirs and consorting with juniors was regarded as eccentric, if not suspicious. Glimpses at Assembly and in the dining hall were James's chief opportunities to check on Hugo and they did not tell him much. Then, one morning, Hugo was absent from Assembly and the gossip about him began at breakfast.

'Howler's in the San again, for worse than howling, this time.'

James had to wait until late in the afternoon before he could sneak into the Sanatorium to find out more. Hugo lay flat in bed, with bandages on both arms and an icepack on his forehead. His face was the colour of a dirty handkerchief and his eyes were sunken. He opened them wide as James stared at him.

'Matron said no visitors,' he whispered.

'I'm not here, I'm in Prep,' James answered, 'so I can't stay long. What happened?'

'I hurt myself.' Hugo struggled upwards onto his elbows. 'Will you tell Uncle Stephen and your mother? I wasn't trying to kill myself. It was a mistake, that's all.'

'Lie still,' James said. 'What did you do?'

'I cut my arms with Norton Minor's penknife.'

'Did the ghosts make you?'

'They wouldn't let me sleep, and I was so tired of their sneers and their boasting.' Hugo spoke in a thread of a voice. 'I thought, when I banged my knee last week, the ache distracted me for a bit, so I thumped my head a few times but that didn't work. Norton's in the bed next to mine and he hides his penknife under his pillow every night.'

That was against school rules but James knew of other boys who did the same. 'How did you find it in the dark?'

'In the moonlight,' Hugo said. 'I just stroked the knife across my skin, just a few times, because the pain was so comforting. I didn't realise how much blood there would be. Then Norton woke up and started yelling.'

'Scared, was he?'

'I suppose.' Hugo shut his eyes.

'How long are you in here for?'

'Don't know. You'd better go before Matron comes back. Will you tell them?'

'Course.' James felt his guilt harden into a black determination. 'And when you come out, we won't wait any longer. If Nick won't tell us what to do, we'll make it up for ourselves.'

Twenty-seven

It took James two weeks to find an opportunity for action. By then, Hugo was living at the Grays' house as a convalescent. His cuts had healed within a few days but the school had taken fright at the whole episode. They refused to have him back on the premises until he had undergone treatment with a mental specialist. Stephen had been near despair when he visited Tilda and Rowan to tell them this.

'How can I expose Hugo to another man who won't believe him? And how can I explain to my brother and his wife if I take him away from the school? What will I do with him?'

'We'll find you a specialist,' Rowan said. 'One of the Wulfings qualified as an alienist. He won't be able to deal with the ghosts but he'll take Hugo seriously.'

Hugo did not talk much about his sessions with Dr. Wulfing but they seemed to make him a little calmer. Meanwhile James had to put up with school and be patient at the weekends with grownups reluctant to leave Hugo alone for long. Various supposed experts among the Exiles questioned James about the afternoon when he had seen the ghosts, but if they had any ideas about how to rescue Hugo, they did not tell him. So he worked out his own plan and did not discuss it with anyone else, not even Nicholas.

He waited until a Sunday morning when everyone was busy.

'Can we go out on the Heath?' he asked.

'Do you want to come with us?' Tilda glanced over at Nicholas. They would tramp for miles, James knew, and both looked relieved when he shook his head.

'You'll go too fast. I'm doing a study of winter bark for biology. Hugo can help.' This was true, though he did not expect to have time for botany that morning.

'Make sure you're well wrapped up,' Tilda said, 'and don't go too far.'

The project was a handy excuse for leaving the house with a bag of equipment. All the same, James waited until Tilda and Nicholas had set off before he gathered the things he wanted to take. Rowan was in her studio by then and Cook's back was turned. Hugo helped to carry the bag without asking questions.

Not far from the entrance to the Heath, they struck away from the path. They walked on as far as a shallow dip in the hillside, with a ridge of gorse bushes above.

'This'll do.' James put the bag down and looked around. They would be partly shielded from the skyline here and as private as was possible without a much longer trek.

A little tree stood to one side of the hollow, its trunk knotted, its thin branches twisted and bristling with thorns. A scant few yellow blooms remained on the gorse bushes but the ground was bare and stony. The sky above them was a pale grey, with rolls of darker clouds hurrying across from the east.

Hugo shivered, despite his jacket and muffler, James knelt down and unbuckled the bag. He had put the rug inside chiefly to prevent the other contents from clanking but now he was glad of it for its own sake.

'Put this round you,' he said.

'What about you?'

'I'll be all right.' James did not want his movements hampered.

Hugo helped him unfold the rug.

'Let's sit on it,' he said. 'We can draw up the edges from the back.'

This worked, after a fashion. They sat facing one another and James took out two old saucepans and two ladles.

'What are these for?'

'Wait,' James said. He lifted out a bundle of newspapers from inside one of the saucepans and unwrapped a decanter, nearly full of a sludgy brown liquid. 'I didn't bring glasses.' They had looked frail and impractical. He unstoppered the decanter and handed it over.

Hugo sniffed it and gasped. 'What is it?'

'Brandy, I think.' He had found it in the drinks cupboard, dusty and untouched, maybe since his father's death. 'And I put in some raisins and banana peel.'

'It doesn't smell like the drink they gave me.' Hugo's voice wavered but James refused to hesitate.

'It's the nearest I could concoct. It'll keep us warm anyhow. Drink some.'

Hugo touched the decanter to his mouth and handed it back. James took a firm hold and knocked back a gulp of brandy. It numbed his mouth, and stung his throat and nose. He wheezed and swallowed hard. Then he held out the decanter again. 'Drink properly.'

Hugo rested the decanter on the rug between them. 'I wasn't drunk that day. I don't think I was.'

'We want this to be different anyhow,' James said. 'Have you ever been drunk?'

Hugo shook his head.

'Maybe it will help you tackle the ghosts better.'

'Why should it?'

'Maybe it will make you laugh at them.'

'I can't stay drunk, even if it does.'

'Drink.' James pushed the decanter with his knuckles. 'We must try something.'

This time Hugo swallowed a good mouthful. He shuddered and opened his eyes wide. 'Better than the knife,' he said.

James reached out for the decanter and drank some more himself. Past the first shock, the taste was vile, like cough mixture blended with ointment, and the fumes clogged his lungs. The hint that Hugo might prefer this sensation to his daily experience with the ghosts worried James, but they could only press on. He handed Hugo a saucepan and ladle and picked up the other set.

'Keep in time,' he said and banged out one of the tunes from the basement game at the Club, as near as he could remember it. After a few missed starts, Hugo caught the rhythm and played along.

A crow flapped sideways across the hill above them, rasping in protest. The banging was harsher than Grimble's drums, muddled and unsteady but powerful enough to drown out James's doubts and worries. He grinned. Hugo did not exactly grin back but the corners of his mouth relaxed, as though he might one day remember how to smile.

James banged harder and changed the tune to a march he had learned for his choir. That was easier to sustain and Hugo joined in promptly.

James shouted, 'Help, help, help!' and nodded to Hugo, who shouted, 'Who are you calling?' James could not hear the words clearly but he could make out the sense of them.

'Anybody. Don't stop. Any friendly Spirit or Thing with power over ghosts. We need your help. We need a champion to fight for us.'

Hugo frowned. 'Help, help, help!' His voice was thin and painful James leaned over his saucepan and banged harder.

'Knights of old, if your ghosts are here, will you fight for us? Spirit guides, Old Ones, Ancient Powers of the land, will you help us?'

And he saw the ghosts, as he had in Burrows's workshop. Their skin crusted with blood, their skulls crawling with maggots, their teeth pointed like claws; they clustered round him and their stench squeezed into his eyes and nose. They were behind Hugo and all around, but not between him and James. James saw Hugo recoil and his drumming faltered. James wedged his saucepan between his knees so that he could carry on drumming with one hand and grab the decanter with the other. He thrust it at Hugo.

'Drink more,' James whispered. 'Drum again, shout again.'

A weight without form pressed down on James's shoulders, an invisible fog. Hugo pushed the decanter back and James raised it to his mouth. He splashed his lips and chin and struggled not to choke, but he must have swallowed a few drops at least and so he carried on drumming.

'Leave him alone,' Hugo yelled. 'Leave me alone, you beasts.'

'Sticks and stones can't break our bones.' The ghosts spoke under the drumming, in little, dark voices, close to James's ear. 'But we like name calling even better. What else can you call us?'

Hugo must be able to hear them as well, because he shook his head as though to drive away a wasp.

James caught his breath and croaked. 'We're calling your enemies, not you. Come and help! Come and help!'

'Nobody will listen to you.' A chill spread out from the ghosts, biting into James's neck and striking through his clothes. 'You'll wear out soon and then you will have to listen to us.'

'Why bother to interrupt us, then?' James nudged Hugo's foot. 'They are afraid this might work, Howler. Keep going.'

They both drummed harder, loud and fast, though without much attempt at a tune now. James looked at the few inches left in the decanter and decided not to attempt another drink. An ache sang behind his eyes in time with the drum beats and he swallowed down nausea with every breath, but he felt he could go on like this forever. Hugo had his eyes shut and James could not see his expression clearly but his arm went up and down steadily.

They took it in turns to shout, 'Old Ones, Cunning Ones, Little People of the Hills, please help us!'

From under their feet came a groan, deeper than all their noise or the snarls of the ghosts. The grass shivered and a wind licked gently over them, then it sucked at them from all directions at once. It pulled their caps from their hair, their hair from their heads, and their voices out of their mouths. James crouched low over his drum and mouthed soundlessly what he could no longer shout.

Darkness fell over him and muffled him. The wind released him at the same time as the stench of the ghosts disappeared.

'Be quiet, both of you,' a voice said. 'How dare you play around like this?'

The muffle was a coat thrown over his head, surprisingly solid by contrast with the pressure of the ghosts. James struggled from under it and saw the angry face of Dr. Hunter. A moment later, Hugo's head appeared from the other end of the coat. The ghosts were gone and so was whatever else had been there.

'You've ruined everything,' James said. 'We nearly did it.'

'I'm going to be sick,' Hugo said and twisted round to vomit into the side of the hollow. James resisted briefly and then stumbled over towards the furze bushes to do the same. When he turned, Dr. Hunter was sniffing at what was left in the decanter.

'No more than you deserve,' she said. 'If your father was alive, young Gray, he'd beat you for this.'

James's head pounded and his legs wobbled. 'Something was on its way and now it's gone,' he said. 'Why couldn't you leave us alone?'

'Something was coming all right. I sensed the boiling in the air half a mile away and the wrath of Spirits insulted by your noise.'

'We never insulted anybody,' Hugo said. 'We were begging for help.'

He shivered. Dr. Hunter picked up her coat and pointed to the rug on the ground. 'Wrap yourselves in that, both of you.'

'Who put you up to this?' she asked when they were huddled together with the rug over their shoulders.

'Nobody.' The question revived James's indignation. 'People promise to help Howler banish the ghosts but nobody does anything.'

'So you weren't just playing.' Dr. Hunter's voice grew grimmer. 'You were deliberately running into danger, invoking forces you had no idea how to handle.'

James wanted to lie down and push his face into the grass, but he was not ready to give up yet. 'Nobody knows what to do,' he said. 'Mr. Fox said so, and Grandfather.'

'Nevertheless, there are things they could have told you not to do, if you'd had the sense to ask for advice. Anyone who remembers Spellhaven could have told you about the Mirkholes, the places of despair made by the Unseen Audience when they loathed the shows put on to entertain them.'

'This wasn't a show,' Hugo said. 'The ghosts are real and I loathe them.'

Dr. Hunter stared at him and nodded. 'I'm not doubting your troubles, boy, but why the blazes should that racket have tempted any Spirit to help you?'

James could not quite remember now where the pieces of his plan had originated. 'I thought they liked drums,' he said. 'We had to try something!'

'Did you indeed? What makes this your fight?'

James wondered if he was going to be sick again. 'It just is,' he said.

'He's younger than me. I shouldn't have let him,' Hugo said.

'You didn't let me.' James clutched harder at his side of the rug. 'This is much more interesting than flying aeroplanes. Men risk their lives in those every day.'

'Not eleven year old schoolboys, however.'

'I'm twelve.' James glared at her. 'Howler was younger than that when the ghosts started on him.'

'Shame you can't argue them to death. I wonder…' Dr. Hunter resettled her spectacles on her nose and studied James for a long moment. She was more formidable than Matron, for all her peculiar clothes, but she was not a bully. 'Are you game for another try, under my instructions?'

James caught his breath. 'Yes, please.'

'Even if it's dangerous? Even if your mother might not approve?'

'He mustn't,' Hugo said. 'Mrs. Gray's been so kind to me.'

'We'll explain to her afterwards,' James said. 'She'll understand, if there's a real chance to help.'

Dr. Hunter emptied the brandy decanter onto the grass and handed it to James. 'I'll leave you to explain that. I was on my way to visit your aunt when I heard you. Let's get you home while I make my plans.'

'But what do you want me to do?' James asked. 'How much longer will Howler have to hang on?'

'Long enough for me to turn a notion into a plan,' Dr. Hunter said. 'He's tougher than you think, or he would have given up by now.'

James was almost too tired to argue properly but he said, 'They made him go to a doctor.'

'I'll be ready as soon as I can.' Dr. Hunter shooed at them. 'Off with you, before you make yourselves really ill.'

'But why did you think making Hugo drunk would help him deal with the ghosts?' Tilda sounded more bewildered than angry, but James felt too limp and sore to explain anything. He was aggrieved at the way Dr. Hunter had interrupted and found fault with his plan. Now that she had gone upstairs to see Rowan, he did not want any more analysis from anyone else, especially his brother.

He looked at Nicholas, who stood beside Tilda in the front hall, his face expressionless.

'It might have helped,' James said. 'He might have liked the ghosts that way.'

Tilda sniffed at the empty decanter and grimaced. 'And why did you try to get drunk as well?'

'To find out what would happen.' That was sort of true. 'Anyhow we didn't get drunk, only sick.'

'Certainly you both look terrible.' Tilda glanced at Hugo, who had not spoken a word. He stared at his feet and shivered.

'You had better both go to bed for the afternoon.'

'We're not ill.' James felt bound to protest. 'We don't need to lie down.'

'Yes, you do. You have to be ready for school by teatime, whatever you feel like by then, and a rest will do Hugo no harm.'

The paving round the Albert Memorial was smooth, with no cracks to be seen. Tilda paced along the front while Darius Fox watched her.

'They must have replaced the stones,' she said, 'but this was the place, facing this way.'

The morning was frosty and grey. People walked past at a brisk pace, with scarcely a glance in their direction.

'What else can you remember?' Fox asked.

'Nicholas stood here, up to his shins in the earth, and Lyulf close by him.' The memory made Tilda more uncomfortable than anything else that had happened, but she did her best not to show it.

'Was the air salty? Did you smell anything strange?'

'Nicholas needed rescue.' Tilda turned and frowned at Fox. 'I didn't pay attention to anything else.'

He returned the frown. 'What if you think back now? What else comes to mind?'

'Nothing.' She did not make the attempt. 'Why does it matter? What can this have to do with Hugo's ghosts?'

'That's complicated.' Fox hunched his shoulders against the wind. 'Walk with me and I'll tell you.'

Tilda had other things to do, but Fox had displayed no silliness towards her since she had turned down his theatre tickets. She owed him some courtesy and there was the faint chance that he might be able to help. She fell into step beside him. They walked towards Kensington Gardens as he talked, his voice low so that Tilda had to stay close to hear him.

'Nobody at the Club knows exactly what Alick was up to before he died, but Nicholas was mixed up in it somehow. If only he would talk to us, we might be able to work out the rest.'

Tilda's hands were cold inside her gloves. 'What has that to do with the ghosts?'

'Nicholas made something happen here. If we understood how, we might be able to harness the same powers against the ghosts.'

Tilda thought about Sallikin. The story was not hers to tell and if it had been, she would not have cared to set Fox rushing down to Hertfordshire with his friends. 'Nicholas did not work any magic,' she said.

'So he says.' Fox walked faster and spoke louder. 'But why else were Lyulf's Masters so interested in him?'

Tilda stood still. 'You've spoken to Nicholas?'

'Only briefly, at the Club.' Fox stopped and looked back at her. 'Maybe he believes what he says-' He caught Tilda's eye and started again. 'I'm sure he does, but that makes the puzzle all the greater. What if the Masters come after him again? Can't you tell me anything that might help?'

Tilda had not forgotten Lyulf's Masters, though Fox's question increased her fears, but she would not be bullied by his arguments. She shook her head.

Twenty-eight

In the winter, Stephen's flat was uncomfortably warm. The heating came from a communal boiler, not subject to individual adjustment, so Stephen was in his shirt sleeves one evening while he laboured over his brief for court next morning. He had not had time so far that week to drop in to see Hugo, as he tried to do every few days. He hoped to go to Highgate after court tomorrow and the better prepared he was now, the faster the hearing should go. He doubted his visits brought much comfort to Hugo, but they might reassure the boy that he was not abandoned by his family, and Stephen could see Tilda, which comforted him in ways he preferred not to analyse. He was careful not to stay long, except when he was formally invited to a meal, but he came away stronger and more cheerful, even from a brief talk with her.

He was surprised at the knock on his door and still more surprised to find Dr. Hunter on the doorstep.

'Is something wrong?' he asked and she shook her head.

'Want to talk to you. Won't take long.'

'Come in. Excuse me a moment,' he said and went to fetch his jacket and tie.

'Don't fuss on my account,' Dr. Hunter said but she let him take her coat and accepted a glass of sherry. She settled into a chair and looked around with open curiosity, especially at the bookshelves. Seeing her here, sturdy and cheerful, Stephen was confused by his memories of her confrontation with Lyulf in the Puppet Theatre. She carried authority in the tilt of her head as well as her sharp glance, but it was the authority of a shrewd, capable woman, not very different in style from the male dons of Stephen's time at Oxford. He could not imagine any of them summoning Spirits or conjuring puppets into movement.

To Stephen's further puzzlement, Dr. Hunter said, 'Rowan told me you were busy. I wasn't sure I believed her.'

'Rowan's helping look after my nephew,' he said. 'I visit as often as I can.'

'I've seen the boy. He needs more than visits.'

Stephen forgot about his brief as his worries about Hugo crashed down on him. 'I don't know what else to do,' he said. 'Should I send him to China?'

'No. Nor Timbuctoo nor the Moon. Why China?'

'His parents are there.'

'When did he see them last?'

'Six years ago, I think. Maybe seven.'

'Half his lifetime. In any case, he doesn't need more people to worry about him. He needs rescue from his ghosts.'

'When I listen to Rowan or young James, I believe that.' Stephen looked out of the window and then faced Dr. Hunter again. 'Other times, I picture myself explaining what I've done to my brother, or to a judge in court. I can't convince them the ghosts are real.'

'Then you're wasting your energies.' Dr. Hunter was not sympathetic. 'You saw what killed Lyulf. Do you doubt that was real?'

'Sometimes.'

'That's what comes of over-education,' Dr. Hunter said. 'I want to try something with the boy. Will you forget your doubts for long enough to help me?'

'Yes,' Stephen said at once, and then, more cautiously, 'unless he might end up in worse trouble. Burrows and Marshall-'

'Are a pair of fools. At least I won't put him in more danger than I put myself and the other players.'

'You want to stage another play?' Stephen's mind sagged at the prospect of learning more lines and strutting about in another absurd costume.

'Has anyone come up with a better plan?'

'No,' Stephen said, 'but what kind of play will please the ghosts?'

'Not the ghosts. Other Spirits who may have power over the ghosts.'

Stephen thought about this. 'Isn't that what you've wanted to do all along? Find a way of connecting with the Spirits as you did in your old home.'

'Just so.' Dr. Hunter's gaze did not waver. 'That's no argument against trying this way to help Hugo.'

'I suppose not.' Stephen tried to separate his unease at his experience in the Puppet Theatre from his worry about Hugo. 'Must he take part? He's had enough to endure.'

'If he's not with us, the ghosts won't be. I'm not expecting to charm the Spirits into my pocket. We'll be lucky if we can gain their attention long enough to show them the ghosts and rouse their interest.'

Stephen looked wistfully at his bundle of court papers. 'Have you got a part for me to learn?'

'I will have, once I've spoken to Rowan.' Dr. Hunter surged out of her chair. 'And meanwhile I'll leave you to your labours. Good night to you.'

In Rowan's studio, the landscapes and abstracts had been turned to face the wall. On the main easel and propped on tables to either side were three large canvases, each featuring a single person.

'Look at these,' Rowan said to Dr. Hunter. 'Look hard.'

Dr. Hunter stood foursquare in front of the paintings and gazed for several minutes while Rowan sat on the couch, making more sketches of her face.

The central picture was of an old man hunched in a chair, his head bent so that his face was in shadow. His hands took up nearly a quarter of the canvas, the knuckles thick as tree roots, the long fingers bony and twisted. A tangled heap of puppets lay round his legs and above his head; to the left, was a roundel in which pale towers rose out of a golden mist. On the other side was the badge of the Varangians, the head of a lion with a mouse peeping out of its mane.

'Domaldi never sat for that,' Dr. Hunter said.

'No,' Rowan said, 'but might Prospero have done? Or even King Lear?'

'Shakespeare's no use. Too many rival performances.' But Dr. Hunter went on looking at the pictures.

In one, a woman wrapped in the Moon cloak stood in a whirl of papers and books, some falling from the ceiling, some in tall piles crammed close together. The face was Dr. .Hunter's but ageless, unlined but too thin for youth. The third painting showed the back of a skinny woman in patched overalls and high heels. She was half way up a ladder suspended in space. A string of beads was looped round her neck and caught on the rungs of the ladder, though whether this would anchor or choke the climber was not certain. The face turned back to stare at the viewer was Rowan's.

'You haven't left any room for the words,' Dr. Hunter said.

Rowan frowned. 'You wanted inspiration, not illustration.'

'Yes but these are complete.' Dr. Hunter waved her hand at the paintings. 'These are good stuff, the best you've done. A brilliant playwright might bring any of these three to life in a new play and people would argue about whether he'd done justice to the pictures, but I want the play to matter more than the painting, and we don't have time to find a brilliant playwright.'

Rowan was too pleased to feel apologetic. If the paintings were right in themselves, she had achieved something. She was beginning to think what Dr. Hunter wanted was unattainable.

'Must we hurry?' she asked.

'I've made a promise to Hugo Cole,' Dr. Hunter said, 'and his uncle.'

'To put on a play for Hugo?' Rowan sat up straight. 'Won't that be dangerous?'

'He can't go on as he is.'

And Rowan had also promised to help him.

'Do you want to look at my sketches?'

'Not for these pictures. Have you any of young Hugo?'

Rowan's old sketchbooks were not shelved in any particular order, but she had known Hugo for scarcely a year, so she was able to pull out the ones with the least faded covers. She and Dr. Hunter sat side by side to go through the mixture of doodles, faces, and bits of pattern or shapes which had caught Rowan's eye. As usual, she discovered images she could not remember making and others much less coherent than she expected. She turned over the pages without comment, until Dr. Hunter put out a hand to stop her.

'That one. What's that?'

The figure was not Hugo but James, helping Tilda wind wool. His arms were stretched out, his mouth open in some argument. Dr. Hunter did not wait for the explanation but said, 'I could work with that. May I take it? And the sketches for Eyes in the Shadows? I'll let you know you when the parts are ready.'

James had too much on his mind these days to perpetrate commonplace mischief at school, so he was puzzled as well as apprehensive when he was summoned to the headmaster's study, late on a Wednesday afternoon. He arrived to find the Head accompanied by Mr. Fletcher, Nick's housemaster, and two boys from Nick's form. The Head's frown lightened when he saw James, which was a further surprise.

'At least you're accounted for, Gray Minor. Do you know where your brother is?'

'No, sir.' James looked at Mr. Fletcher. 'Isn't he in Prep?'

'He hasn't been seen since lunchtime,' Mr. Fletcher answered. 'Where might he have gone?'

'Don't know, sir.' James did not stop to consider the question.

'You must have some idea. Think, boy.' Mr. Fletcher shot a glance at the headmaster, who said, 'You had better tell him the rest.'

The Head stood on the hearthrug, a square, well-padded man, usually unruffled by the antics of any of his pupils. Mr. Fletcher, by his side, was taller and thinner, with a nervier disposition. Tonight, they had the same look, their shoulders up and their balance forward, as though they would have liked to seize all three of the boys present and shake them to pieces.

'Go on, Edwards, Thompson,' Mr. Fletcher said, 'describe what you saw.'

'We were out in the grounds after lunch, kicking a ball about, mostly, but Digger walked round the edge on his own,' Edwards said.

'He didn't want company,' Thompson said, 'so we let him alone.'

'He gets like that sometimes.' Edwards sounded defensive. 'It doesn't mean anything.'

'Understood.' Mr. Fletcher had obviously heard this more than once. 'But then you saw him speak to a man in the street?'

Edwards nodded.

'At the gate where the coal comes in,' Thompson said. 'We weren't spying. I just noticed Digger had stopped and he was still in the same place when I ran past again. Then I saw the man through the bars of the gate.'

'What did he look like?' the Head asked.

'Couldn't see much,' Thompson said. 'He wasn't a delivery boy, though. He wore a hat.'

'Afternoon school seems to be a matter of some confusion,' Mr. Fletcher said. 'I'll deal with that later, but the upshot is nobody has seen Gray Major since that moment. Who could he have been talking to, Gray Minor?'

'Don't know, sir. Sorry.' James could not imagine his grandfather sneaking up to the gate to talk to Nicholas. Maybe someone from the Club might, but Nick would not have paid any attention to them.

The Headmaster grunted. 'You're not trying, boy. You can't make things any worse for your brother than he has for himself. You're usually quick enough with a theory to tackle most situations, as I recall. Tell us where to look for him.'

James was still angry with Nicholas but that did not mean he was prepared to give him away to anybody else. On the other hand, what if Nick had gone into one of his trances, out there in the cold?

'Please, sir, is the gate still locked?' he asked.

'Yes of course,' Mr. Fletcher answered. 'I checked that myself.'

'Did you look in the trees, sir?' James asked. They frowned at him, so he explained, 'He might have climbed up if he wanted to be by himself and – and fallen asleep.'

Outside, the fields were a blank gloom under a blue black sky. The leafless trees round the perimeter changed from formless lumps into complicated silhouettes as Mr. Fletcher shone his torch into one after another. James was impressed that he knew which were the climbable ones without being told. They called Nick's name but nobody answered and they saw nothing larger than a bird's nest. James was shuddering from the cold by the time they headed back inside.

Indoors, Mr. Fletcher turned James to face him.

'We'll give him until after supper. If he hasn't turned up by then, we're calling your mother and the police. If you do know where he is, tell him that. Off with you, now.'

He did not wait for a response, which was tactful, but James could not think of anywhere else to look for Nicholas, on school premises or off them.

Twenty-nine

Tilda sat alone at the breakfast table and pulled dry toast into crumbs which she did not eat. Her tea had gone cold and a grey scum floated on its surface. She had sat up most of the night, in the hope that Nicholas would tap at the garden door or that the telephone would ring with news of him. There had been none and now she longed to take action to find him but she was afraid to leave the house, in case he came. Rowan had gone to the Exiles' Club to ask questions. Hugo was with Gavin Baker, who had been tutoring him so that he could keep up with his schoolwork. James was to stay at school until the weekend. Tilda had nothing to do but worry.

Someone knocked at the front door and Tilda ran out to open it, without waiting for the servants. Darius Fox stood there, breathless and taut with excitement.

'Mrs. Gray, my dear! Tilda!' he said. 'The boy's disappeared, has he? You must be going through hell.'

So he had no news. Tilda let him in, since that was what he seemed to want, and took him to the drawing room, chilly and grey in the morning light. He sat down but then sprang up almost at once, to pace up and down.

'This never crossed my mind,' he said. 'I'd have sworn the boy didn't listen to a word I said, and surely he had the wit to see he was safer at school than anywhere.'

For a moment, this made no sense to Tilda. Then she stood up herself.

'You've spoken to Nicholas. Were you the man outside the school yesterday?'

Fox nodded. 'I took a chance to speak to him by himself, to make him see reason.'

'What did you say to him?'

'Nothing about running away, I assure you.'

'You sneaked up to him without my permission or the school's.' Tilda steadied her breathing. She would be angry later. 'What did you say?'

Fox stood still and grinned at her. 'Only what I said to you in the Park, and I must be right, mustn't I? He wouldn't have run away if he had nothing to hide.'

'You told him he is in danger from Lyulf's Masters?'

'That they would be bound to come after him, sooner or later. I asked how confident he was that he could protect himself, or you or his brother.'

Fox had lost his easy-going manner but he did not seem at all abashed by what he had done. He bristled with so much energy that he used up all the air in the room.

'But you didn't expect him to run away?' Tilda asked.

'I left him to think it over. I promised to meet him again at the weekend.' Fox's face sobered as he looked at Tilda. 'You must let me help you now, Tilda. You're a clever woman and a brave one, but haven't you struggled on long enough by yourself?'

Tilda wished he would go away. She had no time to waste in rebuking him and whatever he was talking about now, she did not want to hear it. 'Thank you for telling me about yesterday,' she said. 'At least Nicholas wasn't abducted by the man in the street, as the police thought.'

'Never mind the police.' Fox's excitement blazed higher as Tilda grew colder. 'If Alick were alive, wouldn't you have trusted him to find Nicholas?'

The answer to that was no. Tilda felt as though she had been kicked in the stomach. She gripped the back of the nearest chair. 'Alick died four years ago.'

'And you need someone to take care of you. His sons need a man to look up to.'

'Do they?' Maybe she should be angry now as well as later. 'What does this nonsense have to do with finding Nicholas?'

'I'm asking you to trust me, Tilda.' Fox came towards her and she let go the chair, drawing herself upright. 'Let me help you find Nicholas and protect him. And after that, there's a lot we could do together, you and I.'

He was a slighter man than Alick but well proportioned, his eyes brilliant under thick lashes, his skin smooth and fair. Tilda wondered, if she had not been hurt so much by her husband's eager charm, would she have been tempted by Fox's warmth and sparkle?

'Trust you how?' she asked.

'Let me hold you.' He stretched out his arms and leaned towards her. She would not retreat but the look on her face must have warned him because he took a step back.

'I think you had better leave my house,' she said.

He folded his arms. 'Would Alick have wanted you to live alone forever?'

'This has nothing to do with Alick. I'm worried about my son, Mr. Fox. Unless you can suggest anything to help find him, will you please leave me alone?'

Fox's eyes narrowed. 'All right, let's go at it that way round, if you'd rather. We'll start with the boy and I'll keep the rest until later.'

'There will be no later between you and me.'

He shrugged. 'I don't give up easily. As for Nicholas, I told you once before what to do. Give me every scrap of information, everything you know or guess about what he did this summer, all the strangeness you have ever noticed in him.'

Tilda walked to the door and opened it. She was almost as angry with herself as with Fox. She could not think what she had done to inspire this stupidity but she ought to have been able to stop him before he encroached this far. 'If I trusted you, I might do that,' she said.

For a moment, he stood quite still, breathing hard, his energy not used up but blocked, his face white. Then he said, 'I'm not the sort to bear malice. Come to me, when Nicholas doesn't turn up and your despair is greater than your pride. I'll be waiting.'

Tilda watched until she was sure he had left the house.

Stephen took a taxi to Highgate as soon as he had finished his afternoon conferences. He had been tempted to cancel them but he did not want to impose his company on Tilda to no purpose. She came out into the hall as he arrived and the strain in her face told him that Nicholas had not been found.

'I won't disturb you,' he said. 'I only came to say, if there's anything I can do, anything at all, you must let me know at once. And to take Hugo off your hands.'

She frowned as though she was translating the words from a language she scarcely knew.

'Hugo's upstairs with Rowan,' she said. 'We're not neglecting him.'

'Of course you're not.' Stephen was horrified at the misunderstanding. 'But you should not have to worry about him as things are. It's all arranged. He can stay with me in the flat for the time being and young Baker will take care of him during the day.'

Tilda's frown eased a little but she asked, 'Is that fair to him? He mustn't think he's a nuisance to us.'

'Then let him do his bit,' Stephen said, 'by moving out of your way.'

'Maybe…' Tilda's voice faded. She looked exhausted, huddled into a cardigan that seemed too big for her.

'Have you eaten anything today?' Stephen asked.

'Rowan made me eat lunch.' She smiled briefly. 'A long time ago. Will you have some tea with me, Stephen, while I decide what to say to Hugo?'

Her hands were steady as she poured the tea. She put her cup down beside her chair and leaned her head back. When James had gone missing, she had looked tense and remote, but not as fragile as this, unless Stephen had not known her so well then. As he thought this, she said, 'Last summer, I believed I knew the worst that might happen to a lost boy. Now I don't know what to fear.'

Stephen wished he knew how to comfort her. 'Would it help to blame me at all?'

'For what?'

'All this might never have happened if I had not dragged you into Hugo's troubles. Nick and James might have carried on as ordinary schoolboys.'

'I doubt that.' Tilda sat up and made another attempt at a smile. 'Sooner or later, their father's world would have caught up with them, however stubbornly I pushed it away.'

'It might have been easier when they were older.'

'Or harder.' Tilda looked at Stephen. 'I can't decide whether my mistake was to keep the boys away from the Exiles' Club for so long or to let them go there at all.'

Stephen stared at his hands.

'After the war,' he said, and had to stop. He had never spoken to anyone about his nightmares and he could not begin now, not to describe them properly, but maybe he could explain another way. 'At the Front, I made mistakes, we all did, too many to count. Afterwards, when I came home, they came with me. I lived through them again, night after night. Sometimes I made the other decision, to stay instead of go, move up instead of down, and every time, as many men were killed, or more, whatever I decided.'

'So all the choices we can make are the wrong ones.'

'There's no way of telling otherwise, at least. We just have to carry on with the next one.'

'Waiting is the hardest,' Tilda said. 'I hate waiting.'

Stephen closed his mouth. I'll wait with you, he wanted to say, play cards or chess, or sit and say nothing, if it helps, but she would not accept that kind of companionship from a friend, and there could hardly be a worse moment to ask to be more than a friend.

'I ought to go,' he said aloud without realising it.

'You must be busy.' Tilda rose to her feet. 'Thank you for coming.'

At midnight, Tilda built up the fire in the drawing room and pulled a chair close to it. She saw no point in going to bed. She would not sleep and she could reach the telephone in the hall more quickly from here. Rowan offered to sit up with her but Tilda said, 'Better for one of us to be alert in the morning.'

Once she was alone, she turned off the lights and stared into the fire. The bright twisting of the flames lulled her into a doze, until she was startled awake by loud, unearthly wails. She shot to her feet, her heart thumping. The wails continued, accompanied by taps and a rattling at the French windows behind the curtains. Nicholas would never make such a noise, even if he was too frightened to utter words. Nevertheless, Tilda pushed through the curtains and shot back the bolts. When she opened the door, the paws which had batted at the glass dropped down and the wails turned into a snarling whine. Tilda could not see much more than a gleam of eyes and teeth, close to the ground. She caught her breath and stepped outside.

'Is anyone there?'

Nobody answered. She looked down by her feet and there was a cat, continuing to whine. As she stared, it picked up something in its mouth, slipped round Tilda, and went indoors. Tilda waited, her eyes and ears strained to their utmost for any hint of another presence nearby. The garden smelled of cold stone and damp earth. Nothing stirred except the wind.

Tilda went back inside and found the cat waiting for her with arched back and switching tail. In its mouth was a lump of fur, almost as big as itself, which it dropped at Tilda's feet. Then it backed away and stared at her. It made a sort of angry purr, a noise she had never heard before.

The lump was a dead rabbit. Tilda winced and began to protest. Then she stopped and focused on the cat, while she tried to think straight. Alick had disliked cats, so she had never kept one in this house, though she had been brought up with them. No doubt plenty of the neighbourhood cats crossed her garden at night but they would never demand to be let in like this or mistake her French windows for their own homes.

This creature was distinctly disreputable, with a rank smell, a torn ear, and a ragged tail. Tilda remembered James's attempts to feed the cat which had escaped from Lyulf's trap. He had never provided much of a description. All the same, Tilda supposed this must be the same beast. Had it given up the struggle to survive the winter on its own or had it come here for a stranger reason?

'You don't have to bring me presents, cat,' Tilda said. 'Do you need shelter? Or is there something you want me to do? Did somebody send you here?'

Her voice shook at that but the cat merely snarled. Tilda crouched down and stretched out her hand, palm upwards. The cat narrowed its eyes, swiped its claws at her fingers, and leaped past her, out into the garden. It had vanished before she could step outside again. She stood and called to it, with the blood dripping from her hand, but it did not come back.

The next night, Rowan sat up with Tilda. They left the curtains open and sat in a draughty gloom, watching the blackness outside. They did not say much, because they had talked themselves out during the day. They nursed a brandy and soda each and they waited.

The wails shocked their ears, even though they hoped to hear them. Both women jumped to their feet. Rowan opened the door and stood aside, ready to shut it as soon as the cat entered the room. Tilda faced the opening and glimpsed the cat's yellow eyes and wild tail, but this time, it made no attempt to come in. It dropped a limp, black crow over the doorsill and leaped away, all in one moment. Tilda tried to follow but she had to give up after a few steps.

She went back inside and said, 'It's gone. What does it want?'

Rowan stared outside and then shut the door. 'Not to be followed,' she said. 'Or to be adopted. Maybe it wants to feed you.'

'But why? Why now?'

Rowan fetched the fire tongs to turn over the crow. 'At least this creature is dead.'

'Do you think the cat knows something about Nicholas?'

'James is the one who fed it,' Rowan said.

'Nick set it free, and it never came before he went missing. If he is out there somewhere, unable to move…why won't it let me follow? What's the use of sending it if I can't-' Tilda pressed her hands to her mouth and felt Rowan's arms around her.

'Nick would manage better than that,' Rowan said. 'Even if he's hurt, he'd find a better messenger.'

James had never been inside a building in the Inns of Court. In Stephen Cole's Chambers, the annexe to the Clerk's room was a dusty basement lined with huge brown books, the leather crumbling on their spines. Two office stools were pushed against a broken desk and on the floor, bundles of papers lay against the walls, each tied with pink tape.

'I'm afraid you'll have to wait in here,' Stephen said. 'I'll be as quick as I can.'

'We'll be all right.' James looked at Hugo, who nodded. 'We'll sit on the floor.'

'Good lads,' Stephen said. 'I'll see if the clerks can smuggle in some lemonade and biscuits.'

When he was gone, James went to the narrow window, which looked out onto a little paved alley and a blank wall.

'Have you ever been here before?' he asked.

'Never.' Hugo sat down and took out a book from his satchel.

'I'd like to see your uncle's room. Do you think he would show us, on the way out?'

'We're not supposed to be here at all,' Hugo said. 'We shouldn't cause any more trouble.'

'What about the lemonade?' James wandered back to his own satchel and lay on his stomach beside it.

'The clerks are all right,' Hugo said. 'It's the senior men, the silks and important clients, who wouldn't like to see schoolboys on the premises.'

'In case we booby trap their doors.' James was disgusted but he looked at Hugo's face and said, 'Don't worry. I'm not going to let your uncle down.'

Both boys were to spend the night in Stephen's flat. Tilda did not want James at home that weekend, so that she could be free to go in search of Nicholas. James minded less about this than he might have done, because he was curious about the flat, and because the next day, they were to meet Rowan at Dr. Hunter's house, to hear more about her plan for a new play. He did not think his mother needed to worry about Nicholas, but she would never listen if he tried to explain why not.

'Digger hasn't run away because of me, has he?' Hugo asked.

'To find you a cure, you mean? He would have taken you with him, if that was it.'

'Didn't he say anything to you?'

'Not a word,' James answered. 'Not even, "don't do anything stupid 'till I get back".'

'Where could he have gone?'

'Maybe just away from everyone.' Hugo looked so miserable that James added, 'Nick goes away inside himself a lot. Maybe this time he decided to go right away, where nobody could get at him.' It seemed mean not to admit that he himself had been one of the people concerned over Nick's refusal to help Hugo, but if he did, that would only make Hugo feel worse. 'He'll come back when he's ready.'

Thirty

The windows of the drawing room in Elephant Cottage were streaked with rain. Inside, Beatrice Gray sat with her embroidery under a standard lamp. The rest of the room was left in shadow, which suited Tilda well enough. She had slept the night before, once she had taken the decision to abandon her vigil at home and set out to look for Nicholas, but the wakefulness of previous nights left her heavy-eyed this morning, while the train journey into Hertfordshire had been stuffy and soporific. Now she wished Mrs. Gray would pay attention to the conversation, instead of her needle.

'Ivar is at the works. If you'd let us know you were coming, I'm sure he would have sent a car to the station.'

'It was a sudden decision,' Tilda said. They had already had this conversation when she arrived but Mrs. Gray seemed reluctant to move onwards.

'If Nicholas were here, we would have telephoned you.'

The embroidery today was a pattern of intertwined reeds, worked in subtle shades of green and brown. Although Mrs. Gray's hands were steady as she stitched, she did not seem relaxed. Her back was rigid and her head too far forward.

'Of course,' Tilda said, 'but there are other places in the neighbourhood where he might have gone.'

Mrs. Gray fastened a strand of silk on its needle into her cloth, chose another silk, hardly distinguishable in colour, and threaded it onto a new needle.

'At home, in the old days, everyone in the city would have recognised a son of the Graysteel Clan,' she said.

Maybe if they started from here, Tilda would be able to push the talk the way she wanted it to go.

'Would all the Unseen Spirits have been his friends?'

'No.' At least the needle paused at this question. 'Nor all the Lords Magician. But a boy could not disappear in Spellhaven. News would reach his family from the Unseen, if not from the neighbours.'

'Have you asked your neighbours here?'

'Ivar made inquiries.' Mrs. Gray's voice thinned. 'Most of them cannot tell one boy from another.'

Tilda had not expected much from that line of inquiry. 'There's a place Nicholas showed me, not far from here: a garden beside a ruined house. Do you know it?'

'My Clan were the Dulcimers,' Mrs. Gray said. 'Our gardens went down deep into the ravine under the Dragon Bridge. Every season we discovered new plants in the corners least visited.'

Tilda could not be sure whether Mrs. Gray disapproved of her too much to answer her questions, or whether she hid inside this mist of vagueness because she could not bear to live in the present, but she persevered.

'Which gardens do you visit hereabouts?'

'The air is too quiet in these parts.' Mrs. Gray stitched away at an even pace. 'I don't go out much.'

'Have you heard any talk of an old garden nearby? Or a family fallen on hard times, who have let their house go to ruin?'

'My sons used to tell me of the places they saw: Alexander, Stilicho, Kendrick. And my other daughter, Ismene.' Mrs. Gray raised her head at last but she did not look at Tilda. She stared into the depths of the room and said, 'When they went out in the mornings, I never doubted they would return at night, but on the day the city broke apart, only Alick and Rowena were at home. I never saw the others again.'

'I didn't mean to remind you-' Tilda said but Mrs. Gray interrupted.

'I tried to keep Alick safe after I lost the others and I failed. I wanted Rowena to stay here with us and now she never comes home. What use can I be to you when I could not hold on to any of my own children?'

'You did your best for them all,' Tilda said.

'And my best led to ill luck and disaster.' Mrs. Gray bent her head and made more stitches. 'Anything I tell you is more likely to lead you wrong than right.'

Tilda could not bear any more of this. 'Don't worry any more,' she said. 'I'll leave you be.'

The woods looked different in the December rain. Tilda walked up to the ridge as she had done with Nicholas in the summer. She found a track which appeared to lead in the direction of Sallikin's garden and set off along it. As she went, her shoes slipped in the mud. Bare branches flicked rain into her eyes and down the back of her neck. Before long, her tweed skirt was crusted with mud, her gloves were torn, and her coat collar was heavy with damp. The outfit suitable for rambles across Hampstead Heath was not hardy enough for these conditions. Tilda thought wistfully of the corduroys she had worn as a youngster, to go out with her cousins.

The track led her further downhill and deeper into the woods than she remembered going last time. She looked for sidetracks which might take her in the right direction or for any signs of the ruins. She had to retreat, once, when an opening led to a black pond with no way around. She pushed her way back from there to a path of sorts, although it might not have been the one she had been following earlier. She tried to head uphill among the oak trees and hazels she remembered from the summer. The bristling arms and heavy trunks of the oaks were unmistakable but their outlines looked unfamiliar, stripped of their leaves, and they became stranger at every turn of the path.

Her felt hat kept her head dry despite the steady downpour of the rain. Her feet squelched and branches creaked as she pushed past them, but the birds were silent. The wood might be empty or it might be full of eyes watching her as she blundered past. Every path she chose seemed to bend round and lead her further away from the direction she wanted to go. When she left the path and tried to force her way through the undergrowth, brambles tugged at her skirts and her ankles twisted on awkward tree roots. Then she stepped into a pocket of rotten leaves and stinking fungus. She had to pull herself free by holding onto an overhanging birch and was glad to stumble back to the path, even though it meant going downhill again.

She was very tired by now and cold. She scraped the worst of the mud from her shoes with a handful of dead leaves, but the smell lingered on her hands and feet. The wind grew stronger as the rain slackened but water still dripped from the trees. When Tilda entered a brief patch of sunlight in a clearing, she stood still to relish the scanty warmth. She looked at her watch and found that she had been in the woods too long. She had left Elephant Cottage in mid-morning and the time now was past three o'clock. There could not be much more than an hour of daylight left and she had accomplished nothing, but even if she decided to head out of the woods at once, she would not know how to set about it.

She had to get moving again, or she would stiffen up. She walked on slowly, turning her head from side to side, in search of any hint that might guide her, and she pushed her hat behind her ears to listen. She heard the wind sweep through the trees above and the patter of raindrops shaken to the ground, but nothing else.

She saw the magpies before she heard them, a swoop of black and white across the path in front of her, then two birds landed almost at her feet. They spread their wings and beat the ground while they made mewing calls, unlike anything Tilda had ever heard from a magpie before. They bounced up and down, turning their heads to stare at her, first from one side, then the other.

'What are you doing?' Tilda was startled by the sound of her own voice. 'What do you want of me?'

The birds repeated their mewing calls, stabbed their beaks into the ground and called again.

'I can't understand you.' This was worse than the cat back in Highgate, which had run away every night after dropping its prey at her feet. 'Do you know where Nicholas is? Or Sallikin?'

232

The birds took no notice of her words. They jumped higher and mewed louder. They must be begging, Tilda realised.

'Are you hungry?'

She had bread and cheese in her coat pocket, hastily packed that morning and neglected ever since. When she unfolded the waxed paper, the magpies went silent, crouched with outspread wings, their beaks open. Tilda was too tired to eat. She pulled off her gloves and broke off crumbs, which she dropped on the ground.

The magpies turned the food over with their beaks and mewed again.

'I haven't anything else.'

Tilda pushed the rest of the food back in her pocket and held out her empty hand. The birds whirled up at her. She felt two sharp stabs in her right palm and threw her arms up to protect her face, but the magpies were on the ground again now, begging harder than ever. Tilda stared at the wash of blood on her hand, where their beaks had cut her.

'That hurt,' she said, more in astonishment than protest, but the birds were not attacking her now. Maybe blood was the nourishment they needed.

She crouched down and let her wound drip onto the crumbs. At once the magpies pecked them up, fast and furious. Then they eyed Tilda again.

Her blood continued to drip. She took out the rest of the sandwich and made more crumbs with bloody fingers. When the food was three-quarters gone, she paused. She ought to hold onto some supplies for later. She wrapped up the rest and put it away. She stood up and the birds ignored her, busy with the crumbs. She found her handkerchief, clean and dry in her innermost pocket, tied it over her hand, and drew her glove on over the top.

She had not walked far when the magpies swooped over her head. She ducked but they landed on a branch ahead, looked back, and chattered at her. When she stood still, they flew towards her and then away, back to the same branch. Tilda went towards them and they flew off in short hops. They headed along a crease uphill between tree trunks, steep and knobbly underfoot. Tilda did not much like the look of it but she was glad to be offered any guidance, however doubtful. She followed the magpies.

They led her on a scramble over fallen trees and round, rough boulders. They came back and scolded when she paused to examine the stones. Each was too lumpy and irregular to have ever been part of a garden, so Tilda kept going. She collected more scratches from twigs which swung back in her face and more rips in her coat, but the birds set a pace which warmed her up and showed her a way she would never have found for herself.

She came to a wedge of rock, an outcrop of the hill itself. She could see birch saplings on an overhang above her head. Below that was a ladder of unclimbable ridges, overgrown with moss and trailing plants. The magpies perched overhead and watched Tilda while she caught her breath.

'I can't climb up there,' she said. She had been a fool to expect help from creatures she could not understand and who probably could not understand her, but the magpies pecked and scraped at the cliff face with their claws. Then they looked at Tilda again.

'No more blood,' Tilda said. The magpies took off, flew round her head, and landed at the same spot. They scraped away at the stone once more. Tilda looked at the dark edges of the moss they had turned over and saw white stone shining underneath. She stepped closer. A patch of the cliff had been cut into a flat panel. Tilda rubbed at the area the magpies had disturbed and felt curved channels and points through her gloves. She rubbed some more and then found a twig to help her clean the panel. The birds hopped to a higher ridge, where they sat and watched her.

She scrubbed at the panel from the centre outwards. To begin with, her movements were careful but they grew hasty and harsh as she became impatient. She hoped to find lettering or a map, something to indicate where she was. Instead, a carved picture took shape as she worked. In the centre was a bearded face, with heavy eyebrows under deep curls twined with ivy leaves. Stems grew out of a grinning mouth and pointed ears, to end in wreaths of oak leaves and acorns. Stone spiders hung in webs on the beard.

Disappointment slowed Tilda down but she carried on working. The wound in her hand throbbed and her legs ached, but she could disregard these troubles so long as she was busy. When the picture was as clean as she could make it, she stepped back. The exposed stone was still grubby but the carven shapes stood clear and the mouth seemed to curve into a smile. Tilda could not guess how the picture might help her. The magpies had flown away while she was busy.

The sky was clear overhead and the sun could not be far from setting on the other side of the wood. The wind had dropped but Tilda could feel a frost creeping over her cheeks, now that she had stopped moving. She could not identify the path that had brought her here. She turned back to the cliff face and saw a fissure a little way to her right, dark and narrow. Maybe if she could find a cave, she would not have to spend the night in the open woods. Before she went to investigate, she looked at the carving once more and said, 'Good luck to you, whoever you are.'

She was only just able to squeeze inside the opening and might have worried about getting stuck, if she had not been so tired. She groped along a short passage into a wider space, where the light was stronger. She was in a round chamber, higher than it was wide, with irregular walls and a dry floor. There was another opening, opposite the point through which she had entered, but she was not tempted to explore further. The temperature in here was a little warmer than outside. Tilda sat down on the floor, her back against the cave wall.

The bumps in her pockets reminded her that she had not eaten or drunk since the morning. She brought out her water bottle and drank a few sips, then more as her thirst sharpened, but she could not bring herself to touch the food. She took off her gloves and inspected her hand. The skin was red and swollen but the cuts had clotted over well. She covered them again and tried to knock some of the grime from her gloves by slapping them in the floor.

Her head felt heavy and tight. She pulled off her hat and combed the fingers of her good hand through her hair. Then she shut her eyes and leaned back to rest.

Thirty-one

'Why did you cut your hair?'

The voice was so deep and the question so inconsequential that Tilda thought she must be in a dream.

'I've let it grow since the spring.'

Her own voice rang in her ears, not her mind, and made her realise that the other had done the same. She opened her eyes and scrambled to her feet, all in the same movement.

A man stood opposite her, a stranger, big as a bear. He wore leather and fur, and his head was large and shaggy. At first glance, his face was that of the stone carving outside, come to life.

'Who are you?' Tilda was too shocked to be polite. 'What are you doing here?'

'In these hills I am the Winter King.' A light shone round him, as though he wore it under his clothes. 'My last human lover called me Thistlebeard.'

His white beard was fine and silky as thistledown but his tangled hair was dark. No plants grew out of his mouth or his ears, but the prow of his nose and his deep-set eyes under heavy brows were the very shapes Tilda had felt in the stone. His gaze at her was intent, maybe amused, but not hostile.

'Then you know this wood?' she asked. 'Please, have you seen my son Nicholas? I'm afraid he's out here, lost.'

'Sallikin's friend? So that's who you are. The boy is a great deal more comfortable than you are.'

'Is he safe?' Tilda leaned back against the cave wall, limp with relief. 'I've been afraid for him.'

'What good did you expect to do for him, astray and starving?'

'I thought I could find Sallikin's garden.' Tilda tried to make sense of what she had been told. 'Do you own these woods? Am I trespassing?'

'Nobody owns the woods.' Thistlebeard's frown bigged his shoulders and lowered his head. His voice was cool. 'The creatures and Spirits that pay me homage seek my protection and goodwill. They are not my servants.'

'Please tell me about Nicholas,' Tilda said. 'Is he safe?'

'Safer than you and much less ignorant.' The flash of anger was replaced by curiosity. 'How did someone so confused stumble into this refuge and summon me here?'

She told him about the magpies and he said, 'Who taught you what to do for them?'

'There was the cat as well.' Tilda felt unable to explain anything and yet, with the challenge of that dark glance upon her, she did not want to collapse into inanity.'

'Not one of my cats,' Thistlebeard said.

'It tried to feed me, because of Nicholas, I suppose, and my other son tried to make friends with it, so I hoped the magpies were also his friends. I just did what they wanted.'

'Your son has the goodwill of many creatures. You are right about that. Why shouldn't he have the wits to find his own way home?'

'I don't know enough about Spirits or supernatural creatures, and what the Spellhaven Exiles told me I don't trust.' Tilda's anger flared as she thought of her endurance of the days since Nicholas had gone missing. 'You haven't told me where he is.'

'With Sallikin.'

'Will you take me to him?'

'The boy ran away from you.' Thistlebeard's amusement grew. 'You should leave him alone until he's ready to come home.'

Tilda winced but she said, 'He ran from the Exiles who badgered him and the Spirits who want revenge for their captivity in Spellhaven.'

'Spellhaven is broken past recovery and years have passed since its ruin. All the Spirits know that, here and overseas. Why should the captives single out your son for their vengeance?'

'Because they don't understand the things Nick can do,' Tilda said.

'He has none of the wiles of the Magician Lords. Sallikin will look after him. But how will you escape from your predicament tonight without my help?'

Tilda looked at him. Darius Fox had offered her help and she had not been tempted, not even for a moment, but Thistlebeard's gaze revived her as much as food and sleep. She could feel the weight of her clothes and the aches in her bones but she no longer cared about them. She tried to think past her feelings and slowly said, 'If I trusted the magpies, I suppose I should trust the person they brought me to.'

'That depends.' Thistlebeard took two steps towards her and stopped, his eyes narrowed and sharp. 'What if they brought you here for my sake, not yours?'

'What do you mean?'

'I have taken human lovers before, beautiful women who have given me much pleasure. The last was a hundred years ago or more. Maybe the magpies thought to offer me another such.'

'I am not beautiful,' Tilda said.

His smile twisted up at one side of his mouth and down at the other. 'Your hair should warm your back and cover your breasts. Why is it so short?'

'I cut it when I moved to London,' Tilda said. 'Most women do, these days.'

'London changes everyone.' Thistlebeard hooded his eyes and drew a deep, slow breath. 'Tree Spirits, deep dwellers, cats and stone eaters, all who brave its dangers. I used to lead my court to raid and riot in London, once every nine times nine years. Not any more.' He spoke to himself, as though Tilda were not there.

'What made you stop?' she asked.

'Too many losses, too little pleasure, when the air grew foul and humans lay dying in every ditch.' He looked at Tilda again. 'I regret the hair. Nevertheless you are beautiful, with your body strong from bearing your children and your face bright with years of sorrow, as well as laughter. I should like to see you naked.'

All her life, Tilda had rejected the compliments men paid her. Now she wanted to share Thistlebeard's smile and see herself as he saw her. She looked at the strong bulk of him and was seized with the desire to touch and stroke him.

'I have had no lover except my husband, until he died,' Tilda said.

'From choice or by chance?' Thistlebeard's voice was a deep rumble and Tilda felt it in her bones.

'Because the hurts of love are greater than the pleasure.'

'Must that always be so?'

'For a woman, maybe,' Tilda said. 'What happened to the others?'

'My companions in London?'

'The other women.' She scowled at him. 'Did they wake a hundred years after their own times, alone and pale on the cold hillside?'

'Never.' This smile was broad and open. 'They lived out their own lives. Some stayed for a night, some for years, and not all the quarrels were of my making.'

'I'm not good at quarrels.' Tilda's confidence drained away. 'I'm not good at danger or breaking the rules of respectability.'

'You underrate yourself.' Thistlebeard's grin faded. 'But I will put no force upon you. Will you dance with me, at least, in return for a night's lodging?'

'Dance?' Tilda's feet turned to lead. She glanced down at the mud clumped on her skirt. 'Like this?'

'It will be easier than you think.' Thistlebeard held out his hand and she took it even as she said, 'There's no room.'

'Listen to the music.' Thistlebeard put his other arm round her waist.

There's no music, Tilda thought and then she heard it, a breathy murmur as though the wind sang to the cave. The tune was an old country dance, familiar from the lessons of her childhood. She had forgotten the steps but she let Thistlebeard lead her round in a circle. Then he changed his hold, so that they clasped hands behind their backs and processed forwards. The cave entrance widened as they reached it and the passage beyond shone under their feet.

Tilda's clumsiness dropped away as she danced. Her skirt no longer thumped against her legs and the weight lifted from her ankles. She stepped as lightly as if she wore ballet slippers and soft linen. A breeze gentled her skin and she took deep breaths of damp air, which eased her throat. She smelled winter scents untainted by rot, of juniper and blackberries.

Out in the open, the music was taken up by fiddles and pipes. Tilda caught only glimpses of the musicians as she danced past them at Thistlebeard's side. Some had pale green skin and hands like tree roots; others shone red as fire, with black snouts and whiskers. Thistlebeard drew her uphill on a path of soft leaves, yellow and red, while creatures came out of the woods on either side to join the dance. Foxes came and badgers, deer and bridleless ponies, who moved in step with the music. Then there were more Spirits, tall and lean like Sallikin, stout and gnarled, or something in between. Other dancers had stony limbs and gargoyle faces or feathered bodies and birdlike heads.

The company spread out when they came to a clearing and the music grew more complicated. Tilda did not know the steps and stumbled when she tried to guess what to do. Thistlebeard steadied her and said, 'Let the music carry you.'

So she stopped guessing and let her mind rest in the music. After that, the steps came naturally to her and she grew confident enough to move away from Thistlebeard. She touched her hand in turn against hoofs, claws, furry noses, many fingered hands of twigs, or lumps of hot earth, but could not pause to look at the faces they belonged to, for fear of losing the rhythm. When she returned to Thistlebeard, he pulled off the handkerchief that bandaged her cuts, raised her hand to his mouth, and licked her palm. The throbbing under her skin stopped and the soreness vanished. She almost lost her balance in surprise but Thistlebeard swept her into another circle and she went on dancing.

The stars were bright overhead when the music stopped. Tilda could not tell how long the dance had lasted but she felt invigorated as if by a cold shower. The strange dancers bowed to one another and applauded the musicians. Tilda joined them and saw that she had danced the mud away from her clothes and the grazes from her skin. Then she found herself at the centre of attention as

Thistlebeard put his arm round her and the crowd all turned to bow to him. He bowed back and Tilda curtseyed to the crowd and then to him. He stepped back from her and grinned.

The crowd parted to line a path to the edge of the clearing. Between the roots of a giant oak was a hollow, well-padded with dead leaves. As Tilda watched, the dancers spread out a layer of rugs over the top and set a couple of pillows at one end, gleaming like silk. Then they turned and moved into the darkness under the trees. Within a few moments, Thistlebeard and Tilda were left by themselves in the clearing. He raised an eyebrow and said, 'Will you be warm enough under those covers, to sleep alone tonight?'

Tilda looked at him. She felt as though she would never be cold again, but if she turned away from him now, she would not be given another chance like this. She stepped closer to Thistlebeard and pulled his head down towards hers. He kissed her and steered her towards the bed.

Much later, they lay tangled together, naked but for the rugs.

'I seldom sleep at this season of the year,' Thistlebeard said, 'and next to making love, my favourite pastime is the hearing or telling of stories. Tell me about your childhood, mother of Nicholas.'

Tilda was drowsy enough to speak without thinking. 'I hated being a child.'

'Because?'

'My parents quarrelled before I was born and neither wanted me. I was all right until I was five, living with my mother's old nurse. Then my grandmother said I had to be brought up as a lady and took me away. I was handed round the family after that, because they said I was sullen and ungrateful.'

'Sullen children are the finest.' Thistlebeard's legs tightened round hers. 'Did you bite anyone?'

'I wish I had,' Tilda said and then realised she hardly minded anymore. 'My father's cousins rescued me. They were so many nobody cared if I spoke or not, and they let me be without teasing me.'

'Where did you live?'

She told him about the farm in Gloucestershire and the countryside round about, but he was more interested in the people and asked questions about each one she mentioned. Eventually, Tilda's voice rasped and she yawned.

'Let me wake you up,' Thistlebeard said and leaned over to kiss her.

When they lay quiet once more, Tilda said, 'You turn to tell me a story.' She lay with her head on Thistlebeard's chest, so that his deep voice rumbled under her ear.

'Of love, war, or hunting?' There was a sardonic edge to the question but Tilda felt too peaceful to indulge him in a quarrel.

'None of those. Will you tell me of your childhood?'

He laughed and his voice mellowed. 'Too long ago. I'll tell you about the Old Woman of the Apple Trees and the thief who raided her underground orchards.'

'Underground? How does she grow apples underground?'

'That's her secret. Her trees bear blossom and fruit both together and she harvests the crop to make cider for a great Winter Feast every year. Dead heroes leave their barrows to come to that Feast, wild Kings ride down from the Northern hills, and great ladies rise up from their river beds to be with us. But once long ago, the Old Woman sent a messenger to me in mid harvest. A thief had made off with a sackful of apples, not once but seven times. She was afraid she would not have enough drink to last out the Feast. She wanted my help to catch and punish the thief.'

Thistlebeard ran his fingers down Tilda's spine until she lifted her head to look at him.

'And did you help her?'

'She put me in a difficulty.' He smiled and Tilda settled back beside him. 'I had my suspicions that the thief was someone under my protection and indulgence, but I had no desire for the Feast to fail. So I laid a trap designed to catch the thief in a place where I could make him return the apples and let him escape before the Old Woman was aware.'

The story became more complicated after that and Tilda must have dozed despite herself. Afterwards she remembered no more than a jumble of strange names and bright deeds. When the story ended, she roused herself to ask, 'Did you ever go to Spellhaven?'

'I visited the land from which the island was torn,' Thistlebeard said. 'Long, long ago, on my travels, I danced with the Great Bears and the Mountain Spirits, before they were bound to the service of the Magician Lords. But I took warning from their fate. Once the city was founded, I would not go near, even when the magic brought it close to these shores.'

'My husband loved the city for its beauty.'

'And its power, doubtless. Both are broken now: you need not be afraid of either.'

Tilda was still thinking about that when she fell asleep in good earnest. She woke to a pale morning and a chill on her skin, despite the rugs heaped over her. Thistlebeard was no longer at her side. She sat up and found him already dressed and on his feet.

'Good morning,' he said and handed her a wooden bowl, full of milk.

Tilda thought briefly once more of Keats's knight abandoned on the cold hillside, but Sallikin's drink had done her no harm and she had trusted Thistlebeard with so much, so she would not hesitate now. She sipped the milk and then drank more deeply, as her hunger awoke.

'Finish it,' Thistlebeard said and she did.

She found her clothes and dressed in haste while Thistlebeard watched her. When she sat down to put on her shoes, he said, 'Stay with me a while.'

Tilda caught her breath. 'I must go back to my sons.'

'Sallikin will look after Nicholas. I'll send my squire to fetch the other one. He can learn the ways of my court.'

That would not be good for James, Tilda thought, and to live as Thistlebeard's lover would not be good for her, though her longing for him was fiercer than any she had ever known. She could do nothing in these woods but love him and that would not be enough, even while it lasted.

'The quarrels would begin too soon,' she said. 'Better for me to leave now.'

'And if you are with child by me?'

Tilda's mind went cold, between hope and fear. 'Am I? Do you have the power to know that?'

'I do not, no more than any lover. It may happen or it may not. If it does, you must not hide the child from me.'

'I won't know how to find you,' Tilda said.

'I'll teach you how to call me.' He held out his hand to her, an acorn on his palm. 'And I'll show you your way home.'

Thirty-two

Dr. Hunter's sitting room was crowded with felt armchairs, pouffes, spindly tables, and a rose patterned carpet. When Rowan had visited earlier in the year, she had realised that the room was seldom used, because Dr. Hunter spent most of her time in college or at the Exiles' Club. But she wanted to hold rehearsals for her new show in a place free from interruption and had invited the actors to come to her house to make a beginning.

Rowan was the first to arrive and helped to push the chairs into a circle. They banished the tables to the dining room and prepared a tray for elevenses, which they set by the fire. Dr. Hunter put a pile of typescripts beside her own chair but would not talk about the play in advance.

Stephen Cole came with Hugo, whom Rowan was expecting, and James, whom she was not. She looked at Dr. Hunter.

'Have you given James a part? Does his mother know?'

'I want to help, Aunt Rowan,' James said.

'His mother has other things to worry about just now,' Dr. Hunter said.

'That's not right.' Rowan looked at Stephen, who stood by the door. 'Did you tell her, Stephen?'

'We hardly spoke.' His face creased with anxiety. 'I didn't want to add to her troubles.'

'You can't leave me out,' James said.

'You can hardly expect him to sit in the kitchen while the rest of us are busy in here,' Dr. Hunter said.

Rowan twisted her necklace of beads and nibbled them while she thought. 'I could take him to visit one of his other friends,' she said.

James went white and his frown almost turned him into the image of his brother. 'I started this,' he said. 'Please, Aunt Rowan, you have to let me help.'

Stephen rubbed the bridge of his nose, between his glasses. 'Today's a first reading,' he said. 'Nothing happened on our first read-through with Lyulf. If James joins in today, we can ask his mother's permission as soon as she is back.'

Both James and Dr. Hunter grumped at this but Hugo said, 'I'll ask her. I wish she could be here.'

That might make matters worse but Rowan decided not to argue any longer. She sat down and said, 'On we go. For today, at least.'

The others settled down and looked at Dr. Hunter, who said, 'One more person to come. Darius promised me he wouldn't be late.'

They sat and fidgeted for a while until Stephen said, 'Won't you tell us about the play, Dr. Hunter?'

Dr. Hunter's hands crimped on top of her papers. Then she nodded and handed round the scripts.

'This is a new notion of mine,' she said.

Rowan glanced at the list of characters, with the cast names alongside.

'Ragnild, Duke Ulfin, the Mountain Bear – you've made a play about the Founders of Spellhaven!'

'I've borrowed most of the words,' Dr. Hunter said, 'from Jacobean tragedies and such, but the story is from Spellhaven.'

'Hildegard, Ragnild's daughter,' James said. 'Why have I got to be a girl?'

'One of you must,' Dr. Hunter answered. 'She's the key to the whole plot and she has more lines than her brother.'

'How can I act Duchess Ragnild?' Rowan asked. 'I'm not fierce enough. Or tall enough.'

'You can act tall.'

'Won't the Spirits be angry?' James asked. They all looked at him and he said, 'The Duchess set traps for them, didn't she, and put them in prison? Won't they hate a play about her?'

'She made a bargain, so the story goes,' Dr. Hunter said, 'and if the Spirits don't agree, maybe they will manifest themselves to argue with us.'

Everyone looked glum at that.

'Let's start the read through,' Dr. Hunter said. 'Maybe then you'll understand.'

They stumbled through a few pages. Rowan found the words heavier on her tongue with every sentence and the others seemed just as daunted. The rat-tat-tat on the front door was a welcome interruption. Dr. Hunter's face was stern as she went to answer it.

'Can't you keep better time than this?' they heard her say.

'I've been making arrangements.' Darius Fox did not sound apologetic. 'Can you come with me at once?'

'We're in the middle of the play reading. Did you forget?'

Dr. Hunter came back into the room, her face crosser than ever. Fox, by contrast, sparkled with excitement.

'Bring the play along. Good morning, you fine Thespians.'

Dr. Hunter sat down firmly and folded her hands over her script. 'We haven't time to traipse about. Bring it where?'

'To Lyulf Lyulf's bolt-hole.' Fox grinned at their expressions.

'The police told us he left no traces anywhere,' Stephen said.

'I don't give up as easily as the police.' Fix took up position on the hearth rug, his hands in his pockets. 'I've been hanging round his old shop in Hoxton for weeks, making friends with the neighbours.'

'I went to Hoxton,' Stephen said. 'Nobody knew anything.'

'I heard about you. They didn't trust you an inch. Nor me to begin with.' Maybe this was meant to be conciliatory but it sounded like condescension. 'But I persevered. I was given my first real clue on Friday and I discovered the place last night.'

'Can you be sure it belonged to Lyulf?' Rowan asked.

'His business cards are there and boxes of glass balls, as well as books and papers. I searched that far and then I decided I needed

Kate to help me. And you too, Cole, in case the police get interested.'

Stephen and Rowan looked at one another.

'What's the hurry?' Rowan asked. 'We promised to do the play this morning, to help Hugo.'

'The hurry is, we don't know what we might unearth,' Fox said, 'or who else might be interested. Lyulf's Masters may have found a new servant by now.'

'What right have we to ransack Lyulf's belongings?' Stephen asked.

'None at all,' Fox said briskly. 'Only a hope we might learn something to help young Hugo, as well as James and his brother.'

Dr. Hunter stared at her hands. 'Lyulf had no family that I ever heard of.'

'If nothing else,' Fox said, 'we can do the play reading there. It's a likelier place than here to catch the attention of the Unseen.'

'There might be people trapped in the glass balls,' James said. 'We can't just leave them lying there.'

'Kate and I can take the boys if you two don't want to come,' Fox said.

'Certainly not!' Rowan jumped to her feet. 'The boys-'

'The boys had more to endure from Lyulf than any of us,' Dr. Hunter interrupted. 'They have the greatest right to come.'

Rowan looked again at Stephen, who said, 'Then we had better all go.'

Darius Fox had a car of his own, so he drove James, Hugo and Rowan, while Dr. Hunter and Stephen followed by taxi. James noticed the car was not as smart as the Gray motors but he was too preoccupied to give it much attention. He had loathed the play reading, much to his surprise. His part had felt creepy and the others had all sounded as though their mouths were filled with glue, but he did not want to let Hugo down, so he could only hope this expedition led to a new plan.

The car stopped beside a narrow field, divided into muddy patches. Some were covered with old carpet, some with rows of stakes or fruit bushes, with sheds in one corner. When the taxi drew up, Dr. Hunter asked, 'Lyulf kept an allotment?'

'He used the hut, anyhow,' Fox answered. 'This way.'

They followed him along the path to a patch covered in dead nettles. The hut was bigger than most and a man stood leaning against the door.'

'Thank goodness,' he said. 'I'm perishing out here.'

James halted when he recognised Piers Marshall and so did Hugo at his side.

'You didn't mention anyone else would be here,' Rowan said.

'I asked Piers to keep an eye on the place this morning,' Fox said. He seemed oblivious of any tension, although Marshall looked as displeased to see the boys as they were by him. Fox unlocked the padlock on the door of the hut.

'Where did you get the key?' Stephen asked.

'I put the padlock on last night,' Fox said. 'Someone forced the old one.'

'Someone?' Dr. Hunter frowned.

'No harm done,' Fox said. 'Come and see.'

He meant he had done it himself, James realised. Fox went inside. James glared at Marshall, who glared back and said, 'This is no place for children.'

'We haven't the time to argue with you,' Dr. Hunter said. 'In you go, boys.'

She was right, even if James wished he could send Marshall away. He stepped round the man and entered the hut, with the others on his heels.

The interior was dingy and damp. Grey light came through a dusty window as well as the open door but was not strong enough to illuminate the clutter around them.

'There's a torch in the car,' Fox said. 'James, be a good chap-'

James could see a stack of boxes like the ones behind Lyulf's stall at the Toy Fair. He lifted the lid from the top one to reveal a row of glass balls. 'I'm going to examine these,' he said. 'Will you help me, Hugo?'

'I'll fetch the torch,' Marshall said irritably.

Without him, the hut was less crowded. The others moved around but James fixed his attention on the glass bubbles. He lifted up one after another and saw nothing except surface reflections, however he tilted them.

248

'We could take them to the door, one box at a time, to see better,' Hugo said.

'They will be empty, you know,' Dr. Hunter said. 'Lyulf must have given the full ones to his Masters.'

'He kept that cat,' he said. 'We have to make sure there's nothing else in them.'

All the same, the check became dull work, after they found nothing but glass in the first box. When they went inside for the third box, James lingered to see what the others were doing.

Dr. Hunter had climbed onto the table to be nearer the light. She held a large book propped against the window pane. She looked black and shapeless, her flamboyant colours subdued by shadow. Fox sat on the floor, unpacking the contents of a trunk and muttering to himself, 'More horrible smocks. More vile pictures. Had the man no taste at all?'

Rowan stood at the table to study a bundle of papers.

'I can't make out his handwriting,' she said. 'James, are your eyes better than mine?'

Marshall arrived back with the torch. As soon as he switched it on, Dr. Hunter's emerald green hat and maroon jacket flared into life, so that she looked like a giant parrot up on her perch.

'Bring that here,' everyone said.

'What have you found?' Marshall panted as he spoke.

'Rubbish.' Fox took the torch and swung it around. The beam glanced off dark bundles, suitcases and more boxes. 'Maybe it's all rubbish, his last little joke.'

'The glass bubbles aren't rubbish,' James said and went back to his task.

'Might as well be.' Fox crouched down, the torch still in his hand, and the shadows jumped round the floor.

'Why not shift the stuff outside and search it there?' Marshall asked.

'And make a public spectacle of ourselves? No thanks,' Fox said.

'Nobody's around.'

Rowan came over beside James to look out of the door. 'We do need more light. James, can we use the boxes you've finished with as an outside table?'

They worked faster after that, with Stephen and Marshall to carry things and to help with the investigation, although Stephen said, 'I don't know what to look for.'

'Anything peculiar,' Rowan told him. 'Call us if you're not sure.'

He would rather have stayed on guard, to judge from his stiff, wary movements, but he sorted through a jumble of shoes and boots from one of the cases and did not call out. As more boxes of glass were discovered, Hugo worked through them methodically but James stopped now and then to see what everyone else was up to.

'Could Lyulf draw?' Rowan asked. She had half a dozen loose pages spread out in front of her. James went over to see them and so did Dr. Hunter.

The pictures were no more than sketches, done in pencil. One showed a lion rampant, its head turned to face the viewer. Its body was slender and ornate, like the beast on a coat of arms, but its roar showed a triple row of teeth and its mane rayed out in black lines, like a dark sunburst. The words underneath were easy to make out.

'This one worries me like a cat does a mouse, and the claw marks are on my skin when I wake,'

Dr. Hunter said. 'His handwriting hasn't changed.'

'We can't tell when these were done.' Rowan sounded grim. She picked up another sketch, of a woman with plaited hair. The words said, 'Siriol is more beautiful than I can draw. Her spiders poison my food.'

James did not want to see any more. He turned to rejoin Hugo, just as Fox said, 'I've had enough of this. Can we make a fire?'

Marshall straightened his back. 'I saw a tin of paraffin inside. What do you want to burn?'

'All this rubbish.' Fox's grin was wild.

'What do you mean?' Dr. Hunter frowned at him. 'We don't know what any of this means yet.'

'Doesn't matter.' Fox's eyebrows bristled and he spread his arms wide, 'If there's anything here that Lyulf's Masters care about, they'll come and save it from a fire. If there isn't, it's worthless to us anyhow.'

'You can't be sure of that,' Rowan said. 'Look at his sketches.'

Fox scarcely glanced at them. 'Come on, Piers,' he said.

'Wait,' Dr. Hunter said.

Fox pushed past her into the hut and she spoke to his back. 'You went to all the trouble of bringing us here, Darius. Have some patience now.'

He came out with an armful of old newspapers and said, 'I want some action, not years of research. We can read your bloody play over the ashes, if nothing else happens.'

He threw down his bundle and pulled up dead nettle stalks to pile on top. Marshall came out of the hut with a tin in his hand. Stephen Cole blocked his way.

'Not yet,' Stephen said.

Marshall handed the tin to Fox and said to Stephen, 'You're the least qualified to decide, old boy.'

'I appreciate that.' Stephen half turned, to keep an eye on both men at once. 'But I think you should listen to Dr. Hunter.'

Fox tugged at the cap on the tin. Stephen reached out to take it away from him but Marshall shoved him in the chest. Stephen pushed back and the two of them grappled together.

'Have you taken leave of your senses?' Rowan asked. 'Piers! Darius! Stop this.'

Nobody took any notice. James would have liked to fight Marshall himself but two against one would not be right. He tried to take the paraffin tin from Fox instead and received an elbow in his stomach, which sent him sprawling. The two women cried out in protest. Hugo followed James's example, with the same result, while Stephen and Marshall swayed to and fro in a wrestling grip.

James climbed to his feet, ready to have another go, just as Rowan threw one of the glass balls at Fox. He ducked and managed to wrench the tin open. Paraffin splashed out and its smell filled the air. Fox had his cigarette lighter in his hand before anyone could stop him. He snapped it and the fire was alight. He jumped back from the blaze and grinned at everyone else.

'You'll have to keep your distance now.'

Stephen and Marshall broke apart, panting.'At least let's save his notes,' Dr. Hunter said.

'Show us what to take away,' Stephen said, but as soon as he moved, Marshall swung a punch at him and the fight started again.

Fox picked up the glass ball Rowan had thrown and dropped it into the heart of the fire. He went back into the hut to find more flammable material. James started after him but Rowan loaded a bundle of papers into his arms.

'Take those back to the street,' she said. 'You too, Hugo. Here you are.'

The smoke from the fire thickened and swirled round them, white and salty. In a few steps, James lost sight of his surroundings and his companions. He stood still, uncertain of his direction, and he heard whispers, endearments in strange, sweet voices.

'Lovely boy, brave cub, little wolfling, come this way.'

Shapes outlined in fire loomed at him, a rearing horse, a lion like the one in Lyulf's sketch, a tree with hands. Then a cord reached out of nowhere to tap his hand.

'Follow our thread,' the voices whispered.

James remembered Lyulf's maze. He dropped everything he held and turned to run, though he could not see which way to go, but the cord became a hook, which grasped his forearm. He tried to push it off but it dragged him backwards into the mist.

Thirty-three

The house in Highgate was empty when Tilda arrived home, after a slow journey on a Sunday train. She was more grateful than surprised. Cook had Sunday off once a month and would not be back until next morning. Stephen Cole had promised to take James back to school this evening and Rowan must be out with her friends. As for Nicholas, Tilda wanted him home, but after last night she was able to wait for him to return of his own accord. Meanwhile, she was glad to be alone, as she struggled to comprehend what she had done.

She went to bed and slept away the afternoon. When she woke, she had a bath and dressed more slowly than usual. She spent a long time staring at the smooth skin on her hand, where the magpies had cut her. When she rubbed cream onto her face, she felt again the touch of Thistlebeard's fingers and the buzz of his voice in her ear.

Downstairs, the house was quiet. Tilda went into the kitchen to make a cup of tea and only then realised she ought to be hungry. She cooked an omelette and ate it with toast. She took her tea into the sitting room, which was cold. She built and lit the fire but did not close the curtains against the dark. She sat and warmed her hands on her tea cup, while she listened and thought. The crackle of the fire was loud against a deeper silence than she was used to: no creaks of movement in other rooms, nobody breathing upstairs. The weather out of doors was not boisterous enough to be heard in the room. Last night, every stir of the wind or rustle of dead leaves had been in the background of her awareness, even if she had hardly noticed at the time.

The yowl of the cat pulled her out of her memories. She stood up without haste, resigned to receiving whatever poor creature she would be offered tonight. Then she heard a human voice interwoven with the noise from the cat and she rushed to open the French windows.

Nicholas and the cat both looked at her. The cat dropped a mouse at Nick's feet and disappeared into the night. Nick crouched down and took the mouse in his hands.

'It's dead.' He spoke in a cracked whisper.

'They die of fright,' Tilda said, carefully. 'Come inside, Nick. We can bury the mouse later, if you wish.'

He put it down on the ground. 'Maybe the cat will come back for it.'

Inside, Tilda turned to face him and took a deep breath. He was covered in grime, with twigs stuck in his hair and stains on his shirt. He looked older than she remembered, not just longer and thinner, though his wrists stuck out of his cuffs and his neck stretched out of his collar. His mouth was set in a firm line she did not recognise and his eyes were sunken. Tilda wanted to hug him but his stance made her wary. She could almost see prickles across his shoulders.

'I'm so glad you're here,' she said.

'I shouldn't have run away. I'm sorry.'

'So long as you're all right. Are you hungry?'

'Not much.' He hesitated. 'Thirsty, maybe.'

'Milk or cocoa?'

They sat by the fire. A tinge of colour kept into Nick's face as he drank the cocoa and ate the sandwich he had not asked for. Dirt was crusted under his fingernails and crumbs of mud scattered onto his chair as he moved, but Tilda was determined not to fuss him. When he stopped eating to stare into the fire, she asked, 'Did you walk all the way home?'

'I went down deep,' he said, without looking at her. 'I had to get away.'

'From school or from the Exiles?'

'From people.' His voice sounded easier now, but dark and slow. 'The earth spirits helped me and the trees.'

'Couldn't you stay with your friend Sallikin?'

He shook his head. 'I hoped Lyulf's Masters would come after me, so that I could draw them away from you and James, but I knew I'd made a mistake as soon as my mind was quiet.'

'I thought you were safe there,' Tilda said.

'I was welcome there but not safe. I listened to the stones and the grass, and Sallikin let me help clear out the bed of a stream.'

'And then?'

'I need to be here, not there.'

'Did Sallikin tell you that?'

He shook his head again. 'She wouldn't, but she agreed I ought to head back towards the smell of danger.'

Tilda's heart quickened. 'Is the danger here?'

'Not right now.' Nicholas hunched down in his chair and his mouth shut hard. Tilda could see he would not bear much more questioning. She sat back herself and asked, 'When it comes, Nicholas, whatever it is, can we face it together?'

He thought this over, slowly. A spasm of anger seized Tilda. He was thirteen years old: she should be protecting him, not asking his permission to share the danger. But she would not know what to do unless he told her, and even if she could lock him up for his own good, his strange friends would doubtless let him out. She swallowed hard and said, 'I came to find you.'

'Sallikin said you were given shelter.' He looked up. 'I didn't mean to worry you.'

'I couldn't help worrying. It will be easier if I can come with you next time.'

He nodded and sat back, his eyelids drooping. Tilda watched him for a while, content for the moment to take comfort in his presence.

When she heard a knock at the front door, Tilda thought that Rowan must have forgotten her key, but Stephen Cole stood hatless on the doorstep, swaying to and fro, his face swollen and lumpy.

'The mist took them away,' he said. 'I tried to pull them back but the mist took them all.'

'Took who?' Tilda demanded and then, as he shuddered, she reached out to him. 'Come in. What happened to your face?'

She steered him into a chair and poured him a whisky.

'Fox said he wanted to call Lyulf's Masters.' He spoke fast, without looking at her. 'Only a mist came. I didn't see any Spirits, not like in the Puppet Theatre. I didn't even see the start of it, because of this stupid scrap with Marshall, but Rowan shouted and I saw James lapped in ropes of mist. I grabbed his shoulder and I made a snatch at Hugo but I couldn't hold onto them.'

'Where were you?' Nicholas came to stand beside him and Stephen stared.

'They didn't get you? I thought you must have disappeared as well.'

'Who disappeared, Stephen?' Tilda asked. 'Was Rowan with the boys?'

'The mist swallowed them all: the boys, Rowan, Dr. Hunter, and Fox. Not Marshall.' Stephen took a gulp of whisky. 'Marshall tried to help me keep hold of the boys. The mist turned into wet sand in our mouths and our eyes, until we choked. By the time we caught our breath, they were all gone.'

'Where's Marshall now?' Tilda asked.

'Gone to the Club to ask for help. But what can they do?'

'Can you take me to the place where it happened?' Nicholas asked.

Rowan stood on a step of polished stone, black and slippery. Stairs rose above her head up to a blank wall of rough stone. The only way to climb higher was to jump across to another, winding stairway, with treads of white chalk. They looked ready to crumble at any touch. Below her, the stairs went down into a wide funnel. More staircases ran down into its depths, the top of each maybe just within reach of a sideways stretch from the bottom of the one above. Or maybe not.

Rowan had groped through the smoke from Fox's fire, trying to find James and Hugo. She had followed their voices through a dense fog into darkness. When her sight cleared, she was alone on these stairs. If she tilted her head back, she could glimpse faint stars high above and below her feet shone red flames. She could not tell how she had come here but she recognised the place. When she was seven years old, she had run away from home and wandered into one of the oldest streets in Spellhaven. She played with some Spirits who had turned out to be less friendly than the ones she was used to. They led her into the Ladder Maze and left her there, not to be rescued for hours. She could remember the humiliation when her brothers had tracked her down and her mother's anger when they carried her home.

She reached out to touch the rock wall, gritty and cold under her fingers. 'Spellhaven is drowned,' she said. 'This can't be real.'

The rock answered her, though she could see no face or mouth. 'Spellhaven is drowned, except in memories.'

The noise was so close to Rowan's ear that she recoiled and nearly fell. She sat down on the steps. 'Who are you?' she asked. 'Where am I?'

'Did you think only human Magicians could make so handsome a prison?' This was a different voice, sweet and mocking. 'We can keep you trapped in your memories as long as you last. Or maybe let you out to serve us as Lyulf did, if you plead prettily for mercy.'

'Not my style.' Rowan forced herself to take deep breaths. 'Who else is here? What have you done with the boys?'

'Built them traps of their own.' The voices spoke together. 'Where's the boy who broke our bubbles?'

So wherever Nicholas was, Lyulf's Masters did not have him.

'If you want me to answer questions, let me see the other boys,' Rowan said.

The rock shook with their laughter and Rowan had to press herself back against the surface to avoid being dislodged.

'We don't need to bargain with you,' they said. 'You have no magic now.'

'I never had much. I don't want to restore Spellhaven or ensnare any Spirits.'

'Then you should have been more careful of the company you keep.'

Rowan had no chance to reply to that. Although she had not been able to see the Spirits, she felt their withdrawal as a change in the air pressure, an absence and a fading of the gleam she had not noticed around her until it was gone. She pulled the collar of her coat up to her chin and tried to think. If this place came from her memories, it would do no good to climb up or down. She called out in the hope that the other traps might be nearby but nobody answered. She called the names of the Spirits she had seen in the Puppet Theatre.

'Lady Siriol! Lord Thurlin! Will you speak to me?'

They did not reply.

The hedge formed a circle round Hugo where he sat cross-legged on the grass. The bushes were too high for him to see over the top, with many tangled branches splayed out from the ground. Instead of leaves they had knives, some thin and narrow, some wedge-shaped or curved into crescents. All gleamed steel-bright and sharp and all pointed at Hugo. The grass prickled under him and he looked down to find tiny, edged blades, too small to cut through his shorts, but strong enough to nick the back of his knees every time he shifted position.

Tears sprang into Hugo's eyes and he wiped them on his sleeve, covering his face to hide his grin. The ghosts had left him. For the first time in two years, two months and seventeen days, he could not see them, even out of the corner of his eye. He could smell nothing but empty air, tinged with salt, and hear nothing but the sound of his own breathing. If the ghosts could not force their way through the hedge, he could sit still in this spot for ever. He did not care if he starved or bled to death from grass cuts, so long as he never had to listen to the ghosts or see them again.

A tunnel opened up in the hedge and a boy crawled through. Or maybe he was not a boy. He was about the same size as Hugo but he looked older and tougher. He turned three somersaults and plucked one of the knives as he came upright. He held it out to Hugo, a miniature spear with serrated edges and no handle.

'Stroke with this and you can cut yourself twice at the same time.' The stranger gazed at Hugo from yellow eyes in an ancient, crumpled face. Hugo gazed back and made no move to take the knife.

'I don't want to cut myself.'

'You did before.' The stranger reached out for two more knives and began to juggle them. 'Have you lost your nerve?'

'Did you make the hedge? Are you one of Lyulf's Masters?'

'You may call me Jollifon the Juggler.' The knives spun towards Hugo. He did not flinch and they dropped harmlessly to the ground. The stranger sat down opposite him, almost knee to knee. He wore soft, close fitting trousers and a dark tunic with golden snakes embroidered on the shoulders. More snakes were tattooed over his bald head. 'I can hurt you much worse than the ghosts you loathe so much.'

'So long as I can stay where they can't reach me.' Maybe he should have pretended not to mind about the ghosts but he felt too peaceful to try. 'You can cut me if you like, if you want me to bleed.'

'You're more complicated than we thought.' Jollifon's frown squeezed the loops of the snakes over the top of his head. 'Where is the boy who broke our glass bubbles?'

'I don't know.'

'Tell me how to find him and maybe you can stay here for a while.'

'I don't know anything I could tell you.' Hugo smiled in relief at the truth of this and closed his eyes. He felt Jollifon's stare increase its strength.

'Then we must find other uses for you.'

Hugo opened his eyes in time to see Jollifon somersault backwards into the hedge. Hugo tensed, prepared for the worst, but the ghosts did not manifest themselves and he was left alone.

James scrabbled his fingers against the cloudy glass, to no effect. He flattened his wrists along the curve and tried to dig in with his nails but they skidded away every time. He gave up and lay down flat, so that he could drum with his shoes and his fists together. The noise boomed inside his ears, just as when he had been in Lyulf's trap.

'Maybe this time it is an illusion.'

The voice spoke from above and he looked up to see a woman's face, crowned by red hair. She was outside the glass but her features were not distorted as Lyulf's had been. James recognised her from Rowan's description and scrambled to his feet.

'Lady Siriol? What do you mean?'

If the trap is in your mind, you should be able to walk out of it. Just shut your eyes and put one foot in front of the other.'

The words sounded helpful but not the tone, and her gaze was not friendly.

'Didn't you bring me here?' James asked. 'Why do you want me to walk away?'

'To see you try and fail,' the lady said. 'Aren't you safer here than wandering about near a fire?'

'Am I? Please, my lady, where are the others?'

'In puzzles of their own. Yours is to do from the inside what your brother did from the outside.'

'I can't.' James's voice wobbled, to his fury. 'I tried and it didn't work.'

'Maybe he could show you how. Tell me how to find him and I'll bring him here.'

So it was a double trap. James sat down and folded his arms.

'No, thank you,' he said.

Thirty-four

Stephen shone his torch onto the path between the allotments, using both hands to prevent the beam from swinging about. Frost had already formed on the grass but his trembling had little to do with the cold. He had not been able to think straight since he had watched his friends disappear that afternoon. When he arrived on Tilda's doorstep, he had only known that reporting to her would be the worst thing and therefore it must be done as quickly as possible. After that, his urge to find a corner and hide himself away was nearly overpowering. He did not believe that Nicholas would be able to track down James and the others, still less set about their rescue. He was not sure Tilda had any real hopes but her support for Nicholas had not wavered. Stephen could not bear to break through her determination, so he had agreed to bring them here.

He did not want to remember his nights in the trenches. The air here was clean, not full of the stench of corpses, and he could set his feet down without sinking into sticky mud, but he had not expected that he would ever again walk in the dark with so little hope and so little power to decide what to do. The further he went along the path, the greater his fear grew that Tilda and Nicholas would be snatched away like the others, and he would be left alone and helpless once more.

The torch light caught the charred remains of Lyulf's nettle patch. Stephen halted and Nicholas went past him.

'There's nothing to see.' Stephen played the torch onto the embers of the fire and on the open door of the hut. 'They didn't leave any kind of trail.'

Nicholas did not answer but he stood quite still with his head bent. Stephen's shudders intensified until Tilda put her hand over his to hold the torch steady.

'This way,' Nicholas said and set off into the darkness.

'How can you possibly tell?' Stephen cried out.

Nicholas did not answer but he paused when Tilda called, 'Wait, Nick. Don't leave us behind.'

He let her catch him up.

'Let me hold your hand, so you won't lose us,' she said.

He pulled ahead but did not break free of her. On her other side, Tilda kept her arm linked through Stephen's and they both held the torch.

They stumbled onto a new path, and then out onto a street where they did not need the torch. Stephen lost all sense of time and direction as they walked between rows of houses and large buildings, dark bulks against the sky. With Tilda at his side, Stephen no longer felt shaken to pieces, but Nicholas set a fast pace, so they had no time to talk. The city seemed deserted. In the distance, the occasional engine growled or a shout rose and faded, but they passed no one, not even a policeman on his beat or a tramp asleep in a doorway.

They came to a set of narrow stone steps and climbed down towards the restless flow of the Thames. Nicholas led them under a bridge where the street lights did not reach. Stephen switched on the torch again, just as Nicholas stopped beside a small iron door in a stone wall. He leaned against the door and muttered words Stephen could not catch. When he stepped back, the door opened of its own accord.

'Not far now,' Nicholas said and went inside.

Stephen was beyond questions. He had to pocket the torch while he followed Tilda down a ladder of iron rungs. At the bottom, he switched it on only for the lamp to flare up and die before he saw more than a glimpse of Tilda's face.

'I didn't bring spare batteries,' Stephen said into the overwhelming dark.

'They wouldn't help,' Nicholas answered. 'Hold onto me and I'll lead you.'

They went forward slowly. The ground was hard underfoot and the echo of their footsteps rang round them. Hallucinatory dazzles pressed on Stephen's eyeballs until he did not know whether he moved forwards or backwards.

When it came, the new light was red and harsh. Stephen stood still and pressed his hands to his face.

'There's no smell of magic in any of you.' The speaker was angry and impatient.

'We don't deal in magic,' Nicholas said.

Stephen lowered his hands and looked around.

They were in a circular pit surrounded by a row of chairs, or maybe thrones, seven of them, set against walls of grey brick, stained with black and green. The dome of the ceiling was as high as in a cathedral but unadorned. The thrones were made of carved marble, red and white. The light came from the bodies of the seven strange beings who sat on the thrones.

'I don't know who you are,' Nicholas said.

'Nor will you, but we will give you the names we have taken, so that you may know them and fear them. I am Parhelion.' The speaker was a tall man with a lion's head, thick maned and golden-eyed. Either side of him were Thurlin and Siriol, whom Stephen remembered from the Puppet Theatre. Beside Siriol was a small man, who sat cross-legged and juggled so fast that his face could not be seen. He gave his name as Jollifon. Then came Stoneheart and Stonetongue, whose bodies were shapeless, their faces like lumps of grey stone with the features scratched into the surface and black holes for eyes. The seventh was a giantess, three times bigger than Siriol, with a round, flat face and goggle eyes, Malaswintha Moonface.

'How did you find your way here?' Parhelion asked. 'What tricks did you use?'

'I don't do tricks,' Nicholas said.

'All your kind are full of tricks. Else you would never have held us captive in Spellhaven.'

'That wasn't me.' Nicholas sounded as though he could withstand any amount of anger or impatience, sturdy as a pony in rough weather. Stephen, by contrast, was unsettled by the eyes at his back. He kept glancing all round the circle, as though he might better understand the seven by meeting their gaze, but their faces were closed to him, stern and cold.

'What's down there?' Tilda asked, her voice sharp with fear. Stephen looked down and realised that he stood, with Tilda and Nicholas, on a ledge several feet below the thrones but above a steep slope. Far below, a heap of sacks wobbled.

'Your friends are there,' Siriol said. 'Soon you will join them.'

'Not yet,' Parhelion said. 'First the boy must tell us his secrets.'

'They are not mine to tell,' Nicholas said. Thurlin raised his hand and a silver whip lashed out. Both Tilda and Stephen moved to shield Nicholas.

'Let me.' Stephen took the blow on his arm. 'I can't do much but I can get in the way.'

'I'm not a magician.' Nicholas spoke with such force that everyone else stopped to listen to him. 'I don't want to learn magic. The walls will tell you that if you let them.'

The whip fell back.

'You want us to listen to the walls?' Thurlin asked.

'Men made this place under the river, didn't they? I don't know why but they sunk machines into the earth and built up the walls with bricks cooked in ovens far away. The walls were used to the darkness before you came, so that they could hear the tumult of the tides above and dream of the fires in which they were made.'

'We hear them,' Stoneheart spoke in a whisper, 'and the earth behind them.'

'Ask them what I am,' Nicholas said.

Jollifon threw his juggles at Nicholas, who caught them as fast as they came, even the one that stung Stephen's ear as it passed him. They were little knives, bright and pointed.

'Iron speaks to you as well as mud.' Jollifon wore a brown leather mask, painted with black teardrops. 'And yet you say you are not a Magician.'

'I listen,' Nicholas said. 'I accept help when it's offered. That's all.'

Parhelion leaned forward. 'Why have you come here, if not to meet our challenge? Did you think we wanted an audience, a human child to listen to us?'

'And how did you break our bubbles, the cunning glass traps we made for Lyulf?' Siriol asked.

'That's why I came,' Nicholas said, 'to rescue our friends from your traps,' but his voice wobbled and he glanced round the circle, as though to count up the opposition.

Parhelion's mane bristled up and sparks crackled from it. 'How can you rescue anyone without magic?'

'I help the glass remember how it was made. I'll show you if you let me.'

The Seven stirred on their thrones. Malaswintha Moonface and the Juggler shook their heads but Thurlin said, 'Let him try,' and Siriol nodded, her hair flickering from red to ash grey in the shadows.

'I want my knives back first,' Jollifon said. Nicholas tossed them up and they landed neatly in Jollifon's lap.

'Down you go, boy,' Parhelion said but Tilda clasped her son's shoulder.

'Are you sure about this, Nick?'

'Not really.' He looked at her, his face drawn. 'But what else can we do?'

Tilda's grasp tightened and she turned to Stephen, her eyes wide, her lips bloodless.

'Let me go with him,' Stephen said and touched Nicholas's other shoulder, but the boy wriggled free and slid down towards the lower pit. A knife flashed towards Stephen and pinned his sleeve to the wall. Another went into Tilda's skirt.

'Stay there, you,' Jollifon said. 'We want to see what the boy can do.

Stephen tugged at the knife, which was wedged fast into a crack between the bricks.

'Wait,' Tilda murmured. 'We might distract him.'

She was trembling, not with the deep shudders which had afflicted Stephen earlier but with a slight, steady vibration like an engine building up pressure. Stephen put his arm round her shoulders and they looked into the pit together.

Nicholas lay sprawled face down on the sacks. He made no attempt to stand up but swept his limbs around like a swimmer. Then he lifted his head.

'There's no glass under here.'

'Lyulf needed the bubbles, not us,' Parhelion answered. 'What can you do to break our own traps?'

Nick's head went down. He felt around some more and said, 'No sacking either. Only nets made of pain and memory.'

'Soul catcher nets.' Jollifon bounced up and down in his seat. 'Traps to let us fondle our prey and drink their souls and gloat, without the trouble of the glass in between.'

'They wear out sooner and die this way but the taste is stronger while it lasts,' Siriol said. 'Can you tell which of the nets hold live souls, boy who is not a magician?'

Silence. Then Nicholas rolled round to sit up, a bundle gathered into his lap. To Stephen's eye, it was a coarse sack, which roiled about as though stuffed with live rats. Nicholas put his arms round it and his head down. He rocked to and fro and spoke so softly Stephen had to hold his breath to hear.

'Layers. From all of you, from the things you loved: white towers, singing trees, dances with the Magicians in Spellhaven.' His voice rose. 'You loved the city you destroyed. You've turned your love into bonds I can't break.'

Malaswintha reached down into the pit. Her arms stretched further than they ought to go, as she scooped Nicholas up and set him beside his mother. The sack remained in his arms.

'Someone's in there.' Malaswintha's voice was sweet and mournful. 'Reach for him and forget our troubles.'

Nicholas leaned back against the wall and shut his eyes. His breathing became hard and irregular, so loud that Stephen felt his own breath pound into the same rhythm. He saw Nicholas's hands spread out and sink into the sack, as if into butter. Then Nicholas dropped to his knees and the sack fell out of his hands to roll down the slope.

Tilda's skirt tore on the knife that pinioned her, as she sat down beside Nicholas. They needed a respite, so Stephen did the only thing he could think of to provide a distraction. He dragged his arm out of his sleeve to step away from them both and looked up at Parhelion.

'Why did you leave me behind this afternoon?'

The seven stares directed at him were harder to bear than he expected. He did not understand the minds behind them and feared he would plunge into madness if he tried, but he could feel their strength and pain.

'You were never in Spellhaven,' Thurlin said.

At least Stephen was trained in argument. 'Neither was Hugo, my nephew, or James his friend. And why should it matter? The city is broken: everyone says so.'

'You have no magic,' Siriol said.

'Neither have the others.' The blank indifference in her glance and Thurlin's, the most human of the seven, roused Stephen into a fury. 'Did our punch up scare you? Were we too rumbustious for your delicate stomachs, Marshall and I, rolling around like a couple of drunks?'

Parhelion's mane flattened and he yawned, while claws stretched and retracted from his fingertips. 'You were nothing to us then. You are nothing now, not worth the trapping.'

'We were no different from the others, except for the fight. Were you afraid we would hurt you?'

'You didn't even sense our approach,' Siriol said. 'We had a big enough haul without the trouble of attracting your attention.'

That rang true but Stephen did not care. 'Prove it,' he said. 'Come down here and fight me, hand to hand. I'll take you on one at a time or all together, just as you please.'

They did not even bother to laugh. Parhelion twitched his ears and spoke in a dark growl. 'We have no ambition to prove ourselves to you.'

'Then I'll come up to you, if I can,' Stephen said. The prospect of action, however desperate, was too much to resist.

He jumped up and caught the top of the wall above him with his hands. Thurlin's whip cut him and the bricks turned hot enough to blister his hands, but he managed to draw one knee over the edge before Parhelion's boot caught him in the ribs. It sent him flying and he lost consciousness before he landed.

Thirty-five

ick's forehead was cold against Tilda's hand. She kept her touch gentle and bent her head close to his. She heard Stephen speak and was grateful for the diversion, but she did not listen to what was said until he made his jump upwards. She saw him fall past her and sprang to her feet, too late to help. She looked down and saw him lying motionless on top of the sacks. She looked at Nicholas huddled at her feet. Then she looked up at the seven on their thrones. She turned in a circle to face each one and they looked back at her in silence. She wanted to scream at them for their cruelty or beg them for mercy, but she could not afford to waste her strength that way. Nicholas had challenged them with magic and Stephen with force. Both had failed. What else could she try?

She did not know enough about them, not even whether their appearances were true to reality, but perhaps how they chose to appear could tell her something of their natures. The stone faces were the strangest, nothing like the elaborate carving she had cleaned in the woods. The features of these were mere scratches, curved lines for brows and lips, with dents for the noses and dark gaps for the eyes. They seemed barely alive. Jollifon and Thurlin had covered their faces but their bodies were eloquent, one lithe and restless, the other graceful as the whip he wielded.

Siriol had a face out of an Italian fresco, grave-eyed and small-mouthed, and she sat as still as a cat at a mouse hole. So did Malaswintha the giantess but her enormous face drooped into the most melancholy smile Tilda had ever seen. And Parhelion sprawled at his ease, his tongue touching the top of his lip, one ear forward, the other back. His mane was a mixture of black and tawny but the fur on his face was golden brown, a shade paler than his eyes. All seven shone and the light from their bodies reached up to show the endless rows of pale, grimy bricks on the walls behind them.

'Do you live down here?' Tilda asked. 'Is this your home?'

She was facing Siriol as she spoke and the faintest tilt of the lady's chin hinted at surprise, but it was Parhelion who answered, 'You have no right to question us.'

'I dare say not.' Tilda looked at the walls again and the black, lightless ceiling. 'But you are all so beautiful. I am bewildered to find you in so wretched a place.'

The giantess tapped Tilda on the shoulder from behind.

'Look at me, Malaswintha Moonface.' Tilda turned to towards her. 'Look well and then tell me I'm beautiful.'

She wore a loose, mud brown robe, out of which her arms stretched down past her knees. Her breasts and thighs were massive and her shoulders heavy, but her skin was smooth and bright and her curly hair held all the colours of mother of pearl.

'I never believed I was beautiful until I was taught to see,' Tilda said. 'You are strong and fair as a sea cliff.'

'We do not want words from you.' Jollifon picked up his knives and juggled them, faster than the eye could follow.

'What do you want?' Tilda turned her eyes away from the dazzle, in case it could hypnotise her. 'Spellhaven was destroyed before my sons were born. Must you stay chained to its memory?'

Parhelion's mane bristled up. 'The only chains here bind the humans we make our prey.'

'That's not so,' Tilda said. 'If you chose this place to keep your victims safe, you have trapped yourselves as well as them.'

Siriol and Thurlin both sat forward and Thurlin's hand tightened on his whip.

'We choose to take our pleasure so, in return for fifteen hundred years when humans tricked us into their service,' Siriol said.

'Down here?' Tilda was afraid to stop the argument, though she had little hope in pursuing it. 'These are not even the people who tricked you. Why should you live in such dreariness for the sake of tormenting them?'

'Lyulf called us.' Parhelion licked his lips. 'He showed us how the people of this land endeavoured to make themselves Magicians, by skinning cats alive.'

'Poor creatures,' Tilda whispered, 'but other Spirits live out in the free air. They live their lives as though Spellhaven never was.'

'What do you know of other Spirits?' Siriol was scornful.

'I've seen them.' Tilda hesitated. 'Some of them make friends with humans without being bound to their magic.'

'So the humans boast, maybe.' Parhelion drew back his lips.

'I don't boast.' Nicholas's voice was croaky and wavering as he rose to his feet and scowled at Parhelion. 'I don't want anything to do with Spellhaven magic.'

'You couldn't break our traps.' Both Parhelion's ears pricked forward as he stared at Nicholas. Tilda put her arm round Nick's shoulder, as much to reassure herself as him.

'But he broke the bubbles,' Jollifon said, 'and he found his way here. How was that done, if not with magic?'

'I had help.' Nicholas's voice rose. 'I listen and I make friends. I don't play tricks.'

'Easy to say,' Jollifon answered. 'Who are these generous friends?'

Nicholas drew in upon himself. 'I promised not to tell anyone.'

'We don't count,' Siriol said. 'You can tell us.'

Nicholas shook his head.

'Call them here,' Malaswintha said. 'One, at least. Surely you have one friend who would come to us for your sake.'

Nicholas went still, then he turned in Tilda's clasp, his face pulled into misery. 'I won't,' he spoke to Tilda, not to the Seven. 'She would wither and die here.'

Tilda hugged him to her side and spoke aloud. 'He's told you the truth.'

'Why should we trust him? Or you?' Parhelion asked. 'You'll mewl and go mad as quickly as the others inside our traps. Your friends will be no use to you there.'

Tilda thought of King Thistlebeard. He had spoken of visits to London and might be tough enough to survive this place. She had no right to summon him except for one purpose and no reason to believe he would help, even if he could, but maybe he would rescue Nick, at least, for Sallikin's sake. Tilda grasped the pouch she wore on a ribbon round her neck and took out Thistlebeard's acorn from inside. She bit into it and let it fall.

'What's that? What have you done?' Siriol asked. Tilda gagged at the bitter taste in her mouth and did not answer. Thurlin's whip flicked out but the acorn rolled away untouched. It stopped halfway down the slope to the lower pit and split open. Faster than a racing tide, roots broke into the floor and a green shoot grew up into a young oak. Branches groaned as they reached out and up, and leaves crackled as they unfolded. The tree trunk opened with a crack of thunder and Thistlebeard stepped out.

He looked bigger and shaggier than when Tilda had last seen him, his clothes stiff with layers of bark like armour plate, his head crowned with a tangle of mistletoe and holly. His glance at Tilda was fierce.

'It's too soon,' he said.

Too soon to know if she was expecting his child.

'I'm sorry,' she said.

Parhelion rose to his feet and his mane flared like a sunburst. 'Are you this woman's slave?'

'No!' Tilda's protest was submerged in Thistlebeard's laughter. 'She is my lover.'

Nicholas lifted his head from Tilda's armpit but he did not pull away from her. She found herself heartened to be so identified and not just because the ordinary conventions did not matter down here.

Thistlebeard stood at his ease on the steep slope. He kept his gaze on Tilda, not on the Seven, and anger still showed through his laughter.

'Sorry is easy to say.'

'Set a penalty and I'll pay it.' Whatever happened now, strength flowed into Tilda at the sight of him. 'But I beg you to help my son and my friends escape from this place.'

The laughter retreated. 'Are you offering me a bargain?'

'I have nothing to bargain with.' Tilda wished she could walk towards him. 'Save them for their sakes, not mine.'

Thurlin and Siriol rose to their feet and spoke together. 'You have no right to meddle here. This place is ours.'

Thistlebeard looked up and round. Frost thickened and gleamed on his crown and his beard. 'London is not my place, that's true,' he said, 'but winter is my strength. What are you doing with these people?'

'We account to nobody since we escaped from Spellhaven,' Jollifon said. 'We do as we choose.'

'Why choose to be down here, where the air is dead and the weight of the city groans above you?'

'We bring our prey down here,' Parhelion answered. 'We care nothing for the city.'

'No humans come here except the ones in our power,' Siriol said. 'We need not fear them or their magic down here.'

'Humans built these tunnels without magic,' Thistlebeard said. 'You're breathing their sweat and the nightmares of the poor fools in your traps.' As he spoke, Tilda saw shadows shift and darken around the Seven. Indistinct hands clutched at their knees, heads leaned over their shoulders, and voices groaned just out of earshot.

'Stop that.' Malaswintha surged to her feet and the shadows leaped round her.

'You should have noticed them before.' Thistlebeard grinned at her. 'Wouldn't you rather go somewhere else to be free of humans?'

'They seek us out,' Jollifon said. 'Their longing reaches us wherever we go.'

'Learn to resist, like the Spirits who swim in London's filthy river or dance in its streets,' Thistlebeard answered, 'or go out into the wilds and learn to forget.'

The air became harder to breathe, hot and stale, heavy with the smells of dung and sulphur.

Parhelion growled. 'We care nothing for you or your illusions.'

'I've lifted the charms that hampered your senses. Had you forgotten them?'

'Get away from us.' Thurlin's whip lashed out, but Thistlebeard caught the end and held it.

'Come down to me,' he said.

Parhelion roared and jumped down onto the slope. His body changed as he moved, so that he landed on all fours, a lion with taloned paws and a black tail. He charged at Thistlebeard, who stepped aside so that the lion skidded into the oak tree behind him.

The tree expanded, its branches stretching out in all directions, thick with young leaves. They rustled in a breeze which sent out whiffs of new air, lost before Tilda could breathe them in.

The hole in the tree trunk deepened as Parhelion hurtled forward. It swallowed him whole and left only his roar behind.

Thistlebeard set his hands on his hips and surveyed the Six. 'Who is next?'

'Where did he go?' Malaswintha extended her arms towards Thistlebeard's back but he twitched his shoulders without looking round. The holly in his crown stretched over his neck and Malaswintha drew her fingers away from the prickles.

'Wherever his heart took him,' Thistlebeard said. 'Where would you go?'

Stoneheart and Stonetongue spoke together. 'Into stone. Into quiet and wilderness. But not at your sending.'

'Then don't rush at me,' Thistlebeard said. 'Look through my door and back away if you prefer.'

'We can fight him if we keep together,' Siriol said.

'Fight for what?' Jollifon stood up on his throne and spun his knives over his head and under his legs. 'Can we put him in a trap?'

'Don't try.' Thistlebeard whistled and the knives flew away from the juggler. Thistlebeard caught them in one hand. He blew on them and they turned into sparrows, which scattered up into the oak branches.

'Give them back.' Jollifon's high, sour voice pulled at Tilda and maybe at the sparrows, for a few started out of the tree, but they settled back into it at the sound of Thistlebeard's deeper, stronger voice.

'Come and get them.'

Jollifon somersaulted down onto the slope and came to his feet in front of the tree. He put his hands either side of the hole and leaned forward.

'What do you see?' Siriol asked.

'Sunlight on the rocks, and the Sea Sprites of Spellhaven.' Jollifon pulled his head back and glared at Thistlebeard. 'That's a lie. The island was drowned when the city was destroyed.'

'And now the Sprites play on the rocks where the island was before the city was founded,' Thistlebeard said. 'Or they search for the ruins of Spellhaven's towers and do not find them. Nobody knows in which dimension of the nine worlds those ruins may lie, from Asgard to the depths of Tartarus.'

'Then I'll join the search,' Jollifon said. The sparrows fluttered onto his shoulders as he walked into the tree trunk and disappeared.

Stoneheart and Stonetongue grunted as they waddled down the slope. They paused, one each side of Thistlebeard and said, 'We could grow big enough to crush you between us.'

'Maybe,' he answered, 'but could you shrink yourselves small enough afterwards ever to leave this place.'

'We could swell until we broke the roof and let in the river to drown us all.'

'Or you might wear yourselves out in the attempt and lie here helpless while the rest of us escaped. Did you learn to gamble in Spellhaven?'

Groans answered him and they surged past him to enter the tree trunk side by side.

Thistlebeard still held the end of Thurlin's whip. He tossed it upwards and said, 'Even in winter, my strength is not inexhaustible. Come quickly, if you are coming.' He looked inexhaustible, his crown now thick with red berries, his silky beard long enough to reach his waist.

'Or shall we wait?' Thurlin asked. 'We do not wither in the spring.'

'We can't stay here now,' Siriol said. 'Not just the three of us in this mirk.'

'Then we go together.' Thurlin broke the stock of his whip across his knee and the pieces melted into nothing. He and Siriol waded down the slope, arm in arm, and went through the hole.

Tilda's attention had been so absorbed in these departures that she had scarcely been aware of herself or her companions. Now, as she watched Malaswintha and waited, her guts ached and her head felt bloated. Nicholas remained at her side, his eyes dark in a pinched face, but he stood upright and steady. She heard a grunt from below and looked down to see Stephen sit up on top of the heap of sacks. He put his head in his hands and rocked to and fro.

'Where shall I go?' Malaswintha asked. 'There is no place fit for my misery.'

'Then find a place you can shape to your liking,' Thistlebeard said. 'Come and see.'

She shrank as she walked down the slope, until she was no bigger than a tall woman, though her head remained large and heavy. She looked round at Tilda, after she had peered through the hole, her face more melancholy than ever. 'The sea shore is empty. What can I do there?'

Tilda did not know what to say, but Nicholas answered, 'Listen to the storms. Lose your misery in theirs.'

She looked through the hole again, said, 'Better there than here, maybe,' and stepped through.

The branches of the oak thrashed about and a cold wind scoured over Tilda and Nicholas.

'We must go too,' Thistlebeard said. 'Hurry.' He held out his hand to Tilda but she stared past him, down into the pit.

'We can't leave the others here!'

'Bring the sacks. Fetch them up, boy, and you, down there. Be quick!'

They formed a chain. Stephen, at the bottom, slung the sacks to Nicholas, who passed them to Tilda. She pushed then through the hole while Thistlebeard held her steady. She was afraid at first that Nicholas would be dislodged from his standpoint, halfway down the lower slope, but a tree branch stretched downwards until he could lean against it. Another branch reached down into the pit to support Stephen. The sacks were heavy but Tilda grabbed and pushed in a blizzard of action, until Stephen said, 'I can't find any more.' He sounded bewildered.

The branches scraped along the ground as they drove Stephen and Nicholas upwards.

'Go through,' Thistlebeard said.

Tilda caught hold of Nicholas and pushed him ahead of her through the hole. She took Stephen's hand and pulled him behind her.

Thirty-six

In the eastern sky, streaks of pink dawned between white and grey clouds. The stone benches in Sallikin's garden were furred with rime. Tilda gulped in the scents of living grass and water, her face turned into the cold wind.

Down below, Sallikin sat in the leafless willow tree and smiled at the company which had arrived so suddenly in her garden. Stephen and Nicholas sprawled near her in a tumble of sacks, just as they had emerged through the hole in the oak tree. Thistlebeard sat on the grass, his head bowed, his crown shrivelled. The skin on his hands was cracked, his neck was too thin to support his head and his chest heaved as he struggled to breathe. Tilda was afraid for him, but before she could think what to do, Sallikin sang out a call, a few wordless notes, high and clear. In response, creatures rushed into the garden from all sides. Some were like the dancers Tilda had met in the woods, with bodies made of reeds or tree faces, but rabbits came, as well as foxes, mice and small birds, crows and jays, even frogs and beetles. They scrabbled all over Thistlebeard and pressed themselves against him. For some minutes he was covered in a mound of fur and feathers. Then the creatures dropped away and Thistlebeard stood up, laughing, sturdy and flushed with new strength.

'That's better,' Sallikin said. 'Now to be rid of this poison.'

The creatures bustled away, keen to return to their own affairs. The humans looked at Sallikin in puzzlement and she pointed a toe at the heap of sacks.

'Nicholas, friendling, your touch will speak to the souls in there more easily than mine.'

Nicholas stood up, wobbly but calm. 'I tried before. I couldn't break the traps.'

'I'll help you. Come over here.'

He sat among the willow roots with Sallikin's hands on his shoulders. This time, when he gathered one of the sacks into his arms, the cloth melted away. Whatever had been inside turned into a black fog and shredded into the air. Nicholas went stiff with alarm.

'I couldn't hold on.'

'You set the soul free,' Thistlebeard said. 'The body must have died elsewhere. Go on.'

The next two sacks were the same. Then came one both smaller and heavier. When Nicholas pulled the cloth apart, James fell out. He sat up and said, 'I tried to run away, Nick. I tried hard.'

Tilda went over to hug him.

'I need to find the others,' Nicholas said.

James saw Thistlebeard and Sallikin and he went quiet, his eyes wide.

The next person to come out was Rowan. 'Tilda!' she said. 'Stephen! What happened to us all?'

'Hush,' Tilda said. 'Wait.'

As he hauled the sacks over to Nicholas, Stephen moved as steadily as a man digging potatoes, but all the time he kept his head turned to watch Nicholas, his frown deeper at every step. Rowan looked from him to Thistlebeard and then scooted over to stand by Tilda.

After more sacks of fog, a stranger fell out of one, a skinny girl with scratches all down her arms and a bruised face. She looked round at them all and snarled, 'Touch me again and I'll kill you.'

'You're safe here,' Sallikin said. We mean you no harm.'

'I'm not listening to you.' The girl's voice rose. 'I'll never listen anymore.'

Thistlebeard stepped forward and touched his thumb to her forehead before she could block him.

'Sleep,' he said. 'Sleep and forget.'

She caught her breath and her eyes closed. Stephen lowered her onto the grass and covered her with his jacket.

Dr. Hunter sat on the ground and scrubbed her face with her hands. 'I'm too old,' she said, 'I can't ride the nightmares any more, not for all of Spellhaven.'

'You should have thought of that sooner,' Thistlebeard said.

She stared at him. She was in worse shape than Rowan, hatless and bedraggled, her clothes stained, her cheeks collapsed. 'We tried so hard when we first came to this country,' she said. I would have had the strength to dance with you in those days.'

'You would have tried to use me to make magic, as you hoped to use the Seven. Sit quiet and be glad you are out of their grasp.'

Another stranger emerged next, a small boy about five years old. He wept and would not be comforted by Rowan or Sallikin. Thistlebeard sent him to sleep.

Then came Darius Fox, who leaped to his feet and glared around. 'I can fight you all,' he said. 'Whatever you do to me, I'll fight.'

'No need, Darius,' Rowan said. 'The traps are broken. Can't you feel it?'

He lowered his head. His hair stood on end and blood welled from scratches on his face, but he dug his heels into the ground and he sounded tireless. 'I don't care which of you did this to me. The Club will find you out and we'll make you sorry.'

'Nonsense.' Dr. Hunter heaved herself onto one of the stone benches. 'Come and sit down, Darius, before you get into real trouble.'

Fox caught sight of Nicholas and prowled towards him. 'You! Tell me how you did this or I'll beat it out of you.'

Before Tilda or anyone else could react, Thistlebeard tapped Fox between the shoulders and marked his forehead when he swung round. 'Be quiet, you fool. Sleep.'

There were only three sacks left now. Nicholas was silent as he worked, his face composed. At moments his appearance changed to match Sallikin's, his skin tinged with green, his chin pointed like hers. Then he would turn his head or lean forward and shift back to his ordinary looks.

Two of the sacks were full of the black fog. As Stephen handed Nicholas the last one, he was so cramped with anxiety, he could hardly let it go. From Tilda's side, James muttered, 'Hugo must be there. He must.'

Stephen turned his head but his glance was unseeing and his frown without hope. Sallikin lifted a hand to reach out to him. 'Wait,' she said.

The frown eased, just barely, and Stephen stepped back. Sallikin returned her hold to Nicholas's shoulders and he set both hands on the sack.

This time the cloth blackened and rose up like a burnt crust. Underneath was a dark mould which bubbled under Nicholas's fingers. He pushed down but the mould pushed back.

'He won't let me in,' he said.

Sallikin placed her hands over Nicholas's and the mould shook harder.

'Let's try another way.' Sallikin slid her hands under the mould and lifted it up. She blew on it and said, 'Be seen if you will not be touched.'

The mould thinned into a mist. Inside sat Hugo, small as though seen through the wrong end of a telescope. Sallikin held him as if he were weightless.

'Hugo!' Stephen, James, and Rowan called out together. 'Are you all right?'

'I'm not coming out.' Hugo bent his head down to his knees and bramble stems grew out of his mouth as he spoke.

'Your friends are here.' Sallikin knelt and set the globe of mist on the ground. She beckoned to the others. 'Call him.'

They gathered round. Stephen crouched down and said, 'Hugo, come back to us.' His voice was a dry croak. He looked pleadingly at James, who said, 'You'll be safe now.'

'I'm safe in here.' The brambles looped round Hugo as they grew, sharp with thorns. 'The ghosts can't reach me in here.'

'The ghosts have gone,' Nicholas said. 'The link must have broken when you entered the trap.'

'They'll find me again,' Hugo said.

'You're not bound to them any more,' Nicholas said. 'I'd feel them if you were.'

'That's true,' Sallikin said. 'Let go your fears, child, and we'll bring you out.'

The brambles thickened into a cage.

'I can't. I don't want to.'

Thistlebeard crouched beside Tilda and set his hands on the cage. 'Come now. Come out.' He spoke in the dark, deep voice which had sent Fox and the others into sleep, but Hugo hunched down within his cage of brambles and shook his head.

Thistlebeard let go and sat back.

'Can you pull him out? Tilda asked.

'Not without breaking his will,' Thistlebeard answered.

'Where is he?' Stephen asked. 'Must I search for him in another dungeon?'

'This is all you'll find of him,' Sallikin said. 'You cannot rouse him until he is ready.'

Stephen stumbled to his feet. 'Should I take him to a hospital?'

'He'll get better nourishment here,' Sallikin said.' He may have a nest in my garden, if you will trust him to me.'

Stephen's face twisted in doubt and pain. 'But I'm his uncle. I can't abandon him to strangers.'

'Then Nicholas shall bring you to visit him,' Sallikin said, 'and I will not be a stranger to him or you.'

'I didn't mean...' Stephen's voice faded away. He looked at Sallikin and drew a long breath. 'I beg your pardon.'

'Can I come too?' James asked.

'Later,' Sallikin said. 'When he has had time to heal.'

The brambles had begun to grow out of the mist. Dark red spikes pressed Sallikin's hands as she lifted the cage and set it down between the roots of her tree. Stephen crouched alongside but made no attempt to touch it.

Thistlebeard caught Tilda's eye and she followed him through the hedge into the outer garden. His crown was bright with holly berries now, and he looked strong enough to knock down the ruined wall at a single blow or to take root in the earth and burst into leaf. His grin delighted Tilda as much as it alarmed her.

'Your sons are in good hands,' he said. 'Now will you stay with me in the woods?'

Her delight ebbed into sadness. 'Would you have me come as a penance? Or out of gratitude?'

The grin widened. 'I only take willing lovers. Remember?'

'I remember.' Tilda was so weary she could scarcely hold her head up, but her blood ran warm at the memories. 'The love would be willing but it wouldn't be enough. I have to find my own work to do, not live in your shadow.'

He looked at her for a long time before he said, 'Then you will never see me again. Your memories will be your penance for your misuse of my token.'

'I wouldn't want to lose them.' Tears thickened Tilda's throat but she swallowed them and lifted her head for Thistlebeard's kiss.

Tilda's feet stumbled and the wind buffeted her face when she walked back alone into the Inner Garden. Nicholas and James ran to her and she put her arms round their shoulders. Rowan came over and asked, 'Time to go home?'

'Oh yes,' Tilda said, looking at the people who lay on the ground, 'but what about all these folk? What can we do about them?'

'They will wake up naturally, Sallikin says,' Nicholas said.

'And what will they do then? We can't leave them here.'

'Nick has told me where we are, though I have no idea how we got here,' Rowan said. 'If he guides me down to the road, I'll hike along to the Gray works. Father won't grudge us a motor or two to load up the sleepers. We can take them to the Club.'

James and Dr. Hunter set about the practical arrangements for ferrying the sleepers down to the road, with Sallikin's help. Tilda went over to Stephen, who stood watch over Hugo.

'The brambles grow thicker every minute,' Stephen said. 'Look.'

'Maybe the looking makes it worse,' Tilda said. 'Leave him be, Stephen.'

'How can I go home without him? I've done nothing to help him, or you, or anyone.'

'You helped us all last night,' Tilda said. 'Trust Sallikin. She's been a good friend to Nicholas.'

Stephen stared away over her head. 'Last night, down that pit, I tried to go mad. I didn't want to face up to anything ever again.'

'I'm sorry I took you there,' Tilda said, 'but we would never have survived without you.'

'Tilda?' He turned to look at her and she took a step back.

'Not yet,' she said, but she held out her hands to him. 'Whatever you want from me, Stephen, don't ask it today.'

His clasp was shaky and cold.

'Just don't give me up altogether,' he whispered and she tightened her grip in response.

'We're ready,' James called across. 'Sallikin wants us to go.'

'The garden wants you to go,' Sallikin said. 'The less you outstay your welcome, the easier you'll find it to come back.'

Stephen and Tilda turned round and she held out a cup of willow leaves, filled with clear water.

'Drink and go in peace,' she said and held out the cup first to Stephen.

Acknowledgements

I am very grateful for all the support I received during the writing of *Ghosts and Exiles*. Farah Mendlesohn helped me get started on this novel and members of the Middle Oak writing group provided valuable feedback. Allen Ashley, the members of London Clockhouse, my fellow Orbiters, and other writers with whom I have exchanged ideas over the past few years have all widened my experience and fed my imagination.

I am also very grateful to my non-writing friends for their interest and encouragement.

Justine, Robert, and everyone at Mirror World Publishing have done another great job with this book.

Finally, the support of my family has been more important than ever, during a difficult year for us all. Thanks once again to Sue, Mark, Eve, Fran, Tim, Sylvia, Georgia, Joyce, and everyone in the wider family.

About the Author

Sandra Unerman lives in London in the UK. When she retired from a career as a Government lawyer, she undertook an MA in Creative Writing at Middlesex University, specialising in science fiction and fantasy, and graduated in 2013. Since then, she has had a number of short stories published. Her latest stories are in *Sword and Sorcery* magazine, June 2017, and *Fall into Fantasy*, an anthology from Cloaked Press. She writes reviews and articles for the British Science Fiction Association and the British Fantasy Society. She is a member of London Clockhouse writers and other writing groups. Her interests include history, folklore and medieval literature.

To learn more about our authors and their current projects visit: www.mirrorworldpublishing.com, follow @MirrorWorldPub or like us at www.facebook.com/mirrorworldpublishing

Or keep reading for a sneak peek at:

By Justine Alley Dowsett and Murandy Damodred
Coming 2018

Prologue

Caralain wasn't supposed to be here. She knew wasn't supposed to return to the Stoa until she was ready to pass her test, but it was late and staying away was just a formality anyway. She let the lantern-light burn low and didn't bother to replenish the oil, watching the raindrops roll slowly down her dorm room window, rather than focusing on the words in the book before her. *A Treatise on the Fall of the Panarch'im.* It was a riveting subject, despite it taking place only a generation ago, and usually she was engrossed by anything to do with politics or history, but her mind and her heart were at odds this evening.

He asked me to marry him...

Caralain kept drifting back to that one thought. It was the source of her distress. She thought she was in love, but her logical brain kept reminding her that marriage, especially to Greyson Seynor, would require so much more than love to make it work.

Tonight is the perfect example of that. He's all the way in the Capital celebrating his birthday with his parents, and I wasn't even invited. Not for the first time that night, Caralain found herself sulking. *They hate me, I know it.*

And that was really the crux of it. *Greyson's next in line for the throne. If I marry him, one day I'll be Queen. Maybe as Queen I would have some kind of chance of changing things for the better...but his parents are young still, they'll rule for a long time. And beneath them, I'll be powerless, even more so than I am now.*

A light in the wet darkness outside her window caught her eye, making her sit up straight and pay attention. It wasn't a lantern or some trick of the storm; it was a Mage's light, borne of majik. Which begged the obvious question, *Who would choose to be out there in this?*

The wind and the rain picked up, rattling her windows. Feeling a mounting sense of alarm she couldn't fully explain, Caralain got to her feet and turned away from the open book on her desk. It showed a picture of her idol, Terrence Lee, the most famous Panarch in history, with his hand resting on the central pillar in a circle of Sentinal Stones.

Abandoning her dorm room, she sped into the hall and instantly regretted not taking her cloak with her. *I'll just run down and satisfy my curiosity, and then I'll come right back,* she thought, justifying her unwillingness to turn back. *It won't take long.*

She made every effort to be quiet on the stone stairwell, despite wearing shoes meant for outdoors. As loud as she was, she resisted the urge to summon a Mage-light of her own. *At least I have the courtesy not to rouse anyone from their beds by flashing lights around.* Caralain smiled wryly. *Not like* some *visitors. I wonder who's out there.*

A part of her secretly hoped it was Greyson, even though he had no reason to think she would be here and even less reason to come even if he thought she might be. Still, she wanted to reassure him that she was thinking his proposal over, even if she didn't have an answer for him yet.

No one was in the school's Great Hall by the time she reached it and there was no sign that the doors had been opened recently. Lifting the latch, she intended to open the door a crack and peer outwards, but the wind caught the door and wrenched it from her grasp. It swung wide and cold rain slapped her in the face, drenching her blue dress all the way to the black leggings she wore underneath.

Soaked now, she took a step out into the downpour, and then another, before she became aware of a dark figure across the courtyard, wearing a cloak and facing the old school's main building, but hunched against the rain.

"Hello?" she called out, figuring that if the person was here, they had to at least be a student or alumni of the school, seeing as no one else knew how to reach the hidden island.

The figure's hooded head slowly lifted. He had broad shoulders and was quite tall. At least, Caralain assumed it was a he. She waved at him, urging him to come inside and take shelter, but he didn't move or make any indication he was seeing her at all.

She summoned a Mage-light above her hand. It did nothing to help her vision, but she hoped it might help him see her. She waved it. "What are you doing out here?! The weather's terrible! Come inside!"

The figure's voice, when he spoke, reached her clearly and easily despite the inclement weather. Majik was the only answer. "Why. Are. *You*. Here?"

"Greyson?" She recognized his voice immediately and it only served to make her more alarmed. "Greyson!"

She ran forward and he took a few steps to meet her, his hood lifting enough that she could see his features. He was clean shaven and his jaw was as strong and proud-looking as ever, but he still somehow managed to look a little haggard. She thought maybe it was his eyes, but it was too dark beneath his hood to make out more than the deep grey-blue colour of them.

"What are you doing here?" she asked him when they were close enough to hear each other over the rain.

"I could ask you the same thing." He smirked wryly, showing a hint of personality.

Caralain smiled, happy to see him, despite the oddity of the circumstance. "Never mind that now. Come inside, you must be freezing!"

"I came here to be alone, but I'm not opposed to having company if it's you. How about we go back to my apartments in the Capital?"

Came here to be alone. His words echoed in her mind, striking her as odd. "What happened? Did something go wrong with your parents tonight?"

"You know how my mother gets." He grimaced, even as he hand-waved away whatever incident he was referring to. "Let's not talk here. I'll tell you all about it when we get to the Capital."

She nodded, but then recalled how she'd left her cloak and bag back in her room, along with her open books. She couldn't risk leaving them behind and having a teacher realize she'd come back when she wasn't supposed to. "All right, you go on and I'll meet you there. I've just got to run back upstairs and grab my things."

"No," he said, a little too quickly. "You don't need your stuff. With what I have planned, you won't need much of anything."

It was clear he was trying to be alluring, but Caralain narrowed her eyes. "Planned? You didn't know I was here until a moment ago. Besides, I can't leave my things behind. I'm not even supposed to be here. I'll just run upstairs and be right back down-"

She felt Greyson's hand clamp down on her wrist, not gently. "I said we need to go. Now."

"Greyson!" she protested, tugging against the force of his grip. "Let go of me. This isn't funny."

"Caralain, why can't you just listen for once?"

She felt the words like a slap in the face. This wasn't the Greyson she knew. She struggled, trying in earnest to pull her hand from his iron grasp. "No, you listen," she told him forcefully. "I don't know what's gotten into you, but I don't like it."

"I didn't want you to have to see this."

The cold whispered quality of his words pierced through her heart like an icicle. She gasped, her eyes going wide as a million possible scenarios flitting through her mind, all of them terrible, yet still formless. "See what?"

Still holding her by the wrist, he looked down at her, his eyes cold and emotionless now. She shrank from him, but there was nowhere to go and he wouldn't let her if she tried. He lifted his other hand, brought it to where she could see it, and snapped his fingers. She found that she immediately did not like this new side to his personality, if that's what she was seeing.

The wind picked up, howling and whipping her dress and hair about. The rain came down harder, drops falling with such force as to leave marks on her skin when they landed. Sand from the not distant beach joined the rains, scoring her flesh like tiny blades wielded by the storm that she now knew was of Greyson's making.

Caralain met and held her would-be fiance's gaze as the ground rumbled at their feet. The ocean rose up from beyond the Sentinal Stones, and they both felt the earth tremble beneath them as the waves crashed up against the Stoa's small island with force. Some of the centuries-old bricks tumbled into the water immediately, making waves of their own; others would take more effort to topple.

She thought she heard someone within scream. She whirled around to watch lightning strike the Stoa, causing some of the windows to shatter and a fire to start in one room where the curtains were now exposed to the elements. Another tremor shook the island, more violently than before, and one of the two turrets fell, just like that, breaking off and falling to the ocean.

Shocked by what she was witnessing, Caralain whirled back to face Greyson, prepared to beg him to stop and consider his actions.

His eyes were stony and focused, his shoulders set, and his feet planted. Every inch of him said he was determined to see this through and would not stop until the Stoa was a pile of rubble far beneath the waves.

"Why?" Caralain demanded, shaking her head in denial even as tears stung the open cuts on her face and raindrops continued to pelt her skin without remorse. "How could you…?"

His response was cold, calculated. "To secure our rule. The people here will one day have the power to destroy everything. Now they can't. I'm doing this for us."

Her eyes locked on to the hand he was using to keep her there next to him and she became aware of something she hadn't seen before. Around his hands swirled a dark kind of energy, unlike the majik she was used to but familiar to her nonetheless. Caralain had read all about the Dark Avatar and the power of the Destroyer; she knew what she was looking at, despite having never seen it in person before.

"You have it too," she whispered, staring at the darkness crackling around her wrist where he held her. "Just like your mother…"

"It's my birthright. And through me, it can be yours to command as well. I would do anything for you, you just have to say the word."

Horror filled Caralain and she stumbled back. This time, for a wonder, Greyson let her go. "I could never…" she began and then she stopped, looking up at him, trying to find some hint of the man she'd fallen in love with. "You're a monster!"

Having said what she could, and still feeling the island she'd called home for the last decade crumble all around her, Caralain ran for all she was worth. She sped past Greyson and down the handful of steps to the only place she could run to: the Sentinal Stones.

Greyson whirled after her. "Caralain!"

She ignored him, staring back at the school she loved so much. There were people within, friends, mentors. As she watched, fire spurted from yet another window and the ancient stone cracked, splitting the building in two.

Greyson stood between her and the rest of the island. Dark power crackled around him like an aura now, and at every clench of his fist, another tremor shook the now uneven ground. His eyes were on her, but he showed no remorse, no sign of stopping, only a desire to bring her, too, under his control.

She choked back a sob. *The Stoa may fall, but I won't let him have me. I have to hope that the teachers get the students out in time, but my power is* nothing *compared to his. I can't stop him… I have to flee.* She realized abruptly where she stood, amidst the circle of tall standing stones this school existed primarily to study. She whirled and located the central pillar with her eyes and hands, scanning the symbols there.

But where? Where do I go? There isn't a place in this world beyond his reach.

Her eyes lit on a familiar symbol. It was the one Terrence Lee had been pointing at in the picture of him she'd spent the last hour half-heartedly staring at. It was on a row she didn't recognize, but that wasn't strange; there was so little they didn't know about the Sentinal Stones. She didn't really know where it would lead, but chances were Greyson wouldn't either.

One last look back showed the school almost completely in ruins, along with the livelihood and possibly the lives of all the people she'd known. And before it all was Greyson, on his knees now amidst the ruins. He hadn't tried to follow her or stop her. Maybe he didn't realize how serious she was about leaving him. She shook her head, letting the tears fall freely now.

You did this, she thought at him, *and it was wrong, but maybe, just maybe there's a way I can undo it all.*

Caralain summoned her majik and poured it into the Stone as she shut her eyes tight against the flood of tears that threatened to overwhelm her and prayed.

Goodbye, Greyson.

Part One.

I.

Mirena hit the ground hard. Rocks dug into the side of her face and her hands stung fiercely where she'd scraped them by instinctively trying to break her fall, even though there was no way she could have anticipated it. Her stomach lurched with the impact as she tried to fight off a wave of disorientation and nausea that threatened to overwhelm her.

A horn sounded. *Two quick blasts.* Despite herself, she counted them. *I made it! I'm home.*

She struggled to sit up. The air around her filled with the sounds of doors and windows being flung open as every person in the Stoa rushed to see who had arrived in the courtyard of their hidden College for talented Magi. Mirena grinned, her expression half grim determination and half hard-won pride. She forced herself the rest of the way to her feet and pushed the remaining nausea aside as nearly sixty students and half a dozen staff members barrelled down on her.

The cheering started as soon as they saw it was her and that she was on her feet and relatively unharmed. Mirena's grin grew wider. *I passed my exam in record time. Only four years study to make it to this moment, where most people take decades. The Mentor is going to be so impressed!*

The gathering crowd parted to let the aging Mentor pass uninhibited. With his presence, the noise died down, slightly. The grey-haired Mentor smiled at the sight of her, leaning heavily on his cane as he alone out of all those gathered made his way down the steeply curving steps to stand just outside the sizeable ring of tall standing stones.

"Well done, Mirena." He very subtly drew upon his majik to enhance the volume of his voice so all could hear him praise her.

Mirena beamed and starting running the minute the words were out of his mouth. She crossed between two stone pillars and flung herself at the Mentor, careful to throw her slight weight at him on the opposite side from where he held his cane, so he'd be able to keep his footing.

There was a collective gasp from the crowd that subsided as they realized the Mentor was still standing. "Whoa, there!" he called out, catching Mirena in one arm. "I know you're excited, but you're not done yet!"

"I know, but I'll do the next part with no problems! You'd expect nothing less from your number one student." She winked at him.

The Mentor shook his head. "Remember what I told you: rushing into things will only lead to a job half-finished. You have to look before you leap." He put a hand under her chin to lift her blue eyes up to his before tilting her chin to the right. "I dare say that you wouldn't have gotten these," he noted the cuts the rocks had left on her cheek, "if you'd been more prepared to make the trip through the Sentinal Stones."

"I would've been more cautious, but I was being chased by a large winged monster!" she exclaimed, stepping back from him so she could wave her arms emphatically. "I had to think fast and perform under pressure, so a slightly bad landing should be understandable…"

"Tall tales, Mirena?" the Mentor asked, but his tone was light and his words kind.

"No, really. It's true, it got my back with its claws, see?" She turned slightly to show him the claw marks that marred her left shoulder and the blood that she could now feel running down the length of her simple white dress.

Now it was the Mentor's turn to gasp. He called back over his shoulder for someone to fetch the Healer.

"It's okay, I'm fine. Just let me finish my test."

He furrowed his brow momentarily, but when the Healer didn't immediately manifest in the crowd, the Mentor had no choice but to step to the side and gesture for Mirena to continue. Nodding once and taking on a serious expression, she faced the spot where the Stoa's headmaster had been standing moments before and applied her concentration to a line cut into the stone in an impossibly straight fashion.

That line was made by generations of Magi passing this test before me, including the last person to graduate four years ago: Terrence Lee. He only beat me in total time by a few days at most. I guess it's not too bad to be second best when you're being compared to the youngest and most talented Panarch in history!

Mirena returned her focus to the task at hand when she realized that everyone was now waiting expectantly. *Everyone is watching. I can't afford to fail. I have to concentrate!*

She furrowed her brow, unconsciously mimicking the Mentor's usual expression. Feeling the wind in her hair and the moisture riding on it from the nearby crashing of waves against the island on which she stood, Mirena took hold of her majik and felt the power of it build within her. She deftly added strength from the earth at her feet and some heat from the sun at her back, and then she added what she liked to think of as the 'secret ingredient'; a tiny piece of her own essence, her soul. Aiming it all at the space before her, directly above the tell-tale crack, she bent reality to her will and forced it to obey her. Two matched silver rings made up of all the elements spun in the air, more expertly controlled than even the best circus performer could have managed, and with a sudden snap they locked together in place and between them she saw herself…from behind.

Mirena grinned once again, showing teeth this time. *Opening a portal in front of you to travel to a spot within your viewing takes a great deal of concentration and skill. Let's see what they all think of that!*

The watching crowd gasped in a most satisfying way. Mirena went to take a bow while still holding the portal open with her majik just to prove that she could, when she took note of the Healer rushing down the stone stairway. *Why is she running? I'm not hurt that bad. Can't she see that?*

But the Healer didn't stop at her side, she brushed past her. Mirena whirled to follow the woman with her eyes, dropping the portal spell in her distraction. Behind her, in the center of the circle of Sentinal Stones, lay a woman dressed in a short light blue dress over black leggings. At first glance she looked to be unconscious and badly hurt; much worse than Mirena had been on her own landing.

Mirena's first thought was that maybe she wasn't the only one to pass her test today, as unlikely as that concept was, but she quickly realized that she didn't know this woman. She wasn't a student or a teacher from the Stoa, she was a stranger. *It's possible she didn't know what she was doing. Perhaps she activated the Sentinal Stones by accident, which happens from time to time. Though usually not here…*

As Mirena pondered the incident she felt the Mentor brush past her, followed by two other members of the faculty.

"Don't crowd around!" the Mentor called out, his voice still amplified above normal volume by his majik. "Give her some room. It looks like whatever journey she's taken to get here has taken a lot out of her. Hemora," he addressed the Healer, "you're in charge. Just let us know what you need."

As the teachers made room for the Healer, Mirena got another glimpse at the mysterious stranger who had stolen her thunder. Despite the bruising on her face and scrape marks similar to Mirena's own, the woman appeared to be about Mirena's age and very pretty, with porcelain-coloured skin and long hair so dark it was nearly black. No sooner had she noted these details did the woman's eyes open suddenly. They were deep blue and piercing, and despite all the people in the courtyard and within the shadow of the tall standing stones, the stranger's eyes locked onto Mirena's own and held them.

⁂

Stop fidgeting! Tendro had to remind himself for about the hundredth time. The application between his hands was beginning to show signs of wear. *How much longer is this going to take?* he asked himself again, looking around the semi-circular waiting room and absently re-counting how many people were still to go before him.

When he realized that number was zero, he felt a lump rise in his throat.

"Tendro Seynor?" The secretary called his name from behind a massive oak desk at the far end of the room. He stood, a little too quickly, and quickly tried to right himself so he didn't appear as nervous as he felt. The secretary nodded at the sight of him. "Right this way, Tendro. The Panarch will see you now."

He nodded and started forward. The only thing beyond the secretary's desk was a round-topped solid wood door. It was unlabelled, but Tendro was fairly certain there wasn't a person in the entire Capital city who didn't know what lay beyond it: Terrence Lee's office.

Tendro realized his palms were sweaty when they slipped on the door's brass handle. It took him two tries to get the door open, but he did it. In the room, Terrence Lee, the most famous Panarch in recent history, sat calmly behind his somewhat cluttered desk, his eyes raised to meet Tendro's and a friendly smile on his perfect features.

"What can I do for you, Tendro?"

"Uh…" Tendro was caught off guard by the Panarch's casual use of his name. *Get it together!* he admonished himself. *The secretary probably told him. It's not like the Panarch has the time to learn the name of every single student at the Collegium!*

Terrence Lee waited patiently for Tendro to speak, his open expression and kindly blue eyes showing no impatience, though there was no way he didn't know about the long line of people waiting to see him in the lobby.

"Uh, yes, well…" Tendro cleared his throat. "I'm here to…uh…drop off my application for the apprenticeship you advertised…"

His voice sounded lame to his own ears, but there was nothing he could do about that. *Hopefully my essay and application will be strong enough to speak for itself. I'm just here to drop it off. If I get selected for an interview, I can worry about my speaking skills then.*

Tendro held out the somewhat crumpled application, but Terrence Lee made no move to take it from him. Instead, the kind-yet-intimidating Panarch seemed to look Tendro up and down from his standard issue black Magi robes to his eyes and back again.

"So, what do you have to offer me, Tendro Seynor?" he finally said, his mouth quirking up only slightly on the left side.

"Uh…" Tendro was completely caught off guard by the question. *Wait…is this my interview?!*

Terrence Lee waited patiently, the small signs of amusement still evident.

"Well, Sir…"

"Lee," the Panarch corrected him.

"Yes, well, Lee…I," Tendro wracked his brain for something intelligent to say. "I suppose what I can offer is…well, my eagerness to learn and um…my complete loyalty."

"I see," Lee said, frowning slightly now. "Is that all?"

Tendro felt the floor fall away beneath his feet. *That's it,* he told himself, *I've completely blown it. The Panarch probably thinks I'm a half-wit. He'll never select me as his apprentice now, no matter how good my credentials.*

"I'm a strong student, Sir." Tendro swallowed and tried to regain his verbal footing. "I think my marks and my essay will speak for themselves." He tried to hold out the crumpled piece of paper again. "I promise I will prove my worth if you select me for this program."

Lee frowned. "It's not a program, Tendro. I'm looking for someone to be my right-hand man. There would be training involved, lots of it, but I'm looking for someone who has the confidence to aspire to be Panarch after me, or at least to stand in my place if it is ever needed. I'm sorry, but I just don't think that you have what it takes."

Tendro hung his head, fighting back the tears of frustration that stung his eyes. After such brutally honest assessment of his lack of abilities, he didn't want to chance further discrediting himself in his idol's eyes. "I understand," he managed. "I'm sorry for wasting your time."

"To try is never a wasted effort," Lee spoke softly. "You'll find the role that suits you, Tendro. Of that I have no doubt."

"Thank you, Sir - I mean, Lee."

With that, Tendro saw himself out and didn't look back at the kind blue eyes he knew to be watching him go.

❧

The newcomer was all anyone could talk about for the next week or so as she recovered. As such, Mirena's feat of managing to pass her test so quickly and so spectacularly was instantly forgotten in favour of juicier gossip.

"Who is she?" they asked. "Where did she come from?" "How did she know how to use the Sentinal Stones?" "Was it by accident?"

Personally, Mirena was getting sick of hearing the girl's name. *Caralain this and Caralain that. I can't wait to get my graduation ring, go to the Capital, and be rid of her. Speaking of my ring, I should have gotten it the day I passed my test, but the Mentor has been so busy with this Caralain person, it must have slipped his mind. Maybe I should just go see him and get it. I just want to be on my way.*

Mirena had never seen the Capital City, but she had a strong image in her mind regardless of what the massive Collegium must look like. As the center of politics and higher education, and the largest city in the world, it must truly be a wonderful place and she couldn't wait to get there and start her master's program.

I can't waste any more time if I am to follow in Terrence Lee's footsteps. I am already weeks behind schedule - how am I going to be the next female Panarch at this rate?

Letting herself out of the modest dormitory bedroom she'd called home for the last four years, Mirena ducked her head out into the hallway and was relieved to find that it was empty. Most people would be in class or studying at this hour in the morning, but having graduated, Mirena no longer had to do such things, and it was nice to walk the halls in silence without being subjected to more incessant chatter about Caralain.

The Mentor's door was slightly ajar, as was his usual custom. It subtly implied that it was okay to disturb him. Mirena tapped on the door as she pushed it open.

"Ah, Mirena, just the person I was hoping to see!"

"Really? You haven't forgotten about your..." It took Mirena a moment to realize that the Mentor wasn't alone in his office, but when she did notice her words trailed off abruptly. *...favourite student,* she finished silently.

Seated in a chair before the Mentor's worn old desk sat a dark-haired beauty. At Mirena's entrance into the room, Caralain stood gracefully and turned to acknowledge her. Just like she'd noted upon the woman's abrupt arrival, she had porcelain white skin and lusciously straight and controlled hair that was so dark as to almost be black. Her eyes were blue and they were perfectly set in an oval face. And now, with the bruises and scrapes beginning to fade, she was even more beautiful. Mirena, with her disobedient white-blonde hair and rail-thin body that refused to even pretend to have curves, was instantly overtaken with an emotion that wasn't common for her: jealousy.

"Of course not," the Mentor answered as if Mirena had finished what she was going to say. "Come in, Mirena, and shut the door. I'd like to introduce you to Caralain Dashar."

Mirena did as she was told and shut the door, though she'd really rather have been anywhere else right now. Having locked herself into this encounter, she crossed the room and deliberately ignored Caralain's outstretched hand in favour of taking the seat next to her with the barest of acknowledgements to the woman who'd been the cause of her bad mood this past week. "Pleasure."

"Same," Caralain returned, taking her own seat and Mirena seethed to discover that even the woman's cool tones were beautiful.

The Mentor seemed nonplussed by the icy tension in the air. "Well, now that introductions are out of the way, Ms. Dashar has a favour she would like to ask of you."

"A favour to ask of me?" This news caused Mirena to sit up straight. "I don't even know her, what could I possibly have to offer?"

"As the Mentor tells me," Caralain began, "you have just passed your test, which means that you are trained in the use of the Sentinal Stones and portal-majik. There are no boats that come to this island, or so I've been told. I would like to accompany you to the Capital City. I have urgent business at the Collegium."

"You seem to be able to use the Sentinal Stones yourself," Mirena pointed out. "Do you really need my help?"

"I'm not a full mage yet," Caralain said, seeming to swallow the emotions this statement evoked in her. "I'd like to finish my training, but…there are more important things. Will you take me with you to the Capital?"

Mirena looked to the Mentor and then back to Caralain. The Mentor's expression was impassive, but the fact that he was hiding his emotions from her told Mirena a great deal.

I feel like I am being put on the spot about all this, like I'm still being tested.

"I suppose that won't be a problem," Mirena answered, aiming for friendly and falling just shy of it. If this was a test, she wanted to pass it, but she didn't have to like this woman. "You said it was urgent business? As soon as I get my graduation ring, I'll be ready to go when you are."

"Ah, yes," the Mentor said, "that's where I come in, I suppose." He slid open the top drawer on the right side of his desk and pulled out a small wooden box. "This is yours. I'm sorry it's taken me so long to get it to you. You passed your test with flying colours, of course. I've just had a lot on my mind."

The Mentor opened the box and slid it across the top of his desk to where Mirena could easily reach it. She snatched up the box, barely waiting for it to leave the Mentor's fingers. She grinned, looking down at the smoky quartz embedded in the thick silver band.

"Remember, Mirena," he warned. "Wear it with pride, but never admit which school it actually comes from. It's near enough to the clear quartz awarded to graduates of Al'legous, the Messenger College. You must remember to say that is the school you studied at."

"Of course I will," she said, hastily putting it on her ring finger and admiring the new shine of silver band, "and thank you. I am one step closer to making my dreams come true."

Climbing to her feet, Mirena circled around the desk and hugged the Mentor gratefully. She hadn't made too many friends at the Stoa, but she was going to miss this old man fiercely. In the midst of her hug, she remembered Caralain's presence. Making eye contact with her, she found that the stranger's blue eyes were dark, watchful, and full of distrust. Mirena shuddered slightly as she loosened her hold on the man she often thought of as a second father, but when she looked back at Caralain, the woman's face was as impassive and seemingly as friendly as it had been before, making Mirena question if she had imagined the shift.

"I suppose we should get going," she announced. "My bags are packed. I'll just grab them and meet you at the Sentinal Stones then."

Caralain nodded. "I am in your debt."

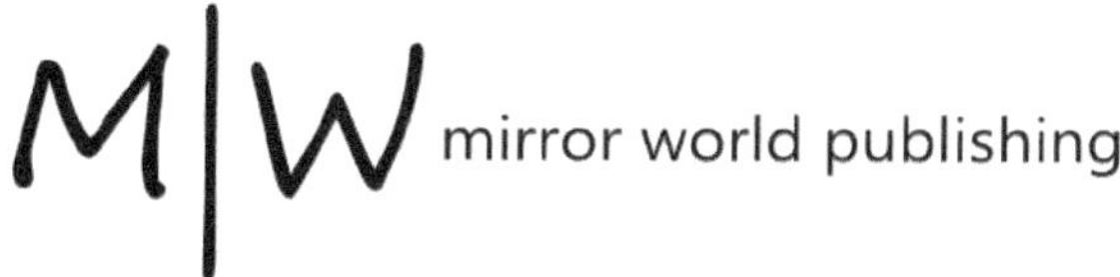

We appreciate every like, tweet, facebook post and review and we love to hear from you. Please consider leaving us a review online or sending your thoughts and comments to info@mirrorworldpublishing.com